~◉ NEWBERY MEDALIST ◉~

CYNTHIA VOIGT

MISTER MAX

THE BOOK of LOST THINGS

Illustrated by **IACOPO BRUNO**

ALFRED A. KNOPF

NEW YORK

THIS IS A BORZOI BOOK PUBLISHED BY ALFRED A. KNOPF

Visit us on the Web! randomhouse.com/kids

Educators and librarians, for a variety of teaching tools,
visit us at RHTeachersLibrarians.com

Library of Congress Cataloging-in-Publication Data
Voigt, Cynthia.
  Mister Max : the book of lost things / by Cynthia Voigt ;
illustrated by Iacopo Bruno. — 1st ed.
    p. cm.
  Summary: When Max's parents leave the country without him, he must rely on his wits to get by, and before long he is running his own—rather unusual—business.
ISBN 978-0-307-97681-9 (trade) — ISBN 978-0-375-97123-5 (lib. bdg.) —
ISBN 978-0-307-97683-3 (ebook) — ISBN 978-0-307-97682-6 (pbk.)
[1. Self-reliance—Fiction. 2. Problem solving—Fiction.] I. Bruno, Iacopo, illustrator.
II. Title. III. Title: Book of lost things.
PZ7.V874Mi 2013   [Fic]—dc23   2012033823

The text of this book is set in 11.25-point Simoncini Garamond.
The illustrations were created using pencil and ink on paper.

Printed in the United States of America
September 2013

10 9 8 7 6 5 4 3 2 1

First Edition

For MY Mister Max

~ CONTENTS ~

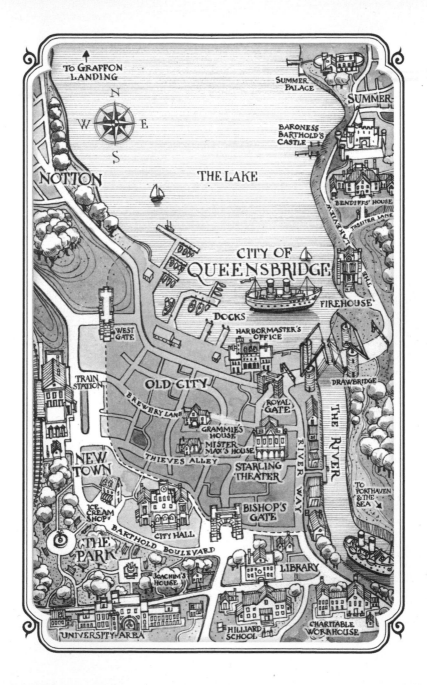

"All the world's a stage."

—William Shakespeare, *As You Like It*

PROLOGUE

On a bright Sunday morning in the early years of the last century, a bellhop from the Hotel Excelsior knocked at the front door of 5 Thieves Alley, the home of William and Mary Starling of the Starling Theatrical Company, and their son, Maximilian. The bellhop, wearing the traditional red uniform with stripes running the length of his trouser legs and with the traditional red cap perched on his head, put a small packet into the hand of the dark-haired, hawk-nosed man who opened the door and accepted the coin offered to him for his trouble. He walked briskly off, unaware of what he had started.

1

In which a surprising invitation
arrives and plans are made

William Starling carried the packet back into the dining room, where his wife and son were seated. In those days, most families did their most ambitious cooking for the midday Sunday dinner, but the Starlings were theatrical, and you cannot give a good Sunday matinee on a full stomach. Therefore, Sunday breakfast was Mary's showcase meal of the week, a matter of sweet rolls and fresh juice, sausages, bacon, and thick cheesy omelets. They ate these breakfasts at a table set with linen napkins, silver cutlery, and the good china. On Sunday mornings, the Starlings could enjoy a leisurely family meal. But when William came back into the dining room, he couldn't contain his curiosity. He pushed his unfinished plate aside. From inside the packet, he pulled two long envelopes, one small, heavy red silk bag, and one thick sheet of paper covered with words arranged in lines as straight as soldiers on a battlefield. He read this letter through silently. When he had finished, he looked across the table to his wife and waited, watching her.

She waited, watching him.

Neither of them looked at Max, who had also stopped eating but did not speak. He knew better than to interrupt the drama they were creating.

William set the letter down on the table, pulled his plate close again, and picked up his fork.

Patient, silent, Mary watched, waiting, until at last she burst out laughing and said, "All right, William. I give up. I'll ask, if you're going to be so . . . so *theatrical* about it. What does the letter say?"

"It says," her husband began, and filled his mouth with sausage. After he had chewed for an irritatingly long time, and swallowed, and savored the last of his orange juice, he said, in a voice that vibrated like a tuning fork, "It promises, my dearling, that a great adventure awaits us."

"That's unfortunate," remarked Mary, with no more interest than if he had just told her she had toast crumbs on her chin. She rose from the table. William was not the only dramatist in the family. "Seeing that we have a full schedule of performances from now until"—she half turned in the doorway and paused, as if to think—"I believe the middle of September. With no time for adventures."

"All right," William said, "all right, Mary. You win. Come back, sit down, and lend me your ears." When she had done as he asked, he announced, as if he were addressing a great crowd from a great height, "On this first day of April, the Starling Theatrical Company has received a letter from deepest India, a letter written by the Maharajah of Kashmir himself, in his own hand. 'The most excellent and skillful William Starling'—I'm quoting now—'and his most beautiful and talented wife' . . . These are his exact words," William Starling said, facing the letter outward and waving it gently, as if his wife and son could read moving script. He used his own voice to tell her, "We've been invited to spend several months, or more, in his raj. In *India,* Mary. We've never been to India. And what do you say to that, my most beautiful and talented wife?"

She answered slowly, "I say it's very odd. Very odd indeed. What use can he have for us?"

"He wants us to create a theater company for him. Like in Elizabethan England, a troupe of actors to entertain his court and to travel among his villages, performing. He wants us to find people of talent and teach them how to act, and introduce them to plays, and show them how to produce a play. He says no other maharajah has his own theatrical company, and he'll be the first, he'll lead the way. Think of it, Mary."

Only then did he pass the paper across the table to her. Max twisted in his chair so he could read it, too.

The letter was written on heavy, gilt-edged paper, embossed at the top with a spiky design, like a series of upside-down Vs of varying height crowding together, even overlapping. The Maharajah offered this opportunity to the Starling Theatrical Company because, he said, he had once seen their brilliant performance of a play, the name of which he couldn't recall, in a great city, although he couldn't be certain just which of the world's great cities it had been. He had, however, remembered not only the name of the Company but also its home base, so indelible had been the impression made on him by the talented couple who were its primary actors. So that when he conceived the dream of having a theatrical company of his own, he resolved immediately to persuade them to come to his "most pleasing and welcoming country, with its most lovely landscapes." He hoped they would be willing to help him undertake his "proud hope." He was looking forward "most blissfully" to the honor of welcoming the Starlings into his "most humble palace."

William Starling spread butter on a cinnamon roll and smiled at his wife, whose large, wide-set dark gray eyes danced with eagerness. "A palace, my dearling. We will live in a maharajah's palace. Imagine it." His own eyes, brown as chestnuts, glowed, and his smile lit the room.

Neither of them so much as glanced at Max.

"They're actors," Grammie often told him, as if that explained everything. She promised him, "When you're older, it'll be different."

Like most librarians and former grade-school teachers, Grammie was proved right. After his eighth birthday, Max's parents began to give him jobs in the theater—prompting actors during performances, keeping track of props, even sometimes appearing onstage if a child was needed as background for a scene. He missed many days of school, but he was smart enough to progress from year to year at the normal rate. After his tenth birthday, his parents sometimes took Max with them when they traveled. Then he was absent not only for rehearsals or after late performances, but also because he was on the road, visiting distant cities with the Starling Theatrical Company.

Max could understand why the other boys and the teachers liked him less and less each year. (You can't know a lot of plays well, some of them written by William Shakespeare, without getting a good understanding of how and why people do what they do.) But he wouldn't have changed his life for anything their friendship and approval had to offer. His parents were the most fascinating people he knew. He never tired of their performances, on the stage or out on a street or even in their own kitchen. Max didn't want to be an actor, although he could carry off a minor role, given the right costume. He thought that, just as his eyes were a mixture of gray and black and brown that made a new, as yet unnamed and possibly unpleasant color, he himself was a mix of their two characters, and therefore different from both of them. And he knew that in their actorish way his parents cared about him, and enjoyed him, and respected him. "He's growing up,"

William Starling liked to say. "Grown up and grown tall in the bargain. After twelve years, a boy's parents have done all they can. He's ready to be independent! Does he look like independence material to you?" he would ask whoever happened to be present for this announcement—which he made for the first time at Max's eighth birthday dinner. "Because he's closing in on twelve. I hope he's ready."

Max had turned twelve the September before. This, despite his father's claim, had given him no noticeable increase in independence, about which Max was more relieved than disappointed. He liked being Maximilian Starling of the Starling Theatrical Company. He enjoyed his father's ebullience, most of the time, and he never tired of watching his mother perform. He laughed and applauded as loud as anyone else when William Starling rose to his feet in some public house or inn to accept a compliment. "I thank you humbly," his father said on those frequent occasions, then he raised his glass to offer the toast. "To my fame and fortune!" he declaimed. "My fame is in your hands, my friends." This was greeted by wild cries of approval and the thumping of mugs on tables. "And my fortune?" he turned to where his wife and Max were sitting to bow slightly and announce, "I break my fast each morning in its company." And Mary Starling would incline her head gracefully toward her husband.

That Sunday morning, with the unexpected invitation on the table between them, William and Mary Starling bowed their heads toward one another, congratulating themselves on this success. They had forgotten Max. Usually, Max didn't worry about being unnoticed, but on that occasion he worried that his parents could be on a boat and halfway across the ocean to India before they realized that someone wasn't with them.

William Starling said to his wife, in a voice that rang with proud satisfaction, "You see how our fame grows? We are now worthy of first-class tickets"—and he held up the two envelopes—"on the *Flower of Kashmir*. We sail at noon, in two weeks and," he looked at a ticket, "three days." Replacing the ticket in its envelope, he asked, "What do we say to this, my dearling? We're promised payment in gold and jewels. An emissary awaits our response, at the Hotel Excelsior. So . . . What do we tell this Maharajah of Kashmir? Who has sent you . . ." He opened the red silk bag, slid its contents onto the table, and whistled softly. "This."

All three stared down at the brooch where it shone against the white linen cloth. Narrow ropes of gold had been wound together, ribbons of gold woven through and around one another, in the same spiky design that appeared at the top of the Maharajah's stationery. Nestled in the curves and marking the points of the upside-down Vs—possibly mountains, or perhaps an unknown Indian letter—were colored stones, polished so that their reds and greens and deep blues gleamed. Studded as it was with jewels, the piece could even have been a crown.

"It's a treasure," Mary Starling breathed. She picked it up. "William? Feel this, it's heavy."

"It's settled!" cried William Starling. "Who could resist? Not me, and not you either, am I right?" His smile lit up the dining room and seemed to reflect from the glass of the framed posters that lined the walls and from the leather bindings of the books in the tall bookcase.

"Yes," Mary Starling said. "Yes."

Max had been waiting, but they had not yet noticed the omission. Finally, he had to ask. "What about me?"

Silence fell over the room like a sudden heavy snowfall. William looked at Mary, who was already looking at him, waiting for her cue. "You'll stay with Grammie, of course," Max's father announced.

This told Mary what role she was playing, the mother who did not wish to be parted from her son. "For such a long time?" she asked.

"She won't mind" was the confident answer.

"But I will," his mother said. "And so will you, William Starling. You know you will, so don't bother pretending otherwise."

Max wondered if they were actors improvising a scene or genuine fond parents unhappy at the thought of being separated from their child. Even knowing them as well as he did, he couldn't be sure.

His father sighed, a long, drawn-out exhaling of breath. "I know. I know. You're right. As well, I wouldn't want to deny him the experience of India. But what can we do?" he asked, and immediately answered the question, giving himself all the lines in this particular scene. "We can refuse, I suppose. The invitation is only for us two, there are only two tickets, and so we cannot accept." He sighed again. "And we will refuse it gladly," he assured Max.

Max was waiting to hear what conclusion his father had in mind for this scene before he made his own suggestions (he could be smuggled into the cabin in a trunk, or they could buy him a ticket—it didn't have to be first class—or he could work as a cabin boy on the ship). Sometimes, his father irritated him.

"Yes, we do have to decline," agreed his mother, equally dejected by the decision. Max expanded his irritation to include his indulgent mother.

"Yes," his father repeated, more slowly and with more longing. Then his head snapped up, as if an idea had seized the tops of his ears, and jerked. "Unless . . . ," he began, and fell silent.

Max knew that if he didn't pick up the cue here it would take a long time to get to the end of this, so he obliged. "Unless what?"

"Unless . . . ," his father repeated, and now he seemed lost in thought. The tension built in the room. "Unless . . . It's obvious, isn't it? The Maharajah must not have known. And how could he?" he asked his wife, looking for his next cue.

"Known what?" she asked.

"Known that we have such an indispensable son!" William Starling declared.

Max relaxed. Of course they would never go without him, off to India for months and months.

"I'll write immediately. I'll accept the offer, but only on the condition that there be a third ticket. For you," he told Max. "I'll promise this emissary that you have all your mother's talent even if you lack my looks. Do you think you can live up to that?"

Max didn't care what promises were made, as long as he got to go. He'd seen photographs of India in the *Queensbridge Gazette,* and he'd read articles in magazines about tiger hunts and the Taj Mahal. Grammie had given him *Kim* for his tenth birthday, and he had read it several times over. The crowded cities, the elegant palaces surrounded by park-like gardens, the high mountains and flower-filled lakes, the thieves and cutthroats and garroters and pickpockets, the temples inhabited by vicious monkeys, the huge golden statues of the Buddha, howdahs like miniature houses on tops of elephants, vipers and mongooses, the spices and sweets—suddenly there was nothing else Max wanted in his life other than to go to India.

"But," his father asked, "what about your painting lessons? Don't tell me you're willing to give up the lessons you *tortured* us about last year?"

"That was almost three years ago," Max corrected impatiently.

His mother pointed out, "He's worked with Joachim for more than two years now, so it wasn't exactly a momentary impulse, and you have to admit that our sets are much improved."

William Starling was not so easily distracted from old grudges that played well. "It *feels* like last year. I remember, remember vividly, the scenes, the tantrums," he said. With a glare at Max, he concluded, "The refusal to eat."

Max, who had never thrown a tantrum in his life, not that he remembered, and who had certainly never refused to eat, did not take this bait.

"Don't tease him, William," Mary Starling said to her husband. "You can't blame him for wanting to go his own way. He's a chip off the old block, and you're the old block he's chipped off of, so go write that letter to our Maharajah."

The response arrived the next day: Telegrams had been sent, to and from India, and a ticket, "for the little boy," would be waiting for them on the boat. A carriage would call for the little family at nine in the morning to transport the travelers and their luggage to the *Flower of Kashmir,* scheduled to leave port at noon. At the docks in Bombay, they would be met by the Maharajah's Daimler automobile.

Max, flush with victory, asked, "Can I take my bicycle?"

William Starling, equally flush, answered, "Your bicycle? Why not? What an adventure!" He rose from the table and held a hand out to his wife. She rose to stand with him, and even though there was only Max as audience, they bowed to one another.

The way in which William and Mary Starling took bows, thought Max, who had spent years observing his parents both on and off stage, was a little drama of its own. Always, of course, there were the smiles, brilliant smiles and shining eyes to tell the audience—any audience, however large or small, whether in theater seats or on a street corner—how much the actors appreciated the attention, the admiration, the applause. Max could recognize the half bow for social occasions, the slight nod of the head for close friends and family, the deep bow with bent knees and lowered heads if there happened to be royalty present for a performance. He liked best to see his parents turn to one another in front of the lowered curtain, where William bowed from the waist to his wife, who gave him in return her best court curtsey. This meant they each felt the other had performed with extreme excellence that evening. It was the opposite of a bow the couple took with their hands clasped between them as their free hands reached out to the audience. Those clasped hands meant trouble for someone.

The very next day they canceled performances and advised the remaining members of the Company to go on the road and share among themselves the major roles usually taken by William and Mary. Notices were posted, one at the entrance to the Starling Theater, one beside the stage door, and even one beside the small, seldom-used back entrance hidden away down an unlit alley. *Closing indefinitely as of April 15,* the notices read, and they were signed in bold, looping handwriting, *William Starling, Manager and Director.* It was arranged that the gas and electricity would be turned off at the theater after the last performance. "We'll give them *Adorable Arabella*," William decided. "It's your most popular role, my dearling, and for good reason. You are Arabella herself. They won't forget us, with your Arabella as their last memory."

William Starling announced his good news to everyone he met. "We are about to embark on the time of our lives!" In restaurant dining rooms and public houses, in streets and in stores, he proclaimed it. Everyone joined in his excitement and applauded his luck, for William Starling was a one-of-a-kind character, vivid, extravagant, larger than life. To be in his presence was to feel more alive yourself. "I'm off to see the world!" he cried joyfully. "I'll send you a postcard!"

Grammie had doubts. On Thursday, the day the theater was dark, she took the well-worn path across their adjoining yards and knocked on the kitchen door. She always knocked and waited to be invited in because, as she said, "When relatives live so close together, it's especially important to have good manners with one another."

When she came into the front parlor, which was strewn with costumes from among which would be selected those to be taken to India, Max's father waved the letter in front of her nose, then folded it up and put it in his pocket. "Show your mother the jeweled brooch," he said to his wife, rolling the last two words around in his mouth like a candy.

Grammie was not won over so easily. "If you can't judge a book by its cover," she said, "still less can you judge a letter by its gilded edges. Think about it, William," she advised, in the schoolteacher voice she had perfected when she was a young widow with a daughter to raise.

"There she goes!" cried Max's father, throwing his hands up into the air in dramatic exasperation. "Dragging books into everything! Raining on our parade!"

Grammie stuck to her point. "I have my doubts about this. Why all the mystery?"

William Starling turned to his son. "Your grandmother, Max, is a stay-at-home, and this makes her an excellent librarian. We, on the other hand, are not. *Au contraire!* We are adventurers! And she"—now he glared at Grammie, as if she were the villain in one of his productions. He pointed an accusing forefinger right between her eyes. "She knows this full well. Full well!" he repeated.

Grammie laughed, as William and Mary and Max all knew she would.

Then Max's mother brought the pot of fish stew out to the dining room table, where thick slices of dark bread were already set out in a bowl, and they all sat down to supper. Before she began to ladle the thick tomato and fish and potato and onion mixture into bowls, Mary Starling looked around at the posters on the walls, at the books and scripts lined up in the tall bookcase, and took a deep breath. She said to her mother, "We talked it over and decided not to have you read the letter." Grammie raised an eyebrow. "You're a good librarian, and you'll look everything up." Grammie opened her mouth. "And then you'll start to teach us all about the country, and its people, and its geography and history, and we won't," she concluded hurriedly, before Grammie could interrupt, "have the adventure of discovering things for ourselves."

She spoke more quietly than her husband, more like a judge than a politician, more like a king than a general.

Grammie admitted, "You're right. Absolutely right about me. I hope that by my age I know the person I am, and you're right about what I'd do. But I'd be foolish not to worry."

"You don't ever need to worry about me," Max's father assured her. "I'm invincible." To prove his point, he thumped his chest with his fist.

Grammie humphed, but said nothing. Max's mother passed around bowls of steaming stew. Max passed around the bread.

"*And* I would never let anything happen to your darling daughter or your precious grandson," William Starling promised.

Grammie humphed again.

Max's mother offered her own kind of comfort. "There's no use to worrying, you know that. And there's no need for it. Not about us," she added, with a quick, glad smile at her husband. "We always land on our feet, don't we?"

"That's all very well for you, but what about Max?" asked Grammie. "What about his education?"

"He'll be attending the School of Life! He'll graduate from the University of Experience!" William Starling declared, although in fact they had made no plans other than to inform Max's teachers that he would be out of school and out of the city and out of the country for the foreseeable future.

Grammie persisted. "He'd be better off staying with me. Attending the school of his *own* life."

Mary Starling spoke gently. "We're always grateful to you for the way you took care of Max when he was little. Always. But he *is* twelve, almost thirteen, old enough to travel in a foreign country and not get himself in trouble. Old enough to get a lot out of the experience, too."

Nobody asked Max what *he* thought, and of course he minded, when it was his life they were having opinions about. He was seated at his usual place at the table, and he looked from one of his parents to the other, minding. He also minded Grammie trying to turn him back into the little boy she'd so often had in her care, for a night or a month, a little boy who couldn't be left on his own in his own house. In fact, the only thing he didn't mind right then was being taken out of school. At school they called him Eyes, and it wasn't a friendly nickname. He said, to nobody in particular, "I want to go. I really do."

With all three of them against her, Grammie could only sigh. "I know, I know, you're always fine, and"—she turned to Max—"you're old enough to look out for yourself. I know. I'd just feel better if I knew where in the world you'll be."

"You'll find that out, my dear little mother-in-law, when you get our postcards."

2

In which Max
loses his parents

Two trunks and three suitcases waited by the front door, early on the morning of their departure. The Starlings had packed for life in a distant and unfamiliar land, where they would be asked to perform as well as to teach. Light summer clothing for when they arrived, and also clothes for the long sea voyage. ("We'll be dressing for dinner, of course. I'll need at least four evening gowns," Mary Starling said, adding, "and you'll both need your tuxedos," although, as far as Max knew, he didn't have any formal evening wear.) A selection of plays had to be included. ("We must have Shakespeare," William Starling decided. "Do you think *Julius Caesar*? Or *A Midsummer Night's Dream*? The comedy," he announced.) Grammie had made sure their trunk carried a supply of soap and toothpaste.

Max had concerned himself with watercolor paints, brushes, and paper. "There are artists in India, and very good ones," his father had protested, "so there are sure to be supplies there." But Max had paid no attention. "When it comes to his painting, he doesn't give an inch," his mother observed, which might have been a complaint, but Max didn't care. "Maybe he's an artist," Grammie suggested, and although Max thought she was wrong about that, he didn't say so. He had in fact insisted on a final lesson on the morning of their departure, arguing that an independent twelve-year-old was perfectly capable of riding his bicycle up to the gangplank on his own, that Yes, he would be there no later than eleven-fifteen, and Yes, he would remember to ask for his ticket from the steward who would welcome him on board, because undoubtedly his parents would be busy, settling in.

They had imagined the start of the journey, the seagoing liner pulled away from the Queensbridge docks by small tugboats, towed through the drawbridge and out onto the river, then cast off after a mile to follow the fast-flowing water down to the seafront city of Porthaven, where it would enter the ocean and cross to foreign lands. "Foreign lands!" cried William Starling. "You don't want to miss that, my boy," and "I don't," Max agreed.

They had worked out the timing as if it were a play. Not

long after Max rode off to his lesson, the carriage would arrive to take his parents, and their luggage, down to the docks. "I want to be the first on board!" William Starling declared, and turned to his wife with a laugh. "I want you to be the second!" To Max he spoke sternly. "Don't dawdle. Leave yourself enough time to get from the New Town to the docks," he said. He warned, "If you miss the boat you have no chance of catching us, and then what would you do?"

"I won't miss it," Max answered.

"He'd go to his grandmother's," Mary Starling said, "and wait to hear from us."

"I said, I won't miss it," Max repeated, impatient to be off. They kept saying that twelve was old enough to be responsible and independent, but they still treated him like a little boy. "I'll see you on the *Flower of Kashmir*," he said, and left before they could think of anything else that might go wrong that they could warn him about.

He rode out through the Bishop's Gate and across the New Town and in twenty minutes had arrived at the house where his teacher lived, a low four-room building with an attached studio and a large walled garden. Joachim's oil paintings were small, detailed pictures of what was growing in his garden: a narcissus, the branch of a pear tree in bloom, red berries against white snow. He sold his work at one of the galleries in the New Town and was reluctant to take on pupils, unless— like Max—they had a clear idea of what they wanted to learn. "Watercolors," Max had told the man when his grandmother had taken him for an interview. "I want to paint the sky, skyscapes."

Joachim did not ask why. His interest was in line and color, in shape and shading, in technique, not people and what made them say and do what they said and did. He considered the boy for a long time, then "I can teach you that," he said, and told Grammie, "Ten per class, one class a week, start tomorrow," before turning back to his easel.

The painter was a gray and gloomy man, gray hair and short gray beard, gray eyes and a gloomy gray outlook on life. His way of teaching was to give an instruction, about technique or color or design, and then get back to his own work while Max tried to apply what he'd been told. Mostly, Joachim ignored his pupil, but early on he had presented Max with a bright red beret. "Work clothes," he'd said, holding the gift out to Max. Max always wore the beret when he painted, and he found that, like any good costume, a red beret made it easier to concentrate, to feel and see like a painter. It seemed to Max that both he and Joachim enjoyed the lessons.

"You again," Joachim greeted him when he wheeled his bicycle in by the garden gate that April morning. Seeing the carpetbag that Max had hanging from his shoulder, he asked, "You aren't thinking of moving in, are you?" but went back to his own easel before Max could answer. On the canvas a perfect blue hyacinth, attended by two plump green leaves, floated on a creamy background. Joachim peered into his picture, almost dipping his nose into the tiny petals. "Don't just stand there," he told Max.

Max put on his beret and got to work. He set his paper on the easel at the proper angle and, with a last glance up into a pale spring sky, mixed what he hoped would be the right amount of cerulean blue with water. Then he picked up a broad brush, to wet the upper third of his paper, and lost himself in his painting. Minute after minute went by unnoticed as they worked, facing away from one another, undistracted by breeze and insect and the occasional bird, until—after a while, long enough for Max to have discarded three attempts and made a good beginning on the fourth—Joachim sighed and set his palette down on the ground beside him.

Joachim often sighed as he worked, since what he could get onto the canvas with his paints and brushes never matched what he was imagining, but he never put down his palette. Max turned to see Joachim running paint-smeared fingers through his untidy gray hair. He leaned closer to his painting, squinting at it as if not quite sure what he was looking at. "I'm too old for this," he said, maybe to himself, maybe to Max.

Max decided to respond, whichever of them the painter had been talking to. "You're not so old." After all, his teacher's hair was gray, not white. His face was no more wrinkled than Grammie's, and *she* certainly wasn't old.

"Old enough to be going blind. And what'll I do then, bat-blind? Who would buy what a blind painter paints?"

Max was imagining what those pictures might look like. "They might be strange," he said, "and interesting."

Joachim gave a sharp, sarcastic bark of a laugh. "Ha ha. I paint what I see in my garden, you know that, and I'm not seeing very clearly these days. Oh, I see the colors all right, but the edges of things are blurry. The details."

"Get glasses," Max suggested. "You're not young—"

"You can say that again."

"You're not young," said the always cooperative Max.

"Very funny."

"Grammie told me that after forty most people need reading glasses."

"And has your know-it-all librarian grandmother also gone to eye doctor school?"

When Max had an idea about how to fix some problem, he grew impatient for the plan to be put into execution. "But will you? Will you get glasses?"

"You know," Joachim told him gloomily, "it could be it's not only my literal vision that I'm losing."

That would be a different problem, but equally serious, Max knew. If Joachim was losing his metaphorical vision, that would be a problem to which Max couldn't begin to imagine any solution. "I wish I wasn't going away just now," he said.

"As if you being here will make any difference." Without turning to look at Max, Joachim picked up his brush and palette to get back to work. "If I'm going blind in not too long a time, I'd better build up an inventory, wouldn't you say?"

"I wish I knew when we're coming back," Max said, following his own thoughts.

"So you could get a quick medical degree and miraculously cure me?" Joachim laughed again, still sarcastically. "Ha. Ha ha. You're a bright boy, Max, but you are no genius."

"No, so I could . . . ," Max thought. What *could* he do, after all, if Joachim really was going blind, or—worse—if he was going to lose his painter's vision, his painter self? That would be like his parents losing the stage; their whole life couldn't be the same if they did that. "If I were here, I could pester you until you went to a doctor and found out for sure about your eyes," he finally said.

"Thank you very much," Joachim said, meaning the opposite. "End of lesson," he decided, and at the same time they heard the bell on the clock tower of City Hall ringing. The bell fell silent. Its final notes seemed to echo in the air. Max had not heard its first notes. "What time is it?" he asked.

Sighing at the interruption, Joachim turned away from his easel. "Noon, maybe. Could be ten."

"I heard it ring ten," Max remembered. He grabbed at his pad and his box of watercolors, and pulled on the traveling jacket suitable for first-class accommodations that his mother had asked him to wear. He slung the carpetbag over his shoulder.

"You were working," Joachim explained, his attention back on his painting.

"It doesn't feel late, but—" Max didn't take the time to shake his teacher's hand and thank him. Or even, he realized as he pushed his bicycle through the wooden gate that opened out onto a back alley, to pay for the lesson. He stopped just long enough to call back, "Ask my grandmother for today's fees. She'll be at the library," and he pedaled off as fast as he could.

A skillful biker, Max was not much slowed on the busy streets of the New Town. He crossed the city park, sounding the bicycle's bell to warn people of his sudden, swift approach from behind, and was relieved to see that the clock on the City Hall tower showed five after eleven. He had more than enough time to make a noon departure even if he'd miss his eleven-fifteen deadline. He raced in front of the cafés and small shops that lined the park to enter Barthold Boulevard, with its tall, three-story buildings, which took him, at top speed, dodging among the trams and carts, carriages, horses and riders, and even an automobile, the long, straight way through the Bishop's Gate and into the old city. There, the streets became narrow and cobbled. They twisted and crossed, offering dark alleyways as shortcuts to someone who knew the old city as well as Max did. Standing up on the pedals to minimize the discomfort and the difficulties of bouncing along on uneven stones, Max rang his bell and called out, "Sorry, sorry," to the people who had to jump into doorways to let him pass. They shouted after him, "You! Fellow! Slow down! What's your hurry?"

He didn't slow down until he entered the crowded waterfront, where ships were lined up beside docks that protruded like fingers from a hand out into the deep water of the lake. The high metal sides of berthed liners and cargo ships loomed over him like fortress walls as he pedaled past them, checking the names painted on banners hung on the sides of the gangplanks that connected the ships to land. The docks

were noisy with sailors and longshoremen carrying out their chores, with businessmen settling last-minute affairs, and of course with passengers arriving in carriages, accompanied by friends come to wave them off. He checked the names on the passenger liners: *Eagle of the Adriatic, Lollapalooza, Queen Eleanora, Arctic Sun,* and then, in its usual place at the far end of the line of piers, the much smaller boat that ferried people and mail around the lake from dawn until dusk, stopping at one small town after the other, *The Water Rat.* He knew Captain Francis, of course; everybody knew the round, friendly ferryboat captain, who with his son was always ready to help you carry parcels, trunks, or crates of carrots on board or to herd an unwilling goat into the animal pen for her journey to a new home.

Captain Francis, his blue jacket splendid with gold braid, his white captain's hat set square on his head, greeted Max. "Why aren't you in school?"

"I'm meeting my parents on the *Flower of Kashmir*." Max was still a little out of breath from his headlong ride.

"That's right, school's out for lunch," said Captain Francis who, like many adults, heard what he expected to from children, which was not necessarily exactly what they said. *"Flower of Kashmir?"* He scratched at his shoulder, thinking. "You sure about the name?"

"She sails at noon, for India," Max told him. "Not literally sails, of course, because she's a steamship."

Captain Francis smiled, showing big white teeth. "When I was learning the trade? It was all under sail. I crossed the ocean twice under sail, once as a common sailor, once as navigator, and I can tell you, these new liners are a great improvement. Much more comfortable. Safer, too, in rough weather. But you're cutting it fine, aren't you?"

"Can you tell me where to find her?" Max asked again.

"Carlo!" called Captain Francis, and his dark-haired son leaned out of the wheelhouse window. "What is it, Pop?"

"Where's the *Flower of Kashmir* docked?"

Carlo shook his head. "No idea. You should ask the Harbormaster. It's his job to know what ship's where."

Captain Francis pointed Max to a little brick building, barely broader than its one narrow doorway. "Leave your bicycle here if you like. I'll keep an eye on it."

"Thank you, but I'm taking it with me. I'm expected, I can't—"

Captain Francis didn't take offense. "You know what? I thought you were one of those painter fellows at first. Must be the beret," he laughed.

Max was already mounting the bicycle and wasted no more words.

"Then I saw your eyes," Captain Francis called from behind him.

The Harbormaster was too important to know who Max was and had his feet too firmly on the ground to know anything about any theatrical company. A tall, thin man in a dark suit and stiff white collar, wearing gold-rimmed glasses and sporting thick sideburns, he was on his way out the door when Max arrived.

He stopped in the doorway, glanced at Max, and bowed slightly. *"Monsieur?"* he asked, speaking French because this fellow wore a beret, and a red beret at that. He couldn't be anything but French, in a red beret. *"Qu'est-ce que vous desirez?"* the Harbormaster inquired. In his position he dealt with ships from different countries, and he was proud of his ability to greet people in several languages.

"What?" Max asked. He asked this impatiently, as if he were his father playing Banker Hermann in *The Worldly Way.* "Whatever are you saying, my good man?"

"Oh. Ah." The Harbormaster switched to English. "How may I help you, Sir?"

"I am expected on board the *Flower of Kashmir,*" announced banker Max, impatiently.

The Harbormaster's eyes widened just a little and a hush oozed out from the small room behind him. The two clerks within looked up from their desks, first at Max and then at the Harbormaster. The Harbormaster's expression grew wary. "The *Flower of Kashmir,* you say? You're sure that's the vessel's name?"

"Of course I'm sure," said Max, the man of few words. But his heart grew suddenly jittery.

One of the clerks spoke from behind the Harbormaster. "Sir?"

Without turning, the Harbormaster raised a hand, to silence his underling. With a sharp-eyed glance from behind round lenses, he said, "No *Flower of Kashmir* is presently berthed in my harbor. What's her country of registration?"

"India," Max guessed confidently.

"Nor are there any Indian registered vessels. We have, presently, one American, one Moroccan, one Dutch, one Canadian, and that's all of them."

Max considered this. "Which vessels sail at noon?" he asked.

"None, as it happens. Though three left their berths by ten-thirty this morning, so as to catch a favorable tide out of Porthaven."

Something was very wrong here. But when Max spoke, it was in character. "Give me the names of those ships."

The Harbormaster rattled off information, proud to have it at his fingertips. "The *Miss Koala* for Australia, the *Eastern Star* for China, and the *Simón Bolívar* for South America. The Australian liner carried four hundred and thirty-five passengers, the Chinese two hundred and twelve, and the South American liner was a cargo ship with only a few staterooms. Those at the docks now will not leave until tomorrow." The Harbormaster waited for Max's next question.

Max's heart grew heavy with dread. This made less and less sense. He asked, "You're certain there is not, and was not, a *Flower of Kashmir*?"

"Certain."

"I wonder," Max asked, the last thing he could think of, "if a letter was left for me?"

"We are neither a post office nor a message service,"

the Harbormaster answered, allowing a little suspicion into his voice.

"Sir?" the voice asked again, from the office.

"Not yet," said the Harbormaster, keeping his eyes on Max.

Fortunately, Max was tall for his age and, since he was acting his father acting Banker Hermann, he looked straight across at the official, unquelled by the man's challenging expression. Max did not smile. He did not move to leave. He waited, and tried to think.

But he didn't know *what* to think. His heart was sinking fast.

"May I ask, Sir, why you inquired about that particular vessel?" The Harbormaster was carefully polite.

Max was not about to utter out loud what he felt like saying and certainly not the way he felt like saying it. He was not about to wail, like a child, "Because my parents are on that boat!" He kept his dignity and his pretense wrapped close about him. "I am to sail on her."

"As I said, no ship of that name has been here," the Harbormaster observed.

"I was expected," Max insisted.

"All right, Fenton," the Harbormaster said. "Now you may come forward."

The clerk was a pale young man in shirtsleeves. He leaned excitedly around his superior to tell Max, "There *was* a message. It was a crook-looking fellow left it, stood like a soldier—but not one of our regulars. More like one of those mercenaries, who carry their weapons hidden. Hangs around the docks sometimes, doesn't he, Sir?"

The Harbormaster didn't respond. He was watching Max's face closely.

" 'Message from actor man for fellow with bicycle,' he told us," Fenton continued. "Exact words. He had a squinty way, didn't look at me proper. Funny ears. Shifty, he was."

Max nodded, important and imperturbable. "What was the message?"

The Harbormaster nodded to the clerk, who took from his shirt pocket a sheet of paper, folded in half. Fenton gave it to the Harbormaster, who passed it on to Max, saying, "A rather odd message, if you ask me."

"You read it?"

"Of course. Anything out of the ordinary could be a danger to the harbor."

Max very carefully did not look either surprised or dismayed, although he felt both. All he said was "I see," and he unfolded the paper to read the message quickly, allowing himself no change of expression, a wily banker who knew more than he was saying. The note, written on heavy vellum embossed with the now-familiar arrangement of upside-down Vs, was only half a page long and made no sense.

Dear boy,

As the greater WS says, there is a tide in the affairs of men. You, it seems, will not be riding on this one with us. A pity, since we are in such a de-luxurious situation here, the eye of man hath not heard, the ear of man hath not seen, such luxury as we are in. Ours alone will be the adventure. And you? You must wait, wait with your grandmother, wait to hear. We wish you farewell!

WS the lesser

You will be glad to know that our adorable Arabella has engaged herself to Banker Hermann.

Max read quickly, nodded importantly, once, twice, pocketed the paper, and held out his hand to the Harbormaster. "Thank you for the information, my good man. You have been most helpful." So. They had sailed without him. His heart hit bottom. He had well and truly missed the boat. But what boat headed for what destination? And why had he been lied to about the time? Max turned to leave, walking his bicycle the way a grown man would, moving at a stately pace among the people and vehicles crowding the busy waterfront.

The Harbormaster and his clerk watched him go.

"What do you make of that, Sir?"

"Something's going on, I'm pretty sure. But not on my docks and not in my harbor, so it's not my problem," the Harbormaster said.

"Who *was* that fellow?"

"He was not who he seemed to be," answered the Harbormaster thoughtfully.

"Could this be a police matter? Maybe we'd better write down a description?"

"Good thinking, Fenton."

But neither of them could remember what their visitor had looked like. He hadn't left any clear impression, except for his red beret. "And his eyes, of course," the Harbormaster said.

The clerk agreed. "Never seen eyes that color, have I? You neither, Sir, I'll bet. Not gray, not really, and you couldn't say brown. Like—like the undersides of mushrooms. You've seen them, haven't you? The undersides of mushrooms?"

This reminded the Harbormaster that he was hungry and had been interrupted on his way home for the good lunch his wife would have waiting for him. "I believe somebody's pulling my leg," he told the clerk, "and I am not amused."

By then, their visitor had disappeared into the crowd. They looked for him but saw only a boy in the distance, a boy riding a bicycle, his schoolbag hanging off one shoulder and a bright red bandanna jammed into his rear pocket. The boy rounded a corner and was out of sight.

3

In which Max and Grammie wonder
what happened, and what to do about it

As soon as he was safely out of sight around two corners, Max stopped. He could go no farther. He put
his leaden feet on the ground and collapsed over the handlebars. The carpetbag thumped onto the ground.

Max felt as if a wagon had whammed into him. A wagon
loaded with heavy stones, a wagon pulled by huge-hooved
Clydesdale horses thundering along so fast they didn't even
swerve for the boy on a bicycle as they whammed into him.
He felt flattened, and stunned, and frightened.

He made himself breathe deeply, the old cure for stage
fright, once, twice, three times. Then he took three more
slow, deep breaths, just to hear the echo of his father's voice

in his head: "One, two, deep breaths, Max, deep, good, three, good."

Then a cart did rattle up behind him, its wooden wheels loud on the cobblestones. "Hey, kid! Outta the road!" a man's voice bellowed. A heavy boot kicked the carpetbag aside and the carter pushed by, muttering angrily, "As if these streets weren't narrow enough. These kids, think they own the world."

There were no sidewalks in the old city, so Max had to pick up his carpetbag, pull his bicycle into a doorway, and huddle there.

He couldn't take it in, what had happened. He felt as if he were floating in a sky with no moon and no stars, just black airless space. He felt hollow as space, empty, frightened.

He took three more slow, deep breaths, and the idea came to him: That note made absolutely no sense, made so little sense that it had—somehow—to make sense that it made no sense.

Grammie, he thought, the fact of her like a candle in the darkness. Maybe she knew something.

Because on fine days Grammie took her lunch out into the garden behind the library, that was where Max found her. He was glad she was alone. She took one look at his face and knew. "They've gone."

Max dragged words up from deep in his stomach. "Without me." He thrust the note at her. "The boat had already sailed, and there wasn't any boat with that name anyway." He sank beside her onto the wooden bench. "Someone was lying all along."

Grammie dropped the uneaten half of her sandwich onto her lap and read the note.

The bench was under a magnolia tree, and the air was sweetened by the perfume of its blossoms, but neither of them noticed that. After Grammie read the note, she covered her face with her hands, wrinkling the paper against her nose and mouth.

Max's own hands were fists on his thighs. "Do you think they knew?"

Eventually, Grammie uncovered her face. "What has he gotten her into now?" she demanded. "What do they expect you to do?"

"Be independent," Max told her glumly.

"Eat the rest of this sandwich, please. I seem to have lost my appetite."

Max shook his head. He wasn't hungry. He thought, in fact, that he might never be hungry again. They sat on the bench for a long time, not speaking, not looking at one another, each thinking unhappy, anxious thoughts. "You'll live with me of course," Grammie said thoughtfully, "but what *was* that invitation about?" The clock tower rang twelve slow notes.

"And what do you mean there was no boat?" she asked. "If they've gone off, there had to be a boat."

Max answered, "I was on *time*."

Grammie shook her head, as if to clear her thoughts, and

took off her glasses to rub at her eyes. Max waited. Grammie was the steady person in his life, the one who almost never got upset or excited.

"And that *note*," Grammie grumbled. "Take your things to my house, and after that you should go down to the docks again and find out everything you can," she decided. "Maybe something will make sense out of this latest . . . this latest *imbroglio* of your father's."

His mother had been just as eager, Max thought; but he didn't say this to his grandmother. He felt incapable of having a single opinion of his own, and he didn't want to have to make decisions, so he got up from the bench and went to do as he'd been told.

"Be back in time for supper," Grammie called after him.

Grammie made spaghetti for their supper, telling him, "It always used to cheer you up to have spaghetti, and I guess you need some cheering up after the day you've had."

On the red-and-blue-striped tablecloth there was also a bowl of salad made with early greens from the garden the two families kept in their adjoining yards. The two little houses were so close together that if Max had looked out his grandmother's kitchen door he would have seen the black shape of his own house, where no light shone in any window.

He didn't look.

"Thanks, Grammie," he said. "I'm hungry enough, but I don't think it *can* cheer me up."

"Well then, it can fill you up," she told him, twirling

spaghetti around her fork. Grammie was now so matter-of-fact about everything that Max became curious to know what she might have been thinking of, over the course of the afternoon.

"You know what?" Grammie asked, as if surprised by her own idea. "They *could* have gotten off the boat at Porthaven. They might be riding the evening train home."

"Do you think so?" Max asked with sudden hope.

Grammie thought about that, and sighed. "I'd be surprised, given that note he left," she admitted, and Max had to agree. "We'll find out soon enough if that's what's happened. Meantime, you'll stay with me," she said again.

Max had done some thinking of his own that afternoon about where he'd sleep that night. The trouble was, his grandmother was bossier than you'd expect from seeing her soft silvery hair worn up in a bun that kept slipping to one side or the other of her head, and her soft grandmotherly shape in the pink and mossy green grandmotherly colors she liked to wear, the loose sweaters and long scarves, the full skirts that swirled around her ankles. However, if you noticed the bright blue eyes behind their heavy tortoiseshell spectacles, you wouldn't be at all surprised to learn that before she was a librarian she had been a teacher and had some very bossy habits.

In the only clear thinking he'd been able to do that long afternoon, Max had decided that he should live at home, which meant he needed to sleep that night in his own bed in his own bedroom. He was a little afraid—which was ridiculous, but also true—and he didn't expect to get much sleeping done, but he had decided. Begin as you mean to go on, that was the advice he meant to follow. He wanted to be as independent as his parents said he could be.

When she saw the expression on his face, Grammie looked sternly at him. "No discussion. No argument. You already have a bag packed."

Max stuffed spaghetti into his mouth. He needed a minute to consider this. Considering it, he remembered: When he was just eight, the Company had presented dramatizations of some Aesop's fables at all the schools in the city, and at the University, too. One of these told the story of a stiff, proud oak tree that was broken in half by a strong wind, while a small, weak reed only bent under its force. Max had played the reed, his mother the oak, and his father the bellowing, billowing wind. And so he decided that just for this one night he would let Grammie tell him what to do. It would make her feel better, too, to have him there in the house with her. "All right," he said. "Just for tonight."

"We'll see about that," she said.

As they ate, they didn't talk much more than to ask for salt or the bowl of grated cheese. Only occasionally did they need to look up at one another. Over the years, they had had supper together countless times, at the same small table in Grammie's warm kitchen with its bright red cupboards and long soapstone sink, so they knew exactly what they'd see if they looked up.

After a long, companionable silence, Grammie said, "So."

Max looked across at her. "What do you think has happened?"

"What happened is they've gone off without you."

"Come on, Grammie, you know what I mean. I mean what do you think is going on? You read that note." Max had had an afternoon and a spaghetti supper, too, to get somewhat used to his situation.

"That note made no sense," Grammie said.

"Maybe it made too much no sense," Max said.

"Unless they planned all along to leave you behind," Grammie said. "Did you ever actually see your ticket?"

"It was supposed to be waiting on the boat. Maybe it was. But, Grammie? Arabella and Banker Hermann aren't even in the same play."

"I *know* that." She sighed and set her fork down on the plate. "I know that, and I recognize the Shakespearean lines. *Eye hath not heard . . .* That's from *A Midsummer Night's Dream,* spoken by that fool who is magicked by fairies. But why did he use those lines? That play is about love, and illusions. Do you think that's what the note is about? Love makes no sense, but it could be saying this isn't the way it looks."

"That would make it a warning."

"I think it's time you told me exactly what that invitation said. And exactly where it was from. And exactly who sent it," Grammie announced. She picked up her fork again.

Max did not argue. He recited the contents of the Maharajah's letter while Grammie twirled spaghetti, chewed, swallowed, and did not interrupt with any questions. At the end, he reminded her about the brooch, and that was what she had something to say about. "I was already suspicious about that. So tell me, what did the Harbormaster tell you about the ships that sailed this morning. Where were they bound?"

"For China and Australia and South America," Max answered quickly. He had made sure of that. "None for India, but a boat going to China or Australia might be stopping at an Indian port, couldn't it? To reprovision, to refuel."

"So your parents are most likely on one of those, rather than the one going to South America," Grammie said. "For which I'm grateful, because South America these days is nothing but little revolutions, one general trying to oust another."

Max agreed with her deduction. "Besides, the boat for South America was a cargo ship. But why have *Flower of Kashmir* tickets if there's no *Flower of Kashmir*?"

"It could be this Maharajah just pretends to himself that it's his private ocean liner. People who have great power and wealth? They . . . they go a little crazy, in my opinion; they don't live in the same world as the rest of us." She thought some more, then reminded Max, "And your mother is right, they do always land on their feet. Imagine how they'd laugh at us if we called out the army and they were lounging around in the lap of luxury in a first-class stateroom. You know what, Max?" she asked, sounding like her normal self. "I think we're going to have to be patient. That's what he said, isn't it? Wait with your grandmother? We're going to have to leave it up to them. They know where you are."

"Patient for how long?"

"Long enough for them to get in touch with us. When they do, this will all make sense. Things tend to make sense, in my experience. Unless"—she smiled—"your parents have been struck down with amnesia."

Max pointed out, "Amnesia's not contagious. They wouldn't both have it at the same time."

"Exactly," Grammie said. "Or it could be—if someone is fool enough to believe in that 'fortune' your father's always talking about? In which case you'll get a ransom note. Unless they've been taken for some other reason. But what could that be? Who would need the use of two actors?"

"It was supposed to be three actors," Max objected. *He* believed in that third ticket, whatever his grandmother might think.

"All the more unlikely to be kidnapping, then," Grammie said. She asked, "Can you live with the worry?" She reminded him, "I know how hard that is, waiting and not knowing, waiting and hoping, waiting and imagining the worst. I remember . . ."

Max had always known that Grammie had lost her young husband to a sudden squall on the lake; that his boat had not been located for a night and a day; and that it wasn't until the morning of the second day of the search that his body had been found. Grammie knew what she was talking about. She said, "It's not easy."

Max looked right back into those brave blue eyes and thought about it. He didn't know where his parents were, but he couldn't imagine that his parents were really lost, gone for good. Not for good, he thought. It wouldn't be for good, it would be for bad, for very bad. He swallowed hard and held his grandmother's glance. "I can wait. I will."

Grammie moved right on. "Not that we'll be doing *nothing*," she said. "I'll be doing research and locating passenger lists, itineraries, reading the newspapers. You'll be watching the mail, and also you should keep an eye on the theater, in case that was what somebody was after. Although, I can't think of why."

Neither could Max. The Starling Theater was an old building, in the old city, not convenient to the New Town. The seats were almost always filled, true, but that was because of his parents. "Any other company would have gone belly-up years ago," his father maintained. "But we have your mother! who is a beauty as well as brilliant."

At which pronouncement his mother would smile and roll her eyes at Max.

"And we have me!"

At which Max rolled his eyes at his mother.

Remembering that lightened Max's spirits even more than spaghetti.

"Which leaves us with the question of what to do about you," said Grammie, fixing him with a stern teacher's gaze.

Trying to match her sternness, Max told her, "I want to live in my own house," and reached out to serve himself green lettuce from the bowl of salad. "Is there dessert?" he asked, hoping that would distract her.

With a grandmotherly smile, to say *You're not fooling me,*

Grammie allowed herself to be distracted. "How do you feel about baked apple?" she asked. "With custard sauce?"

It wasn't until they had done the washing up and were seated side by side in the parlor in front of Grammie's woodburning stove, both pairs of stockinged feet stretched out toward the warmth, that Grammie asked for more details about what Max had learned on the docks that afternoon.

Max reported, "Captain Francis actually saw them. He said they were just getting out of a closed carriage. They waved and looked happy—at least from a distance. Then they went off up the gangplank of a ship, too far away from *The Water Rat* for him to read the name. He said my father was wearing his long green scarf and a wide-brimmed black hat, and looked dashing."

"And your mother?"

"He didn't say." Max's mother didn't get noticed—unless, of course, she was on stage, acting, and even then it was her character, not the actress, that people remembered. "He asked me why I wasn't with them, and I told him I was joining them in Porthaven. He believed me," Max concluded, pleased with the success of his lie.

Grammie smiled. "That was pretty smart, Max. I don't think we should tell anybody. Not until we hear from them, assuming that we will. Not the police, not anybody else, either. We need to be sure they're safe first. If we don't know what's going on, we might . . . put them in danger. If we tell the wrong person, or involve the wrong people. Since we

don't know who the right ones are, or even if there are any. Agreed?"

"Agreed," he said.

"Then, what about your school?"

"Don't tell them," Max answered, so vehemently that she looked sharply at him. He explained, "It's better if the school thinks I've gone off with my parents. I don't want anyone to suspect that I'm living alone." He didn't look at his grandmother, who either didn't hear or didn't feel that she needed to argue the point. "And besides, if I'm going to school, how can I earn the money to live on? I know you can't afford me, Grammie." He'd thought about this, too, during the long afternoon. His grandmother could live comfortably enough, she always said, on her librarian's salary, and she always declined the help her son-in-law offered, thank you very much, but she had nothing to spare, Max knew.

"We could manage," she assured him, but weakly. "Maybe it's lucky after all that your mother had such terrible morning sickness with you. I know you used to want a brother, or a sister, but I'd never be able to support two of you." Grammie gave a little laugh. "Still, it's a pity your father's famous fortune isn't in coins."

Max recited the lines, in as near an imitation as he could manage of his father's rich voice. "My fortune? My personal fortune? I break my fast each morning in its company."

Grammie just shook her head.

For some reason—maybe because they were talking about it together rather than trying to face it alone—both Max and Grammie felt better, not so shocked and frightened and powerless, more as if they had a plan.

"I want to work anyway," Max said, because how could you be independent if you weren't self-supporting? "But I've only ever had my jobs with the Company, and they're not any use outside of the theater, and the Company is the only theater in the city."

"It'll be hard for you to find work," Grammie agreed.

"I can mow lawns, and weed, and prune hedges, I suppose. I can wash windows and clean a house. I could probably clean a business, too, a bakery or a store or an office." He thought. "I can hammer, but I don't know how to build anything, not furniture or even a birdhouse."

"You can paint," Grammie reminded him.

Max knew better. "Even Joachim has trouble earning a living painting pictures."

Grammie had gone back to thinking about Max's education. "I can teach you history and reading, I know the books, and writing, too, and some science, and certainly geography. But I can't teach you mathematics. We'll have to find a tutor for that."

"Another expense," Max warned her. He finished his tea, suddenly tired. "I hope it's not too long before they write."

"We'll be fine," Grammie announced resolutely.

If she could believe that, maybe Max would, too.

Out of the window in the little room he had so often slept in when he was too young to be at the theater with his parents, or traveling with them, Max could look down, across the garden, to where his own house lay, pale in the moonlight, its windows dark. He hadn't really expected to see lights in the windows and the silhouetted figures of his parents moving through the rooms, but he wouldn't have been entirely surprised, either. After the day he'd had, nothing would surprise him. Was this what it was like having an adventure? Because he was beginning to suspect that being independent on your own wasn't as easy as being independent with parents.

Max slid under the blankets and pulled them up around his chin, as if they could warm him against the cold and anxious worries that filled the dark air around him.

4

In which Max doesn't want to get out of bed, Grammie is bossy, and Madame Olenka enters the scene

Max didn't expect to sleep well, but he did. He did expect to feel better when he woke up, at least a little bit better, but he didn't. The first morning after, he awoke to a gentle April rain falling outside the window and to the sight of his own silent and empty house, shrouded by a gray veil. From downstairs came the small sounds of Grammie in the kitchen, but when, after several minutes, he heard her footsteps coming up, he pulled up the blanket and closed his eyes.

He heard the door open, then nothing for a few seconds. The door closed and he opened his eyes.

He couldn't have said why he'd pretended to be asleep, why he didn't want anyone, even his grandmother, to see him.

Once he'd heard her leave the house for the day, he decided, he'd get out of bed.

And then what? he asked himself, and so he did not move, not when the front door closed with a thump, not as the minutes ticked by. Max stayed in bed, motionless under the covers, and tried to go back to sleep. That failed, but still he did not dare to get out of bed. A terrible thing had happened yesterday, and Max did not want to have to face it. As long as he was in this bed he could feel safe.

He wished his father could see him now, see how wrong he was about twelve being old enough to be independent. Max knew he wasn't old enough. If his father stepped into this room, Max would just laugh at him because of how wrong and stupid he had been to say Max was old enough.

He wished his father *would* just step into the room.

Max had been thrown away, like some old rag tossed into the corner of a room, and forgotten, and Yes, he did feel sorry for himself. They had dropped him into the deepest and coldest part of the lake and there was nothing he could do about it. He sank.

He couldn't think what he was supposed to do. If his parents were in danger. If they never came back. If they'd left him behind on purpose. If they couldn't be bothered to leave him anything but that senseless note.

He thought he might be hungry for lunch, but he wasn't. He got up to go to the bathroom and drink a little water out of the sink faucet, but then he skittered back to bed, as if a pack of dogs snarled at his heels. Only the thought of Grammie coming home and finding him still in bed got him up and dressed and downstairs when she returned from work. Once she was in the house with him he discovered that he was hungry after all.

Grammie served leftover spaghetti for supper.

"What did you do today?" she asked him.

Max shrugged.

"I know. Me too," she answered. "I'm going to look at the ships' manifests. I told the Harbormaster it was official city business, so he agreed to send them over tomorrow. Maybe I'll find out something."

Max nodded. The rain slid down the window over Grammie's sink.

After a quiet while, Grammie asked him, "Did you think about what work you can do?"

"Who would hire me?" Max asked. "I'm underage."

Something was making Grammie cross. "Plenty of boys your age have jobs."

Plenty of boys my age are eating dinner with their parents right now, Max thought but did not say. He shrugged.

Grammie sighed but didn't pester him. Instead, she told him about one or two of the people who had come into the library that day, and complained about the newspapers and magazines left scattered all over the reading room. "It took me an hour to put them away, and some are still missing. To think I argued and argued that the library needed a room where people could sit and read periodicals, on rainy days especially. I should have known better."

"Now you do," Max said un-helpfully.

He went up to bed right after the dishes were washed, not because he was tired but because he wanted so badly to be asleep. He didn't know why it should be so, but it seemed that he was more shocked and frightened now, even if it was a day and more after, than when he'd first realized that his parents were gone.

He hoped every day wasn't going to be worse than the one before. There was only so much black emptiness he could swallow without . . . without exploding from it.

The next morning, Friday, the second morning after, Grammie dropped something heavy onto the bed where he was pretending to sleep. "You might as well read," he heard her say. "I've left bread and honey on the table, there's milk in the icebox, and it's stopped raining, so you could do a little work in the garden."

The books she had left for him—for the heavy things were two books—made the day pass quickly enough. He'd read both *Treasure Island* and *Huckleberry Finn* before, and he guessed he knew why she'd picked out those two in particular, but still, he picked them up and turned to well-remembered scenes, reading with only half of his attention.

It was his father's note that really made him angry. Why did everything with his father have to be an adventure and a game? And why hadn't his mother written anything? What kind of parents were they? They said he was old enough to be independent, but they expected him to stay with Grammie.

Probably his parents were just as happy he wasn't with them. Probably they thought he was just moping here, feeling sorry for himself, and they probably thought it served him right for being so foolish as to think he'd actually be invited to go to India, in a first-class stateroom, and that's if it really was first class and not another one of his father's overdramatized pronouncements.

No, he'd seen their tickets. Their tickets were real, he was sure of that.

But why had this happened to *him*? He wasn't adventure-mad. That was his father, with his mother going along with whatever William wanted and probably wanting it herself, too. All Max wanted was not to have been left behind. What was wrong with him that he had no friends and his parents could just leave him behind like that?

"What did you do today?" Grammie asked him that evening.

Max shrugged but said, "I already read both those books."

Grammie said, "Well, I got a lot done. In case you're interested."

She didn't need to be sarcastic at him.

Grammie said, "According to the manifests, both of those passenger vessels are making stops in India. Well, one is in Ceylon, the Australian liner." Grammie looked at him expectantly.

"Miss Koala," Max supplied.

"Yes. She makes port at Lisbon first, then Tenerife, before she rounds the Cape of Good Hope at Cape Town and takes a northern route to Colombo before her last long lap, to Melbourne. She is due in Colombo about the first of June— these sea voyages don't have strict schedules, because they are so dependent on weather." When Max didn't say anything, Grammie added, "Colombo is not far from the tip of India."

"The letter said they'd be met in Bombay."

"Well, the *Eastern Star* actually lands in Bombay, which," she said to the expression on his face, "makes it more likely. It's due to land there about the tenth of May, and it's taking the Mediterranean route, via the Suez Canal, so it's more likely to be on schedule."

Only three weeks, then, Max thought. "Do you think that's the one they're on?"

"It's the likeliest choice, isn't it? That *Simón Bolívar* is a cargo ship. According to its manifest, it was delivering a load of raw copper and carrying back fabrics, lumber, plus some crates of wine for a distributor in New York City and picking up there—the suspicion is arms, but that Harbormaster likes his suspicions, so I don't know if he's to be believed. The ship is going on to Caracas, with a fueling stop in Miami. It's due in Caracas on the tenth of May. Cargo ships don't make good time, you know."

How would Max know something like that? He nodded anyway.

Grammie went on. "I didn't recognize any of the names on the passenger lists. Both of the liners had lots of couples traveling first-class, and before you ask, yes, I looked hard at the entire list, and the crew, too, just in case. There were no

Starlings, not in first class, or any other class. None. And no other names that looked like a clue—no Birdwells or Crowells or Robinsons or Swansons. Nothing. What staterooms they had on the *Simón Bolívar* had all been taken by some Spaniard with one of those *y* names. Carrera y Carrera. I don't know why they have names like that," Grammie grumbled.

Max knew that his grandmother was as unhappy as he was, but he was too unhappy to try to cheer her up.

The third morning after, Saturday, Max woke to the light and to birdsong, and he felt, for a moment, normal. It didn't last long, that good feeling. It didn't last more than a minute, but it was wonderful to be himself for that minute. Before he remembered and sank back down into helplessness and fear and anger. He heard Grammie in the kitchen below. He heard her steps on the stairs. He closed his eyes.

That morning, she made no pretense of believing he was asleep. She yanked the covers off, and when his eyes flew open in protest she said, "If you think you're going to lie around wallowing in self-pity another day, in my house? You have another think coming. If you won't go out and find yourself a job, you can clean up my kitchen. Weed the garden and your mother's flower beds, too, and if I return here at midday and find you still lying in bed there will be trouble."

Max felt his eyes fill with the unfairness of it all.

"You're not the only one who's worried and afraid and bereft. You're just the only one who's taken to his bed," Grammie announced, and she sounded disgusted with him. She turned on her heels and marched out of the room.

On Saturdays the library closed at noon. Usually, on Saturday afternoons, Grammie did her marketing and any other errands, then gave her little house a good sweeping out and washing down, if the weather was bad, or worked in the garden, if the weather was fair and there was gardening that needed doing. There would be no peace for Max today.

Max stormed out of bed, had breakfast without even sitting down at the table, and cleaned up the kitchen. Grammie hadn't even cleared her plate off the table. If she was going to be like that, Max would show her. He would move into his parents' house, his own house, and see how Grammie liked that.

After he had packed his things back into his carpetbag, he carried that, plus his watercolor paint box and pad, downstairs. He removed the key his parents had left with Grammie from its hook beside her back door, then left her house. He locked the kitchen door behind him with the key she kept on a hook under her back steps. Let her come home to a locked house, and wonder. He was angry enough at everyone to be glad to make his grandmother unhappy.

But when he stepped into his own kitchen and put his carpetbag down on the floor, his watercolors down on the table, Max felt different. Entirely different, as if the short crossing between the two little houses had been a long, long journey. The empty house quivered around him. Already its rooms smelled a little musty. Max felt jittery, in his stomach, and it might have been fear, but it might also have been excitement. Because he suddenly realized that he was going to do it—live in his own house, independent, on his own.

He unpacked his clothing and books and then wandered through every empty room, opening windows to let in fresh air. There weren't many rooms: upstairs two bedrooms and a bathroom; downstairs a kitchen, a dining room, and the front parlor, where his parents had left a trunk of the costumes they'd chosen to do without. This was the room where they walked back and forth reciting lines, or sat discussing the plans for a season's productions. Its two windows looked out over a narrow porch across a small front lawn to Thieves Alley. A low white wrought-iron fence separated the lawn from the street; a sweet-toned brass bell hung beside the gate, for visitors to announce themselves. Not that there were many visitors. The Starlings lived an irregular life, at work when most people had time off.

Of course Max also searched each room for any kind of clue, looked in desk drawers and dresser drawers he'd never opened before, but he found nothing of interest or use. Everything was as it had been, everything was in order, everything taken care of in preparation for a long absence. Nothing pointed to any possible solution to the mystery of his parents' whereabouts. So Max went out to buy milk, butter, cheese, and apples. He stopped at the baker's for a loaf of bread, then carried his purchases back to the empty house.

Nothing felt quite right. Buying his own groceries out of

the dwindling number of coins he had in his pocket didn't feel right, and neither did being alone in a silent house that was usually filled to overflowing by the presence of his charismatic parents. It wasn't going to be easy, living here alone and waiting. It wasn't going to be easy not to worry, either. It wasn't going to be easy to live independently. But that was what Max intended to do.

While spring breezes from opened windows washed through the rooms, Max decided to go outside and do a little weeding in the front garden before lunch. With all the organizing and packing and cleaning of the last few days, his father hadn't had time for the gardens, not Mary's flower gardens near the porch and along the fence nor the vegetable garden out back. Max didn't like weeding, but that morning, when he felt more like his old self and yet also like some whole new person, he welcomed the work. It gave him something to be doing. Max dressed for the chore as his father, who always dressed the part, whatever part it was, on or off the stage, would have. He wore overalls without a shirt, and work boots. He tied a red bandanna around his neck and set a wide-brimmed straw hat on his head.

He worked patiently, loosening the soil and pulling up weeds, thinking about the employment possibilities available to a twelve-year-old boy. Could he actually take a job doing this, hour after hour, day after day, in some stranger's garden? He didn't think so, and he was imagining himself saying "No, thank you" to an imagined housewife who was offering him work as a gardener, when the bell rang at the gate.

Max pretended not to hear it. He didn't even turn his head to see who it was. It wouldn't be his parents, they'd walk right in; and it wouldn't be his grandmother, who was at the library. He pulled up a stubborn weed, concentrating on the task.

It rang again, the musical sounds of the round brass clapper striking the heavy brass bell. This time Max turned his head to see who was being so insistent.

A woman stood at the gate. She glowered at him, and then she opened the gate to let herself in. Quickly, Max got to his feet and turned to meet her.

She was not someone he knew. In fact, he'd never seen her before. He glanced at her from under the brim of his hat but did not speak. Max knew, from being on stage, the value of not speaking. The woman wore an olive-green suit, with a row of silver buttons closing the jacket, and a small black hat that fitted close around her head and entirely covered her hair, giving her face a foxy, pointy look. Long silver earrings hung down from her ears. Or perhaps, Max thought, looking more carefully, the earrings weren't all that long. It was her earlobes that were long, he thought, staring. Her earlobes were much, much longer than normal.

She smiled, an unpleasant smile that showed bright teeth. "I am Madame Olenka," she announced in a deep, throaty voice.

Did she expect him to know who that was?

"I did not think to find anyone here, so I have to wonder, who are *you*?"

Max would have reached out to shake her hand and introduce himself, because he knew how to be polite, but his hands were caked with dirt, so he jammed them into his overalls pockets instead, and before he could tell her who he was—and what would he have told her?—she went on.

"The family has gone away," she said, looking past him to the house, not really seeing him, not interested in a gardener. "I know them, the actors and their little boy. I'm here to find out if the house is for rent. Or for sale?" She still wasn't looking at him. "Do you know? Is there an agent?" When Max didn't answer, she asked, speaking very slowly and more loudly, as if to someone simple-minded, or deaf, "Who . . . is . . . paying . . . you . . . your . . . wages?"

"Lady pays," he answered. He concentrated on acting like Greek Jonny, one of the unsuccessful suitors in *Adorable Arabella*.

Then she did look at him, not pleased. "Do you speak our language?"

Max nodded. "Speak good."

"Who can I talk to—do you understand *talk to*?"

Max answered, "Need to work, Missus."

When she sighed in exasperation, the silver earrings danced beside her neck, like long-stemmed flowers bowing to the breeze. "I like live here," she said, pointing to a silver button on her chest and then to his house. "Who let me live here?"

"Me."

"Not you, you ninny. Obviously not you, but who? Who

can I rent—pay coins to—so I live here." She waved a hand at the house. "For my home. You know *home*? Sleep, eat there."

"Me," Max said again. "I live. Here." He waved a hand at the house behind him. "Work"—he indicated the garden—"here."

"Who hired you?" she asked him, and headed for the steps to the front door.

He moved to stand in her way. "Why you doing, Missus?" Of course, he could see that she wore no wedding ring, no rings at all, in fact; but he felt that this was the way the gardener might address an unknown lady.

She stepped backward, to get away from him. "Foreigners," she muttered.

When she stepped back, Max stepped forward, forcing her to move away from the house. He was wearing work boots, and she was wearing pumps with low, narrow heels. His feet looked dangerously large and clumsy next to hers. She stepped backward again, and again, and again, with Max moving right along with her, smiling pleasantly, until she got to the gate.

There, she reached a hand out behind her to find the latch, but before she slipped through the gate she said, "Let me tell you something, Mister. I'm going to talk to someone about you. How you act around here, as if you own the place. What's your name?"

"Name Mister," Max said, and now he glared at her until she had backed through the gate and let it close after her. She went down the street slowly, to let him see that he hadn't

really driven her away, to make it clear that she had chosen to leave. Every now and then, before she turned the corner and went out of sight, she looked back over her shoulder at Max.

He was waiting for this, and watching for it. When she turned to look, he raised his hand to wave at her: Hello, goodbye. . . . When she had rounded the corner, he latched the gate again and returned to his labors. There was something suspicious about the woman, and she might just come right back to catch him out. He didn't want her to think he wasn't really a gardener named Mister, whose name—as he ran the scene through his head—struck him as pretty funny.

When Grammie got home, carrying a basket heavy with a chicken, some bread, butter, cheese, and a box of tea, Max went to join her in the kitchen. After all, he didn't want to make her feel worse than she already did. "Good," she greeted him, then asked, "You've been in the garden? Will you bring me up some potatoes and carrots from the cellar? And an onion, too. I need to get this chicken into the oven."

"I'm moving back," he told her. "Home," he announced, and went down the narrow cellar steps before she had time to say anything about that.

When he returned, hands full, she said, "We'll talk about it."

"I've decided," he answered. He tried to explain, "Otherwise, it's . . . Otherwise I just . . ."

"You're twelve," she said.

"Almost thirteen," he said. "At thirteen I could leave school and go to work. It's the law."

"I *know* the law," she said.

"I was over there today," he told her, and sat at the table to watch her strong fingers pulling overlooked feathers from the pale chicken carcass. "Weeding the front garden, and there was a woman." He began the story of his performance as Greek Jonny. Telling it, he realized something he hadn't noticed at the time. "She said *foreigners,* the way people do who aren't forcigners. So she must live here, and not be a real Madame Olenka, which sounds Russian. Or Bulgarian . . ."

"Name, ears, bad hat, *and* bad manners—I don't like the sound of this woman at all. Not at all. She had no idea who you were, did she?" Grammie looked thoughtfully at the boy. He *was* tall for his age, and accustomed from a young age to being in costume.

"What're you staring at?" Max asked her.

"Nothing," she answered him. "You." He looked like any ordinary twelve-year-old boy, but as she studied him his grandmother thought how unusually ordinary and unmemorable his looks were, always excepting his strange eyes, which had the look of one of the library's oldest volumes that time and damp had turned browny moldy gray. He had normal-length hair that was mostly brown but also looked sort of sandy blond, and his features—his nose and chin, his eyebrows and ears—were unremarkable. He wasn't particularly thin or particularly fat. The way he walked, the way he ran, the width of his shoulders . . . there was nothing anybody would notice in particular about Max. No wonder this Madame Olenka person didn't doubt that he was the gardener, given how he was dressed, and a foreign gardener at that, talking the way he had.

She put the oiled and salted chicken into the oven and joined him at the table to make her own report. "I looked up the Maharajah of Kashmir, in the encyclopedia."

Max put his hands on his knees, gripped hard, and waited. It would be, he knew, bad news.

"There's no such person," Grammie said. "There never has been such a person, although Kashmir is a real enough place, even famous, because it's where cashmere comes from. Your father's green scarf is made of cashmere."

"He was wearing it Wednesday morning," Max remembered, with a sudden sinking feeling. "He said there would be cool breezes out on the open sea. My mother was wearing that brooch."

They both fell silent then, briefly, before they shook off the sadness and unease. Grammie waited for Max to draw the obvious conclusion, and eventually he did: "That invitation really was a trick. A lure."

She nodded.

"But why?"

She shook her head, she didn't know. "That's what we're waiting to find out. All we can do is wait, I'm afraid. I'm sorry to say. This Madame Olenka, however, worries me. I doubt she'll come back on a Sunday, but I'll take Monday off so we can both be at the house. You'd better continue being the gardener. What did she call you?"

"Mister," Max reported with a smile.

Grammie rose to fill a bowl with cold water in which to soak clean the carrots and potatoes. "I don't think you should be living over there alone," she told him then. "But I'll accept it, for a night or two at least. I do expect you to come have supper here."

"But—"

"By six at the latest."

"You're being bossy," Max complained.

"I'm the grown-up around here, for now," she explained. "If you get hungry, you know where I hide my key, and you know where I keep my cake stand. So go back over there and see to the garden, which needs attention. I've got cleaning to do, and we can organize your life tonight after we eat."

Max didn't bother to object. But he knew he'd better make his own plans, or he'd be bossed out of his own life and have no hope at all of independence; and if he didn't have his independence, he was stuck being abandoned and helpless.

That evening, Grammie served a roast chicken dinner, including gravy, mashed potatoes, carrots, and the lingonberry preserves she liked with her poultry. While they ate they talked about the classes Max had been taking at school. Then Grammie outlined her plan to teach the subjects she knew enough about. At the end she told him, "I've found you a math tutor. His name is Ari and he'll meet you at the house—that is, at your parents' house—Tuesday afternoon.

At three. You should pay him what you pay Joachim, and if there's not enough money for both, it's Joachim whose lessons you'll have to miss."

Max had no time to respond as he would have liked to all of these plans made for him without consulting him at all, and all of these orders given to him. What he wanted to say was *No,* and *Wait,* and *What if I . . . ?* But Grammie had gotten up to clear their plates and cut thick wedges of chocolate cake. Finally, after the dishes were washed and dried, the pots and pans scoured and put away, cups of tea were set out on the table and they got down to the most difficult problem, which was: How does a twelve-year-old boy earn a living?

Grammie had made a long list of possible jobs: delivery boy of groceries or newspapers, flowers, food; window washer or dishwasher, dog walker, old person's reader; even gardener— although Max shook his head at that. Her last idea was stable hand, even though Max knew nothing about horses. "You can learn," she promised him. She explained that he would have to be a day laborer, working where the employees were always coming and going so that nobody would ask questions about where he came from or where he was living.

Max suggested that he would rather have a job that was interesting, to which Grammie told him sternly, "You probably won't find challenging work. However, all work is worth doing well. And there are things to be enjoyed about most jobs, that's true, too," she added, in response to something she saw in his face. "That's if you're open-minded. Many people would hate working in a theater, you know," she said.

"Acting. Me, for example. I hope you're smart enough to be open-minded." Then she announced to him that, like his continuing education, his joining her for supper was non-negotiable. "Every night."

"Agreed," Max said quickly. He was almost relieved to think that there was someone who cared where he was at the end of every day. "But, Grammie? If I can't be who I am, who do I *say* I am, when I apply for a job?"

"You'll think of something," she predicted.

At night, at home, lying in his bed waiting for sleep to come out of the hollow darkness and claim him, Max carefully did not think about who was not there in the house with him, nor did he think about how unlikely it was that he could find work. Instead, he considered different names for himself. He'd always rather liked the name Bartholomew, also Tancred, and also—now he started thinking about it— there was Lorenzo. Maybe he would use different names for different jobs. Lorenzo could deliver flowers and Tancred could walk dogs. While Bartholomew—Bart, he'd call himself Bart—sounded like a paperboy to him.

These thoughts kept him distracted in the silence of the empty house. He was alone, maybe abandoned, but he no longer felt so . . . so anxious, so overwhelmed, so helpless.

Or Mister Max, he thought, and smiled, and slept.

5

In which Madame Olenka returns
with reinforcements, and Max seeks
gainful employment

On Monday (which was the fifth morning after some vessel—but which vessel? going where?—had left Queensbridge with William and Mary Starling on board) Grammie was proved right. Immediately after breakfast, she settled herself on Max's front steps with a book.

Max wore the overalls again, and the straw hat, too. He had tied the red bandanna loosely around his neck, and he crouched beside the flower beds along the porch. The front door stood invitingly open on this gentle April morning. A breeze carried the faint city smells of baking bread and horse dung and brewing coffee mixed with the sound of distant carts and, from the lake and river, a certain watery freshness.

Puffy white clouds floated on the surface of a pale blue spring sky.

When the bell rang, Grammie announced in a low, satisfied voice, "I told you. That is a woman with a purpose."

That morning, Madame Olenka wore a suit the color of bricks and the same black hat and shoes. Her earrings dangled down copper on either side of her thin neck. She had a uniformed man behind her, a policeman. Pointing straight-armed at Max, she said, "This is the man." The policeman leaned over the gate to look at Max, who ignored both of them.

The policeman cleared his throat. Max looked up, as if he had heard a buzzing insect, then returned to his weeding, as if the insect was just a honeybee after all, nothing important.

"I've seen that face on wanted posters," Madame Olenka said. "I know I have."

The policeman cleared his throat more loudly. "Ahem? Sir?"

Madame Olenka had no patience for politeness. "He said his name's Mister, what kind of a name is that? He's up to no good, I tell you, he's up to something." She hadn't noticed Grammie before, but now she did because the little silver-haired librarian stood up, a finger marking her place in the book she carried, to approach the gate, with a mild, grand-motherly smile.

"A good morning to you, Sven Torson," she said, and the

policeman quickly removed his helmet to hold it respectfully in front of him.

"Mrs. Nives," he said. The helmet had flattened his brown hair, and he looked shyly down at his black-booted feet. "It's been a long time."

"Since you were a schoolboy," she answered. "What were you, ten? I'd say it's been quite a long time. You do seem to have grown taller."

Now he did look at her, and he grinned. "All grown up. Grew wider, too, didn't I?"

"I'd have thought I'd see you in my library, at least sometimes. You were a good reader, I remember."

"I've got my work now," he apologized.

"So I see," she said.

"And a wife, three children," he said. "A dog, a garden."

"Some other year, then," Grammie laughed. "But why are you here, Sven Torson? And who is this—this person you've got with you?"

"Madame Olenka had concerns about the gardener," the policeman explained.

Madame Olenka demanded, "What do you know about him? What is he doing in this empty house?"

"Do you mean Mister?" Grammie asked, and turned to look at Max, who—as if he had heard his own name—glanced at the group by the gate. He stood up, as though Grammie had summoned him, but he did not move any closer.

"What kind of a name is that? *Mister,*" Madame Olenka

said scornfully. She was standing at the gate beside the big policeman, shouldering her way in front of him to get a better look at Max.

Grammie answered sharply, "No more strange than Olenka, in my opinion. But, Sven Torson, why does this . . . this person—why does she say the house is empty? When the family just left town a few days ago."

"That, she didn't say, Mrs. Nives."

"Well, it's a curious thing. If I were a policeman, it might make me a little suspicious. In any case, the house isn't empty. Mister is to live here and take care of things while my daughter and her family are away."

"Who *is* he, Officer? I demand that you find out."

"But, Missus," Officer Torson said in a patient voice, "this lady says he's living here. She was my schoolteacher, and now she's the city librarian."

"I've known Mister for twelve years," Grammie said to Officer Torson. "More than twelve years, and if there is any question this . . . any questions *she* cares to raise about his character, I will vouch for him."

"Not true!" cried Madame Olenka. "That is Just Not True!"

"Well, Missus," Officer Torson said in not so patient a voice, "I don't know why you would say that."

"The librarian is lying!" Madame Olenka's copper earrings danced angrily in the sunlight.

Grammie didn't even glance at the woman. "You know me, Sven Torson," she said. "Am I a person who lies?"

"No, ma'am," he answered, and turned to his companion. "We'll go back to the station now, Missus, if you don't mind. Mrs. Nives has the right of it. I *am* wondering why you're so interested in an empty house. And how you came to know it was empty."

Her part in the scene over, Grammie returned to her step and her reading. Max got back to his weeding, and the two visitors went off down the narrow road. Even when they had gone out of sight, Max and Grammie continued to play their parts, just in case. Just in case of what, they couldn't have said, but they felt a need to be careful.

After a rather long time—longer for Max, who was on his hands and knees ferreting out deep-rooted weeds, than for Grammie, who basked in the warm sunlight and in fact closed her eyes to let her mind wander—Max went inside to wash and change his clothes. Grammie joined him for an exchange of compliments ("Good job, that," "And you didn't even lie!") followed by a congratulatory handshake and an order: "Go find yourself some work, young man."

"Where?" Max asked.

But Grammie was no help. "That's up to you. The house *does* need to look inhabited, I won't quarrel with you about that, although . . ."

"Fine," Max said. Once he understood that she had no advice to give him, he stopped really paying attention to whatever it was Grammie was saying. Instead, he studied himself in the full-length mirror his parents had hung on the entryway wall. She was a good ally, this grandmother, but she was getting bossier by the minute.

However, he wasn't going to worry about that right then. Right then he needed to see that he looked enough like a student at the University, a rather poor student, someone who needed to find odd jobs to earn a little money for food and school supplies. He had changed into dark cotton trousers and heavy work boots, a collarless shirt, and the old blue jacket his father wore to play the part of the poor but honest farmer who came to ask his rich neighbor for the loan of a cow in *A Miser Made Miserable*.

Max twisted a gray-and-white checked cloth cap in his hands to appear both nervous and hopeful. He watched himself in the mirror and thought, *Overacting*. He tried just turning the cap around and around in his hands, and that was much better.

"I don't know what would have happened if I hadn't gotten suspicious and been here to help," Grammie said. "Do you think you're safe, living here alone? Max, are you paying attention?"

"No," Max said.

"We'll talk at supper. Good luck, *Mister*."

"Who needs luck?" Max asked, admiring himself in the mirror.

Max wasn't feeling so chirpy at the end of the afternoon. He was hungry, and he had failed to convince anyone to hire him. He'd started out confidently enough. He'd ridden his bicycle out of the old city into the New Town, thinking that the people there would have more groceries delivered to their grand homes, would send more flowers to one another, would have more restaurants needing daily, or even twice-daily, deliveries of bread and rolls. Most of the butchers and bakers, greengrocers and florists he had talked to had been polite, even sympathetic. "I know what it's like, being short of the ready," they said. "Never was a university student myself, but I've had to go without, in my day. Good for you, young man, having the gumption to do something about it. Leave me your name and where I can get in touch with you. I don't need someone now, but you never can tell." So he wrote it down, *MAX, 5 Thieves Alley,* and they put the piece of paper in a drawer and turned back to their customers.

The cooks in restaurants were not so kindly. "You think I don't have a boy to do that?" they asked him. "You think my son (or cousin, or nephew, or grandfather) can't do that, and keep the work in the family? You think I can afford to hire some university student—who's going to end up with a high-paid job in some fancy office when all's said and done—to do work any idiot can do? You're supposed to be so smart, you students. Get out of my kitchen and figure it out for yourself."

It was a relief to lean his bicycle against the steps by his own back door, drop his cap onto his own kitchen table, and cross over to Grammie's kitchen for supper. It was good to be welcomed by the rich smells of beef stew on the stove top and biscuits in the oven and look into the face of someone who smiled to see him. "Any luck?" Grammie asked, then, "Do you want a piece of cheese to keep the wolf away?"

"No," Max answered, and "Yes please."

While they waited for the biscuits to come out of the oven, Grammie reported to Max about her afternoon's activities. "I sent a telegram to Bombay. I don't know if you know that librarians are great joiners? We are, and we have many associations we can join, and every association has its own publications, so there are pamphlets listing the addresses of libraries all over the world, along with the names of their librarians. University libraries, too, not just the ones for a public readership, and law libraries, medical libraries, private libraries . . . But only the libraries for a wide public readership might answer. That's what I think. Anyway, I sent telegrams to Bombay and to Colombo." She helped herself to a chunk of cheese and added, "And I asked at Caracas, as well."

"About the Maharajah of Kashmir?" Max asked.

"Why would I do that? We already know he doesn't exist. What I asked about was those three ships, the *Miss Koala,* the *Eastern Star,* and the *Simón Bolívar.* I asked to be told when they landed, and if there was anything newsworthy about them or their passengers. I asked them, in short, to do a little research for me. Librarians love researching things, so I hope I'll hear something back."

She was pleased with herself, Max could tell. But still,

she was shaking her head to tell him, "Although *what* I'll hear back I don't know. Nor when. Now, you tell me about *your* afternoon."

With a little food in his stomach and a dinner almost ready to come to the table, Max could make a report of—if not success—at least many attempts. Grammie was sympathetic. "It's not easy, finding work." Max didn't argue about that.

They ate in friendly silence. "Good" was about all Max said, and "Thank you," Grammie answered. "Do you want seconds?" Max asked, when he got up to refill his bowl. When they were both satisfied, Grammie said, "I've been wondering if . . . Wouldn't you be happier if you at least *slept* here? You could still live over there, but what about sleeping here?"

Max, who had had the same idea, responded quickly. "No, but I'll help with the dishes," he said, before he had any time to think of how much he'd rather not spend all of another night absolutely alone.

"All right, but what about your breakfast?"

"I bought food, and it's not as if I have so much money I can afford to waste anything."

"You could bring it over here."

"I could," Max agreed. It would be easy to do that, and he also knew he'd sleep better in Grammie's house. Then why, he wondered, didn't he want to say yes? And feel safer, feel taken care of, feel cared about?

It was because of that middle feeling, Max realized. In the shipwreck of his life, letting someone take care of him would sink him. It would drown him. It would finish him off. He couldn't let Grammie see that he was wavering. So he smiled, and said, "How can I find my father's fortune if I'm not there on the spot to search for it, day and night? And protect it from marauders?"

Grammie laughed at the well-worn family joke. "All right. It's up to you. You know where I am if you need me."

Max kept it going a little longer. In a voice that shook with the horror of it, he asked, "Are you implying that you don't believe in my father's famous fortune?"

"I'll take you up on the offer to wash dishes," Grammie answered.

In his own dark house, in his own bed, Max lay stiff and still, trying not to think about his parents (Where were they? What were they up to? Were they actors or victims? Would they get in touch with him and explain?) and not to think about the failures of his afternoon and, especially, not to think about the little house across the back garden, where he would not feel so alone.

6

In which Max earns
a princely sum

On Tuesday, the sixth morning after his parents sailed without him, Max's bad luck held firm. He found no employment. He went to hotels, to laundries, to hardware stores, to book stores and stationery stores and even a department store. "No experience? None at all?" they asked, shaking their heads in amazement at his foolishness in expecting to find work under those circumstances. "Try around the corner, tell them I sent you," he was told, but "Does that imbecile mean to insult me? Does he imply that my people are inexperienced?" he was greeted around the corner.

In desperation, he asked for work at a clothing store. The manager didn't even bother to ask his name. He eyed Max's shabby boots and wrinkled trousers. "I could clean. I could sweep, polish countertops, wash windows," Max pointed out, but not with much hope. The manager put a hand on Max's elbow and ushered him out a side door. "Try in the old city," he advised. "They're not very particular," and he turned away.

Max hadn't packed any lunch, so he bought himself a meat pie at a streetside stand and rode into the park that formed the centerpiece of the architect's design for the New Town. This large green space had broad grassy lawns, bright flower beds, and two fountains. Tall shade trees under which benches had been placed lined the walks. Max chose an empty bench, leaned his bicycle against the nearest tree, and sat down to consider what he might try next, as he removed the heavy paper from his lunch. The park was too big to seem crowded, although a throng of people had come out to enjoy this mild spring midday. Businessmen having important conversations, women with small children and large dogs picnicking together on blankets, young shop assistants of both sexes strolling about and laughing, keeping an eye on other young shop assistants of both sexes who were strolling about, looking back at them. Max took a bite of the meat pie.

It was *terrible*! He almost spat it out onto the ground. But he had paid for it, so he made himself chew and swallow. The crust was thick and sticky, the gravy thin and greasy, the meat gristly. The coins he had spent for it would have been put to better use being dropped with a wish into one of the park fountains. He could stand to eat only half, but that was food enough to see him through until he went home to meet with his math tutor. There was bread in his own kitchen, or he might stop in at Grammie's house first, where the icebox and cookie jar were always full.

Lazily, feet stretched out before him, checked cap pulled down low on his forehead, he watched people on the paths enjoying the fine day. City sounds were muffled here, so it was the cries of children and the barking of dogs that filled the air, against a soft, steady background sound of splashing water from the nearby fountain. Three men walked by him, deep in conversation.

Watching them, Max had the idea to ask if businesses might need a messenger to carry important papers and packages between the New Town and the old city, the harbor, the courts, the mayor's office, the hospital. Or he might get himself a little cart and sell his own meat pies; Grammie was sure to have a recipe. Or sandwich rolls filled with cheese and tomatoes, those would be popular here in the park. Or . . . oranges and bananas from a tray or . . . and he had drifted off to sleep. When your dreams have disturbed you, alone in an empty house, even a bad lunch can make you drowsy. But it was only a little light snooze, and Max was pulled gently out of it when he sensed that he was being stared at. Slowly, warily, he sat up.

The staring eyes were big and round and brown as boots. They did not blink. Their face was unsmiling and topped by wispy light brown hair. The body looked almost too small for its head, being so short in the limbs and so narrow at the shoulders. A child, Max realized. A very young child. "Hello," he said, and smiled.

The child wore a loose red cotton blouse, short white pants, and high white shoes made of soft leather. He stood directly in front of Max, staring.

"What's your name?" asked Max.

There was no response.

Max looked around. No adult hovered nearby keeping a careful eye on its child. No mother, no nanny, grandmother, or nursemaid, no sister or brother, not even a large family dog. In every direction there were children in sight and adults around them, but they were all at a distance.

"Where's your mommy?" he asked.

There was no response, no change in the child's serious, staring expression.

What did you do with a child, alone and too young to talk? Max asked, "You want to come sit up here with me?" and patted the bench beside him.

The child lifted his arms, which Max took to mean yes. He bent over to pick him up and set him on the bench beside him, where he sat quite happily, hands clasped in his lap, legs sticking straight out. Max wondered if he'd have to stay where he was, with the child, until the parent or guardian realized he was missing and came looking.

"What's your name?" he asked again, but the child was busily considering the view from this new height and paid no attention to Max.

"My name is Max," Max said. He tapped his chest with his forefinger. "Max. Can you say that?"

The child smiled, showing four little white teeth emerging from his upper gums and four from his lower. "Maah," he echoed, putting his own hand on his own chest.

"No, *I'm* Max. Who are *you*?"

"Momma," the child told him.

Max laughed. "You can't be Momma."

"Dadda," the child suggested cheerfully.

A different approach was needed, obviously. Max asked, "Where's Momma?"

"Maah," the little boy answered, and then, satisfied with their conversation, turned his attention back to the park spread out before them, studying it and apparently thinking.

Should he take the child to the police? Max wondered. He knew that was the logical and the natural thing to do—but the police would ask him questions, and he didn't want to answer any questions. This was developing into a problem, this child. He didn't think he should just put a child into his bicycle basket and wheel it across the park to Grammie's library; but she did know that policeman, Officer Torson, so if no better choice came along, in the end he could do that.

But what if he started crying, frightened at the strangeness of a bicycle and the strangeness of Max? Could Max ride all that distance with a howling child and not be noticed?

The child turned away from Max, twisted over onto his stomach, and slid backward to the ground. He looked up at

Max, extended a very small hand to him, and said, "Eye." Or maybe it was "I." Or could it have been "Aye."

Obviously, he wanted Max to go with him, and Max didn't see that he had any choice. "I need my bicycle," he said, moving toward the tree trunk against which the bicycle leaned.

"Eye!" (Or "I!" or "Aye!") the little boy cried, impatient and cross—if a child that young could *be* impatient and cross—and he ran off, luckily not at much speed. Letting the bicycle fall, Max caught up in three steps.

"Wait, just for a minute," he said. "Wait."

"Eye! Eye!"

"But I have to bring my bicycle. How about—do you want to ride? *Zoom, zoom,*" he offered with a broad, swift swing of his arm.

That interested the child.

"In the basket?" Max offered. Also, that way he couldn't bolt off again. He was beginning to see how the little boy had managed to get separated from his grown-up. "Basket?" he offered again, holding out his hand to the child. "Bicycle?"

Luckily, the child liked the idea and took Max's hand. "Maah," he said contentedly, and pulled Max back to where the bicycle lay. Max stood the bicycle up and let the child spin the foot pedal around and around for a while, then jam his short arms through the spokes of the wheel. At last he raised his arms and gave an order. "Uppie! Uppie!" Max lifted him up into the basket, folding the remarkably flexible legs to fit the basket's shape.

Excited now, with everything being so new again, the

child pointed, shouting, "Eye! Eye!" (Or "I! I!" or "Aye! Aye!") Max didn't dare mount and ride, so he held the handlebars and wheeled the bicycle along the path in front of the fountain.

Twisting around in the basket, the child reached out to push at Max's right hand. "You want to steer it yourself?" Max asked, and he had to laugh. "You're facing the wrong way, just in the first place. And you're much too short." He jabbed his chin at the child when he spoke those last words: much *jab,* too *jab,* short *jab.*

The little boy giggled and tried to jam his small fist into Max's mouth.

Max wheeled the bicycle down the pathway, approaching a group of women who had small children running all around them. There he angled the bicycle so the child could see the group. "Momma?" he asked.

"Maah," the child answered, and pointed away, across the park to the road, reminding Max, "Eye." Then his mouth stretched out flat and wrinkled ominously. "Eye!" he cried, more loudly.

Max thought he could come back to these groups later, to ask if there had been anyone missing a child, but for now he wanted to keep the child quiet, which meant doing as he was told. He didn't want anyone noticing him, wondering about him, looking for explanations. He hadn't yet figured out what lies he could safely tell; he just knew what truths he had to keep hidden. So he kept moving.

They went all around the park, along the paths, among the

trees, around both fountains, and nobody claimed the child. When Max turned reluctantly back, away from the road, to approach the closest group of women and ask them what they knew, the child grew restless and impatient first; then his mouth opened wide as his lips quivered and his round brown eyes filled with tears. He began to wail. "All right," Max said. "We're going, don't cry. Please, don't?"

"Eye," the child sniffled. He twisted around in the basket and pointed.

Max obeyed the pointing finger, moving carefully through the carriages going along the roadway as he crossed Barthold Boulevard, lifting bicycle and child over the tram tracks. Now the child twisted his head around to look at the little shops lining the street.

Max looked, too, but saw no sign of a frantic mother. He saw fruit, books, and hats. He saw four men in suits seated around a table under a wide green-and-yellow-striped umbrella, with plates of food and a waiter bending over to fill their glasses with water. He saw a sign with a chocolate ice cream cone that looked so real he thought he could eat it, after his disappointing lunch. People who painted signs had to be good at it, he thought, and then he wondered if he might earn his living painting signs for stores or restaurants, bakeries, or even ships' chandlers and ironmongers, blacksmiths, goldsmiths, silversmiths; all kinds of businesses needed signs to identify their products. Max admired a large painted wooden shoe hung out over the cobbler's doorway. He would ask Joachim if—

"Eye! Eye!" the child cried, trying to crawl up out of the bicycle basket.

Max grabbed for the little shoulders. "No!" He pushed at the child to keep him in the basket. "Stay there, *please,* don't—" and at the same time he turned to see what the child was pointing at. As soon as he saw it, he understood.

"Ice cream?" he asked. "You want ice cream?"

"I," the child answered, relieved that this large and friendly person had finally grasped his perfectly simple and entirely obvious desire.

Max lifted him out of the basket and set him on his feet, gripping one small wrist tightly while he leaned his bicycle up against the brick wall beside the shop entrance. Maybe, once he had given him some ice cream, the child would point the way home. Or maybe he would have to ask where the nearest police station was so he could take the child there and a parent could be found. Or he could go find Grammie and admit that he'd acted impulsively . . . But she wouldn't want him to have ignored the child, would she? Now he wondered, alarmed, if by putting the child in his basket and riding off, he might be accused of kidnapping. He should have stopped to think. Or at least he should have slowed down and thought. The child seemed perfectly content now, pulling Max into the little shop; but the parent must be frantic.

Should he have just waited where he was, on the bench, with the child safely beside him? It was too late to worry about that. He had made his choice, done what he'd done.

The shop bell jangled behind them, and Max breathed in deeply. He wasn't sure what to say.

The young woman who looked at them from behind the counter had light brown hair held neatly away from her face by a white kerchief, pale brown eyes, and olive skin, and she was as plain—and as appealing—as a mole, or a field mouse, or any other soft little brown thing. The child ran up to the glass-fronted display case, and Max removed his gray-and-white-checked cap, ready to explain, but the young woman rushed out from behind the counter before he could open his mouth.

"Angel!" she cried, crouching down beside the child. *"There* you are!" meaning *here.* "Where have you been?"

"Is this your—" Max started to ask.

She didn't even look at him. It was as if she hadn't heard him. "Your mother is fit to be tied!" She poked the child gently in his stomach. "Momma was just in here, Angel, and she said that you—" and then she did look up at Max, her serious little face hopeful. "Can you go find her? She's a tall woman wearing a red hat with two peacock feathers. It's only been a few minutes since she was here. She's running around like a chicken with her head cut off. Well, of course. She went left, down the boulevard. I'll keep Angel here. He knows me, don't you, Angel? Tell her Gabrielle has him. Do you want some ice cream?"

"I?" the child asked.

"Yes, ice cream. I know, chocolate," answered the young woman, turning back to the child, her face lit by a smile as gentle as early-morning sunlight. The smile did not leave her face as she turned to Max again. "Could you? Please?"

Without a word, Max exited the shop and looked off to the left.

At the end of the block, just past a crossroad, he saw a red hat entering a door under a blue-and-white-striped awning, and he jammed his cap onto his head and took off at a run. He dodged through men and women on the sidewalk, bicycles and a delivery wagon in the street, mumbling, "Sorry, excuse me," ignoring the protests, "Where's the fire, mister?"

She was just coming out of the hotel when he ran up to her and saw immediately that she was a mother looking for her lost child. Tendrils of escaped hair stuck to her temples, her eyes were watery, and the two peacock feathers on her hat tilted so wildly that only a bright silver Z kept them attached.

Max had almost no breath to speak with. He gasped, "It's all. Right. He's."

She looked at him, uncomprehending.

He gasped out, "Angel. With Gabrielle."

Her eyes closed and she sighed in relief. "Thank heavens," and she was rushing off, unable to run in the high-heeled shoes she wore but trying all the same, back the way Max had just come. He jogged beside her, but she didn't notice him at all. He followed her into the ice cream shop, where the child was now seated on top of the wooden counter with both hands wrapped around a chocolate ice cream cone, laughing at the young woman.

"Angel!" cried the mother.

"Momma!" cried the child, and then, "Maah," he added, and held out his cone. "I." Everything now explained, Angel returned to the ice cream.

"Don't you *ever* do that to me again," the mother said, and bent down to kiss the child on his cheek, letting her hand curve around the small neck. "Ever ever ever."

"Momma," the child said, and pushed her away.

Keeping a hand on his head, she turned to the young woman. "I don't know how I can thank you, Gabrielle."

"Don't thank me, thank him," the young woman said. She straightened the white kerchief on her head, smoothed her apron, and smiled at Max. Max smiled back at her. This Gabrielle was the kind of person you would want to keep nearby so you could get to know her better, the kind of person you would want to want you for a friend. That was somehow obvious. "He just brought Angel in out of the blue. Or, rather, off the street."

Then the woman did turn, and did see Max—or, rather, she saw a tallish youngish man, poor by the look of his jacket and boots, turning his gray-and-white-checked cap around in his hands. She thought he looked like a hero. The expression in his eyes—odd, those eyes, almost the color of the tarnish on old silver—was alert and attentive. When he spoke, his voice was an unremarkable, normal voice. "Is Angel short for Angelo?"

"It's short for Humphrey," she answered with a laugh. "My husband calls him Angel because he's so *un*-angelic. He's a runner-offer."

Max nodded. "Yes, ma'am. I did notice that."

"It's the second time this week," she said. "But the other time was out into our own garden. I'm *not* a bad mother."

"You are a lovely mother," the young woman, Gabrielle, said earnestly. "You adore him. He is a happy and lively little boy. I'll make you a coffee—sit down, please—and a pastry?"

The woman set her purse on one of the four small tables and began to take off her gloves. "Look at my hands," she observed. "They're shaking. You naughty boy, you come right here until Momma feels calmer." She picked up Angel-Humphrey, dripping ice cream cone and all, and sat him on her lap. She looked up at Max. "*Thank* you. I don't know how to—won't you join me?"

"Well . . ." He hesitated. He had to continue looking for employment, and he had to be back at home by three to meet his tutor.

"Please, you *have* to," the mother told him. "How else can I gather my wits to thank you properly. Please? Gabrielle has the lightest touch with pastry in the entire city. Gabrielle, bring us two of the almond croissants, and coffee for— What's your name?" she asked, turning back to Max, who was hovering beside the table, making up his mind. Angel-Humphrey paid no attention to anything but his ice cream. "Do sit," she insisted. "Give me a chance to calm down; I was so *frightened*. I mean, when I think how excited we were when he started walking. Those first steps?" She laughed again and straightened her hat. She wore rings on both hands, and when she gestured, jewels flashed and glittered in the sunlight coming through the shop window. Her hands moved now, back from her hat down to her son's narrow shoulder, which she gently rubbed. "Unless you'd rather have ice cream?"

"No thank you, ma'am," Max said. "There's chocolate on your shoulder," he told her.

"Double fudge, it's the only flavor he'll eat. But who *are* you?"

"Max," said Max. He didn't want to reveal his last name, and at that moment Gabrielle put two cups of coffee and two croissants down on the table, so he didn't have to. The mother did not introduce herself—you didn't introduce yourself to poor people, even if they had just returned your wandering child. She picked up a fork and knife to eat her pastry with, because you didn't eat with your fingers unless you were on a picnic. She had an awkward time of it with Angel-Humphrey on her lap, but she managed. Meanwhile, Max was berating himself for not telling her his name was Bartholomew or Lorenzo; now he'd missed his chance, and he should have thought faster.

He picked up his croissant—elegant table manners weren't expected of workmen, or students, or poor people, he knew— and took a bite. He let the taste spread around his mouth and forgot to be cross with himself. "This is really *good*," he said, first to his hostess and then, turning, to Gabrielle, who had retreated behind her wooden counter. "This is *really* good."

Gabrielle smiled her gentle smile. She was used to this reaction.

The mother leaned across the table to say to Max, in a

low and private voice, "Really, she could be the pastry chef in a five-star restaurant. The Silver Spoon, you might not have heard of it, or Zardo's. But apprenticeships cost money, especially at places like that. Which is," she said, smiling, "good luck for us common folk, isn't it?"

Max nodded and said nothing. His mouth was full, and besides, looking at her rings and her expensive clothing, he thought she was—and thought that she knew she was—to be counted among the uncommon folk, one of those who could easily afford elegant meals in expensive restaurants. He stirred cream and sugar into his coffee and sipped.

"Well," the mother said then, opening her purse, taking out a bill—was it a twenty? It might be a fifty, Max thought, but he didn't like to stare at money—and passing it over to him. "I don't know how to thank you, but I hope this . . ."

"Thank you, ma'am," Max said, just as humbly grateful as the Poor Farmer would have been if the Miser had agreed to part with one of his herd of cows. "Most generous." It was, in fact, exactly that: The bill *was* a fifty.

"Not at all. You must have been pretty clever to get him here, and patient, and I think you were kind to my Angel as well. There isn't money enough in the world to pay for all that." She smiled teasingly at him, then, mocking herself, said, "Now if you could just tell me how to keep him from being such a runner-offer, I'd be in your debt forever." Still smiling, she stood up, setting Angel-Humphrey on his feet. The little boy pulled to get free of her hand, but she held him fast. "Put it on our bill, Gabrielle?"

"Already done."

"Thanks again. Max? I really mean it."

Max stood up, too. He said, "A leash."

"What?" The mother was distracted by her son, who was yanking her arm and crying, "Dadda! Dadda!"

"If you had a kind of leash, like people do for their dogs when they take them for walks?" Max said.

The mother sat down again, overwhelmed, but not so overwhelmed that she let go of her son's hand.

"Momma!" he protested, pulling at her. He looked at Max for help. "Maah?"

Neither his mother nor Max paid any attention to him. "That's brilliant!" the mother said.

"Maybe, a leash with a chest harness," Max went on. "A leather worker could probably make one with no trouble." Actually, he agreed that it was brilliant. He was quite pleased with himself. This was what he was really good at, solving problems. He wished there was a job for a problem solver.

"And until I have it I can use scarves, which will be soft and comfortable. I have plenty of scarves," the mother said. "What kind of work do you do?" she asked him. "And where do you live?"

"Five Thieves Alley. In the old city," Max said, confident that she wouldn't know the area, or the street, or the house.

"Because if you're looking for work, I can recommend you to my friends if they need a handyman," she said. "Or to anyone who has lost a child," she laughed, laughing at herself. "To pay you back, to thank you. I'm going straight to the saddlery," she told him, rising again and swinging Angel-Humphrey up into her arms, where he squirmed to be allowed to escape. "A saddlery will know where I can have such a leash made right away. So I won't ever lose my boy again. Oh, that was naughty of you, Angel. But it's all turned out for the best, hasn't it? Isn't life wonderful?"

7

In which we meet Gabrielle Glompf, and Max acquires a lodger

Max stood at the window, watching the woman and her child leave the ice cream shop and turn to walk away down the street. The mother's fingers were wrapped around the little boy's hand. A fist squeezed his heart, and he thought that he wasn't going to be able to wait for word of his parents.

"Max?" Gabrielle asked, as if to call him to attention. "What's your other name, Max?"

Max didn't really hear her, but he did turn to look at her, and he did see her, and that reminded him of who he was and where. "What?" he asked.

"Are you still hungry?" she asked, in the kindest of voices. He noticed then that everything about her was suited to kindness, her soft hair, her round cheeks and gentle eyes, her quick hands, and her quiet way of moving around the shop. "I made a lemon cake with raspberry filling; it's awfully good. May I give you a slice?" she asked, as if he would be doing her a big favor by accepting.

"Yes, please. Thank you." Max sat down again at the little table. While she was busy with the plates, he wondered how to answer her first question.

"May I sit with you?" She gave him a thick slab of cake that had a bright red raspberry stripe running through its center. She set down a second plate carrying a thin slice for herself and sank into the chair opposite.

"Please," he said again, and also again, "Thank you." He took a bite, and another, and then a third, enjoying the tart sweetness of the cake and the sugary sweetness of the jam.

Eventually she asked him, "Feeling a little better?"

How did she know how he was feeling? he wondered, but before he could even start to think about that, she went on. "I once knew a university student. Just like you. I know how hungry you get, with the odd hours you keep and the bad food you eat. Besides," she added, with a smile that made her eyes shine, "I like to show off my baking."

She said this without pride and without modesty, as if she knew without a doubt how true it was; she said it the way Joachim sometimes asked Max to admire a particular petal in a painting, satisfied with the way he had captured the texture and color of it. Max took another bite and looked into her friendly face. "I've never tasted any cake as good. Not nearly as good. *Really,*" he concluded.

She laughed. "It's a talent," she told him. "And what I believe is: If you have a talent, it's wasteful not to use it. Foolish, too. *Do* you have another name, or are you just Max?"

"Mister," Max said, now with a smile of his own.

"Max Mister?"

"Mister Max," he said, hearing how right it sounded. "It's weird, I know."

"Only because it's a name for a round person," Gabrielle said, studying him. "Don't you think? Round head, round stomach, plump arms and legs, little fat feet in polished shoes, pork-pie hat: that's how I picture a Mister Max. Besides," she said, hesitating, fork up in the air. "Since my own name is Glompf, I won't comment on the oddness of yours. I mean, I should have been named something plainer, to go with Glompf, something that matches how I look, something like Bessie or Bertha or Martha." This thought seemed to distract her, and she looked over Max's shoulder briefly before she went on to ask, "What are you studying at the University?"

"Oh," Max said, because he didn't know what to answer and also because he'd been thinking about how to feel round, really *feel* like a Mister Max, so as to *look* more like one. Then, "Math," he said, since that was what he was going to do at three. "I can only take two courses at a time," he added, in case she might expect him to know as much as a normal university student. "I have to work," he explained.

"I know how that is," she agreed, with a seriousness that suited her little mouse face.

"But what about you? Why aren't you apprenticed to a pastry chef?" Max didn't want to talk about himself anymore. He hadn't yet decided what to say to strangers who asked who he was, what he was doing. "Angel's mother says you should be, and I agree."

"There's a black mark on my record," she told him. "A very black mark—and that means I can't get references. You need references."

"I'll give you a reference," Max offered.

"I mean employment references, so everyone will know you are honest and trustworthy."

Max pointed out, "It's obvious how honest and trustworthy you are. Anyone who looks at you can see that."

"It has to be in writing, officially signed and sealed, it has to be . . . And with this black mark," she told him, her smile now as sad as rain, "not even my family will speak for me. They live up the mountain, miles and miles away from the city, but it's a small village, so nobody has any secrets. I have shamed them, and they are angry. Mine is a common story, Mister Max."

Max didn't ask, but she told him anyway: "Girls will fall in love—it's what girls do—and love will turn sour as often as it stays sweet. But," she said, with another of her kind smiles, "sometimes it's very hard. I had a life full of promise and love, and then . . . Well, things change. They get ruined, or broken, and some things can't be fixed, and we still have to earn a living, don't we?"

Max could certainly say yes to that last question.

"There was a time when I dreamed of apprenticeships, but I don't have the heart for it anymore. Somehow. My only hope is that my family will come to feel better about me. I hope that, in time, my family will remember that I'm not the kind of person to steal or lie, even if nobody else believes that. And in the meantime," she said, standing up as a pair of schoolboys entered, "I have my job to do."

"May I buy a piece of that cake to take to my grandmother?" Max said. "She'll love it."

"Of course. You could come back some other day, as well. I'm always baking something, even if I'm not a real pastry chef."

Max said he would, and meant it.

"You're easier to talk to than most people," Gabrielle said then, looking closely at him, as if she was wondering about him. "I think you must have your own story."

Max didn't say anything.

After she gave him Grammie's cake in a bright white box tied around with a dark red ribbon and took his coins, Gabrielle reached out to shake his hand. "It was a pleasure to meet you, Mister Max."

"The pleasure was all mine, Gabrielle Glompf," Max answered, bowing slightly over her hand, as he had seen his father do on stage, playing the mysterious cloaked gentleman in *The Stranger from Across the Sea.*

Max decided not to stop in at any other businesses to ask for work; he had spent the whole morning being told No, and that was long enough for him for one day. Besides, he had a fifty in his pocket. He had just earned enough to keep himself in lessons and in food for over a week. When he thought of that, Max was pretty pleased with himself, pedaling along the busy roads, keeping to an ordinary pace, not too fast, not too slow, nothing at all unusual about him to attract attention. He was just some student, or maybe some working man, riding home from a class, or to a job. He was just anybody, nobody at all.

Except, of course, he wasn't. He was Mister Max, returner of runaway children. He was someone who could pay his own way, someone who was not helpless.

The only person he could boast to was Grammie, so on his way to his tutoring appointment he stopped by her library, across from City Hall. He found her seated behind the wide checkout desk reading a typewritten letter, a serious expression on her face. Wondering if—by some wild chance—the letter brought news of his parents, he waited for her to finish reading. This section of the library was a long room filled with books. There were books on shelves along all the walls, except where there were long, many-paned windows to let in light; in the room's open spaces, books filled tall stacks that were lined up like trees in an orchard; there were even more books waiting in low shelves at the top of the wide staircase up to a special reading room, where periodicals and newspapers were spread out on a long library table; and next to the reading room, there was an entire room dedicated to books for children. The air in the library rooms was silent, full of ideas, the thinking of the writers of books, the thinking of the readers of books. And not just writers and readers, either, Max thought. The ideas and visions of artists emanated from tall, heavy volumes of art history in their special shelves behind Grammie's desk, beside equally tall shelves filled with the decisions of lawmakers and the statistics collected by record keepers. Of course, the air was not literally thick with images and ideas, draped and swaying like cobwebs, but it had always felt that way to Max, who had been a regular visitor to Grammie's library since he was big enough to ascend the stairs, turn left into the children's room, and choose a book. Max was entirely comfortable in the library. He didn't mind waiting, hands in his pockets, smiling in anticipation of her surprise to hear what he had done.

Grammie took off her reading glasses, looking up from her letter to notice him and ask, "Shouldn't you be at the house? What if Ari comes early?"

"I've got plenty of time. I've got my bicycle. I want to—"

"Have you had lunch? I already ate, but there *is* a piece of pie—"

"No, thanks, I had a meat pie. Well, part of a meat pie, about half."

"You bought it at some stall in the New Town, didn't you?" she accused him. "How many times have I warned you—"

He interrupted, "I didn't find employment but I—"

"I've been thinking," Grammie said, and she was so concerned about his reaction to what she was going to say that she folded up her glasses and began tapping them lightly on the desk. This made Max nervous, and halted his proud announcement halfway up his throat.

"I've decided that it would be better, after all, if you lived with me," Grammie said. "In my house. I don't feel right with you all alone in that big house."

"It's not big," said Max.

"It's big for a boy alone," Grammie told him unsympathetically. "And if you can't find a job . . ." She let the sentence go unfinished, as if the end of it was so obvious she didn't need to state it. "In any case, you need someone keeping an eye out."

That didn't sound like independence to Max. He knew his grandmother loved him, so he didn't want to reject her offer without seeming to consider it. But then, how could he reject it politely?

"I'm fine," he assured her. "I don't feel lonely."

"And as headstrong as you are," she said. "You're *very* headstrong," she told him, as if he hadn't heard that a hundred times already in his life.

"Besides, I did earn some money today. I earned . . ." And he reached into his pocket to pull out the bill and show it to her.

"Fifty?"

This was the amazed reaction he'd hoped for. He held the bill out. "Fifty."

"Well." She took it into her fingers and looked at it. "Well, well." She rubbed it gently. "It's genuine. However did you manage that?"

He told her, using his quiet library voice, about the child, the ice cream store, the dash down the street after the mother, and the happy return of Angel-Humphrey, which led to the reward he had earned.

Grammie was impressed, he could see, and that made him even prouder of himself. Then she said, "You can't expect to have a missing child turn up every day."

That was true, and he knew it, but he would have preferred not to have it pointed out right away.

"Take the bill into a bank on the way home and change it into coins," Grammie instructed him. "Nobody will notice if a boy has coins, but they might get suspicious about a bill worth fifty."

This was sounding less and less like independence.

Grammie looked at him sharply. "It's good advice, Max. You aren't going to be too headstrong to take good advice, are you?"

Maybe he would and maybe he wouldn't, Max thought. He said, "I brought you a piece of cake from the ice cream shop."

"Won't it have melted by now?"

"Not ice cream cake, cake cake. The woman is a baker, too, a really, really good baker. Wait until you taste it."

"A better baker than me?" asked Grammie.

One of the good things about Grammie was that she didn't ask questions so you would tell her what she hoped to hear. She asked to find out what you actually thought. "Much. She's good enough to be a pastry chef. You'll see."

"I'll have it for dessert tonight," Grammie decided, and then said, "You can pack a few things after your lesson. This weekend we'll move the rest over."

At that moment, a man entered the library and rescued Max with a request from a city official for information that was needed right away.

Grammie was about to turn into a problem, Max could see that. He felt like hopping onto his bicycle and riding off, fast, to the lakeside or to the Starling Theater, and hiding out. He felt like eating that piece of cake and not giving it to his grandmother after all. He felt like painting a gray and windy skyscape. It would *not* be good for him to be somebody who was taken care of, he knew it. He didn't want to hurt Grammie's feelings, and he didn't want to anger her, but more than either of those he didn't want to live dependently.

In just a few minutes she turned back to him. "We'll talk at supper," she said, having apparently seen something in his expression that told her it was time for her to give in on something little, thus making it easier for him to give in on the big thing later on.

Max grinned at her, and "I'll stop at the bank," he said, giving in on something little himself, with the same plan in mind. "So I'll have coins to pay Ari with."

Grammie continued to study him, her eyes a sharp, thoughtful blue. "I don't need to remind you, do I? That at the moment you're all I have."

Max shook his head, no longer grinning, but did not try to explain that the way things were now, he was just waiting. Waiting to hear from his parents or waiting to hear about them. He hadn't really lost them. He wasn't really alone. Just independent.

Because he had almost an hour before his tutor would arrive, Max decided to try a painting. As three o'clock approached, he stood in front of his easel on the grassy lawn between his back steps and the garden, feet apart and hand raised. He wore the red beret. He had clipped a piece of heavy paper to his easel, set out tins of gray and black watercolors on the easel's tray, and prepared two small bowls of water. Holding his brush with the gentle grip Joachim had taught him, he wet the top of the paper and applied the first streaks of color that he would, he hoped, be able to turn into a turbulent, troubled, stormy sky. At the first brushstroke, his shoulders relaxed and the excitements and failures and irritations and pleasures of the day floated off, drifted away, leaving his spirit calm.

The painting did not go well. He could see it clearly inside his head, but as so often happened, the picture did not turn out as he imagined. Also, with watercolors, you have to do your thinking in advance because you can't erase or paint over your mistakes. Max wanted the sky in his painting to look windy, but wind itself can't be painted; it can only be suggested, just as actual wind can't be seen but only felt as it blows by. Wind is visible only in the effect it has on branches and flags and, for Max's purpose, the speed of clouds across the sky. When Max stepped back to look at his work, he saw that he had failed. He consoled himself with the knowledge that he'd try again. He could figure out how to paint the wind, if not immediately then eventually, maybe. He would have to be patient with this wind, he thought as he studied his unsuccessful effort.

He had entirely forgotten about his tutorial appointment.

A faint pounding sound, like a rubber mallet landing over and over again on a chunk of wood, reminded him. He dashed around to the front of the house, where a tall red-headed man knocked and knocked on the door.

The man looked older than Max had expected. He looked like a university graduate, not a university student. He wore a dark blue cardigan sweater under his brown jacket and a fedora on his head. His ill-fitting trousers were a light brown, and his boots were worn down at the heels. His briefcase looked softened and scraped by hard use. However, when he turned to look at Max, his eyes were a lively bright brown. Also, the man was entirely handsome, like a marble statue of one of the Greek gods, Hermes, perhaps, or Apollo. "You must be the grandson," he said.

"I must and I am," Max answered. "Are you Ari?"

"The mathematics tutor. Let's get to work. I'm on a tight schedule."

Max led him around to the back door, wondering what the man would say about his skyscape, but the tutor didn't even look at it. He seemed unaware of the easel and the garden, unaware of anything other than his immediate business. Inside, he went right to the little kitchen table and opened his briefcase to pull out his books and papers. "I hope you have a pencil? Paper? Sit here."

Ari was treating Max like a little boy, so "First I'm going to make a pot of tea," Max announced.

"Oh." The tutor turned to look at him again. "I take mine with milk and sugar, if you have them," he said, now as much a guest as a teacher, which was Max's plan. It wasn't just Grammie from whom his independence needed protection, he thought. It was everyone.

Max filled the kettle with water and set it on the stove. He pulled down teacups, the sugar bowl, and the small pitcher for milk, at the same time telling Ari, "I know all the functions. Add, subtract, multiply, divide. There's bread and jam, would you like some?"

The tutor took a few seconds before answering, a shade of reluctance in his voice, "Yes, I would. Please. I don't seem to have had any lunch."

From the look of him and the way his eyes lingered on the loaf of bread as he waited for Max to cut slices, Max guessed he hadn't had any breakfast, either. But why should a university student who was so well spoken and so tidily, if shabbily, dressed, and also had fine manners, go without food all day?

Ari, however, couldn't be asked that question because he set to work tutoring, even as he ate slice after slice of bread and jam while drinking cup after cup of tea enriched with milk and sugar. He had Max sit down beside him at the table and tested his student's claim about addition and subtraction, multiplication and division, at the end setting him a difficult problem in long division. "I guess you *do* know the functions," he concluded. "Good. You're someone whose self-evaluation can be trusted. Good again. What about fractions?" and he emptied his teacup. He seemed, at last, to have eaten enough, and in fact only the heel of the bread remained.

Max worked a page of fractions, adding, subtracting, multiplying, and dividing, while Ari watched, nodding every now and then.

"Good for the third time. So we can get right to work on geometry," Ari said. "Geometry's my favorite part of math. Everything makes sense, everything can be proved, everything has a place and a purpose. Unlike the world we live in," he added, in the tone of voice with which people greet an idea they have to admit is true but wish weren't. He pushed his plate aside and opened one of his books, *Euclid's Elements, Vol. 1.* "Triangles, parallels, and areas," he announced. "Definitions first, of course. If you want to learn something, you have to know the vocabulary. Let's see how adept you are at memorizing, shall we?"

Max didn't mind this one bit. He enjoyed using his brain. One of the things he liked about acting was the work of memorizing lines, and just as much as setting colors on paper, he enjoyed figuring out how to put together a painting. Even schoolwork often interested him.

Ari opened the book between them on the table.

From the very first definition, "A point is that which has no part," Euclid required close attention to exactly what was said. Ari had Max first read the definition aloud and then draw on a piece of paper exactly what the words meant. In this situation, Max was happy to do as he was told. There was something about envisioning parallel straight lines, "which, being in the same plane and being produced indefinitely in both directions, do not meet one another in either direction," that pleased him with its precision. At the end of the lesson, Ari wrote down each of the words on a sheet of paper and asked Max to write as many of the definitions as he could remember. "You won't get them all, not yet, but let's just see how you do," he said.

Max set to work, trying to remember Euclid's exact phrasings. For several minutes, the only sound in the room was the scratch of his pencil on the paper, then that was joined by a deep, regular breathing. Max looked up to see that Ari had put his head on the table and fallen asleep. Max studied his profile, the longish, proudish straight nose, the dark curve of eyebrows, the strong jaw. He thought that Ari awake looked older than Ari sleeping, and returned to the definitions.

When he had written as many as he could remember, which was only twelve out of twenty-three, he set his pencil down on the table. As if he had only been waiting for that small sound, Ari sat up, eyes alert. "Done already? Let's take a look." He reached out.

Max kept his hand on the paper. "You're overtired."

Ari didn't argue. "I've learned to take catnaps. They say Napoleon did that. And he was always fresh, always ready to run a country or fight a battle." Ari smiled then, a subdued smile, just a lifting of the corners of his lips, as if he didn't think he had the right to smile brightly, or widely, or entirely happily. "I'm not Napoleon, you may have noticed? I don't want to be a Napoleon, either, even if I do have . . ." He did not complete that thought. "The truth is that I have too much work, two regular part-time jobs, plus whatever I can pick up tutoring, plus the university courses. Life's expensive," he told Max. "Textbooks are expensive, too."

Max knew how to solve this problem. It was pretty simple, after all. "Couldn't you take fewer courses?"

"I could, but here's the difficulty: I'm already only taking two courses a year, and I need the degree as much as I need the money. I save most of what I earn for . . ." Again he let the thought drift off and rephrased it. "I need to save most of my earnings. There's a specific sum I need to have, and I'm almost halfway there. The only un-minimal expense I have is housing. In order to keep to my schedule I need to be close to the University, and housing in the New Town is expensive."

"How much do you pay?" Max asked.

"Forty a week. I have my own room. Weekdays I wash dishes at a restaurant near the City Hall, the midday shift—I can eat there those days—and three times a week I'm the night clerk at a hotel near the University. I can study then, too, because almost nobody comes in after midnight, and I kill two birds with one stone, as they say. Which *is* pretty Napoleonic," and he smiled again, that same subdued smile. "I guess that's more than you want to know."

Max relinquished his paper and watched the tutor read over it. "You're working hard," Max remarked, and then asked, "Do you do well in your classes?"

"Quite well sometimes, and others well enough. You're a pretty curious fellow, aren't you? This"—he put a finger on the paper—"is not bad, not bad at all. A good beginning. I think I'll enjoy teaching you, but now," and he got busy packing up his books, selecting from his papers a sheet on which he had copied out all twenty-three of Euclid's definitions, "I have another student to see, calculus, and he'll be waiting at the library, which is a half hour's walk, so if you'll give me my fee— What are you paying, by the way?" he asked, and took a small notebook out of the briefcase. He uncapped a pen.

"Ten," Max said, taking his purse out of his pocket. "But—" He was busy thinking about Ari's financial difficulties. "But why—?" He didn't know how to ask this question.

The tutor paid no attention. He opened the notebook and found the page he was looking for, which was already lined with two columns, headed with names that Max couldn't read from where he sat, and numbers beneath the names.

"What are you saving up for?" Max asked. "Why do you *have* to have a degree?"

Ari looked up. He ran his fingers through his dark red

hair. "Oh," he said. "Well." He shrugged. "I made a mistake, years ago, and . . . Well, I lost everything of value that I had, but I was a spoiled young man and it served me right. The bad part is I cost somebody else everything, somebody who had much less to lose than I did, so her everything was much more valuable."

"Very mysterious," Max observed, hoping to hear more.

Ari ignored the hint. He wrote the figure 10 in the numbers column. "What's your name?" he asked. "I have to pay taxes on what I earn, so I have to keep records, and I can't just put down Grandson."

"Mister Max," said Max, wishing again that he could say Bartholomew or Lorenzo, since he wasn't sure how far he could trust this tutor, although he did instinctively like him. And Grammie had approved him, too. Max did, however, have an idea about a way to solve at least one of Ari's difficulties, and one of his own at the same time. "Why don't you have a room here, in exchange for the tutoring," he suggested.

Ari shook his head. "It's a long way from the University, and the hotel, and the restaurant. Not to mention the library."

Max had an answer to that: "There's an extra bicycle in the cellar." His father liked to take early-morning rides beside the lake. Max told Ari, "You could use that one. I ride mine everywhere, and it only takes twenty minutes by bicycle to get almost anywhere in the New Town."

Now Ari was tempted. "What would your grandmother say?" he asked.

It was what his grandmother was saying that Max was

trying to avoid. "Grammie doesn't live here. She has her own house, the one across the back garden, behind this one. I live alone," he told Ari, "so it's up to me, not her. There's a big room upstairs, a worktable, too; you could save that forty a week, which would be actually only thirty since I won't be paying you for lessons, but still, thirty is something."

"Thirty is a lot," Ari said. He looked around the kitchen.

"I have dinner with my grandmother every night, so you'd come, too."

"Let me think about it."

"She's a really good cook," Max could promise him.

"I once knew a really good cook," Ari said, and Max knew then that the tutor would move in and he'd solved the problem of Grammie not wanting him to live alone. It made him feel good to know that at the same time he'd solved a bit of Ari's problem. In fact, Max felt pretty pleased with himself, and clever, too. He felt so good that he immediately thought of two new ideas about how to address the problems with his windy skyscape and was impatient to go back outside and try it again.

"My rent's due tomorrow," Ari told him, standing up. "I pay Wednesdays, a week at a time, in advance."

"Then you better plan to move in here tomorrow," Max said happily. William Starling was right, and Max was proving it: Twelve *was* old enough for independence.

8

In which Max is
offered a job

After the satisfaction, and excitement, of earning that fifty, and the success of his plan to continue living in his own house, Max thought everything would be different. He thought his luck had changed. For the next few days, he walked confidently out into the morning. He always went by the Starling Theater to reassure himself that it was being safely neglected, and then made his way along narrow, winding streets and alleys of the old city looking for work. He went to Soapmaker's Lane, Cobblers Way, Miller Street, asking at any kind of business. "I can learn anything," he promised shopkeepers. "I can't afford to hire you," they answered, some apologetically and some angrily. "I have a family to feed," they pointed out, or "Do I look that busy to you?" they asked.

At first, Max was un-discourageable. He talked to fishermen by their boats on River Way ("My wife mends the nets") and the firemen in the firehouse on The Lakeview ("Our apprenticeships are all taken"). Some people made suggestions. "You should try at Bendiff's factory. He's a good employer, they say, if you don't mind wearing a uniform." "Icemen always need young men, especially now with summer coming on; those blocks are heavy for an older man." "Have you thought of asking in the New Town? They have a lot more money there."

Many wished him well, but by midday Saturday Max had still not found work. He had also spent most of his fifty. His parents had been gone for eleven days. Eleven days and no word! His spirits were once again sinking.

It turned out that he was glad to have studies. With the work Grammie and Ari assigned him, and with his painting, at least he always had something to do. Without them he would have had only worrying to do, about finding a job, about his independence, and about his parents. "You can't give up," Grammie advised him Saturday evening. "Not about anything."

"I haven't," Max pointed out. "I won't," he promised, not entirely confidently. As long as he didn't let himself start imagining all the nasty possibilities—William and Mary Starling trussed up in some dark mountain cave waiting to be ransomed, in chains in the dark and airless brig of a ship living on bread and water and headed where? for what purpose?—he was able to be patient, mostly. He could even hope, sometimes, that they were crossing some wide ocean in first-class luxury. In fact, he was pretty sure that they were captives and nothing worse. Because why would anybody cook up such an elaborate scheme just to murder them?

"No, I mean literally, you can't. You have no choice. You have to find work."

On Sunday morning, Max sat at the kitchen table with the book of Greek myths Grammie had assigned. It was pretty interesting, their idea of how in the early days of the world the old gods fought a huge battle against the younger gods to decide who was going to rule over the world and all the creatures in it. Max was thinking about this. Older people wanted things to stay the same, he decided, with themselves being more powerful and important than younger people, who hadn't yet done anything significant or, really, difficult. Younger people, of course, wanted the older people to step aside, get out of the way, so they could have room to make all the changes they wanted, and improve things. Those gods were pretty extreme about it, the father swallowing his newborn children so they couldn't grow up and overthrow him, the children cutting their father into pieces and tossing the pieces every which way so he couldn't put himself together again and regain mastery. Max wondered if he felt a little bit that way about *his* parents, with his wanting to be independent. Then he wondered if his parents felt a little bit that way about him. These weren't the most pleasant of thoughts, but they might well have some truth in them. Those Greeks didn't sugarcoat things.

Grammie had asked him to write an essay in answer to the question "Which of the young gods would make the best king?" three to five pages in length, which struck him as unreasonable. After all, it would take only one word to answer. And he still had his geometry homework to do, which would take up the rest of his morning. After lunch, however, he hoped to spend some time painting. He could feel himself getting edgy, and painting, he knew, would calm him.

Max had every intention of starting out again Monday morning. He hoped that by then he would have had some idea, any idea . . . and then he did have one. A balloon man. Couldn't he sell balloons at the park? Max wondered briefly how much it would cost to set himself up as a balloon man—it couldn't be very much—then wondered, was that too far-fetched? It was the only idea he had. What if he never had another? What if he never found work? He felt himself becoming even more edgy. Which didn't do any good at all.

So, instead of worrying about earning a living, he forced his attention back to the Greek gods. He knew Grammie thought Apollo would make a better king than Zeus, but Max thought Athena was the best choice. Could a goddess be king of the gods?

By late morning, Max could put his papers into a neat pile, ready for the next lessons, and feel satisfied. He was prepared for his tutors. He still had coins in his pocket. He could go outside and paint. He'd work out front so Grammie wouldn't see him and ask him to help her with some cleaning task or to come eat something or ask if he was feeling sad and worried, trying—the way she did—to make him feel as if nothing had changed. Even though things *had* changed, and of course he *was* feeling sad and worried. Partly. He was also feeling independent and eager, and curious about what might happen next to him, *and* he had a painting to work on. He wanted to try the stormy sky again, to see if he could use darker shadows in the clouds—or maybe the shadows should be blue?—to make it look as if the wind was grabbing at them and pulling them to pieces. Setting the red beret at an artistic angle on his head, he put on one of his father's worn, faded blue work shirts and carried his easel, its block of heavy paper clipped in place, out through the front door. He had both good light to paint in and an interesting problem to solve.

He was concentrating so hard on strokes and shading that the ringing of the bell startled him. His head jerked around and this made his hand draw a long black line right across the whole sheet of paper, from top to bottom, from left to right, from thick to thin.

The picture was ruined.

If Max had been a swearing person he would have sworn. But he wasn't, so he didn't, and besides, since April 18 he had a different idea about what might be worth swearing at. He just groaned softly in exasperation and turned around, paintbrush in hand, ready for long-eared Madame Olenka to be once again at his gate.

Instead, he saw a man in a dark suit and a tall black hat.

The man's high, stiff collar shone white in the sunlight, and with him he had a girl, younger than Max, perhaps nine or ten. Her brown corkscrew curls were neatly organized, her honey-colored eyes looked hopefully up at the man, and a little smile rested lightly on her mouth, ready to fly away.

Before Max could say or do anything, the man had opened the gate for himself and, herding the girl along in front of him, came down the path. His polished shoes crunched on the gravel. The girl hurried to keep a step ahead. "Would this be Five Thieves Alley?" the man asked, brisk and businesslike.

"Yes?" Max asked, as if to say *And if it is?*

"Would you, then, be Mister Max?"

"Ye-e-es," Max said, drawing the word out, as if to say *And if I am?*

"Would you be that same Mister Max who was so helpful in finding Humphrey Henderson?"

It began to make sense. Max wondered if this was the mother's husband, and Angel-Humphrey's father, and if the girl was then his sister. He hoped not, because these two looked too smug for the warmhearted woman with her bright red hat and her eager ways and her little boy with his adventuring attitudes. "Yes," Max said, and this time added, "Although it was more a matter of finding *her*. Humphrey had already found me."

"Irrelevant," the man announced. Max decided he must be a lawyer or someone important in the government, with that quick, decisive manner. The man looked closely at Max. "She said this Mister Max person had odd eyes."

Max could be decisive, too. He stood a little taller and asked, "Would you be a friend of Mrs. Henderson?"

The man shook his head impatiently. "Not to speak of, although I do know *him,* the husband, slightly. He's in banking, so of course we have some dealings, but we're not what you'd call friends." After saying that he fell silent, as if he might have given away too much.

Max had never practiced law or worked in the government, but he *had* appeared on stage. As if he were the Miser, full of self-importance and money, safe in his large leather chair behind a big wooden desk, he asked, "Would there be a reason why you are here?"

The girl tugged on the man's dark sleeve. "Papa? Tell him what Brenny told Mama."

"I'm taking care of this," he snapped, and she looked down at her feet, which were shod in laced leather shoes, the same deep green color as her velvet coat and the ribbon in her hair. The man said, "I'm offering you a job, Mister Max. I presume you are some sort of detective, and I want to hire you to find . . ." His voice faded as he tried to decide how to put his request.

Max waited, as relaxed as if people were always stopping by to interrupt his painting and ask him to do things they didn't know how to say.

"My daughter has lost her dog," the man said at last. "I want you to find it. What do you charge?"

Calculating as fast as he could, Max tried to figure out what he could ask without raising suspicions. Too low a sum would be just as suspicious as too high a figure, he knew. Because he was busy thinking, he didn't answer.

The man misunderstood his failure to respond and asked impatiently, "Is it that you want to know how we heard of you, before you'll agree to undertake the work?"

"Yes," Max said, although he already knew that. He needed the time to calculate: Angel-Humphrey's mother had paid him fifty without batting an eye. So fifty was a good number, but should he ask fifty per day? Fifty per job? Fifty when the job ended? His mind sorted the options while his face waited to hear what the man said. Maybe he should ask for a hundred, he thought, seeing how richly dressed the girl was and the diamond tie pin in the man's cravat.

The man said, "I've never heard of you, and nobody I asked has heard of you, either. You must be a beginner in the detective business."

Max nodded. *Was* he a detective? Did beginners have to charge less? How much less was enough less?

"Papa!" The girl stamped her foot. She turned to Max. "Our parlor maid, Brenny, has a sister who works for the Baroness Barthold. You know her, don't you? Everybody knows about the Baroness. She's the old witch who lives all alone in that castle on The Lakeview, halfway up to the Royal Promontory. It's as big as a palace, Brenny says. The one with a stone fence so high you can't see over it? She's very rich and very important; you have to know who she is."

Max did.

"Martha—but that's not really her name, it's just what

the Baroness calls her—told Brenny, who told us, that when Mrs. Henderson was paying a call on the Baroness she told her about how you found Humphrey, so when I lost my dog, Mama asked Papa to ask Mrs. Henderson about you, and he did. She said— What did she say, Papa?"

"She said she gave you fifty," the man said to Max with a stern look. "She didn't say you were an artist," he added, and did not need to say that for him this was *not* a recommendation.

"I'm a little bit of everything," Max answered. He had made up his mind and spoke with all the confidence of the Miser with bags of gold piled up safe in the cellar. "I'll take the case, twenty-five paid now, plus another twenty-five if— and only if—I succeed in finding the dog."

"Done," said the man. He reached into his jacket pocket to take out his wallet.

Max put the bills in his pocket and turned his attention to the girl. "Now," he said, all business, "what's your name, Miss?"

"Clarissa," she answered quickly, and waited—with a little nervous licking of her lips, as if he were a teacher, testing her, and she didn't want him to find out that she hadn't studied. He wondered what she was trying to keep hidden from him.

"What kind of dog is it, Miss Clarissa? What color, what breed? What's the dog's name?"

"Her name is Princess Jonquilletta of the Windy Isles, because she's gold and white and expensive and because—"

The father broke in. "It's a golden retriever. My daughter

had to have a golden retriever, nothing else would do, nothing smaller, nothing that didn't shed. Nothing"—with a sharp glance at Max—"more intelligent and trainable. Just this one breed, just this exact dog. And now she's lost it."

Max ignored the interruption. "That's a long name. What do you call her for short?"

"Princess Jonquilletta—but she doesn't obey, but then she doesn't have to because she's always on a leash on account of she won't come when she's called." She looked up at her father. "It wasn't *my* fault. I told you, I tied her up. Somebody must have untied her. I *didn't* lose her." The girl looked up at Max to say, "I didn't really *lose* her. I didn't forget her or anything like that. I know exactly where she was."

"Where was that, Miss?" Max asked, because that would be the place to start his search.

"At the Hilliard School, over near the University."

"Do you know the school?" the father asked, and Max did. It wasn't that far from Joachim's house. The father informed him, "Hilliard is the best money can buy."

Clarissa explained, "Dogs can't come to school. But there's a fence just across the street from the play yard where we tie our dogs and cats while they wait for us. Princess Jonquilletta of the Windy Isles is the most beautiful pet of all."

"She should be, the money we pay to have her washed and brushed," the father grumbled.

"Everybody says," Clarissa assured Max.

Max concentrated on being a detective, looking for clues. "I gather that the dog hasn't come home?"

"Not yet," Clarissa told him. "Not by this morning, so it's been two nights. It wasn't my fault. It wasn't, was it, Papa?"

"My daughter is very upset about this."

She didn't look so upset to Max, but maybe she was pretending, or being brave, or keeping her hopes up. Just because she didn't look sad and anxious didn't mean she wasn't. Max knew about not letting everybody see just how you were feeling. Although, Angel-Humphrey's mother *had* looked sad, and anxious, and a little terrified, too.

"When can you get to work on this?" the father asked.

"A lost animal?" Max answered, as if he were speaking from experience.

"Or stolen. The dog *is* quite valuable," the father said.

"With a lost animal, it's better to start immediately, of course. Today is Sunday, and you lost the dog when, Miss? Friday?"

"I told you, I *didn't* lose her. I think somebody at my school, somebody jealous, took her."

"She's been gone over thirty-six hours," Max reminded them. "Have you searched for her? Have the police searched?" He didn't know what he should do if there were police involved. Given his present situation, he didn't want the police anywhere near him, and he didn't want to go anywhere near the police. Maybe it wasn't such a good idea to pretend he was a detective.

"Police? Of course not. We're talking about a *dog*," the father snapped.

"I thought she'd come home," Clarissa said. "Like before."

"I knew better," her father said.

"She's been lost before?" Max asked.

"Only twice, and never for all night," Clarissa answered hastily. "And it wasn't my fault. She pulled the leash out of my hand, for a cat once and once for a bird. A chicken, actually. She's *strong*." Her eyes got a little wider, and her mouth quivered a little, and she said, "Can you find my dog for me, Mister Max? Please? I'm very sad without my pet, so can't you please, please, *please*? Find Princess Jonquilletta of the Windy Isles and bring her back home?"

"This is the address," the father said, reaching inside his jacket to pull out a flat silver case, from which he took a business card.

"I'll do what I can," Max told the girl as he put the card in his pocket. "I'll do my best."

Whatever that might be, he thought.

It wasn't until they had disappeared from view that he realized, like the sun breaking through clouds, *This is a job!* and he realized also that, whether he succeeded in finding the dog or not, with this twenty-five added to what was left of Mrs. Henderson's fifty, he had enough to get through the next two weeks at least. By that time he might well know something—mightn't he?—about his parents' whereabouts. Then he thought it again, *A job!* and set to work.

Max had changed out of his painting gear into something more appropriate for finding a lost dog and was washing his lunch dishes, his back to the door, when he heard Ari come in the kitchen door, home from dishwashing for an afternoon of study. "Who the devil are you? What are you doing here?" Ari demanded. "Where's Mister?"

Max turned around. He wore a train conductor's flat-topped, stiff-brimmed hat from *Trouble on the Tracks* and the private's jacket from *A Soldier's Sweetheart,* which had no medals or gold stripes sewn onto it. This struck him as a good uniform for a dogcatcher. The butterfly net from *The Lepidopterist's Revenge* leaned against the counter at his side, and he wore one of his mother's aprons so as not to get his costume wet.

"You heard me," Ari said, stepping around the table, his hands clenched into fists. "Where is Mister?"

Max turned back to the sink to hide his grin.

Ari spun him around by a shoulder, glared threateningly into Max's face, then recognized him. "Oh," he said. "It's you."

"It is," Max agreed. He turned off the water and reached back to untie the apron, which he lifted over his head and hung on a hook beside the sink. "I'm a dogcatcher."

Ari had stepped back. Now he studied his young landlord, shaking his head, and asked, "Exactly what are you up to, Mister Max?"

"Also, actually? My name is just Max," Max told him. "Mister Max is just—it's the name I'm using."

Ari's head switched from slow shaking to slow nodding. "All right," he said thoughtfully. "Just Max. Makes more sense. Any last name?"

That Max wasn't going to say. He shrugged.

"All right," Ari said. "Then why a dogcatcher?"

"To catch a dog." Max was enjoying mystifying Ari, but he didn't want to upset his tutor, so he explained, "It's a job."

"It's a job. I see. All right. A job doing what?"

"Dogcatching," Max repeated patiently. "So, if you'll tell Grammie, in case I'm late for dinner? Tell her, even if I have to miss dinner I'll stop in to see her when I get home, so she doesn't have to worry about me. I hope to be on time, but . . . Do you think she'd save me a plate if I'm late?"

"I'll tell her. I don't know what she'll say, though. I'll be there, too," Ari said, perhaps a promise or maybe a threat, "because I wouldn't mind hearing the explanation of this— this dogcatchering."

9

The Lost Dog

• A C T   I •

The Hilliard School had once been the home of a wealthy jeweler whose diamonds had been revealed to be paste imitations, so his three penniless daughters had to turn their fine home into a school, and their fine educations into classroom lessons, in order to put food into their mouths. The spreading lawns were now playgrounds and playing fields, the elegant painted bedrooms held desks and chairs and chalkboards, the grand salons had been chopped up into offices, and the great dining room was now filled with tables that seated only eight or ten, where students and teachers practiced table manners and polite conversation during lunches prepared for them in the large kitchens. The school fees were high enough that the students came only from the wealthier families of the city. There were no scholarship students at Hilliard, no deserving poor; it was not, its faculty pointed out, a university, to accept every applicant. Not that the students at Hilliard were allowed to be lazy or uneducated; a boy or girl who did not, or could not, do the work of his or her classes was asked to stay home, perhaps with a tutor or governess. "It is a privilege to be here," the teachers told their classes, and the students told one another, and the administration told its faculty. "You are the lucky ones."

When Max rode up on his bicycle, the butterfly net held at his side while his free hand steered clumsily, the great iron gates were locked, the grounds and buildings unpeopled. Max dismounted across the street from the gates and stood at the fence to which he thought Princess Jonquilletta of the Windy Isles must have been tied. He looked up the street and then back down it.

To the right, the wide avenue passed in front of the arched brick entrance to the University before it became a busy commercial street of the New Town. To the left, it narrowed to a single paved roadway that ran between walls, some lower and some higher, some red brick, some gray or golden stone, some stiff pikes of wrought iron. The walls protected the privacy of homes belonging to the wealthy people who inhabited this quarter of the city. If he were a dog, Max thought, and if he were running loose, where would he go? He would have his nose to the ground, exploring, going . . . into a busy city street? or toward the lawns and gardens hidden behind the walls? Max had played many parts in Starling theatrical productions, and he could guess what might anger a Russian cavalryman and even what Puss in Boots might say to a king, but he had never played a dog, and certainly not a dog who had been saddled with the name of Princess Jonquilletta of the Windy Isles. Who knew what such a dog would think, if a dog could think at all?

He couldn't *know,* but he guessed that the smell of grass and trees would attract a dog more than the smell of horse dung and carriage oil, so he turned left, away from the University and down along the quiet street.

The first entrance posts he came to towered over a brick wall no higher than his waist. He left his bicycle against the wall and, carrying the net, walked along a brick driveway that curved up a low hill at the crest of which stood a brick mansion with wide green lawns stretching away along curving slopes. Stone pillars lined a curved central section, like a row of footmen, while two long wings rose up, three stories high, and a dozen chimneys reached into the sky. The mansion stood on its hilltop as if it were a palace. Not one of the huge, important palaces nobody can imagine being a home, of course, but one of the smaller palaces, where a royal family could go for quiet, more private, times together.

Max stepped between two of the pillars and walked up slate steps to the wide oak doorway. Its brass shone with polishing, and a fat bell knob gleamed in the afternoon sunlight. He pulled it.

There was no sound from within, not even a distant

ringing. Max waited, and after a few minutes—as if there were a great distance to be crossed—the door swung open.

A man blocked the entry. Tall, stiff, silver-haired, and solemn, he wore a long-tailed morning coat and white gloves. He did not invite Max to step inside. "Yes," he said, and it was not a question. There was a lot of No in that Yes, most clearly a No Entry.

"I'm the dogcatcher," Max began, but he got no further.

"Trade goes around to the side," said the man—the butler, Max guessed—who then stepped back and closed the door.

Max thought about pulling the bell again and making a pest of himself, because he didn't like being talked to in that way—or, rather, he didn't like *not* being talked to in that way. Also, he didn't like having a door shut in his face. He was a city official, practically, and that was no way to treat a city official. However, because he was, after all, only the dogcatcher, he retreated to where the bricks turned into a gravel driveway that led to stables and outbuildings and a yard where an automobile was being polished by a uniformed chauffeur and a row of shining carriages could be seen through the open stable doors. A short path led him to the back entryway, which was a much less important, smaller, painted door, and which opened immediately. This time it was a woman who blocked the entrance, as tall for a woman as the butler had been for a man, and even less welcoming. The apron that covered her black dress was stained with chocolate and dusted with flour. "What is it," she said, but before Max could answer she decided that she already knew. "We don't need any nets, thank you, nor brushes nor anything else you're hoping to hawk here."

"Actually, it's a dog I've—"

"Nor any animals. We've got a big tom for the mice, not that there are any mice in *my* kitchen, so get off with you, mister."

"—come to find," Max persisted. "I'm the dogcatcher," he told her, as sternly as if he actually were an official official and offended by her rudeness.

"Well then," she said. "In that case. I can assure you there are no dogs in here, and I haven't seen one on the grounds, either. If you turn around and look, you'll see that there's not many places a dog could hide itself on this property. So you had better move on down the street to where the lawns aren't so carefully kept nor the homes so well taken care of." She clasped her hands together over the waist of her apron and pursed her lips in satisfaction with who she was and what she had just said.

"You haven't seen any unknown dog?"

She let out an exasperated breath. "And didn't I just tell you that?"

Max could be as brusque as she was. He nodded and, without a word of farewell and especially without a word of thanks, turned away, bearing his butterfly net down the long drive and out through the gates. Nobody watched from behind the windows or the doors of the great house to be sure he did what he'd been told. In that house, people were accustomed to being obeyed. As he got back to his bicycle, he heard the distant bells of the clock tower ring four times, warning him that the afternoon was almost over.

When that low brick wall ended, a pale yellow stucco wall began, a wall so high that even if Max had been twice as tall, he still would not have been able to see over the top of it. He rode along beside it until he came to a pair of stucco pillars, each topped with a statue of a fierce-looking eagle. The thick, high wooden gateway between the pillars stood open, so Max once again parked his bicycle and toted the net onto the grounds. A cobblestone drive led straight between short rows of thick-trunked beech trees to a two-story square yellow stucco mansion, its entire façade decorated with red-and-green-painted diamonds and small balconies. This house was surrounded by wide beds of flowers, the daffodils and tulips in bloom, and azalea bushes that were bursts of bright pinks and whites. The house glowed among the gardens like another, much larger and much fancier, flower.

Max had learned from his first experience not to go up to the main entrance. Instead, he followed a slate pathway around the side to a back entrance. There he knocked loudly on another white wooden door.

There was no response, although through an open window he heard voices. He knocked again, *bam-bam-bam,* pounding with a fist. The voices fell silent.

It was a little round man, shorter than Max, who opened it. Like the other cook he wore an apron, but his was stained with reds and the occasional streak of bright orangey yellow, where an egg yolk might have fallen. He had suspicious eyes, like little gray pebbles, and restless, impatient hands. "What are you doing here?"

"I'm the dogcatcher, looking for—"

"You don't look like no dogcatcher to me. And that net'd never hold anything much bigger than a butterfly, so don't try your tricks on me, mister."

Max took a deep breath and insisted, "Have you seen a dog running loose in the area, a large—"

"I know a gypsy when I see one," the man said. "Don't think you can try your thieving tricks in this house, Mister Gypsy. And don't try giving me that evil eye of yours, neither," he went on. "You've got the eyes for it, I can see that. So I'll tell you about the dog. Dogs, really," he added with a little mean smile. "There won't be any wild dogs here, not with our two." He expanded his chest like a bird and leaned up at Max. Max stepped back. "That's right," the man said. "Rottweilers, ours are. I've half a mind to call them and introduce you, but if you scarper off fast enough I'll just go quietly back to preparing dinner for the doctor and his guests. Who might be very disturbed to know that there is some gypsy horse thief going up and down the street, getting a look around with who knows *what* mischief in mind."

With as much dignity as he could muster, or would have been able to muster if he *had* been a real dogcatcher, but also with the little swagger he thought a gypsy might want the cook to see, if he had been a real gypsy, Max retreated. He went down the drive and through the gates without a backward glance, the net angled over his shoulder like a rifle.

Max kept to the same side of the street, riding beside a fence of tall iron bars, each one topped with a pointed tip, like a row of soldierless spears standing at attention. The metal had once been painted black but was now rusting, much of its paint worn away by time and weather. Through the fence, Max saw an overgrown lawn and a two-storied gray shingle house with a long porch across its front. At each end of the house, the porch became a covered walkway leading out to a gazebo. Both gazebos looked out over what must have once been gardens but were now bushy tangles. Despite looking so worn-down and worn-out, like a much loved stuffed bear or a frequently read book, this was a house Max could imagine living in. It didn't *feel* like a mansion, although it was of the right size and on the right street for one. It had once been a fine home, that was evident, and it could be again, if its owners wished. This house was quite possibly the very place a dog who was accustomed to good food and a soft warm bed might choose. Max went up the weedy dirt driveway and around the side of the house, without even looking at the windows to see if anyone was inside. He didn't expect to find anyone living in this house. He only chose to go to the back door out of officialdom. A dogcatcher, like any city official, would do things the proper way. After knocking, Max turned around to look for a shed or open stable door through which a dog might slip, and so when the house door opened behind him, he swung around in surprise.

Two old ladies, wearing identical high-necked, long-sleeved, and long-skirted black dresses, stood in the doorway, the taller one in front, the shorter peeping out from behind. They both had round heads covered with short white curls; they were both staring at him out of identical pairs of round, faded blue eyes. Neither of them spoke.

Max took off his cap. "Good afternoon. I hope I'm not disturbing you? I'm the dogcatcher and—"

The taller one interrupted, turning to say to the shorter, "I told you, Sister. I told you someone would claim her. I did tell you, you remember, don't you? That I wouldn't be surprised if someone came looking."

The shorter one peered out at Max from behind her sister's shoulder and asked, "Can you give us a description of the dog you're looking for?"

"It's a golden retriever, young but not a puppy. Female," Max said, in what he hoped was a dogcatchery manner. This seemed description enough because the two women looked at one another, as if to confirm what he had said.

"The dog was lost on Friday," he added.

"No," the shorter one corrected him from her sheltered position. "That dog wasn't lost. That dog ran away. There was a leash, but it was chewed through. Not cut," she pointed out with an emphatic nod. "Chewed." Then she added quickly, "If it's the same dog."

"Ask him if the dog he's looking for had a collar," advised the taller sister.

"Did she have a collar?" the shorter asked.

"I wasn't told," Max answered. "I imagine so. Also, I was told she was groomed, bathed, and brushed. Professionally bathed and brushed."

Their expressions clouded over, and once again they looked at one another. "Oh," and "Oh dear," and "I'm afraid," and finally, "It's her," they said.

"We didn't know what to call her," the shorter sister told Max, "so we called her Sunny, because she's so sweet and happy. She always came when we called her, so maybe Sunny is her given name?"

"Is she in the house now?" asked Max.

"Oh no," the shorter sister assured him.

"Tell him why, or else he won't know the kind of people we are," the taller instructed the shorter.

The shorter sister did. "We knew she had to belong to someone. It isn't right to take someone else's dog into your house, where the dog might get used to being there and want to stay. But you're a dogcatcher, you probably already know that."

The taller sister had been studying Max during this explanation. Now she turned to report, "He understands that dogs don't like to be tied up."

Max tried again. "Where is the dog now?"

"Somewhere nearby. She doesn't go far. I can call her,

if—" The shorter sister stopped speaking and studied Max carefully. After several seconds, she looked up at her sister and said, "He has a kind face."

"But can we be sure?" her sister asked. "Find out why he's looking for her."

"Exactly why do you want to find this particular dog?" the shorter one asked.

Max looked from one face to the other as he answered. "The family that owns her, the little girl, actually . . . Well, her father, really . . ." He put it officially: "Inquiries were made."

"Hmmh" and "Hunh," the sisters said, not satisfied. Two sets of pale blue eyes now looked right into Max's face, and he knew what they were thinking. He thought the same.

Then the taller one turned to the shorter to say, "But you know, Sister, we couldn't keep her here, keep her for ourselves. We're too old, and who knows how long we'll live? What would happen to her then?"

The sister agreed, although reluctantly. "You're right. I know, I know. There wouldn't be anyone to take care of her. And we can't walk her, either." She explained it to Max: "A dog like that needs exercise. But you already know that, too, don't you?"

Max concentrated on thinking like the kindly dogcatcher they thought he was. "We never know everything about dogs, any more than we do about people," he told the sisters, a kindly and philosophical dogcatcher.

A few minutes later, he was walking down the driveway with his net over one shoulder and a large, brown-eyed, feather-tailed golden retriever loping along at his side. He had a rope tied to her collar, but she showed no sign of wanting to run away. From time to time she looked up at him, as if pleased to be in his company. Her tail waved enthusiastically. This was a happy creature, maybe not all that smart but easygoing and friendly and, most important, like all dogs ready to love. Max looked down at her and had to smile. "What made you run off like that?" he asked.

She wagged her tail even harder and then looked to the road ahead with bright, curious eyes.

"No, I mean it," he said, as if he expected her to answer. It was, he knew, an important question.

The late-spring twilight was slipping in among the winding streets and low houses of the old city when he finally leaned his bicycle up against his back steps, leaned the net against the bicycle, and ran across to his grandmother's house, famished.

Grammie and Ari were playing cards at the kitchen table, their cleaned dishes drying on the rack by the sink.

Max stopped in the doorway, surprised. He'd never known Grammie to play card games. He'd thought she would find them, like most games, a waste of time that could be spent much more usefully doing something else, reading, perhaps, or cooking. They seemed equally surprised to see him, although they had been waiting for just this, for him to arrive.

He ate the good dinner Grammie had kept warm for him and told them about finding the dog and leaving her in Joachim's garden. "I had the net and the dog and the bicycle.

It was—it was like walking with snakes winding around my feet, and I couldn't ride."

They imagined his clumsy progress across the avenues and boulevards of the New Town, and it seemed to amuse them.

"So I thought of Joachim's garden, with the wall all around it, and he said as long as the dog didn't insist on sleeping inside it was fine, as long as I come back tomorrow to take care of things."

"That was good thinking," said Ari.

"Very well done," Grammie agreed.

Max ate his meal and accepted their compliments. "You're quite the detective," Grammie said.

Max didn't see it that way. "I didn't really detect anything. It's not as if there were clues. I just—it's more as if I was acting a part on the stage."

"Are you an actor?" Ari asked curiously, but before Max had to answer, Grammie asked, "Don't you *want* to be a detective? I thought all boys did, and many girls, too. I certainly did when I was a girl. What about you, Ari, didn't you want to be a detective?"

"No," Ari said, distracted by a memory. "Far from it. I wanted to be a shepherd, or a goatherd. I wanted to lead a simple life. Or even a cowherd, as long as I could live up on the high meadows with my flock."

"Cows don't come in flocks," Grammie pointed out to him. "And anyhow, everybody outgrows their childish dreams."

"Not everyone," Ari said. "Not every dream. Have you ever seen the high meadows? With mountains all around, and heard the quiet?" Ari asked. "And the stars and—There's so much time in the high meadows. It feels like there's more time there, more hours in every day. There's space for children to play, and nobody cares if they get dirty. They can learn how to not get lost, they learn what's really important. A boy who lived in this high meadow wouldn't—he couldn't—"

Grammie interrupted again. She had something she wanted Max to hear. "Detectives see people at their worst. It can be unsafe to be a detective," she warned him.

"I'm not a detective," Max told her. "But I'm ready for bed," and in part he *was* tired, but also he wanted to head off a quarrel he could see looming up over the metaphorical horizon of Grammie's kitchen.

"What are you going to do about that dog?" Grammie asked, then told him, "You should take her back to her mistress tomorrow and collect the rest of your fee. Your fee for *not* detecting."

"I'm thinking about it," Max said. "It's not that simple."

Back in his own house, on his way with Ari to the stairs leading up to the bedrooms, Max saw an envelope lying on the floor just inside the door, under the mail slot. On a Sunday, it must have been hand-delivered. Ari was in front, so he bent to pick it up. He looked at it, turned it over to look at the back, then passed it to Max with an odd expression on his face. Actually, his face had no expression at all. His eyes were stony, his mouth stiff, and that was what was odd about it.

The envelope was made of heavy, cream-colored paper and the name *Mister Max* was written on it in bold, swooping strokes of very black ink. There was a crest engraved on the back, a long-necked bird with a frog in its beak. Max went to the kitchen to slit it open with a knife. This was not the kind of envelope you tore at with your fingers.

Ari followed him. "You know," Ari said, running fingers through his dark red hair as if to better arrange his thoughts, "when I came in this afternoon? I didn't recognize you."

Max looked up. "I was being a dogcatcher."

"I didn't think of a dogcatcher, not with *that* net. I thought maybe rat-catcher. I thought you'd maybe come in through the back door, looking for rats. But it's made me realize: I don't know anything about you, do I? I mean, you aren't going to school, and you were living here alone until I arrived. I don't even know how old you are. You're young, but I can't figure out *how* young. I know you've got a trunk full of all kinds of clothing— You left it open, Max. I don't snoop. And there's this huge mirror in your hallway, a dining room with theatrical posters on the walls and a bookcase of plays in it, so whoever owns the house is probably theatrical, but . . . And you have a grandmother next door, I know, and I've known Mrs. Nives for years at the library. And there's this detective business . . ."

Max stopped in the act of extracting the thick sheet of paper from its envelope, sensing danger. "But you *do* know me," he told Ari.

The tutor doubted this. "Only as a tutoring student. Only

for a few days, a few dinners. As far as I know, you don't even have a last name. What about your parents? Where are your parents? Who *are* you?"

Max chose his words carefully. "I can't say," he said, and tried not to think about the reasons why he couldn't, each one of which could make him feel . . . more alone, more worried, more frightened than the one before. "Really, I can't," he assured Ari, then reminded him, "You *do* know Grammie."

Ari's response to that was another odd thing: He entirely changed the subject. "Go ahead and read your letter," he said. "I can tell you want to." However, he didn't turn away to let Max read in privacy. He stood watching, close enough to read over Max's shoulder, and that lack of good manners in his tutor was, Max thought, perhaps the oddest thing of all. But he decided to ignore Ari, and read.

It wasn't a letter, not really. It was a summons. It might have had a *please* attached to it, but it was a summons all the same: *Please come to the home of the Baroness Barthold at half past ten tomorrow, Monday, morning. She wishes to speak to you about employment.* It was signed, in that bold handwriting, *Baroness B. PS,* it added, *do not make the mistake of thinking that because the Baroness is a wealthy and important personage you can therefore charge an exorbitant amount.*

"Well?" asked Ari.

"Why would she want *me*?" asked Max. "I've never met her. I've only seen her two or three times when—" He cut his words off, because he didn't want to tell Ari that he'd been on the stage and looked out to see the magnificent elderly aristocrat seated in her private box. "When she was out in public," he finished, hoping that the Baroness did go out sometimes.

"Is that the truth?" asked Ari.

"Of course it is." And because it was the exact and precise and honest truth, Max could demand, "What do you think?"

"I don't know what to think," Ari said, rubbing at his temples with his fingertips. "I think she doesn't know you at all, to say that to you about exorbitant fees. I think she's a terrible old woman." Then he ran his fingers through his hair again, as if it had been messed up and he was tidying it. "I think I'm so tired I'm seeing ghosts."

Max asked, "What do you suppose she wants?"

"You, apparently," his tutor said, and yawned, and—finally—smiled. "Mister Max."

10

The Lost Spoon

• A C T   I •

What the Baroness Barthold, seated in the carved ebony armchair that had enthroned the Barons Barthold for over five hundred years, saw standing before her was a rather un-noteworthy person in a definitely un-stylish brown suit, hair slicked down across the crown of his head, pork-pie hat held awkwardly in front of a round stomach over which his bright blue waistcoat stretched tight. This was neither a distinguished nor a dashing figure; he was not the kind of person you would want to be introduced to. She studied him and he studied his boots, which while clean had obviously *not* been polished.

Neither of them spoke. Each was waiting for the other to begin.

The Baroness couldn't even have guessed the detective's age, although that, she knew, could be the result of her weakened eyesight. His portliness, his rounded shoulders, his clothing, all seemed those of middle age, but his skin looked unexpectedly youthful. Perhaps he wore makeup? Detectives were such questionable types. Their work brought them into the company of the worst kinds of people doing bad things; and the Baroness had lived a long time, so she knew just how many worst kinds there were, and how various were those bad things. She cleared her throat. The man looked up.

For a moment she was distracted from her own interests by his eyes, a most unusual and perhaps unpleasant color, like certain dirt-and-lichen-encrusted rocks in the forests of her childhood. "I am having my doubts about you," the Baroness said.

Max, in the costume of one of the unsuccessful suitors from *Adorable Arabella,* was not surprised by the bad manners of the old woman, with her sharp beak of a nose and her clawlike fingers gripping the side of the massive black chair before which he stood. Her white hair was pulled back tight along her narrow skull, her dark blue dress had no adornments, neither jewels nor lace, and her narrow lips looked as if it had been years since a smile had been asked of them. Her eyes gleamed like vengeful coffee beans, and she added, "You don't look like much."

The unsuccessful suitor, too middle-aged and dull and unhandsome and humorless for the lively, lovely, spoiled young Arabella, did not argue. Max said, "Maybe I'm *not* much."

"That's not what I've heard," the Baroness snapped. It seemed that she didn't want him to agree with her.

"Then maybe it will depend on what you want from me," said Max.

The Baroness shifted in her seat. The chair didn't, now that he looked more closely, appear at all comfortable; the bumps and angles of all those carved high mountains with long-necked cranes circling their peaks would stick into your back. In fact, this whole room didn't look comfortable. Like the other great rooms of the castle he'd glimpsed on his way to this one, it looked expensive and important and magnificent, altogether the opposite of welcoming. The large fireplace, for example, with its thick stone mantel, might be big enough to stand up in, but it didn't do a very good job of producing warmth. Many portraits of many men, all dressed in one sort of uniform or another, military or civil or church, stared out from many thick gilt frames on the dark walls. The stone floor was thickly covered with dark oriental rugs; dark, fat-legged tables held atlases and painted globes. The room needed books, he thought, it needed windows, it needed something. It had no life in it, just things, things and this unpleasant old woman.

However, Max was not his own self. He was on a job. So, patient and humble as the unsuccessful suitor, he waited to hear what the Baroness would say next.

"I will ask you to find something that was lost many years ago," she at last announced. "I have no hope that you'll succeed, but I've reached the point—reached the age, more accurately—where even an unsuccessful attempt to find it, or find out what happened to it, is better than doing nothing."

Max continued to wait in silence. She hadn't actually told him anything, and she hadn't asked him to pull up a chair and sit. There was nothing for him to say or do.

"Not exactly chatty, are you?" she complained. "It's the Cellini Spoon. Of course. You'll have heard of the Barthold Cellini Spoon?"

Clearly, Arabella's unsuccessful suitor was not the right role for this situation, so Max shifted to Inspector Doddle from *An Impossible Crime* and asked cagily, "Why don't you refresh my memory? I like to hear things firsthand. It can be of use."

She looked at him sharply, suspicious, as if she had just noticed something unpleasant about him. Apparently, she was deciding what to do about him, and apparently, what she decided was *not* to have him shown out of the room. The Baroness leaned forward in her great chair to say, "I don't believe in wasting words myself, either. Benvenuto Cellini, 1500 to 1571, born in Florence, Italy, and died there, too, but for most of his life he didn't live there. A scoundrel and a trickster but a gifted craftsman. In many ways an artist."

That word reminded Max of Joachim, and he wondered what the painter had done about the dog he'd left out in his garden last night. He could only hope . . . but he didn't know what he could hope for from his teacher in regards to an uninvited dog in the garden. However, thinking about that distracted Max from his present work, so in order to gather his thoughts again he took a small chair from beside the wall and carried it over to where the Baroness was enthroned. He sat facing her, the round hat balanced on his knees, and hoped that the pillow at his waist would not slip off sideways.

Displeased, or maybe just surprised, the Baroness stared at Max for a long moment. "Or perhaps," she said eventually, "Cellini was only a rapscallion. Greedy, like everyone else; that, too. Have a seat," she added sarcastically.

"Thank you," said Mister Max, playing the imperturbable Inspector Doddle looking alertly at his hostess, awaiting the rest of her story.

"My family, that is to say, the Barons Barthold, has had in its possession for over a hundred years a Cellini Spoon. This is not a teaspoon, nothing as ordinary as that, but a large serving spoon, one of a pair that Cellini crafted to gain favor from a pope. Paul the Third, I believe it was." The Baroness looked at Max as if waiting for what he had to say about that.

"Hmm," Max said importantly, confident that Grammie would know about these Cellinis and popes. "Yes. I see."

"The Moses Spoons," she went on. "So-called because, on the handle of each spoon, Cellini depicted a scene from the life of Moses. The Barthold Spoon pictured the infant Moses about to be discovered by the daughter of the Pharaoh of Egypt, who—as you know?—adopted the child and raised him as a prince in the royal household. Moses' mother and sister, who had contrived this plan to save the infant's life, can be seen peeping out through the bulrushes. It is a magnificent piece of art."

"I can imagine," Max said.

"You can do better than that—you can see it. Right there," and she pointed. "In the portrait of my great-grandfather, who"—she hesitated, then decided—"brought it into the family."

Max rose to go searching among the portraits that lined the walls to find a man with a spoon.

"Do not be so hasty," the Baroness snapped. "Sit down." She continued: "The whereabouts of these spoons, about which Cellini boasts in his autobiography (although it must be acknowledged that he boasts about all of his works), has always been known. That is, until ours was lost. Was stolen. Disappeared."

"Where is the other?" Max asked, too curious to stop himself.

She ignored the question. She had her own way to tell the story. "Almost a century ago, the pair of spoons was being sent as a gift from the Vatican to Napoleon, a bribe most likely; but the ship was attacked by Barbary pirates, and the young French officer entrusted with the spoons offered them up in exchange for his life." She sniffed. "The act of a coward."

"That's as may be," said Inspector Doddle. If Max's parents had been taken prisoner by pirates, he would be glad if they had something in their possession with which they could purchase their lives and freedom.

"Humph," she said, and glared for a minute, her fingers clutching the carved arms of her chair. Then she went on. "The pirates, for once, kept their word and set the officer

ashore, which is how we can trace the whereabouts of both spoons. When, not many years later, that same pirate captain was captured, one of Cellini's Moses Spoons was among the treasures in his possession. He was brought to land to be tried and hanged, but the Governor of that colonial island—a man who had been a successful general in his younger years, a hero of his country—made a startling appearance before the tribunal. He testified that this pirate captain was in fact a spy, whose information had saved many lives. Nobody believed this, but nobody has ever dared stand boldly up to a Barthold, so the pirate was given a generous reward and sent off to South America, for his own safety. The booty he'd taken belonged, by law, to the crown." The Baroness watched Max's face as she concluded her story: "There was no mention in the inventory of that treasure of the Cellini Spoon."

"Hmm," Max said. "Yes. I see." And he did. Almost as if it were at a play, he saw the filthy, unshaven pirate offering the many-medaled official a large spoon, and he saw the Governor place it in a desk drawer, then lock that drawer with a small key and turn back to the pirate, but not to shake his hand. No handshake concluded that particular deal.

"That Governor," the Baroness announced defiantly, "was my great-grandfather. It was only after his death that his son, that is to say, my grandfather, dared to exhibit the spoon. The Barthold Cellini. They tried to claim it for the Royal Museum, but my grandfather refused to part with it. No king," she announced with satisfaction, "was ever powerful enough to bend a Baron Barthold to his orders. They tried and they failed." This drew what might have been a smile from her, but it might have been only indigestion. "Uncontrollable, that's our reputation—and no king ever hesitated to make use of a Barthold to govern some wilderness of an island or to lead some marauding army. They despised us, but that didn't stop them from using us when they needed our kind of help. My grandfather took great pleasure in displaying the Cellini Spoon on its carved wooden holder—and knowing it was in his possession, not the King's. The spoon was priceless, of course."

"Of course," Max agreed, although he didn't think it could literally have been without price, since it had already been enough to purchase two lives and since, as well, there were people rich enough to pay any price for something they wanted. He waited, but the Baroness did not go on.

"I think you said there was a second spoon?" Max asked.

She didn't seem displeased at the proof of his grasp of the situation. "One of the pair was immediately sent as tribute to the Grand Bey of Baghdad. It is known that in exchange for the Ottoman Empire looking the other way, as they say, the pirates put a portion of their takings into the Bey's coffers. That spoon is presently displayed in the Pinacoteca of Baghdad. I have never seen it."

Max inclined his head. A true inspector—he had seen his father play the role—said as little as possible and was always aware of his own importance. He stood up again. "The portrait?"

The Baroness did not rise—and now he wondered if

she *could* stand or walk. She indicated with an outstretched arm and a pointing finger the portrait of a handsome red-haired man in a green military uniform with gold epaulettes at his shoulders, one hand resting on the hilt of his sword, his glance resting on something in the distance behind Max. "There has always been a Barthold in his country's service," the Baroness told him. "Which is why I am—as far as I presently know—the last of the line, since so many men chose military service and, as you would predict, died with their boots on. My grandfather had himself painted as a wedding gift for his bride. Her name was Lily."

Max went to stand in front of the picture. He knew enough about the craft of painting to recognize a bad portrait when he saw it, especially in the stiffly awkward gesture of the soldier's free hand toward the items on the table beside him—a spray of lilies of the valley in a small glass vase and beside it, on a wooden stand, the spoon in question. The flowers, however, were wonderfully well painted—their ghostly white color, the delicate small curves along their bell-shaped blooms, the sweep of leaf up from the pale, slender stalk. For a moment Max admired the flowers, and then he turned his attention to the spoon. This was indeed large, long enough to reach stuffing out of the belly of a roasted turkey. On its shallow bowl the gold gleamed as smooth as water. The painter had copied the famous carving with care, so Max could make out tall bulrushes at the top of the spoon's long handle and the hidden faces of two women who looked anxiously at a basket that floated nearby. The basket had not yet been seen by the tall, crowned woman who was approaching the riverside, up the length of the handle.

"What do you think of him?" the Baroness asked from behind him.

"The baby?" But the baby could not be seen over the rim of the basket. Only a trailing blanket told you that there was a baby within. "Or do you mean the spoon? The spoon must be a wonder."

"No, *him,* my grandfather. Never mind, don't tell me. You'll just utter some pleasantries, some lie, about how handsome he is. All the Barthold men are well featured, but you know what they say about redheaded men and their tempers. However, he did us the favor of dying of fever, during an African campaign, not long after his marriage, which was a mercy for his wife and the two children she had already produced for him." Now the Baroness spoke sharply: "Do stop that staring. You've seen the portrait—*Sit.*"

Max did as he was told. "The Cellini Spoon," he said, nodding thoughtfully, once again Inspector Doddle. "It will have come into your possession?" he hinted.

"The Baron," she continued, as if he had not spoken, "left those two children, a son and a daughter. The son became my father and inherited the title—and I his only child—while the daughter, my aunt, married badly. Married for love, married against her brother's wishes. Her son, handsome like all Barthold men but soft as his mother, died young, in an earthquake in South America on a climbing holiday with his wife, leaving their young son to me. That boy was my heir, as you can imagine. To the title, the fortune, and all the properties."

A real inspector, Max sensed, would take charge now, but what about a hired detective? Would he just sit and listen, or ask his question yet again. "The spoon," he decided. "What about the spoon?"

She sighed. "Disappeared seven years ago."

Inspector Doddle nodded. "Stolen, you said."

"I believe so."

"Do you suspect anyone?"

"Oh, I *know* who took it. The kitchen maid. Martha."

"It was a woman you called Martha who showed me to this room. Is this the same person?" Max was wondering if the Baroness was in her right mind, and how you could tell if so old and important a person was *not* in her right mind.

"All of my maids," announced the Baroness, "are called Martha. I do this for my cook. Zenobia has been with me since we were both girls. Zenobia is not clever, except in the kitchen, but she is loyal as a dog and I promise you, loyalty is much undervalued these days. Zenobia is not good with names, a handicap in a house with so many servants, so it is a condition of service in this house that the girls—I hire no men—take the name of Martha. None complain."

If they did complain, Max guessed, they would be immediately let go. The old lady seated across from him glared, daring him to question her right to do exactly as she chose, with the same expression that appeared on several of the portrait faces. Looking at the portraits, as Inspector Doddle rather than as a novice painter, he observed, "There are no portraits of women. Weren't there any women in the family?"

"Don't play the fool with me. After all my time and trouble, you aren't going to prove useless, are you? That Mrs. Henderson is charming, I'd never say otherwise, but she's not . . . she's not solid. I couldn't tolerate her company more than once or twice a season, and she must feel the same about me. But she seemed sure of you. Naturally there are portraits of my ancestresses, but they hang along the upstairs gallery. They are not for just everybody to see."

She didn't have to tell Max that he was less than a just everybody. He also knew better than to ask if her own portrait had been done, when she was a younger woman; that would be too personal a question for her hired detective to ask of a baroness. So he said, again, "The spoon. It was stolen by the kitchen maid. What did the police say?"

"The police were not brought into it."

Max sat silent.

The Baroness, too, sat silent.

Silence suited that dark room.

Finally, the Baroness lifted a hand from the arm of her great black chair, then lowered it again. "It was the last dinner I ever held. After that occasion, I didn't have the heart for another, and why should I? That night there were twenty-four distinguished guests at my table, the finest Sevres, the best wines poured into Venetian glass goblets. With every course Zenobia outdid herself. It was a splendid dinner, a great success—except that the spoon was never returned to its accustomed place on the sideboard. Zenobia had last seen it in her dishpan. She always washed the goblets, the silver, and the Cellini Spoon herself. It had to be that Martha. All the other servants had been in my service for years, so I knew it couldn't be any of them. Moreover, that Martha bore a grudge. Against me. As if I would let my great-nephew and heir marry into the scullery and the girl nothing but a round little scrap of a nobody. What he saw in her I never understood. She didn't even have the wits to flee the house before the theft was noticed."

Max was assembling the details in his mind. "You noticed it exactly when?"

"The next day, as soon as I entered the room for my midday meal. There it was. Or, rather, there it wasn't."

"And the Martha?"

"In the kitchen, if you can imagine the gall of the girl, just going on with her duties as if I wouldn't know who was guilty. I summoned her and she denied it, even pretended shock, surprise. She actually asked that my great-nephew give his word that she wouldn't have taken it, wouldn't do such a thing. But what could he say? As I pointed out to him, we knew nothing of her family, and that stopped him in his tracks. And she . . . She asked that the police be called in to prove her innocence. As if she really were innocent. I knew she had merely hidden the spoon away, somewhere, although she denied that, too. She even wept. The boy had fallen in love with a woman who *wept* when things went against her. He saw her tears, but he didn't say a word, just opened and closed his mouth like a fish in a tank. I thought he was silent for shame, and I was glad. I admit it."

"Had Martha left the house at any time that night?"

"Not possible. The doors and windows were all locked and shuttered. I see to that myself, every night, as I have every night since my father's death. What is truly important must never be left to others."

"Where is Martha—that Martha, I mean—now?" Max asked. He thought it would be useful to have somebody else's version of the story. "And your great-nephew, where is he?"

"Gone, both of them. I turned her out, watched her pack her belongings myself. The next morning he was nowhere to be found. He'd left everything behind, except for what he wore out of the house—left all his fine clothing, the pictures and the books, even the books for his university courses. He wasn't to be found at the University, nor anywhere in the city. The last words he spoke to me—after all my years of care, the ungrateful wretch—were 'You are a fool.' I did not deign to respond."

"You haven't heard from him since?"

"He seems to have vanished from the face of the earth, just as she has."

"They might be together, then." They might, Max thought, have stolen the spoon together, sold it, and fled with the proceeds to South America or Mozambique, Ceylon or Bali.

She shook her head. "That, at least, was accomplished.

When he was standing there, pale and silent as if some cat had in fact got his tongue, as if he couldn't remember how to talk even, she told him he was spineless—as of course he was, otherwise how could she have gotten her claws into him? She would have spoken up for him, she said. She never wanted to see him again, she actually told him that, in front of me. I would have laughed—who was she to reject the next Baron Barthold?—except that I was so disturbed by the loss of the Cellini Spoon, by the success of her thieving scheme . . ." The Baroness's mouth worked but no more words came out, the ones she wanted to utter being so huge and hard that they couldn't make their way up her throat, as if those words were bricks or stones or chunks of wood.

Max waited until the red angry spots had faded from her cheeks, then asked, "Are you certain that the Cellini Spoon didn't leave the house? With one of your guests, perhaps?"

"Not with one of *my* guests, I'm sure of that. But I have also Zenobia's word that the spoon was in her dishpan at the end of the evening. She knew the spoon's value to me. She knew its importance, even if she knows nothing of Cellini, or any history to speak of. She had washed the spoon as usual that evening, she remembered."

Max nodded, and considered the situation. He tried to imagine the night the spoon disappeared, but his imaginings were too sketchy and uninformed to be useful in solving this mystery.

The Baroness grew impatient. "Can you find it for me?"

Max put his finger to his lips—*Patience. Let me think*—and thought.

The Baroness did not wait well. She shifted in her chair. She puffed out irritated breaths. Luckily for him, before long Max had a plan.

"Can you tell Zenobia you are giving a dinner party?" he suggested. "Or a luncheon, it doesn't matter which."

"I haven't entertained in years," the Baroness protested. "Zenobia is grown old."

"So that you can bring me into the house, to help her in the kitchen, just for the occasion," Max continued. "I need to be here in the house, where it happened. To study the actual scene."

"I've been too long absent from the social and political world of the city," the Baroness protested. "Many of my acquaintances are no longer alive. How will I know who to invite?"

"You don't need to actually *give* the party," Max explained. "The party is only an excuse for me to be in the house. If I'm here in the kitchen, I'll have a chance to look around. To see how things work."

"No man sleeps in my house," the Baroness announced.

"Agreed," Max said.

"Are you a trained cook? No, I didn't think so. You're a fakir, a pretender, a . . ." She waited for the most accurate, most insulting word to come to her, and it did. "An actor." She drummed her fingers on the arms of her chair, then decided, "I'll do it. I'll hire you to be the scullery maid. *Maid,* I said. Not *boy.*"

Max looked right at her, his expression giving nothing away. "After a day or two of working here, of being here, I may know something."

The Baroness sniffed. She huffed. "I won't have Zenobia upset. I do not, as anyone can tell you, have a warm heart hidden within this imposing exterior, but I am a good mistress to those who serve me well."

Max said nothing. He believed her.

"Those who do *not* serve me well, like that Martha? They do not remain long in my service. Nor," she did not need to add but she added anyway, "if I have anything to say about it, in the service of anyone who cares about my good opinion." She glared at Max. "Point taken?"

Max nodded. "My fees—"

"I wondered how long you would wait before mentioning those."

Max was not about to be bullied, or distracted, by her rudeness. "Twenty-five at the start, another twenty-five if I am successful."

"And if you fail?"

"If I fail there is nothing more due to me."

The demand came quick and sharp: "Will you fail?"

What kind of a question was that? The kind of question designed to get him in trouble, Max decided. "You can give me the first payment when I arrive to work" was all he said.

She nodded, apparently satisfied, apparently agreeing.

"You may go now. An envelope will be waiting for you in the kitchen. I will tell Zenobia to expect you Thursday morning. At the servants' entrance, and early," she told him. She rang a little long-handled silver bell set out on the dark mahogany table beside her to summon the servant, Martha. As he followed the woman out through the door, the Baroness called after him, "In this house, early means before eight and no later."

11

The Lost Dog

· A C T   I I ·

SCENE 1

It was not until Max had ridden his bicycle back along The Lakeview, across the wide drawbridge, and through the Royal Gate into the old city that he remembered the dog. How could he have forgotten the dog? he asked himself, changing direction and riding as fast as traffic allowed through the Bishop's Gate and out into the New Town. The Baroness had so filled the room with who she was and what she wanted that everything else had been driven out of Max's mind. How did she do that? he wondered, and he wondered— who wouldn't?—if he could learn to do it himself. He'd like that, he thought, as he dismounted and turned the latch.

Joachim's gate was locked.

But the gate was never locked during the day. During the

day, Joachim worked in his garden, especially on a bright, warm day like the one that was pouring sunlight over Max's shoulders.

Max called out, but there was no response. Leaving his bicycle in the alley, he hurried back to the street and around to Joachim's front door. He pulled at the bell, then knocked, loudly. Still no response. Puzzled, he tried the doorknob— and it turned. The door swung open.

Joachim never left his front door unlocked.

Why would Joachim lock the garden and leave the house open? And where would Joachim *be* in the late morning of a sunny day, if not at work? Not to mention the most urgent question: Where was the dog? The house was empty, no Joachim, no dog, all the rooms as usual, everything put away in the sitting room and kitchen, the studio filled with light, painted canvases leaning against the wall and one on the easel, the bedroom tidied, and towels folded neatly in the bathroom. Max went through the house and out into the garden, looking around for any sign of man or dog. He was getting worried.

Then he saw what had happened. Or, rather, saw something that had happened in that garden, and when he went back inside, he saw that it had happened in the studio, too. The paint on the picture on the easel outside, and also on three of the paintings set on the floor against the studio wall, seemed to have been swept across by soft brooms. These had blurred the images and stretched out their shapes. Joachim's careful, clear lines had—some of them, many of them—been ruined. His bright colors had overflowed into one another and grown muted. The flowers now seemed to be seen through a veil, or looked at through a lacy curtain, or hidden behind thin clouds.

Max could imagine Joachim's reaction to this ruination. His teacher was already uneasy about both his inspiration and his eyesight; this destruction of his work might break his spirit. Or drive him into a rage. Max closed his eyes and hoped the dog was not to blame.

But he knew. The dog had to be to blame. *He* was to blame.

Max stood motionless in the garden, horrified, his back turned to the painting because he didn't like to look at what had been done to his teacher's work. He could imagine it happening—the dog somehow finding her way into the house, tempted to enter the studio by the presence of a person working in there, wagging a hopeful tail, brushing it across the wet surface of pictures Joachim had set down against the studio wall to dry. It was all too easy to imagine. He should have thought of that before he left the poor dog with Joachim, whose temper these days was even touchier than usual. He should have thought longer about all of it, before leaping into that solution to his doggy difficulty.

He didn't know if he should wait for Joachim to return—and where would his teacher have gone, with the dog? Where might he have taken her? Maybe Max should assume that Joachim had dragged the poor dog to Max's house, or maybe even to Grammie at her library, and get over there on his bicycle as fast as he could. But if he did that, and Joachim had *not* taken the dog to Max's or to the library, Max would have wasted precious time. Where else might an angry man go to get rid of an unwanted animal? What else might he do? Think, Max urged himself. He wanted more than anything to ride off, fast, ride off anywhere, just to be doing something, but he made himself stay where he was, and think.

At the end, he could see that he had to make a choice. He could stay where he was, waiting, or he could go looking. If he went off, he could leave Joachim a note, and he would be able to swing back by his teacher's house at regular intervals while he searched the New Town, the old city, the lakefront, the riverside, in hopes of seeing a large, friendly, sun-colored dog wandering around loose. If he waited, it might be hours before Joachim returned, although he could be sure that the painter *would* eventually return.

Max didn't like any of his choices, which made it hard to decide between them. He stood in Joachim's garden, uncomfortable in the ill-fitting brown suit and tight, bright blue vest, his pork-pie hat in his hand, the sun warm on the top of his head, and tried to make up his mind.

They burst in on him, almost before he had time to turn at the sounds of their arrival and see them. Joachim came to an abrupt halt in the doorway, a cloth shopping bag in his hand, staring as if he had never seen the person standing there, but the dog pulled forward, pulled her new green leather leash free from the painter's hand, and jumped up on Max's chest. She almost knocked him over with her big paws and heavy head. "Down," Max said, then more firmly, "Down!" He smiled weakly at his teacher over the dog's wriggling body, then stared. "You're wearing glasses?"

"Max?" asked Joachim, taking the glasses off to see if this unexpected sight was what it used to look like. When Joachim was working, painting, he never wore any hat and he protected his clothing with a long artist's smock, but when he went out he liked to wear a beret as well as paint-streaked trousers, so that everybody could know what he was and keep to a distance, as people do when an artist or beggar or crazy person comes into view, someone you can't count on to behave by the rules. "You *are* Max, I can see that." He replaced the round, gold-framed glasses. "What about this dog? This dog is trouble," Joachim announced.

"I know and I'm—" Max started to say.

"I had to go out and get glasses," Joachim complained. "How else could I really look at what she's done to my paintings?"

"I saw and I'm really—"

"I could see that the paintings had been changed, but I couldn't tell exactly how, so— Don't you *see*?"

"I do."

Bored by the conversation, the dog was sniffing around the garden wall, tail high in the air.

"I've had to get an entire set of new brushes."

"She chewed your brushes?"

"Why would she do that?" Joachim demanded. "Dogs have more sense than to try to eat turpentine. Even golden retrievers know better than that, and everyone knows they don't grow a brain until they're seven."

Max made himself say it: "It's my fault she's here. So it's my fault this happened. I'm sorry, Joachim."

"*And* I had to buy her a leash and replace that collar, too. What does a dog want with glass jewels in her collar? What is *wrong* with the people who own her? She's not yours, I take it, and now I think of it . . ." He looked at Max, surprised. "Do I take it that your parents changed their mind about your much-vaunted tour?"

"Things changed, yes. Things have changed and I'm still here, at home, and I want to continue the lessons if you— I really am sorry about the pictures."

Joachim walked over to the altered picture on the easel. "Are you? I'm not. I don't think I am, anyway. I think—I'll have to study it carefully, the effect—it's like a curtain waving, or as if you could *see* the wind. The sunlight is *flowing* over those clematis blooms, don't you think? I might have to work with a feather. A peacock feather might give that effect," he said, speaking to himself. Then he turned to Max. "It's not as if I can train her to wag her tail on cue. It's not as if she's my dog. Sunny?" he called, and the dog trotted over. Joachim scratched her behind the ears as she pushed her muzzle into his leg.

Then Max felt a faint hope fluttering inside him. He asked, hesitantly, "So you could keep her a little longer?"

"She'd better stay for a day or two at least. I spent good

money getting food for her, and a bowl. It'll be entirely wasted if she leaves right away. So, are you going to come for a lesson at the usual time? Because I'd like it if you left now. I've got a lot of work to do and— There's a technique I can use to duplicate this, I'm sure there is, but I have to figure it out."

Joachim had taken off his beret and was standing bareheaded in the sunlight of the garden, in front of the easel, staring at the painting with his glasses on, then taking them off to stare some more.

Curious, Max went to stand beside his teacher and study the picture. *Wind,* Joachim had said, and Max saw that. He wondered if, somehow, that feathered brushing of the damp surface could be used to create the impression of wind blowing through heavy gray clouds. He wondered how he could try to reproduce it in watercolors for his stormy skyscape. He turned to look at his teacher and did not ask what he'd meant to. Instead, he wondered, "When did you get the glasses?"

"I'm not going blind, whatever you were thinking. I know what you were thinking, Max, but I'm just getting older. Doctor says. He says I'm healthier than I have any right to be, although what health has to do with rights he couldn't tell me. And I've asked you once to go away. I've got work to do, even if you don't."

Just as Max was going out the gate into the alley, Joachim called after him, "And get out of that ridiculous costume. You look like some . . . some middle-aged lowlife, some detective. Don't you have someplace to be? Like school?"

12

The Lost Dog

• A C T I I •

SCENE 2

That first Wednesday in May, the bell in the town hall had just rung twelve times when the substitute teacher strode through the Hilliard gates and up the steps into the school building, without even a glance for the children who chased one another about in some game or, in the case of the older students, stood talking in the spring sunlight. The two teachers assigned to watch over noon recess that day paid him no attention. He could have been a university student, in his light gray trousers, seersucker jacket, and a round straw boater on his head. He was skinny, as so many young men are, and long-legged. He might have been applying for a position in the school, or maybe putting his name down in hopes of finding tutoring work. But the two teachers had enough to do keeping an eye on things, and the young man was nothing to do with them. When, however, he emerged from a side door onto the playground, with its climbing bar and swing sets and sandboxes, with its benches and tables where children could gather and gossip, overlooking the long field where boys of all ages kicked a ball and ran after it, the teachers tried to think of which teacher might have fallen ill and had to go home. But didn't the young man know that he wasn't required to take recess duty? Hadn't anyone told him? Perhaps he preferred being outside to waiting inside for the long recess to end. Young men had almost as much energy to get rid of as did schoolchildren. It would do no harm to have him join their vigil.

Madame Celestine, the French mistress, was the one who approached the substitute teacher as he stood beside the spreading chestnut tree, looking about him. He seemed a pleasant enough young man, with an intelligent enough expression on his face. "A good day to you," she said, holding out her hand. "I am Madame Celestine. May I welcome you to the Hilliard School?"

He had a firm handshake and was not, now that she was closer to him, quite as tall as he had first appeared to be. He introduced himself with a quick smile—"Lorenzo Apiedi"—and then turned his attention back to the activity on the playground.

"What an odd name," she said.

"Yes, isn't it?" he answered, and turned his head to give her another of those brief smiles, which did, she checked, reach his eyes and were therefore genuine. But what odd eyes the young man had, like the truffles of her homeland, slightly gray and very dark brown. It didn't do to stare, so she looked back at the children playing on the grounds and said, "I don't know if they told you?"

Max, dressed for the role of Lorenzo Apiedi, the tragic young hero of *A Patriot's Story,* spoke boldly and frankly, as had Lorenzo to the judge who would sentence him to death. He could say with total honesty, "They didn't tell me anything."

"Ah, well, it is the lunch hour—they will have left their desks," Madame Celestine explained. "I can assure you that our students are as a rule well behaved, even in their games, but they are still children, and so there can be . . . mishaps? mischiefs? And even sometimes meanness. Some of our students haven't learned to control their tempers when they are not under our eyes in a classroom. But they are good boys and girls at heart. And why should they not be, coming from the families they come from?"

"The world will not have been very hard on them," the substitute suggested, and the French teacher, who felt the world had sometimes, maybe even often, maybe even unnecessarily often, been hard on *her,* nodded in agreement.

"I must return to my post. It has been a pleasure to meet you," she said.

He gave her a last smile, a brave one, she thought, and so, thinking he might be substituting for the first time and a little fearful, she promised him, "It is not so difficult. You will see."

"I hope I do," Max agreed, and resumed his observation. He wasn't sure exactly what he was looking for, here at the school.

He had passed by the line of seven dogs and two cats, tied to the railings across the street from the school gates. The cats had made themselves comfortable, in the way of cats. They had curled themselves up close to the fence, where passers-by would not be likely to disturb them, and gone to sleep. The dogs were not so philosophical. They rose to their feet and wagged hopeful tails, seven hopeful tails wagging at Max, fourteen dark, imploring eyes. "Good dogs," he said, noticing the nine water bowls, some of delicate porcelain, some decorated in bright colors, and one—belonging to one of the cats, he hoped—entirely encrusted with glass chips, perhaps trying to look like diamonds. "Good dogs." Some dogs had plain leather collars, a couple sported a bejeweled collar like the one Sunny had worn until Joachim replaced it, and a heavy-jawed bulldog even had a collar with spikes all around it, as if he dreamed of a more dangerous life than a house pet could hope for.

When Max had stepped past them and into the street, the row of dogs sighed and lay down again, their heads on their paws. He could see them now, patiently watching, waiting. Max wondered if their masters came out to give them fresh water or treats during recess, if the students were allowed to leave school grounds, and he wondered what happened in bad weather, rain or snow or even the kind of chilly, damp fogs that often rose from the lake on early spring mornings.

Max was undisturbed if not unnoticed as he considered the groups of children, and tried to identify the animal owners. A small group had gathered around one girl who was seated on a bench, and he recognized her as Clarissa, mistress of Princess Jonquilletta of the Windy Isles, otherwise known as Sunny. Clarissa wore the same blue pleated uniform skirt and white short-sleeved blouse as all the other girls on the playground, but she had a thick black ribbon in her hair, and she wore a black mourning band around one arm. The others bent toward her in sympathetic attitudes. As Max watched, Clarissa raised one hand to her eyes to wipe away tears. In the background, the excited voices of the younger children filled the air, like cries from flocks of small, busy birds, nuthatches or sparrows. Clarissa's grief stood out all the more in contrast to this happy background.

Clarissa saw the substitute teacher watching her and managed a watery smile and a subdued toss of her brown curls, but she didn't recognize him as the Mister Max her father had hired to either find, or confirm the loss of, her dog. She said something to the girls around her, who turned briefly to look at Max—by then he had looked away and only sensed their attention—before returning to the satisfyingly sad task of offering comfort to Clarissa.

Toward the edge of the playground, close to the high fence railings and just across the street from the animals, two boys stood talking. These were certainly pet owners, Max decided, seeing the way that every now and then one or the other boy would look out across the street and one or the other of the dogs would stand up and wag its tail. The cats, of course, paid no attention.

Max moved around the tree to see what was happening on the other side of the playground, and almost as soon as his back was turned a ruckus erupted behind him. There came cries, not at all like birdsongs. These were shouts of anger and alarm, and he saw that a fight had broken out, between the two boys at the fence, he thought.

Well, boys liked to fight, especially boys of eleven or twelve, thought Max, who now felt years older than that. For a few seconds he watched the flailing arms and tumbling figures as he would have watched any of his own schoolmates having a good fight. Then he heard someone calling, "Lorenzo Apiedi! Come help! Mr. Apiedi!"

At the repetition of the name, Max remembered who he was, and where. Of course a substitute teacher, and a man at that, would be expected to help break up the fight. He ran down to the fence.

The fight was not between the two boys after all. A third party had joined in the fracas, a long-haired person—a girl?— but who was fighting whom, he couldn't tell. He reached in, grabbed an arm, and pulled. At the same time, Madame Celestine pulled another combatant loose. This left the girl alone, panting, her fists clenched, her long white-blond hair pulled loose from its braid. Then her fists unclenched and she grinned angrily, as if she wished the fight had not been interrupted.

"Thomas? Hector! You are coming with me right now! Mr. Apiedi, you take Pia."

"Yeah, let *him* deal with Pee-pee."

"That is enough from you, Hector. We do not call names at the Hilliard School. It is also against the rules—as all three of you know—to fight on school property."

Pia, the girl, was brushing dirt from her skirt and pulling up her socks. Her fingers pushed her hair messily back into place. The boys left their shirts untucked and their hair untidied. The children refused to look at one another.

"Before school lets out, you will all apologize," Madame Celestine predicted grimly. "You'll apologize to your classmates, to one another, and to me. If you plan to return tomorrow, you'll apologize today. Yes, even you, Pia. *This* time you'll apologize, or . . . Because if you don't, it may not matter how much money your father has. Come along, boys. And tuck your shirts in, for goodness' sake."

Max was left with the girl, whose hair shone like snow even on that overcast day and who had started the day with a bright red ribbon tied at the end of her long braid. Now the ribbon hung limply, its bow undone. The girl glared, still grinning, right at his chest. In her fury and frustration she didn't look at his face, for which Max was grateful. Few adults, he had noticed, really looked at things or people. Children, however, were a different story.

And then—without warning, like the sudden gust of cold wind that comes before an icy rain—Max remembered who he really was, and where, and why. He had a sudden vivid memory of his parents, his lively, laughing mother, his father with those dramatics and enthusiasms—and he wished with all his heart that they had not left him behind. He wished they would be waiting for him at home even if that meant they'd lay claim to his time and energy for their own uses. He wished he was not a boy alone. That wishing and longing, and the sadness it dragged along behind it like a huge, heavy chain, made Max shiver, despite the sunshiny warmth of the day. The girl saw this and she stared into his face, frankly curious.

Max was in danger of being discovered.

Luckily, he knew what a teacher would say, and so he asked, "Do you want to tell me what that was all about?" In Max's experience, teachers often asked questions they knew wouldn't be answered, and by asking that kind of question he turned himself back into the substitute teacher.

She continued staring into his face and said, "No." Her eyes were a dark blue and her eyebrows unexpectedly, dramatically, black. She was eleven, he guessed, maybe twelve, short and solid, with a stubborn jaw and broad shoulders. Hands on her hips, she glared up at him, waiting to see what he'd do next.

"As you wish," Max said, and he smiled down into her angry face.

This confused her. To confuse her further, he then looked away from her, across the street to the row of patient pets, as if *they* were what really interested him. A wagon rattled by, loaded with wood, the horse's hooves clopping on the macadam. An automobile went by in the opposite direction, heading out of the New Town, going perhaps up into the hills or maybe as far as the distant mountains. The voices from the playground had recommenced their bird-like cries. When Max looked back at her, the girl was biting at her lip and her forehead was wrinkled. She said, "I suppose I have to tell you."

He didn't answer, the adult being patiently grown-up while the child figured things out.

"They called me Pee-pee. You heard. They don't like me, that's all," Pia said. She shrugged, and grimaced. She had a wide, flexible mouth, good for grimacing and grinning and probably sneering, too. Her nose had a bump in the middle, as if it had been broken in a fistfight.

"You, on the other hand, want to be everybody's friend," Max said with gentle sarcasm. She smiled then, quite a pleasant smile. He smiled pleasantly back, and she gave a little happy laugh. "You're no teacher," she said.

Max ignored that. What could he have said, anyway? Instead, he asked, "Why *don't* they like you?"

"Nobody does," she explained. "Not the girls, not the boys, not the teachers—although the teachers are polite about it." She thought for a brief time. "Especially the girls don't like me," she concluded cheerfully. "It doesn't break my heart. It's not as if I'm worried they're better than I am. It's not as if"—and this thought made her laugh again—"we're going to be in school for the rest of our lives. It's true, isn't it? That things are really different after school. My father says."

"You don't have *any* friends?"

She shook her head, and looked defiantly up at him as if she expected him to deny that.

But Max figured that she would know if she had a friend, and he knew what that was like, being friendless at school. They called *him* Eyes, so he also knew what it was like on the receiving end of name-calling. He asked, "Are you new to Hilliard?"

"This is my third year here."

"Did you ever have friends? Or even just one friend?"

She shook her head, No and No.

"Did you ever want one?" he asked. She was interesting, this Pia. She wasn't feeling sorry for herself, and she certainly wasn't creeping around the edges of one group or another the way some people did, hoping not to be pushed away even if they knew better than to hope to be asked in.

She thought about his question, as if it was something that hadn't occurred to her before. "No, I don't think so," she decided. "I have brothers and sisters at home," she told him. "My father enjoys my company. I'm not lonely. But what are you doing here if you're not a teacher?"

"Who said I wasn't a teacher?" Max asked.

"Me," she reminded him. "I did."

Max avoided the girl's question. "If you've been here for three years and never had a friend, what was there to fight about today?" he asked her.

"What there always is," she told him. "My father, the name they call me. Plus, they don't like my ideas about some things.

And I don't like being told not to have the ideas I have," she announced, and glared again. She was a good glarer, this girl.

Max waited, letting the silence grow.

"My father was a brewer," she explained, although that explained nothing. "He still is, but now he's more, too. My father is a successful businessman. *Their* fathers are bankers and lawyers, doctors, professors, and their grandfathers are just the same, but my grandfather was a dairyman. He took care of cows for a rich farmer. *Their* mothers were all debutantes and speak French, and the girls will all be debutantes, too, but you couldn't make me do that if you paid me a million." She thought a little more, then added, "Unless, of course, I needed the money. Which I probably wouldn't, because my father's beer is in every bar and pub and restaurant. That's not even counting his other businesses. That's why we're so rich," she explained, "even if we're not good enough for *them*." She gave him a broad smile and assured him, "Not that I want to be good enough for them."

Max nodded. "What is it they don't like about your ideas? I mean, other than that you don't admire them for the reasons they want to be admired."

She turned to look through the fence to the street and across to the other side. "You see those animals?"

"Yes."

"Don't you think it's wicked to leave an animal tied up there all day? Especially a cat. I mean, really wicked, like Attila the Hun. It's cruel, and stupid, it's—"

"Well, *I* wouldn't like it," Max agreed.

"It's just showing off," Pia announced decisively. "It's just a contest they have, to be the one with a pet everybody else wishes they had." She wheeled around. "You see that girl?" She pointed to the bench where Clarissa was still sitting, still surrounded by sympathizing friends, still holding her handkerchief. "The pretty one, with a black armband? You'd think her sister had died or something, her father. But it's her pet, a dog. A nice dog, I admit, but . . ."

Max asked, curious, "Her dog died?"

"If she has, I bet Clarissa wouldn't care. Not really. It's all pretending. If they really loved these pets, don't you think they'd leave them at home instead of keeping them tied up here all day? They just . . . I don't know why it makes me so angry . . . it's not as if I care whether or not they're good pet owners. I don't know why I get into fights about it. But what do *you* think? Don't you think they're hypocrites?"

"Not everybody has a pet tied up there," Max pointed out.

"Only people who think they'll win the contest bring their pets. The rest just talk about them, what Fluffy did that was so cute, that kind of boring stuff. If I didn't have my classes to think about, I'd die of boredom here. I would, and if I didn't die of boredom I'd kill myself from boredom."

Max laughed.

She scowled at him and her dark blue eyes narrowed, ready to be angry. "You think I'm lying?" she asked.

"I don't think you're a liar," he told her.

"I'm not," she agreed, and that was the end of her anger.

"That might make you unpopular, too," Max said.

She looked back to the playground, and the expression on her face changed again. It grew wary, maybe even a little frightened. But before he could turn to see what was upsetting her, "Listen," she said, speaking fast. "You're no teacher, whatever you pretend, and I think they've figured it out, so if you don't want to get caught you better run."

Max was too much the actor to turn his head, but he didn't have to. Someone called out, and not in a friendly fashion, "Mr. Apiedi! Lorenzo! I wonder—"

Pia reached out to shake his hand. "I'll create a diversion. Good luck." And then she jerked her hand away and cried out, "I'm not sorry! I won't say I'm sorry! You can't make me! And you can't catch me, either!" She took off at a run toward the gate.

Max moved behind her, letting her draw ahead as he heard the voice shout angrily, "Pia! Where do you think—? Pia, stop! Stop right now! You're not allowed to—!"

At the gate, Max sped up to pass the girl and run out onto the road, crossing it between a brougham and a group of three workmen in dirty overalls busy arguing with one another. He took off his hat and jacket as he ran so that when Madame Celestine—Pia held firmly by the wrist—looked for him, the substitute teacher had disappeared. The only person she saw of the right general size was a tall, skinny boy, probably playing hooky. But not from the Hilliard School, she thought with satisfaction.

13

In which Max and Joachim
discuss thorny topics, and Grammie
has a strange encounter

Max was troubled by what he'd learned. He doubted that Clarissa cared about the dog at all. That was a problem for him. Also, he didn't want to return the dog to a life of being tied to a fence, day after day, as if it were a prisoner in a jail, as if being a pet was committing a crime. On the other hand, the dog did belong to Clarissa. Legally, he had to return Sunny. Didn't he? It would be dishonest not to, and it would also count as a failure for Mister Max.

But what about the dog herself? How could it be a success for Mister Max to do that to the dog?

Max was not unhappy to have this thorny question needing his attention, and as he rode his bicycle home he was so concentrated on the Hilliard pet problem, which was the

Sunny problem, that he barely noticed when it began to rain. But the bad weather and the difficult thinking added together convinced him to pay a visit to Joachim and the dog to see how they were getting on. He leaned his bicycle against the garden wall and let himself in. If Joachim was working, he wouldn't want to put down his brush to answer the door. If Joachim was eating lunch, he wouldn't want to put down his spoon, or sandwich, and get up from the table to answer the door.

The truth was that whatever Joachim was doing, he wouldn't want to answer the door.

Max found Joachim in the studio, in front of an easel that held one of the paintings Sunny had ruined. His teacher ran a dry brush along the streaked lines her tail had made on wet paint, imitating the strokes. Then he dipped his brush onto his palette and, using the same long, stroking gestures, painted over a canvas on another easel, a fresh painting of the flowering branch of an apple tree. He put his glasses on to see the effect more clearly; he took his glasses off to perceive the effect more feelingly. He mumbled to himself and called to the dog. "Sunny? Come here, girl."

The dog rose from where she lay on the stone floor and padded over to Joachim, her tail wagging gently. "Good dog, good dog," the painter said, studying the movement of her tail. He turned back to his easels, the dog returned to her original place and position, and Max cleared his throat.

The dog raised her head and wagged a welcoming tail, but Joachim ignored him, so Max went out to the kitchen, where he deduced from the lack of dishes that Joachim hadn't yet eaten lunch. Neither had he, so he heated a vegetable soup he found in the icebox. He set a loaf of bread and two spoons out on the kitchen table, filled two bowls with the hot soup, and not until then did he go back to the studio door to announce, "There's lunch ready."

Joachim sighed deeply, put his brush into a jar of turpentine, and took off his smock. "Shouldn't you be in school? Because this is the third day you've been here this week. Sunday, Monday, and now again today." In case Max couldn't do the math, Joachim concluded, "That makes three days."

Max waited until Joachim had eaten half of his bowl of soup before saying, "I need to ask you—"

"Are you here for your lesson?"

Max had forgotten about his lesson, and he welcomed the distraction. "Yes!"

"You didn't bring supplies," Joachim pointed out. "I gather your parents don't want a dog? Not that I blame them, and especially a large dog, but if they are changeable enough to cancel this long tour, which I thought everybody was so excited about, *and* cancel it at the last minute, can't they change just a little more?" Joachim demanded.

Max almost laughed.

Joachim looked at him suspiciously. "You told me you were leaving the city."

"*They* left," Max said.

"Without you? I don't believe it."

Max set down his spoon, took a deep breath, and told his

teacher what had happened. It was not, after all, a very long story. Joachim spooned soup into his mouth and listened. At the end, he looked up at Max. "It's not good," Joachim said. "It can't be good."

For some reason, that gloomy prophecy allowed Max to hope that the best was just as possible.

Joachim mopped up the last of his soup with a thick slice of bread and ate it slowly, bite by bite. When at last he spoke, he was concerned about Max, not Max's parents. "The city authorities will want to send you to an orphanage." Before Max could say anything, Joachim conceded, "Maybe they wouldn't be able to, maybe they'd have to let you live with a blood relation. But your grandmother is old—"

"No older than you," Max protested.

"—and there are laws about these things, there are laws about everything having to do with children. You know, if they can put you in an orphanage, the city authorities will be able to sell your house, *and* the theater. They'll say it's to cover the expense of keeping you, and educating you, feeding and clothing you, training you for some work. Somehow, when the authorities get involved, they end up a little richer."

This was terrible. "But it's my parents' house and their theater, too. That makes them mine now."

"I'm not saying they *will* do that. I'm just saying they might want to. I suppose your grandmother could hire a lawyer, but lawyers don't come cheap, and librarians don't earn much."

Max couldn't argue with that.

"So whatever you do, you don't want to let anyone know your situation," Joachim advised.

"I don't plan to." Max had never thought of any danger to him personally. Had Grammie? He hoped not. She already had more than enough to worry about.

"But only for a few years, only until you're sixteen. So it's not for *that* long." Joachim got up to ladle more soup into his bowl. For him, the subject was settled; he'd said all he had to say on it.

Max, on the other hand, had lost his appetite. New worries and fears washed over him. "I don't know," he said.

"Exactly," Joachim agreed. He ripped a chunk off a slice of bread, dipped it into his bowl, and offered it to the dog. "Sunny? Try this." Tail wagging, the dog padded obediently over to accept the treat.

To distract himself from the dismal possibilities Joachim had introduced into his situation, Max said, "Sunny? Come," and patted his thigh. To his surprise, she obeyed, settling her head where his hand had indicated. Without thinking, he began to rub at the bony top of her head and pull gently on her ears, which for some reason soothed him. He could feel his anxiety easing as he stroked her floppy, soft ears. Then he wondered, Why *did* the dog refuse to come when Clarissa called her?

"What about Sunny?" Joachim demanded now. "Where did you get the dog?"

"From two elderly sisters. On Hilliard Road," Max said.

"I know who you mean and they never had a dog." Now Joachim spoke sternly. "Unless you can swear to me that wherever she came from *wasn't* a place she wanted to escape from," he said, "or the people, too—it's people *and* place that make a home—I won't have Sunny taken back there. You're going to have to think of something else."

"That's what—" Max began.

"What's the truth about her?"

"Her owners hired me to find her when she disappeared from where she was tied up, outside the little girl's school," he said.

"Tied up? Why at a school? Don't they know anything about dogs?"

"The little girl likes to take her to school," Max explained. He didn't want to go into the whole long story. "She's not the only one. It's . . . it's a kind of contest, I think, a way of showing off, like . . . like talking about your marks on a test."

Joachim thought about this and decided, "You can't take her back to those people."

"But I accepted the job."

"You're a detective now? You have a license?"

"And I need the money, or I *will* need it. They paid me twenty-five."

"I'll loan you money if I have to. Even better, here's what I'll do," Joachim offered, and for him, Max knew, it was a sacrifice, "I'll give you lessons for nothing, and that's as good as putting coins in your pocket. Pay me back when you can. If you ever can."

"But the dog does belong to the girl."

"Only legally."

"The law is important," Max said. He thought but did not say—not ready to argue this point with Joachim right then— that just because a law didn't always seem fair to you personally, or wasn't working in your favor, that didn't mean law wasn't necessary.

"What about what's good for the dog? The law doesn't protect the dog, so we have to. Don't tell me *you* want to give Sunny back to her."

Max stroked the golden head and agreed, "Of course not. But is it right not to? Isn't that stealing?"

"It's right for the dog," Joachim said. "Sometimes you have to break one law to obey another, more important one."

"I don't want to be someone who breaks any law," Max said stubbornly.

Joachim ignored this. "Can't you keep her yourself?"

That would be unwise, Max knew. "They might see her with me, for one thing. For another, I'm often away from home, and I don't see that being left alone in a house is much better than being left tied up to a fence. At least tied up near the school there were other dogs around for company. And besides," Max concluded, "how can I earn my living finding things for people if I don't succeed? I'll get a bad reputation."

"You'll be lucky to get any reputation at all," Joachim pronounced gloomily. "And anyway, you're no detective."

"I know I'm not," Max agreed unhappily. "I don't know what I am. What *am* I?"

Surprisingly, Joachim laughed, although it was not a cheery sound. "You're in trouble, that's what you are, and I don't know how you're going to get yourself out of it. What could your parents have been thinking of, going off without you?"

"They wanted me with them," Max said.

"Although it may be a good thing you aren't," Joachim announced, rising from the table to take his soup bowl to the sink. "Did you ever think that it might have been your lucky day when you missed that boat?"

No, Max hadn't, and he didn't now. "I'm going to see what Grammie says about the dog."

"What does she know about dogs?"

"She knows about right and wrong," Max said stubbornly. "I trust her."

"She looks like a trustworthy type," Joachim admitted.

Max planned to put the Sunny problem to both Grammie and Ari that evening over supper. Knowing his next step made him feel a little better—despite feeling a lot more worried about what could happen to *him*—so when he got home he settled down to his schoolwork first and then more eagerly to another attempt at a windy skyscape.

Max might have had his own plan, but that evening, standing at the stove, her back turned to her two guests so they couldn't see her face, Grammie announced, "I had disturbing news today. And a very odd visitor. At the library." She turned around then and came to sit at the table. Looking at

Max, she said, "I think we ought to tell him. If he's going to live in your house, I think we have to."

Max stood up. He walked to the kitchen door and looked out. Now he was the one with his back turned, concealing his face.

"Tell me what?" Ari asked. "What's wrong? What news?"

"Tell you about . . . ," Grammie began. "About the . . . the situation. My daughter and her husband . . . They're actors, the Starling Theatrical Company."

"The Starling . . . Your daughter? They're Max's parents? Which explains the posters," Ari said.

Max went to the stove and pretended that the dinner needed his attention. He picked up a long-handled wooden spoon and stirred at a pot of boiling noodles. Behind him, Grammie told Ari about the letter from a nonexistent Maharajah, the strange note left for Max when they sailed without him, the possibility that the unpleasant Madame Olenka was somehow connected, and how she and Max had decided that they had to wait, for a few weeks at least, to see if they heard anything from William and Mary Starling. "When you don't know anything, it's often better to stay still, stay put, and find out what you can," she explained.

Max took down three dinner plates.

Ari protested, "But *anything* could be—" and fell abruptly silent. It was as if his thoughts were so dark and unpleasant that he didn't want Grammie and Max to even know he was thinking them.

Max carried the noodle pot over to the sink and drained it, listening.

"I never guessed," Ari said to him. "I never even thought of anything like this. How old *are* you, Max?"

"Old enough," Max answered, and quickly returned to the stove, carrying the colander of noodles.

Ari looked from one to the other of them. "You must— both of you . . . You must feel . . ." He couldn't find the word. Max didn't want to hear the word, whatever it might have been. "No wonder you look so tired, Mrs. Nives."

"We do," Grammie assured their friend. "I am. Max?"

Max was serving noodles onto the plates and didn't turn around, but Grammie knew he was listening.

"I heard from Cape Town," she said. "I cabled city librarians around the world about the ships," she explained to Ari, "and today I got my first answer. Storms at sea have delayed shipping and the *Miss Koala* is two days overdue. They assume she was driven off course, and he'll cable me when . . ." Her words faded off. Shipwreck was always a possibility, even with the larger, safer, steam-powered ocean liners.

Max spooned the goulash over the noodles and set the three plates on the table, along with a bowl of buttered brussels sprouts. All three ate slowly and thoughtfully for a few minutes, fortifying themselves with hearty food against the news to come, because Grammie had not yet explained why her visitor had alarmed her. "Now Ari knows the background," Grammie said at last. "That catches us all up to today." She took a deep breath. "Today . . ." But that was all she said.

"What's happened?" Max asked. Had a city official come to inquire about him?

"As I said, I had a disturbing visitor at the library today. Late this morning, just before we closed for the lunch break. There was a man." She looked significantly at Max. Max looked to Ari, who just shook his head. Neither of them had any idea what Grammie would say next.

"When he got to the front of the line, he had a book. I think it was an atlas, anyway it was a reference book, and you know those are never loaned out. It's library policy." She chewed and swallowed a bite, remembering. "I had just started telling him that when he leaned over, close to my face, as if he didn't want to be overheard. He was interested in local theaters, he said, and he had heard there was a good theatrical company here, in the old city, and could I tell him anything about it. That was when I looked at him." She watched Max. "Really looked."

Max had a mouthful of food, but he stopped chewing. What had she seen? To upset her?

"He was an ordinary-looking man, middle-aged, short gray beard, curly gray hair, brown eyes, chunky, muscular. He wore trousers and a jacket, but it wasn't a suit. He looked like just anybody. Except—he had rather long ears."

Relieved, Max swallowed. This wasn't the worst possible news. When you've been fearing the worst, something that's merely worrisome is almost *good* news. He asked, "You mean long earlobes?"

"Exactly," she said.

"Madame Olenka," Max explained to Ari, "had very long earlobes."

"Not a common characteristic," Ari pointed out.

"It isn't," Grammie agreed.

"An inherited characteristic," Ari added. "It's a recessive, not dominant, gene and therefore, according to Mendel's findings—"

"Exactly," Grammie said again. Turning to Max, she explained Mendel's experiments with beans and their results.

Max could draw the conclusion. "You think they're probably related, this man and Madame Olenka."

"If that's anybody's name at all," Grammie said.

"What did you tell him?" Ari asked.

"I was so surprised, I didn't say anything. So he kept talking, 'The *Starling* Theater,' he said. I asked him to step aside so the person behind him could check out and he did, but he stood there, waiting. While he was waiting, I checked books out, and thought."

"That was smart," Max said. He had gone back to eating; the goulash was very good, meaty and flavorful and rich with sour cream. He suspected that his dinner might not taste nearly as good if he waited until the end of Grammie's story to eat it. Ari apparently thought the same, because he, too, had recommended his meal.

"Well, I needed my wits about me if I was going to find

out anything from him and keep him from learning anything from me. When everybody else had gone, he stepped up right in front of me and asked, 'Is the theater ever going to re-open?' 'Why ask me?' I asked him, and he said, 'Librarians know everything.'"

"So he knew it was closed down," Ari observed.

"He also knew your parents were out of the city. He said someone had told him that. Your father talks entirely too much," she said to Max.

"My father likes to be larger-than-life," Max explained to Ari. "More vivid, more . . . My father always wants things to be adventures, and he makes adventures out of everything."

"He must be a lot of fun," Ari said. "I'd have liked that when I was a boy, someone dashing and flashy, someone every-body noticed and—probably—enjoyed," he said wistfully.

"He's not a bad father," Grammie allowed. "And he's a good husband, too. But he does talk too much. People know too much about him. Or, and this might be more danger-ous, people *think* they know about him. This man today, he said he wondered if the theater needed a watchman, or if the house needed guarding or caretaking. 'Starling is a wealthy man,' that's what he said, exactly. 'I wouldn't know,' I said, and opened my drawer to take out my purse and lunch. I swear he followed me to the door, as if he was going to follow me out to the garden and sit down right beside me, hanging over my shoulder while I ate. So you know what I did?"

Grammie looked at Max and Ari with mischief in her eyes and the kind of smile Max had not seen since his parents disappeared. Max and Ari shook their heads, they didn't know, they couldn't guess.

"I went into the ladies' bathroom. And I stayed there for a long time. When I came out, he'd gone away, I don't know where. So, what do you two think?" Before either one of them could speak, she added, "I'm not ashamed to tell you, he was a little frightening. Or, maybe, more accurately, alarming. Whatever has your father gotten himself mixed up in? What do they want, those Long-ears? Do you think it has something to do with this fraudulent Indian escapade?"

Those questions drove the problem of the dog entirely out of Max's mind. The three of them spent the rest of the evening trying to guess who the Long-ears were and what they were after and if they might be connected to the phony Maharajah of Kashmir. . . .

14

The Lost Spoon

• A C T I I •

enobia would have said something, but maybe it *was* a girl after all. Zenobia was an old woman, she knew, and it sometimes seemed to her that the weak mind she started life out with had grown weaker every year. What had she ever known about young people, anyway? It was only food she ever knew anything about. But she did know that if it hadn't been for the Baroness, nobody would have suspected she could do *anything* useful. As a young girl, the Baroness had watched Zenobia chop vegetables for a soup and seen how she used her eyes and hands and nose, too, to do the job. The Baroness might not be clever in the kitchen, but everywhere else she was smart, and strong, and bold. She always had been, from girlhood, and from that same time, Zenobia had clung to her mistress, like someone shipwrecked in the wide ocean with only one broken spar to keep her afloat. To Zenobia, the world beyond the kitchen was as treacherous and unpredictable and stormy as any ocean.

Zenobia had felt, at times, as if she might be sinking into that stormy world. She couldn't, now, remember precisely what troubles had happened during those times, but it was absolutely clear in her mind that the Baroness had always been there to keep Zenobia safe. She would never protest any decision her mistress made. If the Baroness decided to hire a new scullery maid, Zenobia would train her as the Baroness wished. Luckily for Zenobia, who had never been good at remembering names, this girl was named Martha. They were all named Martha, in fact, all the maids in the castle, as if there were a conspiracy of mothers, all of whom wished their daughters to go into service for the Baroness.

This Martha was plump as a partridge, tall and clumsy as a turkey, and wore a red bandanna to cover her hair. Her eyes made the cook think of saucepans forgotten on the flame, burned a browny black-gray. She was not particularly pretty, but Zenobia knew from experience that it was not the prettiest girls who made the best pastries. There had been cakes tasting of strawberry or lemon, chocolate or vanilla, oh, and raspberry, too. Where had that Martha gone?

Zenobia wished she could remember all the things she'd forgotten, as she watched this Martha wrap an apron around her thick waist and prepare to be told what to do. Loose-cut they might be, but the cook would have sworn the girl was wearing trousers. But Zenobia never commented on the styles young people chose. The young wanted their own style, and if an old woman didn't like it, who cared? "Martha," she asked, "do you know how to polish silver?"

"I can learn," Martha said. "Just tell me how to do it."

Zenobia couldn't explain anything to anybody. She just knew how, so she seated the girl at the far end of the long wooden worktable and mixed a large bowl of the white paste for her. She put a pile of soft cloths to one side and spread a wide strip of cotton over the tabletop. She didn't speak as she did this, and having done it she wiped her hands on her apron and stood back.

Max waited. The cook had a short, square body and a squished-in square face, which gave her a worried expression. This was not at all what he'd thought someone would look like after a lifetime spent in command of a baroness's kitchen. Her white hair was covered with a yellow-and-blue-striped kerchief tied at the nape of her neck; arthritis had thickened the knuckles of her strong fingers. Over a black dress Zenobia wore a long, bibbed apron, already stained with what was probably jam, coffee grounds, and perhaps an egg yolk. The apron had two deep pockets, from which several spoons stuck out, some wooden, some metal. After a long minute of staring at him, Zenobia nodded, as if satisfied with how things were going, and went back to her own end of the table, which ran almost the whole length of the cellar room. There she sat, paying him no further attention.

For a while, Max watched her and considered the scene and situation. He had dressed in the costume his father wore to play the title role in *The Caliph's Doctor*: loose-fitting blue silk trousers with a loose long-sleeved yellow silk shirt. To conceal his boy's haircut, he had covered his head with the red bandanna. While he waited for whatever would happen next, he unbuttoned the cuffs of the shirt and rolled up his sleeves. When Zenobia began to talk, however, it wasn't to tell him how to polish silver or where to find the silver he was supposed to be polishing. She seemed to be speaking to herself. "Lamb," she said, "but she never liked lamb, not that I remember. How long has it been, Martha," she asked Max, "since that last dinner the Baroness ordered?"

"Years," Max answered.

"A sad dinner, I think. Do you remember?"

"No," Max said. "What do *you* remember?" While he sat waiting to be shown how to polish silver, he might as well do a little detecting.

"Beef Wellington," she told him. "A whole tenderloin sent down from our farms in the hills, wrapped in pastry, the tenderest, flakiest pastry—you can't imagine it. The Baroness was unusually pleased with us that night. It was a good party. There were three great men at the table—a scholar, a senator, a doctor—the nephew, too. I *think* that was the night the senator dined here, but it might have been the poet. The poet was a favorite guest, he talked so well, but I never could remember names. Why was it sad? Do you remember?" She took a pad of paper out of her apron pocket, and a pencil. Her fingers wrapped around the pencil in a child's grip.

As she talked, Max looked around, detecting. This kitchen was the last place the Cellini Spoon had been seen. The dark table where he sat filled the center space of a brick-walled, stone-floored room, which had only small, high windows to let daylight in, and those only along one wall. The castle kitchen was in its cellar, as if this room was the foundation on which everything else stood. A large range was set into the fireplace, eight burners and three ovens, and the wall nearby was hung with copper saucepans and copper molds and small buckets holding wooden spoons and metal spoons, ladles and spatulas of all sorts, long-handled cooking forks, tongs. One old woman couldn't possibly eat enough to need all of these utensils, and even though it had probably been years since any of them had been used, they all gleamed. Shelves along the walls held Dutch ovens, roasting pans, soup pots, cake tins, baking sheets, cooling racks, and rows of mixing bowls in all sizes. He couldn't imagine the dining room such a kitchen had been built to serve. Except, he corrected himself, to imagine that it would have dark wood and poor lighting. That seemed to be the style the Barons Barthold preferred.

This long, gloomy cellar was reached by a narrow, twisting staircase that Max had himself descended just before eight that morning. Food would have been carried on wide, heavy trays up along that staircase to the dining room, and dirty dishes brought down, unless there was a dumbwaiter. Max looked for the little shuttered window that would house a dumbwaiter but didn't see one. A long soapstone sink with an even longer soapstone drainboard stood opposite the range. On the rough wall behind the sink were pipes that brought water to the long-necked faucets. He turned to look behind him. The three closed doors must lead to pantries and iceboxes.

This kitchen was entirely too large for any one old woman, whether she was upstairs being served or downstairs preparing meals.

"Today I make the broth," Zenobia said, "and the Bavarian cream, to chill. Tomorrow the lake-fish mousse." She wrote as slowly as she spoke. "Martha must go to the butcher today, greengrocer tomorrow." Then she looked up and saw Max. "What are you sitting there for, Martha? You have work to do."

Max rose to his feet to show how obedient and cooperative he was, then said, "I don't know where the silver is, Missus Cook." He had never played a scullery maid, so he didn't know exactly how he was supposed to address Zenobia.

"Stupid," she said, but it seemed she was talking about herself, not her assistant. "It's been so many years, how could anyone remember?" She pointed to one of the doors behind Max and said, "In the pantry there, in the cupboards, you'll see glassware and china." She looked back down to her list. "Asparagus?" she asked herself. "Courgettes?"

Max went to the door, then turned back to ask, "The silver will be . . . ?"

"In the drawers, where it's always been."

"Yes, Missus," Max said.

The pantry was another dark, narrow room, lit by a single bare bulb at the center of the ceiling. Max pulled on its string and saw a row of glass-fronted cupboards. Some held stacks of plates and bowls of all sizes, dinner and lunch, dessert and salad and butter plates, soup and fruit and finger bowls; others held glassware of many different sorts, water goblets and champagne flutes, wine glasses and brandy snifters. Wide drawers lined one side, and when he pulled the top one open he saw that it was filled with silverware, stacked up neatly in small racks, dinner forks and salad forks and lunch forks and dessert forks and fish forks, all in a row. The drawer beneath held the spoons, dozens and dozens of teaspoons, as well as round bouillon spoons and oval dessert spoons, long-handled iced tea spoons and doll-sized demitasse spoons. He opened a knife drawer, where some blades sharp enough to cut meat with and some only sharp enough for fowl lined up beside butter knives and lunch knives and fish knives. The lowest drawer was a jumble of serving utensils—large spoons and big forks, carving knives, ladles of all sizes for everything from soups to sauces, fish servers and stuffing spoons and sugar tongs, berry spoons, delicate little forks for which he couldn't imagine the use, and an array of spoons with which to put small servings of jams and marmalades onto a plate. If the Cellini Spoon was lost among the silver, it would be in here. Loading his apron with as many pieces as it could hold, Max went back out to the kitchen and let it clatter out onto the table.

Zenobia looked up, nodded, and looked down again. Painstakingly, she finished what she was writing, then said, "I'll get the bowl for you," and rose from the table to make her way over to the shelves. She chose a large bread bowl, which she filled with water at the sink and then set down in front of Max. "Rinse off the dirt before you apply the polish. I need to ask my Baroness to approve the menu," she said, and took off her stained apron, dropping it with a rattling of the utensils still in its pockets at an open door behind Max, to put on a clean one. She saw Max watching and smiled at him, perfectly friendly. "We have a laundress, and my Baroness is particular. After you have the tarnish off the silver, wash it all in soap and warm water in the sink. You must polish it dry, Martha. To bring up the shine, the way we always do in this house."

Alone in the dim, cavernous kitchen, Max thought: The cook hadn't emptied her apron pockets before she dropped the soiled garment on the floor; might a laundress have found the Cellini Spoon and kept it? He got up from the table and went to see what the laundry looked like. There, a mangle occupied one wall, and two round machines with wringers stood opposite, while clotheslines hung across the ceiling. Anyone putting the kitchen laundry through the wringer would certainly have noticed the Cellini Spoon, but would she steal it? If Zenobia had absent-mindedly dropped it into her apron pocket, it would certainly have turned up in the laundry. But the laundry would not have been done that same night, would it?

The Baroness, moreover, had sworn by every servant in the castle, except the Martha who had fallen in love with her great-nephew. Also, Max didn't think the Baroness would have failed to look everywhere, including the laundry room, for her lost treasure. Max was still betting on the drawer of serving utensils—unless of course the spoon had been somehow removed from the kitchen. Up to a bedroom? Down into a wine cellar?

In the meantime, he had his disguise to maintain. He returned to the table, dropped a handful of the serving pieces into the bowl of water, chose from them a long-handled stuffing spoon blackened with time and neglect, dipped one of the soft cloths into the white paste, and began. He might get lucky, he thought. This might be the exact thing he was looking for.

When Zenobia returned, Max had cleaned only eight of the largest spoons and had not found the Cellini Spoon. He couldn't even be sure how clean the eight were, because the paste was smeared all over them. He was lining them up on the cloth in front of him. The dirty rags, blackened with tarnish, he dropped on the brick floor beside his chair. Zenobia mumbled and muttered—was she grumbling? Max wondered—and sat back down at the table, pulling her pad of paper back in front of her.

"Foolish woman, it was always only a lunch," she mumbled. "You remembered it wrong, all wrong. You're more trouble than you're worth and it'll be the poor farm or the workhouse for you. A beef consommé," Zenobia said, and wrote slowly. She thought, and said, "Lake fish with beurre blanc. She always liked beurre blanc, and who else knows what she likes the way I do?"

This question Zenobia seemed to direct down the length of the table to Max. Then she rose and rushed at him. "What are you doing? We'd never need all those serving spoons at once, Martha. What are you thinking?" She went into the pantry and came back with handfuls of forks and spoons and knives, which she dropped into the bowl of water. "Service for eight, no more," she said, with a quick and, to Max's surprise, entirely alert glance. She selected out the remaining unpolished serving spoons from the bowl, setting them aside. "You'll find that's enough to keep you busy."

"Yes, Missus," Max said. "It won't happen again." He made the apology as he thought a scullery maid might, but Zenobia's unexpected energy had already left her.

"It's not as if she ever was nice," the cook told him. "Not kind."

Thinking that he knew of whom she spoke, Max agreed, "No, Missus."

"Not as bad as her father, though, and how should she hand out kindness having never been given none?" the cook asked, returning to her seat. "A chicken salad, do you think?" she concluded. "Martha must go immediately to the butcher."

Max took a luncheon fork from the bowl and dipped a clean cloth into the polish. "Yes," he agreed, even though Zenobia appeared not to hear anything he said. The cook summoned a maid and gave the order, then returned to writing on her pad. Max rubbed hard. It was actually sort of satisfying, the way tarnish came off onto the rag, leaving behind glimpses of glowing silver. These forks were thick and heavy, and they had an ornate *B* carved into their handles. He couldn't imagine eating with such utensils. How could you help being proud, eating with forks like this?

Zenobia looked up to remind him, "The boy had kindness. I used to think—but I never said, not to her or anyone—that all the kindness of the family had been saved up for that poor boy to have, and what good did it do him? It just made him fall in love." But just as Max thought he might learn something interesting, Zenobia got up so suddenly that her chair clattered backward. "It's time! It's almost time, I mustn't forget!" she cried. "There's the meat to set out, there's the little salad to make," and she was off, into the iceboxes, into the pantries, filling a wide silver tray with napkins and gleaming silver utensils of a plainer pattern than those Max was working on, kept handy in a dark wooden chest on a low table beside the staircase.

Max was going to need to look through all the drawers in this whole huge kitchen, and he thought there must be twenty or thirty of them. He didn't see how he would have the time to do all that searching and still get this silver polished. He sped up his work and finished both fork sizes, eight of each, then turned to the knives while Zenobia worked at her end of the table, her fingers nimble with the julienne of carrots and celery to lay on top of soft green leaves of lettuce, her hand adept with the encircling quarters of cherry tomatoes. He thought she must be two different people, a simple-minded girl and a clever cook, living together in one old woman's body. She carved slices of a cold roast beef onto a gold-rimmed plate, then set everything onto the tray, with a woven silver basket holding two soft rolls, a small gold-rimmed plate with pats of butter arranged in a circle, and a carafe of ice water. When all the rest was ready, Zenobia quickly washed, chopped, and sautéed spinach, spooned it onto the plate beside the beef, and picked up the tray.

"Let me carry that," Max offered, seeing how wide and crowded it was, thinking how heavy it must be.

"You keep to the kitchen," Zenobia told him. "But I like your good manners." Her glance drifted off over his shoulder, and he almost turned around to see who was there, but he knew better. The cook was just looking back into the past. "There haven't been good manners in this kitchen for years, but that doesn't mean I don't recognize them."

She left the room. Max went back to polishing the silver. He was getting more efficient at it and was coming to the end of the service for eight. Eight place settings of three forks, two spoons, and two knives each, plus the serving utensils—it made a little hill of silver, filmed with white paste, ready to be washed clean and then polished dry. It was peaceful, working with his hands like that, his mind free to consider the various puzzles and problems he was dealing with. He rubbed paste onto a teaspoon and rubbed tarnish away and thought about the dog. Whose welfare was it most important to think of?

His own? Because if he hoped to earn a living, he needed to succeed at a job he'd agreed to undertake. The dog's? Because she couldn't, she obviously didn't, want to spend her weekdays tied to a fence across the street from the school, and also—he had noticed how she obeyed Joachim—he suspected that the dog had little affection for her mistress. There was the welfare of Clarissa and her father to be considered, too, because they were the owners. They had purchased, fed, and groomed the dog; they had a legal right to her. And then there was the law itself. But how did you even *begin* to think about what was good or bad for the law, as if the law were as real and actual as a dog?

If Max took Princess Jonquilletta of the Windy Isles back to Clarissa, it would benefit three out of those four. But the one it would not benefit was the one least able to defend herself. This was definitely a problem.

The chickens had arrived by the time Zenobia returned, and she set immediately to work. She took onions and carrots out of a pantry drawer. She removed more celery from one of the iceboxes. She sat down at the table with a wooden block in front of her and took a broad-bladed knife from a drawer to begin chopping. "Mirepoix," she whispered to herself, "and rosemary and lemon, salt and pepper, and oil to rub into the skin." Little squares of carrots, then onion, then celery cascaded from the knife blade.

Max piled the silver back into the big bowl and carried it over to the sink to wash off the paste before beginning the final polish. How long would it take him to search through the pantries and laundry room, and the maids' rooms upstairs, in the whole castle? Three days? A week?

But that, as it turned out, was not necessary.

It was when he carelessly shoved a clean fork onto the disorganized mound of washed silverware he was piling up on the drainboard that Max found it. He had shoved the fork onto the pile and reached down into the warm, soapy water to pull up the next spoon, or fork, or knife, when he heard a clattering sound. He knew what had happened. One or more—he hoped not many more—of the freshly washed silverware pieces had been knocked down into the narrow space between the brick cellar wall and the cabinets under the drainboard.

Zenobia looked up from where she was arranging three pale chicken carcasses on a bed of chopped vegetables in a long roasting pan.

"Sorry, Missus," Max apologized.

At the same time she asked him, "Did you light the ovens?"

He was drying his hands, trying to think of how to recover whatever had fallen into that narrow slot. He barely heard her question, and it made no sense to him.

"Did I ask you to light the ovens?" Zenobia wondered, and now worried, she said, "Don't tell me I didn't ask you. I meant to ask you. After all the years you've worked here, Martha, you don't still need to be told, do you? If my Baroness knew . . ."

Max went around the end of the drainboard and tried to

see into the dark space. He pushed the sleeve of his shirt up to his shoulder to make his arm as skinny as possible.

Zenobia watched this, and then unexpectedly she laughed, a round, happy sound. When Max looked at her, he glimpsed the girl she might once have been. "My arms are too fat now to fit into there," she said, and held them out in front of her. "But I was once as slim in the arms as you are, can you believe it?"

"Of course I can," Max said, crouching down to reach in.

He heard Zenobia get up, but she didn't walk toward him. "What was that temperature?" she asked, but Max couldn't have told her. He grasped something with his hand, and pulled out one of the oval spoons he had so carefully removed tarnish from, which was now covered with dust. He reached in again, in case two had fallen onto the narrow slot. The next fork he removed had *not* been polished, and was in fact a dinner fork, larger and heavier than the lunch forks. So he reached in again.

The Cellini Spoon was the fourth or fifth utensil he pulled out of the damp darkness, and he knew what he had as soon as he saw it, thick as it was with seven years of dirt and dust.

A quick glance at Zenobia assured him that she was still in front of the oven, consulting with herself about temperatures. Max returned to his seat at the table and to the bowl of polish. He was not at all surprised when, after several minutes of vigorous work, there appeared on the long, broad handle of the big spoon the bas-relief image of a reed-lined riverbank and a tall figure approaching it. He laughed out loud,

victorious and glad, and Zenobia said, "It's not often we hear that, in this place. There was a time, though. Do you remember the times?"

When Max had finished re-presenting the Cellini Spoon to the light of day, or rather, to the dim light of the kitchen cellar, he held it out to admire. It was an incredibly beautiful piece of work, and it glowed gold. The floating basket, in which the infant was hidden, was about to be discovered, the story of the exodus from Egypt was about to begin, and the craftsman had somehow filled his image with promise and hope. How had he done that? Max wondered, studying it. With the curve of an arm, a ripple in the water, the two smiling faces hidden among the bending reeds . . .

Zenobia's voice interrupted his dreamy thoughts. "That one has a stand in the dining room. I'd best take it up. If she sees it not where it belongs, she'll have one of her tempers."

15

The Lost Spoon

• ACT III •

Spoon in hand, Max dashed across the kitchen. "No!" Zenobia cried. "No!" she cried again, as he stormed past her. "Martha, don't!"

He ran for the stairs.

The cook came after him as fast as she could, which was not nearly as fast as Max. "We never go in the dining room when my Baroness is—" she called.

But by then Max was bounding up the narrow staircase, bearing the Cellini Spoon. There was no difficulty in finding the dining room. An open door at the head of the stairs led onto a short hallway, lined with drawers and cupboards, the content of the drawers a mystery but the cupboards lined with more glassware, more plates, and some tarnished silver candelabra. Beyond that another door stood open, revealing a dimly lit dining room furnished with a long, dark table at the near end of which one person sat alone, her back to the door, almost invisible in her tall chair.

The Baroness didn't respond to Max's footsteps, almost as if she didn't hear the movements of servants. Max approached her chair, the spoon held out before him, as if he were presenting her with the keys to the city or with her newborn heir. Only when he reached her side did she turn her head to see who it was that dared disturb her meal.

Then she recognized what it was Max held in his hands, set down her fork, and took it from him. She studied it for a long minute before she glanced up at Max. "Well," she said, unsmiling. "That's the Cellini Spoon. Beautiful, isn't it?"

"Beautiful," Max agreed, entirely sincerely.

"It has such luster . . . Where did she hide it that so little air got to it?" the Baroness asked. She couldn't seem to take her eyes off the spoon, which she cradled in her two hands. "You'd expect *some* tarnish, after seven years, but— Just *look* at it." She turned it over.

Max saw that the back of the spoon had also been carved to show the same scene, but from the rear. Now you saw the backs of the two women, hidden among the reeds, and the proud face of Pharaoh's daughter, her hair falling straight from under her high crown. The river rippled along, but no more than a round edge of the basket was visible as it floated away from the reeds and toward the Pharaoh's daughter. "It's wonderful workmanship," he said.

The Baroness looked sharply up at him. "You know something about art? No wonder the portraits failed to impress you."

"Well, the lily of the valley, at least, is—" Max began, but he was interrupted.

"I *told* her," Zenobia panted from the doorway, stepping forward but not coming too close to the woman seated at the table. "Martha, I told you, and you disobeyed. She disobeyed me, my Baroness. I promise, I did tell her."

"I know you did," said the Baroness. "You may return to the kitchen, Zenobia, and I will deal with Martha. However, I find I've changed my mind and there will be no luncheon on Saturday. It seems that I know no one to invite."

Zenobia didn't agree. "There's the doctor and his wife, for one."

"That's two, and he died five years ago. Moreover, the widow has gone to live with her daughter in the capital."

"I'm sorry to hear that," said Zenobia. "He cured my headaches," she told Max.

"Back you go, Zenobia," the Baroness said, but not at all impatiently.

"I'll admit it, my Baroness. I'm not sorry. It was all going to be so . . . so hurried, and the silver only once polished. Not that I couldn't make you a lovely luncheon."

"I know you could. Nobody cooks for me but you, Zenobia. Another time, when I've found some guests, we'll have our luncheon. By then I promise you a better scullery maid, too. One who knows her place, and stays there." She looked sternly at Max.

Max knew it was an act, but even so he resented it. Hadn't he just recovered her priceless family treasure? Zenobia didn't need to see him scolded like that, like a servant. Even if as far as the cook was concerned he *was* a servant, the Baroness knew he wasn't.

"Yes, my Baroness," Zenobia said, and turned away. The two in the dining room listened in silence as she went slowly back through the butler's pantry. Then the Baroness turned her attention back to Max.

She did not tell him to make himself comfortable. He ignored that and pulled out the chair catty-corner to hers and sat, although he was careful not to rest his elbows on the table.

"Well," she said again, and set the Cellini Spoon down beside her plate, where it shone gold against the bright white damask cloth. "Tell me," she ordered.

"The spoon was never stolen," Max told her. He explained where he had found it and suggested that someone might want to investigate more thoroughly, perhaps with a broom handle? Because who knew what had fallen into that narrow space over the years. He did not tell the Baroness what else he was thinking.

He didn't need to. She was thinking the same thing. "I made a mistake," she announced.

This was too obvious to need any response.

"It was an entirely reasonable error," she went on, "but an

error nonetheless. I acknowledge that. I have paid dearly for it," she reminded him.

"You are not the only one." Max spoke as Inspector Doddle, a man with a deep concern for justice. "And you've paid the least, as it seems to me," he added, speaking for himself, Max Starling. Then he wondered. The young couple had lost one another, but maybe they had gained something, too. Maybe the Martha had gained a worthier lover. Certainly the nephew had gained independence—and Max could imagine how hard this imperious, scornful great-aunt would be to live with. The nephew had lost his inheritance and gained independence. Did independence always have a price? If so, Max hoped he didn't know the price of his. Then he realized that his case was more like the Martha's because the nephew had had a choice, but she, like Max, hadn't.

The Baroness interrupted his thoughts. "What's done is done. What's lost is lost. Time flows in one direction only and thus what's past is gone. *Quod erat demonstrandum*."

Max had had just enough geometry to be able to say, "Not QED. You haven't actually proved the proposition."

The Baroness didn't care about mathematical certainty, it seemed. She knew what she meant, and that was good enough for her. "I will be able to tell Mrs. Henderson of your usefulness when next she comes—and she'll have that child with her, leashed I hope. She speaks highly of you, and I agree that *she* has good reason." The Baroness didn't say *Although I don't,* not out loud, but Max heard those words as clearly as if she had spoken them.

He got to his feet. What else was it she had expected of him? He thought that she had expected either nothing or the discovery of the spoon in some place that absolutely proved the Martha's guilt. It didn't seem that the spoon was what she was really after. But if it wasn't the spoon, what was it? Just to have been in the right?

The Baroness held out her hand, but before Max could take it she pulled it back and set it beside her plate, clenched into a fist, and said softly, "I was very wrong." She looked up at him.

Max couldn't think of *what* to say to that. She was an old woman, she was a baroness, she had only said what was true—what did she expect him to say? Not *It's all right, we all make mistakes,* he was sure. But if not that, then what? What more did she want of him?

"Well," the Baroness said, for the third time. Once again she held out her hand. "I should thank you for finding my spoon." *At least you did that much,* Max heard in her disappointed tone of voice.

Max shook her hand and almost didn't remember, "I believe the second payment of my fees is due?"

She had been waiting for him to ask, and she thought less of him for asking. Scornfully, she opened a small reticule she had set beside her on the chair, took twenty-five out, and gave it to him. Max took his fee and he walked out of the room without hesitation, but the Baroness had succeeded in filling him with doubts. Had he really succeeded at this job? Or, for that matter, had he actually succeeded at any of the jobs he'd been paid for? It had been only by accident that he found the spoon, he knew that. Just as he had found Angel-Humphrey only by accident. In two out of the three cases, he had succeeded only by chance, and the third, which he *could* claim as his own success, refused to resolve itself. The lost dog that he'd located was simply presenting him with a different, and more serious, problem. But what was the Baroness thinking of? Why wasn't she satisfied? What more did she expect from him? If he hadn't known how little she enjoyed his presence, he would have thought she didn't *want* him to be done and gone.

He rode his bicycle slowly down the long flagstone drive between two rows of ancient beeches, their thick gray trunks reminding him of the elephants he had thought he'd be riding on in the faraway country he'd thought he'd be going to with his parents who now— This was not something he wanted to pursue, so as he turned onto The Lakeview, he thought instead about how hungry he was. He should ride over to check on Joachim and the dog, but he could do that later in the day, after he had eaten. He wished he felt more sparkly and successful. He certainly *should* feel that way. It might have happened only by chance, but he *had* after all found the spoon, something nobody else had been able to do, not for seven years.

To his right, the lake opened out wide, its surface ruffled by a light spring breeze. On his left stretched high walls and the occasional ornate gate, behind which lay the wide estates of Queensbridge's oldest and wealthiest families. He pedaled along the paved road, alert for the sound of a motorcar, which could approach so quickly that its driver wouldn't see him until it was too late.

Max emptied his mind, not thinking or remembering or even, at that moment, worrying. For that brief time, he wanted to be just a boy on his bicycle, riding beside a lake, admiring the silvery blue color of the water and the light blue, cloud-streaked sky above it. It couldn't be any other month but May. Only May shone with a sky of that particular color and produced such long streaks of cloud. Max would like to paint that skyscape. He thought that if he could paint it well enough, everybody who saw it would know that it was May. Then he had a large idea: a calendar of skies, one skyscape for each month. He wondered if he could do that, if he was talented enough, patient enough, clever enough. It would be hard to make clear the differences between the gray winds of a March sky that cleared the way for spring and those of a November sky, which blew in the cold of winter. Hard also to show how much hotter August is than July, with only colors and brushstrokes. Max picked up speed. He would have time, at home, to try to capture this May sky on paper and begin the project. His mind was full of possibilities.

He sped among the narrow roads to Thieves Alley and lunch.

He rounded the final corner, his heart high. It was all there, the gate with the brass bell hanging beside it, the little front garden, the small stone house and—

He saw the thing happen in chunks, as if it was taking place at two different times. But it wasn't. It happened all at the same time. The front door of the house burst open and a man emerged. The man did not have red hair, and he didn't close the door behind him. He leaped down the steps. He was a man running away.

At the same time, a bicycle approached from the other end of the street, a bright red bicycle, ridden by a girl in a blue school skirt. She wasn't going fast, just riding, her head turning from side to side as if she was searching for something particular. Her white-blond hair was in a long braid tied at the end with a red ribbon. She looked familiar, but Max had the man on his mind.

He pedaled hard. Why was the man running away out of *his* house?

The running man burst through Max's gate and did not close it behind him. His jacket hung crookedly off his shoulders, as if someone had grabbed it and pulled, hard.

The girl had seen the man, and she turned her bicycle toward him. Did she know him?

The man—he had dark hair, Max noticed, but things were happening too fast for him to notice more than that—dodged to the right to avoid running into the bicyclist.

The girl swerved, too. As if she *wanted* to run into him.

Max was coming close to the pair of them. He knew the gate and door to his house were both wide open, but he couldn't worry about that, not now. He wanted to catch the man.

The running man dodged left.

The girl swerved right, to stay in his path.

The man looked back over his shoulder, saw Max, and increased his speed.

And the girl ran her bicycle right at the running man. When he saw what she was doing, the man raised both hands and pushed at her, shoving her hard. She tumbled off her bicycle, yelling "Hey!" not in fear but to object. "What do you think you're—?" and she thumped down onto the hard ground, her legs tangled up in the bicycle frame.

While the man ran off, around a corner and out of sight.

Max didn't hesitate. He knew he had a good chance of catching the running man, since he was on a bicycle, but the girl was lying on the ground, and if she was hurt— It was more important to make sure she was all right and get her to a doctor right away if she wasn't. The man's hands had been empty, clenched into a runner's fists, Max remembered. So if he had taken anything it was something small.

Max skidded to a halt and dropped his bicycle to the ground. The girl was just who he thought, but what was she doing in Thieves Alley? "Pia?"

Her eyes opened. She didn't smile. She tried moving her hands and arms gently, then she flexed her feet at the ankles. "I'm all right," she told him, and began the process of extricating herself from the metal frame. But she kept sitting there on the ground. "It looks like my bicycle's OK, too." She pulled the skirt of her school uniform down over her knees.

"What are you doing here?" Max asked. Then he looked back to the open door. "I have to—" He turned to his house.

"Give me a hand up? You're Clarissa's Mister Max, aren't you?" she asked as he pulled her to her feet. "Why are you wearing a clown costume?"

"Hunh?" he asked, trying to sound confused, trying to figure out if it mattered if this girl knew who he was and where he lived. "Mister who?"

"I tricked her. She thought she was proving how rich and smart she and her father are, boasting about hiring a detective to find her stupid dog." The girl grinned at him, and her dark blue eyes sparkled. "It really *was* a stupid dog; golden retrievers are. Sweet-natured and gentle, but not smart. If I were a dog, I'd be a poodle. Except not the kind of well-groomed poodle you see, so maybe a mongrel, half poodle the other half . . . Alsatian," she decided. "What about you?"

"I need to—" Max turned around and started for home.

"I'm coming with you," Pia said.

Max was too concerned about what he might find to argue with her. They picked up their bicycles and rolled them inside the gate, which they shut and latched behind them before racing up the steps into the house, to find whatever was waiting there.

16

In which the Long-ears reappear

What happened in here?" Pia's voice asked from behind Max, but Max moved right through the mess of overturned chairs, dismantled bookcases, and scattered posters to the body that sprawled facedown across the dining room table. He rolled it over and, as he expected, as he feared, saw his tutor.

Ari's eyes were closed and his skin colorless. A trickle of blood came from his cheek, but that was the only blood Max saw. With no expression on his handsome face, Ari reminded Max of someone. Just as he was about to remember who, the eyelids fluttered, so Max got down to the business of finding out if his tutor was seriously injured and finding out what had happened, after which he would decide what he was going to do about it, after which—now he did look around the room—he could start dealing with the mess.

"He needs a doctor."

Pia's voice reminded him that she was there and he told her, "Out the kitchen door, across the garden, there's a house. It's my grandmother's. The key is in the geranium pot on the step. There's ice in the icebox."

Without a word or a question—although he'd have guessed she was the kind of person who tended always to have a word or a question—Pia ran off.

"Ari?" Max asked, and the eyelids fluttered open. Ari's eyes were angry, hard, scornful, and once again Max had the feeling that he had recently seen someone who looked enough like Ari to be his brother.

Then Ari's face assumed its usual expression, the dark eyes sympathetic and alert. "Max?" He slid unsteadily to his feet and buckled at the knees. His hands flew out to Max's shoulders.

Max righted one of the chairs and gently pushed his tutor down onto it.

Ari closed his eyes. He put a hand up to his head, just behind the right ear. "That hurts," he admitted. "It's pretty tender."

Max gently touched the place. "You're getting a real goose egg."

"I think he hit me with *Shakespeare's Complete Works*. Or maybe one of those posters?"

"Probably a book," Max decided. "It's not bleeding," he explained.

Ari groaned. "Would one of those frames have hurt less, do you think?" He folded over at the waist and rested his head on his knees. "I feel . . . bad."

"What happened?" Max asked.

"Really bad," Ari said, and he raised his head so that he could lean it against the back of the chair to admit, "I'm no good in a fight." He tried to smile but couldn't, and closed his eyes again. "Never was."

Max realized that this was not the time to ask what had happened, so he turned his attention to the room. Books were scattered all over the floor, some lying open, some on their sides. Also scattered all around were the scripts of plays the company had produced or were thinking of producing. The walls that had been lined with his parents' proudly framed advertising posters were bare, and the posters had been dropped onto the floor with such force that a couple of the frames had split, although at first glance, Max could see no broken glass. That was one good thing. If the room was going to have to be set to rights, it would be a lot easier if he didn't have to look out for shards of broken glass. Then he had a thought. "I'll be right back," he said to Ari. "Don't move."

"No danger," his tutor assured him.

"She's getting ice," Max said, and went to check the front parlors, where there was no damage. The kitchen, however, was a mess. Plates and glasses had been shoved aside, drawers emptied, chairs upended, pots and pans scattered, oven door wide open, and bread dumped out of the bread box. Had the intruder come in the back door, then? Max went to check on Ari.

Pia returned with a cloth-wrapped chunk of ice in one hand. In the other she held a sprig of mint and a vanilla bean. "I bet your grandmother's a good cook," she said, stepping around Max to help Ari press the ice against the right side of his head. Then she asked, "Where's your teapot? Mint tea, with a little vanilla, it's a restorative. My nurse knows about these things," and went back into the kitchen. Max, watching to see that Ari was able to hold the ice steady against his head, heard water running and then, when that stopped, her voice calling, "The old lady was just getting home. Is that your grandmother?"

"She's not so old," Max called back.

"She's just changing her shoes," Pia told him. "She'll be right over. Does she have a *job*?"

Ari groaned softly, and Pia came into the room. "The infusion will take a few minutes, but it'll help." In case Ari hadn't heard her the first time, she repeated, "My nurse knows about these things. She says if people are going to take you for a gypsy you might as well know something about what gypsies know. But really, she isn't one. Which is too bad, if you ask me, which nobody does. Who was that man who pushed me over?" she asked Max. Then, "Is this your brother?"

"Do I look like him?" Max asked. He'd never thought of himself as handsome, but if he looked like Ari, maybe he was.

"Not really, but you don't look like much of anything in

particular. You could be anybody's brother, even mine," the girl said. "Except for your weird eyes, I mean. Also, neither of my brothers would ever wear pants like that— Your stuffing has slipped, by the way. No, I just thought if he lives with you he must be related."

"How do you know he lives with me?" Max asked, pulling free the pillow, which he'd entirely forgotten in the excitement of the attack on his house and his tutor. He put the pillow on the table with not one word of explanation.

"Well, this is your house, and you're more worried about him than about chasing the person who was running out of it. Who probably wrecked all this. And hit *him*."

Pia was pretty logical, Max thought but didn't say. Instead, he asked, "How do you know this is my house?"

"I know your name, don't I?" she answered, and smiled, like a cat with a mouse's tail hanging out of its mouth. "That Clarissa . . . she's pretty silly. All I had to do was pretend— and it wasn't even really pretending anything. I let her suspect I thought she'd lost her dog because she was careless, and she blabbed and blabbed about her father and the detective. You're Mister Max," she told him. "*Are* you a detective?"

"No," Max said, but she ignored him.

"Because I wanted to tell you—"

Grammie's voice and the slamming of the door interrupted her. "Max?" She called out her news: "The *Simón Bolívar* docked in Miami yesterday, nothing out of the ordinary, and there's still no word of the *Miss Koala*. Ari? Are you home? Who was that girl? What's happened here?" Then, "What has been going on?" she demanded from the kitchen doorway. But when she saw Ari's pale face, for the next several minutes she was busy pressing her fingers onto his skull and looking into his eyes, and she wasn't interested in whatever anyone said.

While Grammie was seeing to Ari and the herb tisane infused, Max and Pia put the chairs back in place around the table. Max piled books and scripts into stacks while Pia set framed posters on the table. "I hope you didn't get hit with one of *these*," she said to Ari. "You'll have a concussion for sure if you did." She disappeared into the kitchen and after a few minutes brought out four mugs and a pot of tea. "My nurse swears by this."

"Aren't you too old for a nurse?" Max asked.

"My father doesn't like to let good servants go," she told him, pouring a light brown, sweet-smelling liquid from the teapot. "If you ask me, he just doesn't like to fire anybody. Although sometimes"—a grin lit up her face—"he helps them want to quit."

What did that mean? Max wondered and would have asked her, but Ari was blowing over the top of his drink to cool it, and this was such a relief to Max that he finally realized where he had seen Ari's face before. However, Grammie was still fussing beside the young man, so he couldn't ask his tutor if he was by any chance related to the Barthold family. And then, as he watched his grandmother adjust the ice pack and heard her grumbling that she didn't know what things were coming to around here, Max found bits of information fitting together in his head like pieces of a jigsaw puzzle: Ari's odd reaction to the Baroness's note, the frequent appearance of good pastries, that red hair and handsome face, and the reasons for the Baroness's low estimate of her great-nephew's character. About which, in Max's opinion—that is, if his hunch was correct—the old lady was much mistaken.

"I want him to see a doctor, but not here," Grammie announced. "You two, help him across to my house."

"I'm fine, there's no—"

"You, young man, would do well to save your strength for your trek across the garden. Because until we know what's going on, I don't think we want anyone official making inquiries in this house. Do we?" she asked Max, then, "Who are you?" she asked Pia, whom she seemed to have just noticed. "Never mind, you two take him across to my house, and I'll bring the doctor. It's not far. I'll be right back."

She was as good as her word, but the doctor wasn't with her. "He has two people in his waiting room, but he'll be here in less than an hour. You two, sit," she ordered Max and Pia. Then she said to Ari, "You look a little better. Precisely how do you feel?"

"My head hurts."

"Dizzy? Nauseous?"

"I was dizzy at first but not anymore. No nausea."

"We left his tisane behind," Pia realized.

"Are you going to tell me who you are?"

"Pia."

Grammie looked at her for a long minute. "You're not a reader."

"Yes I am."

"You don't come to the library."

"I go to Hilliard. We have our own library and it's a good one."

"Not as good as mine," Grammie said. "You should take a look."

"I will," Pia answered, and Grammie nodded, satisfied.

"Go get him that infusion, then," she said, and as soon as the door closed behind Pia, she asked Ari, "What happened? Be quick."

"I was studying and dozed off, but the noise woke me—a lot of crashing and swearing, from downstairs. There was a man. Tearing the dining room apart. I tried to—"

"Who was it?"

Ari shook his head, then pressed his hand to it with a muffled groan.

"What did he want?"

"He was mumbling something about 'too clever by half.'"

"What did he look like?"

"Youngish, dark hair . . . medium height, but"—he looked at Max first, then Grammie, not hiding his concern about this—"he had pretty long ears. Long earlobes, I mean. I asked him what he was doing, told him to put down the book he was holding, and grabbed him by the arm when he started to run away. Then he hit me."

Grammie looked at Max, who reported, "He was running out of the house when I rode up. Pia tried to block him—at least I think she did. Anyway, it looked like that was what she was doing. But he shoved her over and ran off. I couldn't just leave her there and chase him. I didn't know if she was hurt."

"I didn't say you should have. But who *are* these Long-ears?"

"What does your policeman friend know?"

"I didn't ask him."

"Maybe," Max suggested, "you should?"

"And what is that girl doing here?" Grammie demanded.

But Pia was at the door and answered the question herself. "I'm here because of the dog he was hired to find."

"*That* dog?" Grammie asked Max, and he nodded.

Ari told Grammie, "I can't wait for the doctor. I have to be at work."

"You're not going to work. You've had a bad blow to the head, in case you've forgotten."

"I'll be fine, Mrs. Nives. I'm the night clerk. All I do is sit behind the desk."

She shook her head. "The doctor needs to look you over. Max will tell them at the hotel that you won't be in."

"I *need* that job."

"He'll think of some good excuse. Won't you?" she asked Max sternly.

How could Max answer that? He had no idea what he might say to the manager of the Hotel Iris to explain Ari's absence.

"If he doesn't, I will," Pia promised.

And what was she doing, butting into his business like that? But before Max could ask Pia who she thought she was, Grammie said, "Good girl. Max, you better change into something more . . . less . . . exotic, then it's off with the two of you. We'll tackle this new mystery later."

17

In which Pia
is irritating

By the time they stood in front of the manager of the Hotel Iris, whose gold-rimmed spectacles gleamed as brightly as did the polished wood of the receptionist's desk and the polished brass hinges and handles of the doorways in the lobby, Max had thought of an excuse. "Ari is sick. He has a fever," he told the man.

"He can have his fever as easily here as home in bed," the man answered, rubbing his bald pate in frustration. "What am I supposed to do for a night clerk at the last minute? It's not as if the job's very difficult . . . Unless, did he send you in for a replacement?" He glanced at Pia, who stood just behind Max. "Not you. I don't hire children, and especially not little girls."

"I'm not a little—"

Max cut her off. "No, Ari just asked us to tell you he won't be able to come to work tonight."

"In which case, I am asking you to tell him that if he doesn't come in tonight he needn't bother coming back, because there won't be a job waiting for him," the manager said. He looked a challenge at Max. Clearly, he thought Max wasn't telling the truth, which, since Max wasn't, seemed fair enough. Except, since he didn't *know* Max was lying, seemed pretty distrustful, of Ari if of no one else.

"I'll tell him that right away, because I know how much he wants to keep this job," said Pia, who now stepped up to stand beside Max. "He'll probably come in and be sick here, and it probably isn't too serious, because he's had a temperature for about a week and it's only just today gotten really high," she told the manager, with as wide-eyed and innocent an expression as if she were Clarissa asking her father to hire Mister Max to find her beloved Princess Jonquilletta of the Windy Isles because she would just die of sadness if her dog was lost forever. "We don't think it's typhoid," Pia assured the manager, who at the word looked sharply around to be sure none of his guests were close enough to listen in.

"There's been no talk of typhoid in the city," he said nervously.

Pia nodded. "I know, and I wouldn't have wondered myself if his mother hadn't died of it last—"

The manager stepped back. He rubbed his head again, this time in anxiety.

"But I know he'll want to come in, once he knows how you feel," Pia assured him.

"No, no need, I'll cover it myself if there isn't anyone else to be found."

"We couldn't ask you to do *that,*" Pia told him, with a guileless smile. "You're the manager—you have to work all day. I'm sure Ari can do it. He's stronger than he looks."

"No, no need for that. Tell him I'm holding the position for him, tell him to take all the time he needs," the manager said. "Now, I better find that replacement—if you'll excuse me?" and he hurried off, almost as if he was running away from them, as if he thought they might be carrying the dreaded disease themselves.

Max did not dare to look at Pia until they had exited the building and were climbing back onto their bicycles. "You think fast," he said, and then allowed the laugh he had been holding in to break free. "Did you see his face?"

Pia grinned. "That was fun," she said.

"Thank you for helping out," Max said, and then he had an idea. "Let me buy you an ice cream, I know a really good shop. Unless you'd rather have a pastry? The pastries there are better than anything." He really was grateful to the girl, and now he remembered, "Besides, didn't you come looking for me?"

"Sort of. Well, yes, actually, I did," she admitted.

"Why did you want to see me?" Max asked. It would be another case for him to work on, and he was feeling so confident about himself that he was mostly just curious about this new job. Because this girl struck him as the kind of person who would rather figure things out for herself, so it might be an interesting and difficult one.

"I'll tell you when we get to your ice cream shop."

When they entered Gabrielle's workplace, they had to wait for a few minutes while a large family (parents, one grandfather, four children ranging in age from about six to sixteen) bought themselves pastries for a special dessert after that night's dinner and then ice cream cones for their present pleasures. Eavesdropping on the conversation, Max deduced that it was somebody's birthday, and probably, he further deduced, one of the grown-ups, since there would be pastries rather than a cake with candles. Pia apparently agreed because she said, "What's your guess? I think it's the old man's birthday," standing on tiptoes to speak quietly into Max's ear.

"Then why is he paying?"

"It's what people do on their birthdays when they get older, grown-up. They give themselves the present of having ice cream with you, or something like that. My mother says her grandmother said—she's dead now, of course. The grand-mother, I mean; my mother's very much alive—one of the things you learn if you get to live a long life is how important people are to you. The people you care about, I mean. My mother's grandmother told her there don't even have to be that many of them. She said just one can be enough. Do you think one can be enough?"

"How would I know?" Max asked, but he thought that

maybe this great-grandmother knew the truth of it. He had only Grammie, but worried as he was about his parents, worried and anxious as he had been for two weeks and one day now, he was managing, wasn't he? With Grammie's help. Without Grammie, he knew, it would be much harder. Not impossible—he'd learned that about himself in the two weeks and one day—but much much harder, and lonely, too. He said, "It's like having just one friend at school. You don't need more, do you?"

"I wouldn't know," Pia said, but without any trace of self-pity, and Max laughed. He did not say, *Me either,* although he could have.

Instead, he turned his attention back to the family, listening in while they discussed flavors and then ordered their ice cream cones. The grandfather didn't want any ice cream. He stood to the side, a couple of Gabrielle's white pastry boxes tied with scarlet ribbons on the counter in front of him, his wallet in his hand, not talking to any of them, a contented smile on his lips. Max watched all this, then turned to Pia. "You might be right."

"I am," she told him in the same confident tone of voice that she had used to assure the hotel manager that Ari would be able to come in to work despite perhaps having typhoid fever. Remembering his first meeting with her—was it just the day before?—Max decided that she knew how to talk confidently, but you couldn't always believe what she said. He looked back to the grandfather, who was putting change into his pocket and passing out the boxes for others to carry.

"Happy birthday, Mr. Bassett," Gabrielle said to him with one of her smiles.

"Thank you, Miss Gabrielle," the old man answered with a bow, as if she were a lady at an opera.

Gabrielle turned her attention to her next customers, the young couple, the tall young man, and the girl—his sister?—her attention caught by the bright white-blond hair. Then she looked again and asked, not quite sure but—now that she looked a third time, looked carefully at his eyes—really asked without any doubt, "Mister Max? It's good to see you again. Is this your little sister?"

"I don't have any sisters," Max said.

Gabrielle smiled. "Well, it's not your brother, and she's too young to be anybody's girlfriend."

"I'm his assistant," Pia announced.

Max turned to look sternly down at her. "You know I don't have any assistants."

Pia smiled, all innocence. "But you could. You should."

Now Gabrielle laughed. "What can I get you two? I have chocolate cake with mocha cream filling. I've got lemon curd tarts, chocolate croissants, and the ice cream, of course."

Talk of food distracted Pia. "Are the pastries good?"

"Try one," Gabrielle advised. "Cake for you?" she asked Max, and that was exactly what he wanted most . . . *after* he satisfied his hunger to put Pia in her place. They moved to one of the small round tables and sat down facing each other, like opponents in a chess game.

Pia apparently decided from the look on his face that she

should change the subject. "That lady seems nice. Is she a friend of yours? What's her name?"

Max told her firmly, "I don't want an assistant, and I don't need one."

"Maybe. But I'm the one who thought of typhoid."

"Yes, I know, and it was a good idea." She waited, until he added, "A very good idea. But"—and now *he* changed the subject—"why *were* you there at my house?"

"Looking for you, of course."

"Why?" Max asked again. He was losing patience.

Gabrielle came over and put two plates down on their table and offered them lemonade or coffee. Max chose coffee, to go with the chocolate cake, and Pia asked for lemonade. Gabrielle looked down at them for a minute while they looked up at her, waiting to hear what she wanted, until she said, "People should always try to understand each other. Especially young people." With that pronouncement she went back behind the counter.

Pia looked at Max. "All right," she said. "I know I'm irritating and I should try not to be so impatient. It's just that"—she raised her pastry, ready to bite into it—"sometimes, other people are so *slow.*"

"You think I'm slow?" Max asked, too amazed to be insulted.

"No, the opposite. Well, mostly the opposite." There was a little silence as they both took a bite and then—quickly, eagerly—a second bite, and a third. "This is really good, you're right," Pia said, and quickly, before Max could say anything, she recommenced talking. "I was coming to see you because I know you're a detective. But I don't think detecting about dogs is the same as detecting about people—"

"I'm not a detective," Max repeated patiently.

"So probably there's no danger you'll find the dog, but I wanted to tell you that Clarissa is the worst of all of them, about her pet. She's the kind of person who should never have a pet, but if she has to, if she has to have something to show off? She should have a pet flea."

Max laughed.

"That's more like it," Gabrielle said softly as she set their drinks down on the table. She did not linger.

Pia flushed but went on. "No, I mean it, except a flea would probably escape. Like the dog did, if you ask me."

Max didn't say so, but that had been just what he was wondering about.

"A goldfish, maybe. Except she never would, because anybody can have a goldfish. So if you do find that dog, I don't think you should give it back to her. Do you think you will find it?"

Because he already had, Max could say honestly, "No, I doubt I will."

"But you might, because you were smart enough to come to school to find out what could have happened. I think you're probably a pretty good detective."

"I told you, I'm not a detective."

"And I think I'd make a pretty good detective's assistant. I'm like my father, we have really good ideas, we're always thinking up something new. That's why he's rich. I'm going to have a piece of that cake," she said, and went up to the counter, returning with a second plate. *"And,"* she explained, sitting down again, "if this cake is as good as the pastry, I'm having one of my best good ideas."

Of course Max was curious, but he wasn't about to ask. He watched her take a couple of bites and didn't say anything. He guessed that Pia liked her ideas so much she wouldn't be able to resist boasting about them.

He guessed right. She looked across the table at him, eyes sparkling, to say, "She could have her own pastry shop, or restaurant. Or she could work in a private house, if the people were rich enough to have a private pastry cook. Like us," she said. "My mother loves sweets, and she's almost never happy with what she gets. She'd be happy with this." She ate another bite of the cake.

Max didn't want Gabrielle put on the spot, so he leaned forward to say quietly, "She doesn't have any recommendations."

"Why not?"

Max shrugged. "I don't know. She said she can't get them, and that even her family won't have anything to do with her."

Pia thought about this. "What could she have done that's so bad but she's not in jail?"

"I told you, I don't know."

"But she has the job of working here, so it couldn't have been *that* terrible. You're the detective, why don't you find out?"

"I'm not—"

"Don't you care? She seems really nice, and she likes *you.* I can tell. If I can find out what she did, will you let me be your assistant?"

"No!" Max cried. "I've told you, I don't want an assistant." She was relentless, this girl. Granted she did have good ideas, and granted she was probably brave, if the way she ran her bicycle into the man running out of his house was any example, but he already knew that she didn't listen, and his guess was that she wouldn't be any good at doing what she was told.

"We'll see about that. I bet I can find out anyway," Pia said, and she took her plate of half-eaten cake up to the counter, where she engaged Gabrielle in a quiet conversation. Every now and then one or the other of them looked over at Max, but he paid no attention. He drank his coffee slowly, pretending he didn't notice them, the Absent-Minded Professor from *The Lepidopterist's Revenge,* and he looked out the window at the busy boulevard. People hurried along the sidewalk, going home at the end of the day. There were fewer delivery wagons on the street, but Max saw three automobiles go by in just the time he sat there, waiting for the two of them to be through with their chattering and pretending he had forgotten that he hadn't come in alone.

In reality, Max never forgot how alone he was. He couldn't forget it, he could only figure out ways to be distracted, to be finding other things to think about. Really, now he thought of it, he was a lot like that Absent-Minded Professor, and he scratched gently at the back of his head in the same gesture his father had used when playing the role.

Eventually, Pia returned, her face wearing a smug smile. "I'll tell you when we're outside," she said, although Max had not asked her what she'd learned. "See you soon, Gabrielle," she called over her shoulder as they left.

"You too, Mister Max," Gabrielle answered. "It's always something good when you come by." She smiled as if she meant it. "He's the one who found that little boy," she told Pia. "Did he tell you? No, I didn't think so. He's not a boaster, our Mister Max."

Pia and Max claimed their bicycles and stood side by side in front of the shop window. "Well," Max said, beginning his farewells.

"Come to the park, it's just across—"

"I know where the park is. But why?"

She didn't answer. She just mounted her bicycle and rode off, her braid bouncing from one shoulder to the other. She was right about being irritating, Max thought, but he followed her anyway, in case there was something useful she might tell him. Besides, he remembered, he hadn't thanked her for trying to stop his thief. He didn't follow her all the way into the park, however. He halted by the first tree and dismounted. "I'm not going any farther. I've got something to do," he said. "So what is it?"

Pia turned around to come back and join him. "I didn't find out anything, really. She won't go into private service ever again, she did say that, but she didn't say why, only that I shouldn't fall in love if I could help it. I told her I could help it for sure. But I'm going to bring my mother there, tomorrow if I can. I know she'll like Gabrielle's sweets and she'll tell Poppy, and he'll think of something. When he's thought of his something, things will happen. Poppy does what he sets out to do," she told Max. "He does what he says he will, and he knows everybody."

"Is that so," Max said, careful to act uninterested. He changed the subject. "I didn't thank you for trying to stop that man. That was really brave," he said, and held out his hand to shake goodbye.

She didn't accept his hand or the compliment. "It didn't do much good, did it? But, Mister Max, why was he there? What did he want? What are you going to do about it? It's attempted robbery, and he could have killed Ari. Are you in danger? I can come by Saturday morning to help clean things up."

This girl made him tired, with her barrage of questions and her refusal to go away. "I don't need any help," he said.

"Your grandmother's old, and Ari got a real bump on the head. He should take it easy, and besides, those picture frames are awfully heavy. And we could talk some more about me being your partner," she told him.

"Partner?"

"If you don't need an assistant."

"If I don't need an assistant, what would I do with a partner? And anyway, I'm not a detective," Max said, yet again.

"Then what *are* you?" she asked. "Because people hire you, don't they? What do they hire you to be?"

18

In which Mister Max plies his trade, whatever that might be

With every round of the pedals, Max's bicycle went faster and his thoughts, too, went faster. Pia really got under his skin. Up his nose. On his nerves. He *did* have ideas on his own. He had plenty of ideas. In fact, he usually had too many ideas whirling around in his head at the same time. Just now, maybe, his brain wasn't working as efficiently as it usually did; but what did anyone expect? With his life entirely changed. With needing to earn a living and trying to figure out why those Long-ears would break into his house. With his parents who knew where and maybe even— some things were *not* to be thought about, and his imagination scurried away from the possibilities like a mouse fleeing the cat—

Who was Pia to tell him what to do about Clarissa's dog, anyway? Or, what not to do.

Too much was happening too fast, and he had no time to think about anything. He guessed he shouldn't be surprised if some little girl thought he needed someone to give him ideas. But she was wrong, entirely wrong. He could take care of things himself. Wasn't he living independently? Hadn't he found work he was good at? *Yes,* he answered his own questions, and *Yes.*

Max wheeled through the gate into the old city, dodging carriages and carts, sounding his bell to warn people that he was right behind them, moving fast. "Mister Max, coming through," that's what his bell rang out. "Important business."

At the supper table, Ari ate with a good appetite, but Grammie kept a worried eye on him even so. She was pleased with the excuse Pia had given to the hotel manager. "That's a resourceful girl you've found yourself," she told Max.

"I haven't found myself anyone," he told her.

"I'm sure you haven't," she answered, soothing him in the way grown-ups have of seeming to agree with you while implying at the same time that they know better.

Max had too many other things on his mind to wonder if his grandmother was treating him like a child. He had the dog and his handsome red-haired tutor to think about. He had his parents and those persistent long-eared people. He had the problem—because he had to admit Pia was right about this—of what to call the job he was doing and getting paid for, since he had, probably, to accept the idea that his parents were gone for . . .

For how long? And where? And especially, why?

Max did not enjoy a good night's sleep, and he woke late to find that Ari had already left for one of his classes. *Remember, we meet at three this afternoon,* Ari's note read, from which Max understood that his tutor had entirely recovered from the blow to the head and that Max had better address his schoolwork after cleaning up the kitchen. Only then would he be free to take his watercolors and easel out to the back garden, and have ideas.

By the time he had the kitchen in order and finished making a map of the lake and all the towns around it, then reading about Napoleon's rise to power in France and memorizing the names of the largest bones in the human body, not to mention preparing three mathematical proofs, it was almost lunchtime. But that Friday, the dark thoughts of the night before driven away by May sunlight and schoolwork, Max was more interested in painting than eating. He took his equipment out to the garden and stood in front of the easel, looking at the blank sheet of paper. He dipped his brush into the water, and began.

He spread sky colors and cloud shapes across the moistened paper, while his mind forgot about maps and congruent lines and war-making to turn its attention to the artistic problems he was working on. His thoughts drifted like clouds, floating inside his head, seeming, like clouds, to have no purpose or direction for their motion although actually swept along by high, invisible winds. He painted his sky, and while he painted, other images and ideas floated across his mind, Clarissa with her black armband, the glowing golden bowl of the Cellini Spoon, and, unexpectedly, long copper earrings dangling down. He smiled as he remembered the way Joachim leaned forward, the new glasses on his nose, to understand what he had put into a picture, to discover what he might find there.

Max looked at his own picture, into which he had put a sky crowded with clouds, but he could not tell if they were about to move off, leaving a bright sunny blue, or to close in, loosing rain. This picture was a question, not an answer, and—in a sudden tumbling blowing about of ideas—it reminded him of Pia, because while painting it he had figured out that, whatever she might claim for herself, her real talent was for asking questions. The girl was always asking questions, and some of them were just what Max needed to hear in order to discover his own ideas.

He didn't need an assistant. How could he need an assistant when he didn't even know himself what he was doing? What he really needed was a name for his job, which was, in fact, one of the questions Pia had raised.

Max washed his brushes and carried the picture on its easel into the kitchen to finish drying. He put on his everyday trousers and shirt, because he needed no disguise where he was going.

At the pet store, Max considered the various choices on

display, the painted turtles, kittens and puppies, the monkeys and parrots and parakeets, snakes and even insects, and, of course, the brightly colored tropical fish. Then, his purchase in the basket in front of his handlebars, he rode over to see Joachim and Sunny. He found his teacher having a snack of bread and cheese in the garden, two new pictures—one in the old style, one in the new—set out side by side on the easel in front of him. The painter studied the paintings through his spectacles.

Max came right to the point. "Do you want to keep the dog?"

Joachim turned to look at him and asked, "What are you doing here? Again. Are you going to turn into a pest?"

Max stuck to his point. "Do you want this dog for your own?"

"I take it, then, you've chosen which law to overrule?"

Max took a deep, patient breath. "My question is, do you want to keep the dog?"

"Sunny?"

At the sound of her name, the dog rose to her feet and trotted over to where the painter was sitting. She lowered her haunches and sat there, looking up at him, wagging her tail hopefully. Joachim stared back at her, not happily.

"I guess. If I have to."

"You don't have to," Max said. "Do you want to?"

"Then yes, if you must know," Joachim snapped. "I do. Is there anything else?"

"I'll need to borrow her for an hour or so on Sunday," Max

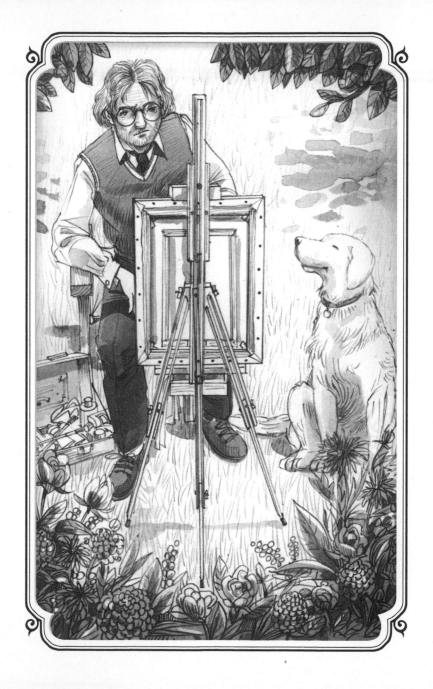

told him, and left abruptly, knowing that what his teacher really wanted to do right then was *not* hear a brilliant plan but to get back to work.

Max, too, had work to get back to, even if he didn't know its name. He returned home—relieved to find that no new breaking-and-entering had taken place, not that he really expected another attack so soon after yesterday's. He found his mother's best stationery in the little writing desk in the parlor and took some to the kitchen. There he wrote a brief note, asking Clarissa's father to bring his daughter to 5 Thieves Alley on Sunday at half past twelve. *The investigation is complete,* he wrote, and signed himself *Mister Max.*

He wished he had a profession to put under the signature to make it look more official. But what would it be? Detective? Detective-at-large? Private Investigator? Nothing seemed right, so he just slid the folded paper into its envelope and copied the address from the business card Clarissa's father had presented to him.

Then he wrote another note on another sheet of paper. This one was more difficult to find the right words for. *Honored Baroness,* he wrote, and then stopped to think. He could ask her to call at the same time he was scheduled for a math tutorial and let the old woman and Ari confront one another. That was certainly a scene he would enjoy watching. But he couldn't be sure she would accept his invitation, and besides, she was so very proud that any audience to the reunion would cause her to become the Wronged Baroness, wrapped up in her righteousness and her dignity. Proud people made things hard on themselves, Max reflected, and with that in mind he wrote, *How often are we given second chances?* This note he didn't sign. He didn't think it would be very difficult to persuade Ari to deliver it to the Baroness, especially since he could assure his tutor that in the matter of the Cellini Spoon, his Martha was known to be innocent.

Those two letters written and one slipped into a nearby mailbox, Max returned to the house and waited for three o'clock, congratulating himself on how well prepared he was, for the lesson and for the next steps in these two cases.

In part he was right. His geometric proofs were flawless, and after the lesson he had the note ready to give Ari, asking him to present it to the Baroness "in person." But he was not prepared for his tutor's rising from the table, cheeks red, eyes flashing, looking entirely too much like one of his unpleasant military ancestors.

"What do you know?" Ari demanded, his shoulders high and stiff. "You don't know anything. If she hired you to hunt me down . . ." He couldn't finish that furious thought.

"No. Wait. Listen." Max stood up, to face Ari across the kitchen table. "She has no idea where you are. She asked me to— Ari? I found it! I did, the spoon, the Cellini Spoon. It had fallen behind the sink in the kitchen. That's where it's been all these years. She *knows* she was wrong."

Ari froze. Then his shoulders relaxed and curiosity shone in his dark eyes. "You found it? Really? How did you do that? I looked everywhere, including the kitchen."

"By accident, really. Sit down. Can I get you some water?

I didn't know . . ." There was much Max hadn't understood about Ari, but he did know that Ari could walk out of the house and disappear. He waited.

Ari sat. Max brought him a glass of water and took the chair opposite to explain what he'd worked out. "I know who you are, the great-nephew. Or I think that's who you are."

Ari nodded, but his face was stiff and expressionless, a bad portrait.

"The Baroness has the spoon," Max said, and then added, "so you don't have to save up money any longer, you don't have to have all those jobs, you can go back to being just a university student. You can even"—he made himself admit this—"go back to live in the castle. She hired me to find the spoon, but she didn't expect me to be able to do it. She really believed it had been stolen and sold. But I think, too, you might be right about her. Maybe she really did hire me to find you if I could."

"It looks like you could," Ari said with one of his sad smiles. "But it's too late."

"That's what she said."

"No, I mean . . . it's my own fault. I should have stood up for her. My Martha. I knew she'd never do anything like that, and I never doubted her, not for an instant, but I didn't say anything. I failed to protect her. I was looking for words when she—the Baroness, I mean—started carrying on, about how Martha had stolen me then stolen the spoon for revenge on the Baroness, and it was all so . . . Ugly, it was just ugly, what she was saying, and Martha was kind and gentle, she would never have— I'd never seen my great-aunt like that before, so cruel, so shrieking. I was stunned. All of the ugliness in the room choked me, I couldn't— But Martha thought I believed it, and I don't blame her, what else could she think? The way I stood there with my mouth just flapping and not defending her. She was *weeping*, Max. My heart broke for her. By the time I found words, my great-aunt—she's terrible, a terrible woman—had already sent my Martha out of the room. And Martha had seen how weak I was, spineless, just like my great-aunt always said, and she never wanted to see me again." He buried his face in his hands. "She was thrown out, with no references, no recourse." He looked up at Max to add, "I would have followed her but I was sure I could find the spoon and rub that old woman's face in the truth." His voice became muffled. "I didn't even know Martha's name, and anyway she was finished with me. And I don't blame her. I'm as bad as all the other Bartholds after all. What I did was even more terrible than what the Baroness did." He lowered his hands, looked Max in the eye, and corrected himself. "What I didn't do."

Max could see why Ari felt that way, and actually, he agreed. What Ari had done was weak, even cruel, and it didn't matter if it wasn't what he meant to do or wanted to do. "So you won't deliver this note?" he asked.

"I can't forgive her."

Max thought, and then he asked, "Wouldn't you like the chance to ask Martha's forgiveness?"

"How can I find her after all these years? She's probably

married and a mother. If I hadn't been such a blind fool, she'd be married to me and the mother of my children, but instead I stomped all over her heart."

"But if you could?"

"Of course I would!" Ari snapped.

"Then the castle is the best place to begin looking, and you might also think of how the Baroness would feel if you went to see her. Not to forgive her," he added hastily. "But not to be lost to her."

"She'll accuse me of being after her fortune, and the title."

"I'd guess she knows you better now."

Ari sat silent.

Max waited.

Finally, "Not today," Ari said.

Grammie handed him the postcard when he and Ari were sitting at her table that evening. She held it out to him without a word and then pretended it was nothing special, while Max—heart racing—studied the photograph on the front.

This was a black-and-white picture of an ocean liner on an empty sea, the long hull a dark charcoal gray, the water a rough rocky gray, the sky the clear gray of old ashes but the clouds so white that you knew the sun was shining. He wondered if that was his parents' ship. He wondered what the ship would look like if they could take photographs in color. Before he could turn it over, Ari was saying, "I suppose he told you who I am."

"Nobody has told me anything," Grammie said. "Who are you, then? If you're not who I think you are."

"Let's eat first," Ari said. "And I've been thinking. Max?"

Max looked up.

"You're right, I can quit the night clerk job at least. But do I have to move out?"

"No," Max said, relieved. "You don't. I was afraid you'd want to," Max admitted as he turned the postcard over.

It was addressed in his father's unmistakable thick black lines and loops.

"Why do *you* have this and not me?" he asked his grandmother.

"They sent it to the Queensbridge City Librarian. If you notice."

Max looked down and noticed. He looked up again. "What does it say?" He didn't dare to read.

Grammie stared at him, her eyes bright and her expression serious.

Max made himself look at the message.

The great bard WS says it best: "The rich oft underestimate beauty's lasting embrace," he read, and looked up again, confused. "That's not really Shakespeare."

Grammie shrugged. She had no answers.

Well, our dear Arabella has riches and beauty both now, the card said. After that, however, his father wrote something that actually sounded like him: *The adventure is under way!*

There was no signature, not even initials.

"That father of yours would rather sound mysterious than make sense," Grammie grumbled, taking the postcard from Max.

Max reclaimed it and read it again. "Do you think he was drugged?"

"He sounds like his normal self at the end," Grammie pointed out.

"Where is it postmarked?" Ari asked.

They passed the card back and forth between them as if different pairs of eyes might be able to puzzle it out, but all they could be sure of was that the postmark ended with an *A*.

"It's as if someone blurred it with a finger," Max said.

"India? America?" Grammie suggested. "China, Australia, Argentina?"

"Panama, Kenya," Ari added unhelpfully. "Tanganyika, Malta, Bermuda."

"Do you think it was smudged on purpose?" Max asked.

"He's right," Ari said. "It could have been done on purpose. I didn't think of that."

"That's why he's the detective," Grammie agreed proudly.

"I'm not a detective," Max said. It seemed to him that was all he was saying these days.

"They didn't say where they are," Grammie complained. "I don't know why they wrote at all."

Max had an idea about that. "To let you know, if I wasn't here, that I might be in trouble," he guessed. "Or maybe to let me know, if I was here, which I am, that they're safe." He was beginning to suspect that he knew, with this talk of riches, what the Long-ears were expecting to find somewhere near one of the tables where his father sat to eat, but he had more immediate concerns. "Who do you think blotted the postmark? My father? Or someone else? It would have to be someone in a post office, wouldn't it?"

"I didn't think of all that," Grammie said. "That's why he's such a good detective," she announced proudly to Ari.

"I'm *not*—"

"He certainly is," Ari agreed, and smiled, if not merrily at least without the shadow of sadness. "And he does his homework, too."

19

In which Pia
has her uses

That night, dreams stalked Max. Tall, dark-cloaked, long-eared men chased after him, and he ran through all the secret places he knew in the theater, but with their long ears to the ground they kept following, always closer, never quite close enough to grab him if he could force his legs to keep running.

Max woke in darkness, heart pounding. He hadn't checked on the theater in days. What if something was wrong there, a fire, rats, squatters . . . ? When he slept again, in his dreams he was the hunter and his parents the quarry in some familiar but unknown city, the kind of place nightmares construct, where tall buildings crowd the sides of half-remembered roadways down which we wander, searching.

It was the postcard, he realized, waking with relief into morning light. That postcard made him feel both a little better—to know they had come safely to land, to know they had been able to send it to him—and at the same time much more anxious. Misquoted Shakespeare? What was he supposed to make of that? As he got out of bed, however, something about those dreams made him remember that he might know what the Long-ears wanted.

His father's fortune. That is, his father's alleged fortune. They must have heard William Starling's claims about a fortune and thought he was speaking literally. Max could picture the scene, some restaurant or pub, his father flushed with the pride of a successful performance, one during which the audience gasped and wept and roared in anger at the satisfyingly right times and to a satisfying degree. His eyes aglow, with a sweep of his arm his father would have said to whoever was listening, "Fortune? My personal fortune? I break my fast each morning in its company!" Meaning, Max knew, his wife, his son, and the tall bookcases where he kept scripts. His drama-loving father liked to proclaim his favorite lines over and over, whether they came from his own head or from a play. Probably, the Long-ears had heard him and taken William Starling's theatrics for the truth. It was a Long-ear, probably, who had delivered that message to the Harbormaster. Hadn't the clerk said something about his ears?

Sometimes Max wished his father wasn't the kind of grandiloquent man he was. And where would this fortune have come from? Theatrical people didn't make fortunes, and neither William nor Mary Starling came from a family that had a fortune to bequeath. But the Long-ears wouldn't know this.

That morning, Max and Ari breakfasted in companionable silence. Ari probably wanted to be left to his own thoughts and decisions, Max thought. But before he went out the back door to ride off to the University, Ari turned around to say, with a thoroughly mischievous smile of a kind Max had never before seen on his tutor's face, "You know, Max, I was thinking. Now that you've found that wretched spoon? I have so much saved, I might just quit *both* of my jobs." He was gone before Max could say anything.

So some good had come from the finding of the Cellini Spoon; one life, at least, had been improved. It was Max's life that hadn't, and he couldn't help but think of that.

Yes, a postcard had arrived, and yes, it did make him feel less abandoned. For about an hour. After that, questions began all over again, prickly questions that stung and scraped at him, burned him like a patch of nettles. Where had the postcard been mailed? Someplace not much more than a week distant by steamship, that was all he knew; after that it was all guesswork. Had his parents debarked? Or had they gone on, and if so, gone on where, and gone on by land or by sea? What was their ultimate destination? What was happening? And what was he supposed to do? Just wait for another disturbing communication? But what else *could* he do but wait? And how many jobs could Mister Max hope to be offered? Not many, probably. He had already been lucky, he knew, and how long would his luck hold? Not long, probably.

Max buried his face in his hands, and a feeling like a wet black cloud wrapped itself around him. If he'd been a weeper, now would have been the time for tears, tears of worry and frustration, of anger, of fear and loneliness. But he wasn't, so he rubbed at his eyes, hard, and decided that he'd put away the breakfast things first, and then do the dining room, and maybe find his father's fortune, too, ha ha. Putting things back in order would at least be something to do, a distraction. That morning, Max badly needed distracting.

The kitchen took almost no time to tidy, and after finishing there Max went to the dining room. With only empty hooks on its bare walls and only the top two shelves of the bookcase full, with posters and books scattered on the table-top and chair seats and even in clumsy piles on the floor, the dining room looked like the half-finished set of one of the Company's productions. Looking around, thinking about the Long-ears, Max couldn't help considering possible hiding places for a treasure. He agreed with the Long-ears about one thing: Any possible fortune would be hidden in a room with a table at which people sat down for breakfast. Even if it came to nothing, a careful search would put the room to rights. Also, a treasure hunt would carry him even further away from the thoughts that had disturbed his sleep.

Their intruder hadn't gotten up to the top bookcase shelves before Ari interrupted him, so Max decided to start there, with the long line of Shakespeare's plays in individual volumes. He reached for *All's Well That Ends Well.*

He had gotten as far as *Hamlet,* lifting down each volume,

feeling its weight, checking its binding for mended places, fanning gently through its pages to see if anything fell out, and then replacing it on the shelf, when he heard the bell ring on the front gate. He climbed down from his ladder but had gotten no farther than the front hall when the door opened and Pia entered. "I didn't say come in," he greeted her.

Instead of her school uniform, she wore a blue flowered dress and sandals. She was carrying a white box tied with a scarlet ribbon, and her braid shone in the sunlight that followed her in through the open door. "Good morning to you, too, Merry Sunshine. Is there an apron I can put on? I'm here to help clean up. Don't you remember?"

In fact, Max had hoped that *she* wouldn't remember.

"What kind of an assistant would I be if I left the hardest, most boring work to you?" she asked.

"Pia, you know perfectly—"

"Have you had breakfast? Because I haven't. I had to sneak out of the house before breakfast or they would have noticed I was going out and either told me not to or sent me in the automobile, and you don't want anyone involved in your private life, isn't that right? I got enough of Gabrielle's croissants for all of us, if Ari's here." She headed into the kitchen, saying over her shoulder, "Do you want a glass of milk or some tea?"

"There's nobody else around," Max told her.

"Then you can have two croissants," she answered.

When he and Pia returned to the dining room, she wore one of his mother's aprons over her dress, and she asked,

"Should I begin by rehanging these posters?" and then "Have you decided what you're going to call what we do?"

Max couldn't help it. It was just the way he was made: Ask him a question and he answered it. "I thought maybe Finder, and it's not we, it's me. I, I mean. It's what *I* do."

Pia opened her mouth, then shut it. She sighed loudly, the way a teacher sighs at a troublesome student, and asked, "What about Finder of Lost Things?" She set to work as she talked, picking up the framed poster of *Trouble on the Tracks*. "Or just the initials, FLT, which is sort of mysterious. Why do you have all these posters, anyway? Are you some kind of theater fan? How about Tracker? Or do you like Discoverer? I do—Mister Max the Discoverer. Or would the Un-coverer be better? Or how about just The Discoverer?"

Pia asked questions but didn't seem to care about answers. She went about her self-assigned job, apparently not noticing the one-sidedness of this conversation. "I told you I'd take my mother to Gabrielle's shop, didn't I? Although it's not actually hers, she doesn't own it. I wonder who does? Because it's a successful business, even without the pastries." She checked that a hook was securely set on the wall before hanging a framed poster on it. "And why are these frames so fancy? What's so special about these posters? It's just the Starling Theater Company, not the Royal Shakespeare or anything. Anyway, I *told* you my mother would like Gabrielle's pastries, didn't I? Because she did. So do I, a lot. Don't you?"

Max went from one volume to the next, moving slowly and carefully, checking each thoroughly. It wasn't particularly interesting work, and he had to admit to himself, but never to Pia, that it was less boring with her voice chattering away like some farmyard flock of hens.

"Can you believe this? My mother tried to hire her. As soon as he got home yesterday, she sent Poppy back into the New Town to ask Gabrielle to come work as our private pastry chef, and do you know what else? He offered her a little house, there's one for an undergardener or married groom just behind the gatehouse, it's even smaller than this one, to live in. But do you know what she said to him?"

After this question, Pia waited for a response. Max looked over his shoulder to ask, "What?" but then told her, as soon as he saw what she was doing, "*A Soldier's Sweetheart* goes to the right of the kitchen door. Look at the dates. They're hung chronologically." He turned quickly away, sorry he had explained anything. The less anybody knew, the better for everybody. Especially, the less this busybody girl knew.

"So I should check the dates on the posters before I rehang them?" she asked. "That makes sense, chronologically in a clockwise direction. Why's this one so heavy?" she wondered, putting *Adorable Arabella* back in its place. "It's a pretty ugly frame, don't you think? All those bumpy squares and knobs." She searched for the next poster and went on talking. "Probably you like it, since this is your house and your picture. It's a good thing I'm so strong. That comes from horseback riding, if you want to know. Do you ride? Because we have a stableful of horses." Without stopping to take a breath or to look at Max's face to see if he was listening, she went on. "But do you know what Gabrielle told my father? She said she would never work in a private home again because rich, important families didn't care much about the truth, or even justice." Pia turned to look at him and asked, "You're the detective, what do you think happened to her?"

"I'm not a detective."

"All right then, what about Explorer? We need a sign, for the fence outside: 'Mister Max, Explorer . . . and Partner.'" She hung *The Caliph's Doctor* in its place, looked at it for a few seconds, and suggested, " 'Mister Max, Discoverer . . . and Partner.' "

"I don't have a partner."

"What am I, then?" she demanded.

"A pest," Max muttered, but low so she couldn't hear, because she was, in fact, being sort of a help right then. "A pestilence," he added in an equally quiet voice.

"What?" she asked, but chattered on, "So my father—I told you, he's like me, he looks like me, too. We both have ideas. He likes to have ideas that will make money, and maybe mine will, too, eventually, but— Anyway, my father already wanted his own restaurant, fancier than some of the popular places in the New Town but not as fancy as The Silver Spoon or Zardo's. Poppa likes to go out for dinner to good restaurants. And guess who would be his pastry chef?"

"You," said Max, deliberately stupid. He didn't turn around but he could feel her sharp glance on the back of his neck.

"How did you know?" she asked. "So I guess you've lost your partner in the detecting business."

Then he did turn around to see what she was up to. She

was staring at *Adorable Arabella*. "It would be fun to have a job that let you wear dresses like that," she said with the teasing smile of the person who is two steps ahead of you in everything. "Those purple panels, that lace . . . What if I switched the frames and put this poster in the one with ivy painted on it? *The Caliph's Doctor* would look better with these squares and knobs. Did you paint those ivy leaves for the frame? Or do you only paint the sky?"

"How do you know I paint?" Max demanded. "How do you know what I paint?"

"Clarissa," she told him, this time not wasting any words, and Max remembered that he had been painting in the garden when Clarissa and her father had come to hire him. "Then there was a portfolio in the kitchen when I was in there yesterday, so of course I looked at it." All of these things settled to her satisfaction, Pia returned to her previous subject. "Gabrielle said she'd think about working for my father in a restaurant if he actually opened one and really wanted her to bake for it. Do you think that means she will? Because *he* will. He likes putting his ideas into action. He's like me. He wants to open his restaurant somewhere in the old city, maybe on the river or maybe a little out in the countryside. Do you want to come home with me and meet him?"

Meet another person just like Pia? Max wasn't sure. "Let's take a break," he said. "I'm halfway through the books, you've hung all the posters back up, it's a good time for lunch, and I'm hungry. You bring out bread and cheese while I go over to Grammie's to raid her cookie jar."

When they were seated across from one another at the small kitchen table, Pia dunked a snickerdoodle into her mug of tea, ate it in one bite, and asked, "If you're not a detective and not an investigator, what do you think you are?"

Max was glad his mouth was full so he couldn't answer.

Pia seemed to think he was avoiding the question. "I mean, what would you tell someone you do?" she insisted.

Max thought about what he *had* done. "I find things."

"So you're a finder. Like I said."

"Sort of. I guess."

"Sort of find things or sort of a finder?"

"Both."

She thought about this, then asked, "Why do you keep your ant farm in the kitchen?"

Max had forgotten the ant farm on the kitchen window-sill. He wouldn't need it until tomorrow, so he had set it aside in the tomorrow corner of his brain.

"And what do you want with an ant farm, anyway? You're as bad as those people at school, Mister Max, wanting to have something nobody else—" Then she stopped speaking and stared at him. "That's why, isn't it? You're going to give Clarissa an ant farm instead of a dog. Is that it? Because it's brilliant if it is. Do you think she'll take it? See, you *are* a real detective. I told you. You're a great partner for me."

"That's not detecting," Max pointed out. "That's . . ." He thought of what it was, really, that he had done. "It's figuring out a problem. It's solving, not detecting."

"If you say so," she said, to let him know she had her own better idea.

"That's what I really am," he realized. "A solver." But he didn't care for that name, which among other things sounded too much like *salver* or even *silver*. He tried a synonym, silently, inside his head, and liked it so much he said it out loud. "A solutioneer!"

Pia shook her head. "That's not a word."

"Why not? Like a mountaineer or a privateer or an engineer." The more he said it, the more perfect it sounded. "Musketeer, charioteer, solutioneer . . . That's my job, it's what I do, and I don't care if you don't like it, and also I don't plan to have any partner." With that question settled, Max felt settled, too. When he knew what its name was, he knew what he was doing. "Ever."

"All right," she said, taking another snickerdoodle. "All right. You don't have to be so—" She bit into the cookie, chewed thoughtfully, swallowed, and picked up her teacup to take a sip, all without taking her eyes off Max's face. Then her eyes brightened, as if she had just had a particularly good idea but wasn't going to tell *him* about it.

What might that idea be? Max wondered, and then he wondered if she had had any idea at all. Was she an actor, too? he wondered, and then he thought, *She might be a pest but she isn't boring,* and that thought made him smile at her across the table with an irritating secretiveness that matched her own. But what she asked next surprised him. "Why *do* you only paint skies?"

Before he could think of how to answer that, not to mention if he wanted to answer it at all, Grammie came up the back steps and into the kitchen without knocking or calling out, as if this was her own house, where she was living. She was carrying a plate of snickerdoodles, which she set down on the table beside the plate they already had. "That explains *that*," Grammie said. "I couldn't think where all those cookies might have gone. Too bad for you, Max, I was going to refill the jar with chocolate-chip cookies, and now you'll have to wait. I heard voices," she explained, sitting down to join them. "I didn't know who was here, and I thought . . . I thought if you were someone official it wouldn't hurt to look like I lived here. I don't live here," she said to Pia.

"Why would you?" Pia asked.

"He's my grandson and . . ." She fell silent and looked at Max, who was desperately thinking, *Don't say it, please don't say it.* As if she could read his mind, "Is there any tea left in the pot?" Grammie asked.

Max brought her a mug while she announced, "I talked with Officer Torson this morning. About Madame Olenka." She turned to Pia. "Has he told you about Madame Olenka?"

"Why would he tell me that?" Pia asked.

"Ah," Grammie said.

"Who is she?" Pia asked Max. "Or is that a secret, too? How many secrets do you have?"

Max ignored these questions and instead asked Grammie one of his own. "What did you find out?"

"I found out where she lives." Grammie put sugar into her tea and stirred. "In Graffon Landing, that little village right at the head of the lake where summer tourists like to go because of the waterfall. There's a father and a brother, and both of them also have those long ears. None of them has a regular job—she claims to be able to tell fortunes—and yet they always seem to have money for dinners and drinks. She dresses well and the house she rents is right on the lake. It's expensive, and how can she afford it? Funny business gets reported to the police, nothing exactly illegal but nothing violent . . . The local policeman keeps an eye on them when there are tourists around."

"Tell me what you're talking about!" Pia demanded. "What's going on? Does it have something to do with whoever attacked Ari?"

Grammie explained, "Sven Torson is a policeman and an old student of mine from when I was a schoolteacher, so he knows I'm trustworthy. That's why he's willing to give me this information, even if it is, properly speaking, police business." Then she turned back to Max. "That's as much as he knows." She nodded at Pia. "How much does *she* know?"

Pia answered for herself. "I know this has something to do with one of his cases, even though he won't admit he has cases. I know that he wasn't surprised about the intruder. I mean, not surprised that there *was* an intruder—not that he expected it, but he wasn't . . . outraged. Or shocked. Neither were you and neither was Ari, although I don't think any of you know what's going on. Is that right?"

"Certainly the end part is," Grammie said.

"I think I might know," Max said. "You know how my father likes to boast about sitting at his breakfast looking at his fortune?"

In the background he heard Pia's questioning voice. "Your father? What father? Why would he say that? Is that why you're checking every book? What are you looking for? What about a mother, don't you have a mother?"

"If one of those Long-ears heard him . . . ," Grammie said.

"And took him literally," Max agreed.

"So the intruder took down the posters to look for a wall safe?" Pia asked, apparently not noticing that she wasn't being listened to. Or perhaps she didn't care. "I didn't see any sign of one, and we have three, so I know what they look like, even disguised. Do you think those pictures could hide something? Bonds? Deeds? Do you think he'll be back? What's going on, Mister Max? Why won't you let me help?"

"You're checking every volume, I hope," Grammie said. "Just in case?"

"Why doesn't anyone answer me?" Pia demanded.

"I'm not finding anything," Max told Grammie. "I don't think there's anything to find, but how can we convince *them* there's nothing here? Because I don't want them coming back. Ari could have been seriously hurt."

"Where is that boy, anyway?" Grammie asked.

"I'm not sure," said Max, because he only hoped he knew where Ari would go after attending his classes and quitting his jobs.

"Why do you call him a boy?" asked Pia. "He's even older than Mister Max."

Grammie looked at Max then, and then at Pia, a long, long look at each of them. "Has anyone ever told you that you ask a lot of questions without"—she held up her hand to keep Pia from speaking—"listening to the answers?"

"I didn't notice anyone answering me," Pia grumbled, but she had to ask, "Do you really think I talk too much?"

Max and Grammie answered together: "Yes!" and Pia grinned.

"I'm Pia Bendiff," she said, and reached across the table to shake Grammie's hand. "Pleased to meet you." She had apparently decided it was a good time to show that she could have good manners.

Now Grammie was silenced. Finally, she asked, "Bendiff's Beers and Ales? Bendiff's Cheese and Crackers? Bendiff's Jams and Jellies?"

Pia nodded. "I told you my father was successful," she said to Max.

"What's he going to start up next?" Grammie wondered. "I'm Max's grandmother the librarian. Mrs. Nives."

"The trouble is," Max said to his grandmother, not giving Pia the satisfaction of being the one he actually admitted this to, "that when she talks— All those questions? I can't help but try to answer them."

Grammie nodded, understanding. "Which gives you ideas."

Max nodded.

Pia smiled smugly and for once didn't say a word.

Max spoke to his grandmother so that praise wouldn't encourage the girl to talk even more. "She claims that she has ideas, too, but she doesn't. She just asks questions."

"I'm right here," Pia objected. "I'm listening. I don't agree, but I don't feel like quarreling about it right now."

"Good," Max said.

"Because I don't have the time. I have a riding lesson. It's only dressage, but I have to get home and change," she explained, as if they had asked her about that.

Max *had,* in fact, had an idea or two, so now he asked Pia a question. "Can you give me your address?"

"We have a telephone," she told him.

"Maybe you do, but I don't," he told her. She was aggravating but useful to him; he could see that, he could see what Grammie meant. As long as she didn't know too much, as long as she knew nothing that her constant jabbering would reveal to anyone and everyone, she might be a help, sometimes.

"It's One Eleven The Lakeview," she said with a defiant look. But Max didn't mind if she was rich and lived in a mansion and had a father who could start a brand-new restaurant business just because he wanted to and whose wife could hire a private pastry chef. Max didn't care if the people he knew were rich or poor; he just wanted them to be interesting.

"You said you'd come to my library," Grammie reminded Pia. "You could just look."

"I could," Pia agreed. "Maybe I will," and she left them.

So it was his grandmother who helped Max check and

replace the books and scripts on the lowest shelves of the bookcase. They found nothing.

As they washed their hands, "Your father," she began, but didn't finish because "Actors are different," Max said quickly.

"And he's a fine actor," she allowed. "He's a fine man, too. It's just that—his way of being so extravagant, so *dramatic*—right now it's making difficulties for you. What are you going to do about these people? Take an ad in the paper? Saying—what? *My father wasn't speaking literally? My father is only an actor?* This could be a serious problem for you, Max."

"Problems have solutions. That's what I do," he told her, made cheerful at the memory of the quarrel with Pia. "I'm a solutioneer. What do you think of that for a job?"

Grammie decided, "I like it better than detective. It sounds less dangerous."

Max leaned down to kiss her on the cheek because he knew she was more worried—about him, about his parents, about everything—than she wanted him to know. He was worried, too, but not at that very moment. At that very moment he was mostly pleased to be Mister Max, with this particular problem to work on. He told Grammie, "I think I have an idea about how to get rid of Madame Olenka and the rest of them. So I need to paint."

Grammie understood this. She went off right away, leaving Max alone with his ideas, plans, hopes, and possible solutions. Although he had no idea what to do about Pia and didn't dare think about his parents, he no longer felt so helpless, so trapped in a nightmare.

20

The Lost Dog

• ACT III •

A mild Sunday morning followed the rainy night. Even in the old city, the air shone fresh and clean. As the first church bells rang out, Max set off on foot for Joachim's house. It was a good morning for a long walk. Windows and doors were propped open to catch the breeze, so voices and cooking smells floated along the winding streets. On the broad boulevards of the New Town, couples and families and solitary strollers had come out to celebrate the morning in a variety of ways, some to worship, some to picnic, some to wander about aimlessly.

As he expected, Max found Joachim in his garden, glasses on his nose, painting one of his perfect flowers— a single butter-yellow tulip cradled between two long, curving green leaves. "I need Sunny," Max told his teacher.

Joachim didn't take his eyes from his canvas. "She's already eaten. She'd like a walk."

"I'm taking her to my house," Max answered. He held out the leash he had taken down from its hook by the door.

"When will you have her back?" Joachim asked inattentively.

Max hesitated. "That, I can't say."

Then Joachim did turn his head, to take a long, long look at Max. At last, "All right," he said, and called the dog. "Sunny? You do what Max says. Whatever that turns out to be," he added in a voice full of foreboding.

The dog approached, tail wagging.

"Max is the detective," Joachim told her. "He knows what's what."

"Not a detective," Max objected as usual, and he was pleased to be able to offer, "a solutioneer."

"Solutioneer?" Joachim put down his brush. "Like puppeteer?"

Max nodded, subduing his smile of victory at having surprised his teacher and, if the twitching of Joachim's mouth was any indication, amused him. "Solutioneer," Joachim said again, and gave in to good humor to the extent of a short barking sound that caused Sunny to prick up her ears and wag her tail even faster. "Then go get to work solutioneering. You've figured this problem out, haven't you?"

"It might not work," Max admitted.

Joachim had already turned back to his painting. "The way you did mine," he concluded.

When Clarissa and her father arrived at midday dressed in Sunday finery, they found Mister Max in his front yard sporting a red beret and a baggy blue shirt, slender paintbrush in hand as he stood before the long-legged easel, behind which was a rather odd, narrow glass box filled—most peculiarly—with what looked like dirt.

A dog, a large golden retriever, had been tied to the low fence with a rope. As the father and daughter approached, the dog—apparently bored by her long wait for something . . . anything . . . anything at all to happen—jumped up, barking eagerly, leaping at them, long tail frantically wagging. Until the rope pulled her up short, onto her hind legs.

Clarissa took shelter behind her father, who hesitated. Max looked up from his easel. "She's just being friendly," he called to them.

The girl hovered behind as the father opened the gate—narrowly, narrowly—and they squeezed through.

The dog was desperate. Her tail wagged wildly. She lurched at the man, who shoved her aside with his knee, and then she nosed behind him to jump up on the girl.

That day Clarissa wore a yellow dress, embroidered along its hem and high neck and narrow wrists with bright red flowers and bright green leaves, with matching flowers on her yellow shoes and twined around the crown of her yellow straw bonnet. When the dog jumped up on her, she gave a little scream and pushed it away, but the skirt already had long brown streaks on it, because Sunny had worked off some of her energy digging in the flower patch by the fence while Max painted and waited, his pet store purchase set out in the grass behind his easel as if he wanted to keep it hidden.

"Down, Princess Jonquilletta of the Windy Isles!" cried Clarissa, and the dog jumped up on her again. She stepped back. "Down! Sit! Play dead!" The dog paid no attention to the order and lunged again and again, pulling at the end of her rope, hoping that she could get loose to play with this lively, shrieking person. "Daddy! Help!"

"You, sir!" the father called. "You! Mister Max!"

Max put his brush in a jar of water and wiped his hands on his shirt.

Clarissa fled across the lawn toward him.

Sunny barked twice, then sat down again, resigned. to boredom.

"You summoned us," the father announced, approaching Max at a dignified pace. "I have luncheon guests waiting."

"Yes," Max agreed, keeping an eye on Clarissa as he stepped forward, hand outstretched. Seeing that she was making her stealthy way to his easel he said over his shoulder, "That's private, Miss."

As he expected, the girl pretended not to have heard.

"Is this the dog?" the father asked.

"That would be my question to you." Max wanted to stick to the exact truth. "She was running loose in the New Town. She answered the description."

The dog was sitting back on her haunches at the end of her tether, panting, her tongue hanging out of her mouth, her tail brushing back and forth across the grass of the lawn and the dirt of the garden, her dark eyes fixed hopefully on Max. The father studied her.

"She's not wearing a collar. Ours had an expensive collar, set with semiprecious stones. She's quite dirty. Ours was never dirty. Ours didn't jump up like that, or bark. Ours was quiet and well-behaved."

Max said nothing.

"Clarissa?" her father asked. "What do you think? Is this your dog?"

Clarissa had arrived at the easel and was staring at the picture on it. She turned her head to call the dog by name, her voice high, as if she were speaking baby talk. "Princess Jonquilletta of the Windy Isles!"

Sunny didn't turn her eyes from Max.

"Who was responsible for feeding your dog?" Max asked.

"That would have been the maid Brenny or, if Brenny was occupied with some other duty, the cook."

Max nodded solemnly.

"We're a very busy family," the man said.

"Come see this, Papa," Clarissa called. "It's a painting."

The father went to join her at the easel. Max followed, murmuring, "Private, I said. Private."

The father looked at Max's unfinished—and now that it had started to dry, unfinishable—watercolor. "It's just sky. With clouds. Are you going to put the birds in after?"

"Not—"

"There has to be something going on in a painting," the father instructed him. "Something to engage the viewer. I know a good deal about art. I'm pretty well-known at several of the galleries, and I've earned a reputation in the New Town as something of a connoisseur. This painting will never sell."

Max didn't argue.

"As a subject, there is nothing so commonplace as the sky. It's everywhere. It's absolutely ordinary. Who wants a picture of that?"

Clarissa had moved on. She bent over the ant farm, then crouched to get a better view. She tapped with her finger at the side of the dirt-filled, narrow glass box. "What is this?"

"That's mine," Max said quickly.

"But what is it? I've never seen anything like it. Is it a terrarium?"

"Your little girl is awfully nosy," Max said to the father.

He sprang to her defense. "Curiosity is a valuable quality in a growing mind," he announced. "As everybody knows. Is there some secret about this . . . whatever?"

"You're here about the dog," Max reminded them.

"*That* isn't my dog," Clarissa announced with absolute finality. "You can't make me take it."

"You heard her," the father said.

"Where can I get one of these?" Clarissa asked, still staring into the glass. "There are little tunnels, see, Papa?"

"This is the only one in the city," Max could tell her truthfully, since that is what the pet store owner had told him yesterday. *"Got the thing last summer, thought it would be a novelty and sell like hotcakes. Or, to be precise, a hotcake. But nobody wanted it. Are you sure you do? It's been in the store for months and I have to tell you, it's pretty boring. But if you're sure? I'll be glad to take your money and I'll give you a good price, too."*

Max told Clarissa, "It's a formicarium. An ant farm."

"It is really strange," Clarissa said. "Have you ever seen one before, Papa? A formicarium," she murmured, practicing the word.

"What do you do with them?" the father asked Max.

"You look at them," Max said. "Like a painting, except there's always something going on in there. You study them and learn. Ants are a good example to us all," he declared. "As everybody knows."

Clarissa reached out a finger to touch the glass. "I wish I could have one." She sounded sad, as if she were a poor, hungry girl looking at a plate of sandwiches that was about to be carried out for somebody else to enjoy.

"What do you feed them?" the father asked Max.

"Honey water," Max answered, as he had himself been instructed. "Plus a little piece of fish every now and then. For protein."

"Ah, protein," said the father, to show that he understood nutrition. "Yes. They aren't any trouble, are they?" He looked over at the dog. *Their* dog had been a great deal of trouble.

"Doesn't look like it, does it?" said Max. If you don't want to tell the truth, which in this case would have been *I don't know,* you can always answer a question with an echoing question.

The father said to Clarissa, "I guess nobody at your school has a—what did you call it?—formicarium?"

"I'd be the only one." She stood up and looked hopefully right into his eyes.

He smiled, reaching down to touch her cheek. "You'd like that, wouldn't you, my little princess?"

"He says there aren't any others, not in the whole city."

"There are other cities," her father said. "It's your vacation week, so your mother could take you down to Porthaven on Wednesday. She's free on Wednesdays. You two girls can take the train, have a day's shopping."

"But I want it *now*." Clarissa's eyes filled with tears.

"Sometimes," her father told her, older and wiser than his little girl, "we have to wait for the things we want."

"That's the truth," Max agreed, irritating Clarissa.

She looked from one to the other of them. At the gate the dog barked, as if to remind them of her presence, and anger crossed the girl's face, swift and light as a cloud blowing across the sky. She stood on her tiptoes to say, in a whisper too loud not to be overheard, "He *said* he'd find Princess Jonquilletta of the Windy Isles for me. He *said*."

The father looked at Max, then back to his daughter. "He didn't promise."

"He *said*," she insisted, and a tear or two spilled onto a cheek.

Max told the exact truth. "It's not that I didn't try."

"You can't say that you succeeded," the father told him.

Max could have, but he didn't. If things turned out the way he planned, he would only have succeeded in a secret, unacknowledged way. But that way happened also to be the best solution he could think of. He said, "I don't expect you to pay the second half of the fee."

The father laughed, a little scornful, the way successful people can be. "I'd hope not, although you can't tell me you couldn't use the money. You can't be making much of a living, not with *those* paintings, and I don't imagine there's much business coming in for a detective. An unknown detective. With only the one reference, because *I* can't give you one, can I?"

Max shrugged.

"Tell you what, though. I'll buy that ant farm from you, for the twenty-five you'd have gotten for the dog if you'd found her."

Max hesitated, as if he had to think about that.

"You *have* to," Clarissa scolded him. "You *owe* me."

"And I'll throw in another ten, since you won't be able to replace it," the father added. "That's my best offer. Take it or leave it."

"I guess I'll take it," Max said, in just the voice the formerly rich and now terribly poor man used when he was offered only a third of the original price for his last remaining silver fork in *A Miser Made Miserable*.

"And you'll have to get rid of that," the father said. He pointed to the dog.

Pleased to be noticed at last, the dog jumped up, barking eagerly and happily.

"It's not going to be easy," the father predicted with satisfaction, a man who liked getting more than what he paid for in a deal.

Puffed out with proud and happy energy at the success of his plan, Max rode—*fast*—through the winding streets of the old city with Sunny running beside him on her leash, at last getting the exercise she had longed for all the long morning. Max couldn't stop smiling. Everything had turned out just the way he had hoped, and planned, and worked for. Everything had turned out for the best: The dog had a good home; Joachim, by means of the dog, had a new vision of what his art might be, and that caused him to go out for glasses and thus discover that he wasn't dying of some blinding brain disease; Clarissa had a pet she could show off but not neglect; and Max had money in his pocket. The lives of his teacher and the dog were both better. Even Clarissa's life was improved, since it couldn't be good for a person to misuse a helpless creature. This solutioneering felt like something he had always been meant to do. He was using his best abilities and finding out how good they were. *And* he was being paid for doing it. He was truly independent.

Max felt as if at any moment he would spread his arms and fly, up into the air, up among the clouds. That feeling made him laugh out loud, which made a woman passing by with her two young children look up in alarm, which made him laugh again. He pedaled as fast as he could. Sunny ran easily beside him.

Max was bursting with ideas.

He left Sunny with Joachim and rode—even faster along the wide boulevards—across the New Town and out to 111 The Lakeview, slowing down only a little at the long, steep approach. Pia's home might not have been as large as the Baroness's castle, but it was a very grand edifice nonetheless, with an arched gateway, a gatehouse, and a paved drive leading to a cobbled courtyard that fronted the perfectly rectangular three-story mansion. The glimpse of foyer Max caught before a tall, broad butler blocked his view had shining marble floors in black and white squares like a chessboard. Still wearing his red beret and painting shirt, Max was breathing heavily from the speed of his ride, and the liveried man looked mistrustfully at him. "Yes?"

Max asked if Pia was at home.

"Is Miss Bendiff expecting you?"

"Probably not," Max said with an inappropriate laugh.

The man looked again carefully, to make up his mind. "Wait here if you would, Sir."

Max spoke quickly, to slip his words through as the big door swung closed. "Tell her it's the Solutioneer."

That evening Max and Ari ate alone. Grammie had been invited to have dinner with friends at a restaurant and go on to a concert, but she had left a pot of chicken stew simmering on her stove and a platter of biscuits on her kitchen table, along with a bowl of chopped kale for Max to sauté and a lemon sponge cake for dessert. In honor of his independence, Max decided to carry dinner over to his own house. He wanted to be the host at his own dining room table.

Ari didn't even ask the cause of this perhaps rebellious behavior. He just sat at the table in the dining room, which Max had set with two places. Neither did he comment on the way the room had been cleaned up, posters rehung, books and scripts replaced in neat rows on their shelves. He touched the swelling on his head only occasionally.

Max poured them each a tall glass of cider and served the two plates. They ate without speaking for several minutes before Ari, with a shake of the head as if to clear his brain, broke the silence. "You look like the cat that swallowed the canary."

"Are there feathers on my face?" Max joked.

"I guess you *should* be pleased with yourself," Ari said, not laughing. But he was smiling and a smile suited his handsome features. "I've quit *both* of my jobs," he announced.

"That's good news," Max said, and then, seeing Ari's expression, "Isn't it?"

Ari nodded as he took another bite of Grammie's chicken stew. "It's very good news. Now I can sign myself up for more courses at the University, and I'll be able to complete my degree in a year's time. By the start of next summer I'll finally be a graduate, and I can tell you, it's been a long wait for that accomplishment." He picked up a biscuit, split and buttered it, and ate it with pleasure, all without taking his eyes off Max's face. He was waiting.

Max waited right back at him.

At last, with a sheepish smile, Ari admitted, "I did go and see her. I took her that note. I did it this afternoon."

Max put down his fork. "The Baroness."

"My great-aunt, yes."

Max waited. Ari waited. Finally, "And—?" Max prompted.

"Oh. Well. She apologized, and rather nicely—nicely for her, that is—about the way she had treated me. And she did admit that she'd misjudged Martha. Then she started in telling me what to do. You know: move back, see a tailor, study economics so I can manage the estate I'll inherit, buy myself a horse and carriage and even one of those new automobiles, start going out with the right kind of people to meet the right kind of girl. Because I'm going to be Baron Barthold," Ari said, and it was an apology.

"Are you going to do that?" Max asked.

"Get some new clothes? Maybe. Probably. Boots especially. But—Max? I hope it really is all right if I continue living here. I can pay rent and I'm happy to, I'd like to. I don't want to move back into that castle. It's not as if all the apologies in the world can undo the damage or bring back what I lost—for which I know I'm as much to blame as Great-Aunt is. I do understand that."

"You don't mean the Cellini Spoon," Max said. "I guess what she wanted all along was for you to be found."

Ari nodded. "I know," and he handed Max a thick white

envelope. "She wants me to give you this. Ordered me to, actually. Great-Aunt doesn't ask. She's still a terrible old tyrant."

"At least she enjoys it," Max pointed out, opening the envelope and finding in it a typically brief note, which did not say *Thank you* or *Well done* but proclaimed in dark ink, *You may use my name for a recommendation, should it suit your needs.* He put the note back in the envelope and set it aside on the table. Then he said to Ari, "What *you* want is to find Martha."

Ari could only nod. It mattered too much to him to say even just the word *Yes.*

Max was pretty sure he knew where Ari's Martha was, and who she was. He had opened his own mouth, in a rush of happiness and pride, to announce the good news to his tutor, but something stopped his headlong solutioneering dead in its tracks. The something was a thought. The thought was: Sometimes it's better for people to solve their own problems, if they can; sometimes it's best if they work out their own solutions. Part of a solutioneer's job, he thought then, might be to recognize those times and keep his own cleverness to himself.

Max guessed this might be one of those times. "How are you going to go about doing that?" he asked Ari.

"The problem is," Ari said sadly, "that Martha isn't even her name."

21

In which Madame Olenka
is dealt with

Captain Francis watched the two of them cross the short gangplank from the deck of *The Water Rat* onto the dock at Graffon Landing. The female—youngish, prettyish, broad-shouldered—was expensively dressed in striped purple silk with flounces at the hem and lace at the wrists, a short purple cloak tied at her neck, and purple leather gloves protecting her hands. Her hair was so blond it seemed white under her straw bonnet; her dark blue eyes were thickly lined with kohl, which made her look exotic and queenly, like an Egyptian statue on one of the picture postcards sailors like to carry to call up memories of their more exotic voyages. She was, however, in the company of a man so unlikely that for the entire uplake journey Captain Francis had kept a close eye on the pair.

They had no luggage. They had a round-trip ticket.

The man looked to be not much older than the young woman, but Captain Francis couldn't guess *what* he might be. Something about him reminded the Captain of the many dubious characters—gamblers, pickpockets, confidence men, and cutpurses—who rode *The Water Rat* in summer, going from one small lakeside town to the next looking for victims, looking for profits. The long overcoat and the broad-brimmed black hat he wore low on his forehead, as if to conceal his face, raised the Captain's suspicions. He might even be a gypsy run off with his stolen bride, the old song come to life. On the other hand, the long white silk scarf that flowed off behind him in the wind was a bohemian touch, and he wore fine brown leather gloves. He might not be a gentleman, although she was clearly a lady, and from her dress and bearing a titled lady, even—the Captain had thought, watching as she leaned against the rail to admire the little waves that ran along beside the hull, entirely unconscious of the man who stood a few feet behind her—a countess or duchess or baroness, if not a princess. Perhaps the man was not some dancing master who had persuaded her to go off with him for a day's romantic adventure, or for the rest of her life, but only her personal guard. She didn't look at him the way a young woman should look at the man with whom she was abandoning her family and friends, for love.

Captain Francis couldn't imagine what their errand might be in the little lakefront town, unless—and this was also possible—she was fleeing across the mountain pass to safety. Such things happened among great and powerful families, as Captain Francis knew from the many novels he had read in the long evenings since the death of his wife many years ago. If the couple was not waiting on the Graffon Landing dock to catch the midafternoon ferry back to the city, he might read about her in the newspaper. Captain Francis determined to observe the two carefully, should they make a return voyage. There was something familiar about the lady's traveling companion, but Captain Francis couldn't see his eyes or his hair, and the long dark coat he wore concealed his physique. The Captain couldn't put his finger on who the man reminded him of, and that puzzled him.

A puzzle, a little mystery, added excitement to the Captain's days.

As the ferry pulled away, he kept an eye on the young couple. They looked around themselves, uncertain about which direction to take. They faced one another, conversing, and it seemed as if the man was her equal. Perhaps, after all, he was no more than the lady's artistic cousin with his long white scarf, and they had come to see the waterfall in search of inspiration. But he carried no sketch pad, no case of supplies. A poet, then?

Curiouser and curiouser, thought Captain Francis, as the ferry pulled out into the lake.

Max and Pia walked the short distance into a town that had grown up so close to the waterfall that tiny rainbows floated in the moist air and the steady sound of water splashing down a cliff drowned out the voices in the street. Because of this, and because he was once again following several paces behind Pia, Max spoke loudly. "This is a pleasant village," he observed, adopting the humble voice of the Medical Man's Valet in *The Caliph's Doctor.*

She did not deign to answer him. However, the slight rise and fall of her shoulders told him, and anyone who might be watching, that he might think as he would, she could not be bothered to disagree.

Without hesitation she approached the town's one small store, whose windows displayed yarns and loaves of bread, shoelaces and dishcloths, little jars of patent medicines, boxes of stationery, knives, and a bowl of eggs. "Wait here," she said.

Max obeyed.

Although he stood and spoke as if he might be her servant, Max wore the white scarf, slouched hat, and long coat of the Royal Spy in *The Queen's Man,* and he carried in his inside coat pocket a small notebook along with three small sharpened pencils. He was ready to play any one of three supporting roles—servant, artist, or biographer. Pia had the starring role in this performance. He waited patiently in the street, his gaze fixed on the doorway through which she had entered the shop. When Pia emerged, she set off without a word to him, knowing he would follow, Arabella herself promoted to royal (or at least aristocratic) status.

Madame Olenka had rented a large house, white brick with

black shutters, set on a green lawn that sloped down to the lakeshore. Red azalea bushes bloomed around it. The wide front porch was comfortably furnished with wicker furniture. Wicker chairs had cushions in the reds, yellows, and bright blues of tropical birds. Delicate wicker tables had painted china candlesticks set out on them beside little glass vases filled with pink and white sweet peas. This would be a pleasant place to spend long summer evenings. Even on this May morning, the sun-washed porch was warm and welcoming.

Pia pulled on the chain that rang the little brass bell beside the door while Max waited at the foot of the steps. A gray-haired woman in a pale yellow dress, a little lace apron at her waist and a white lace cap on her head, opened the door. "Do you—" she started to say, but Pia cut her off, as rude as any baroness.

"I am here to see Madame Olenka," she announced.

"Do you have an appointment?"

"You may tell her that she will profit from hearing what I have to say. I will wait inside. You"—with a gesture to Max—"come along." What could the servant do but step back before her?

The hallway they entered was filled with light, and the servant led them into an equally bright room, furnished with spindly-legged little sofas and chairs upholstered in pale embroidered silk materials, little round tables crowded with filigreed lamps and china figurines of shepherds and shepherdesses, although no sheep, as well as painted china bowls. Bouquets of flowers filled the two crystal vases on the carved wooden mantelpiece, and the long silver mirror hanging above it reflected the room back to itself.

Pia approached the mirror and arranged a lock of her hair. Max took a position beside the long windows. Neither one of them removed cape or coat, hat or gloves. Neither did they speak.

Eventually, Madame Olenka entered.

She had apparently spent the long interval in perfecting her dress, warned by her servant that someone of importance, or at least wealth and arrogance, had called. Madame Olenka's long ears dangled diamonds over a sky-blue velveteen suit. Her close-fitted jacket's top buttons were open to reveal the folds of a heavy satin blouse the color of beeswax candles. On her feet she wore delicate high-heeled blue boots with a row of tiny pearl buttons. She barely glanced at Max before she spoke directly to Pia. "*I* am Madame Olenka."

Pia did not introduce herself, as if she assumed that Madame Olenka already knew who she was, and Max had to admire the girl's acting ability.

Madame Olenka spoke again. In her own home, Max noted, her voice rang soft and deep, full of mystery. "You will have come for a reading," she said. "We go into here," and she opened a door leading to what seemed to be a windowless closet, if a closet could be as large as one of Max's front parlor rooms. A round glass ball shone on the square table at its center.

Pia did not move. She said, "I do not desire a reading."

Madame Olenka closed the door. "So, so. You will be wanting a consultation." She shut her eyes and reached her hands toward Pia, palms outward as if to receive invisible messages emanating from the flesh of her visitor. "It is a matter of the heart," Madame Olenka said, her voice soft with sympathy. "There is a quarrel in your poor heart. The future makes you afraid, I think?" She opened her eyes to ask, "This is so, yes? But I cannot tell you more unless we make the arrangement. I would give from my gift freely to all in need, but I too must eat, and live." She waved her hand to indicate the room they stood in, the house beyond. "I was not born to high position and great wealth, as are some others."

But Pia was not about to apologize for her own good fortune. "There are as many different gifts as there are uses for them," she announced, as mysterious as her hostess. "I sent word that you might profit from talking with me. Now that I have seen you, and heard your voice and that paltry excuse for a prophecy, I know that I am correct. But I will not stay any longer in here." She indicated with a gloved hand the room around them, the rest of the building. "The air is so thick with lies and greed that it chokes me. We will talk on the porch, Madame Olenka."

Madame Olenka drew herself up to protest, perhaps to mock or even to refuse, but Pia—gesturing to Max to follow her—swept out of the room. She spoke over her shoulder, "You may, of course, decline to hear me out."

Madame Olenka sighed dramatically and did not decline.

Out on the porch, she seated herself on a wicker chair and indicated that Pia should take one of the others. She continued to ignore Max.

Pia took a chair, arranged her skirts, and looked over at the blue-suited woman, then up at Max, who kept a respectful distance. "You may begin taking notes," she told him, then turned back to Madame Olenka. "This man is my biographer."

At that point Madame Olenka did glance at Max. Then she looked more sharply.

Max took out his small notebook and a pencil, flipping the small pad open to a particular page and wetting the tip of his pencil as fussily and slowly as Inspector Doddle readying himself to take down information. Madame Olenka lost interest in him and turned her unfriendly gaze back on Pia. As their conversation continued, Max didn't raise his eyes from the page on which he was writing.

Pia said, "It is I who have the true gift. *You* are a fraud and a cheat. Don't bother protesting. This is as clear to me as it is well known to you. I have come this afternoon not because I sympathize with you or pity you or wish to catch you out. I have come because you have disrupted my sleep. So. We are agreed that you are an imposter?"

Madame Olenka pursed her lips.

"Do you deny that you take money from those poor fools whom you persuade to trust you?"

"If someone wishes to pay me, I do not refuse the coins."

"At the end of this road a lightless place awaits you. What

it is, I don't know—a dungeon, a prison cell, an abandoned attic, a mountain cave. I only know I dreamed of you in such a place, among chests, iron bars, chains, cries of terror, and sobbings of despair, some sunless place. I don't know if it was you who cried out in the dream or some other miserable creature. But I do not like to have my sleep disturbed, and so I have come here to tell you what awaits."

"How would you advise me?" Madame Olenka sounded scornful, but her earrings trembled. "If I were to ask."

Pia took a long time answering. She folded her gloved hands in her lap and stared at them, letting the minutes pass slowly by. When at last she did speak, without lifting her eyes from her hands, her voice was oddly flat and distant.

"Where the road forks, I see—a journey? A white city in the desert? I see . . . is it a stallion? Perhaps not, perhaps it is only a man . . . I see . . . No," Pia said in her proud, confident voice and looking directly at Madame Olenka, "I see no more."

"Do you think I am not familiar with such tricks? This is my own trade, and I have practiced it here, successfully, for three years and more. How do I know that *you* are not the charlatan?"

Pia shrugged and rose from her seat. "That is of no interest to me. I am only here to win back unbroken slumbers in order to keep my own energies pure and return clarity to my own vision. You can believe what I have said. Or not. Come," she said to Max.

Max closed his notebook.

Madame Olenka did not move. She said, "Wait. Please. You will let me ask one question?"

Pia sat down, resettled herself, and looked up at Max. "Continue."

Max opened the notebook again.

"If you don't see anything more than that ahead of me, can you tell me what lies behind?" Madame Olenka asked.

Now Pia closed her eyes and did not hesitate, so sure was she of herself. "Behind lies a house, a small house. Empty but not empty. A closed gate, and I see flowers and . . . is it a name? No, only letters. There is an *M*. I see just the single *M*." She opened her eyes. One glimpse of the expression on Madame Olenka's face told her that she had been believed.

Madame Olenka did not give up so easily, however. "You wish to drive me out and have all the business of the lake to yourself," she maintained, but her hands gripped one another in her blue velvet lap and she didn't quite dare to look Pia in the face.

Pia laughed and once again stood to leave. "Perhaps I do. Or perhaps I am not what I appear but am instead an agent of the police, and what my biographer has been writing down is not notes pertaining to this application of my gifts but your confession, and he will now open his coat to reveal a policeman's badge on his chest, and he will take handcuffs from his pocket."

Madame Olenka half rose in her chair. She glanced quickly at Max and then as quickly away.

Pia laughed again.

"Miss?" Max said, as if reminding her. "If I may, Miss?" Pia was not the only good actor in the room.

An irritated inclination of Pia's head gave him permission.

Max flipped back in the notebook and, looking at an earlier page, said, "When you told me the dream, you said this woman—with her long ears? She was alone but not alone. There was an uncle, you said," he went on, apparently undistracted by Madame Olenka's sharp intake of breath. "Or a cousin, or perhaps both an uncle and a cousin? In the dark place with her. I only mention it," Max said to Pia's expression, which was turning to anger at his interference in her performance, "because when you told the dream to me, you seemed to feel this was important." He turned the notebook page to face her, as if she could read the words across the distance.

Now Madame Olenka stared at Max fearfully. She thought she *might* know him from somewhere, but she was too upset by this unexpected call, and too afraid that she might in fact know him from her time in the police station in the city— trying to persuade Officer Torson that she was an innocent bystander who only meant to be a good citizen—to be able to locate him in her memory. If she hadn't been so worried by this *person,* with her purple gloves and haughty manner, she would have had the energy to demand that the man take off his hat and give her a good look at his face. But she was too distressed and distracted and afraid to be bothered. Already, she was thinking of what she could pack and what leave behind.

Pia decided to go along with Max. "I had forgotten those

two. Yes. You should make a note of that, Biographer. On this morning I forgot something; and I remember now that I did intend to mention it, if only to assure myself that the dreams would not recur. They were"—she turned back to Madame Olenka, who stood motionless, speechless—"alarmingly unpleasant dreams. I would not wish to be you."

They left her there, Pia once again ten paces ahead and Max tucking the notebook into his pocket as he followed behind.

It was not until they had walked away from the docks where the *Flower of Kashmir* had never been berthed and moved beyond the range of Captain Francis's curious glances that Pia turned around to demand, "What was that about, about an uncle and a cousin? I thought they were her father and brother. That's what your grandmother said."

"I was guessing," Max admitted proudly. He stepped up beside her and they went together through the narrow streets to Thieves Alley. "Didn't you hear her gasp? That's because I guessed right. There was nothing in that house a man could like, everything so fragile and fussy. I didn't think those two men were living with her, but if they were her father and brother they *would* live with her, wouldn't they? But they still had to be related, because of the ears. And because of the way the three of them seemed to be in cahoots. It was a good guess," he pointed out.

Pia said nothing. For the rest of their walk, both were silent, thinking.

When they had changed back into everyday clothing and were standing in Max's kitchen, Max acknowledged, "We did a good job up there."

"I make a good partner," she agreed. She took up from the table the long, rectangular package she had placed there when she arrived that morning and was hurried into the front parlor to dress for her role. Before Max could make his usual objection she held it out to him.

"I don't need a partner," he said anyway.

"I know." She grinned. "Open it."

He began taking off the heavy brown paper in which it was wrapped, but before he did, he had an announcement to make. With a grin of his own, he told her, "I could, however, use a part-time—only occasional, mind you—assistant."

"Really?" she asked, a schoolgirl again in her pleasure. "Really and truly? I was afraid you were the kind of person who made up his mind right away and after that couldn't change it. But can I really be your assistant?"

"Sometimes," Max allowed. "For certain specific occasions. Like today." He had surprised her, and that was pretty satisfying. "But you can't tell anyone."

"I wouldn't. I won't. I promise. Open the package," she urged.

When he had the brown paper off, it was his turn to be surprised and hers to be smug. What he unwrapped was a long, rectangular wooden sign with two thick brass hooks on its back by means of which it could hang on a gate. Golden letters had been painted onto its glossy red surface:

Out in Thieves Alley, Max and Pia admired the sign for several silent minutes. Then she mounted her bicycle to ride home, but not before reminding him, "Don't forget, I'm on holiday all the rest of this week if something comes up."

Max felt so grateful to her right then, and so pleased with his own problem-solving abilities, that he responded, "I won't. Thank you for your help today."

"You are most welcome, Mister Max," she called over her shoulder, and pedaled off.

Max lingered a little longer outside his own gate in the golden light of the May afternoon admiring the sign. It was plain and clear for anyone to see: MISTER MAX, SOLUTIONEER. He had the sign, he had at least two references, he was definitely in business. He was independent. All of those thoughts pleased him, and he reached out to pat the wooden rectangle, just a couple of small tapping pats, for luck. The luck he hoped for was employment, problems to solve. He had completed everything, and no new job awaited him. He had enough money for two weeks, maybe, maybe less. How far would forty-five take him? If he gave up cheese, and milk, could he hold out until another job came along? Assuming, of course, that another job would come along. Max tapped the sign one last time and went through the gate and up into the house, to wait for whatever would happen next.

22

The Library Job

• ACT I •

What happened next was . . . nothing happened.

Max waited for mail, and none arrived.

He waited for unexpected callers, and none came to his door.

He waited for lucky accidents, and none occurred.

Nothing at all, not a thing, happened.

Of course the sun still rose and set, the business of the world went on. Pale morning mists floated on the silvery lake, then melted into the day like sugar in hot tea. Nights unfolded gently over the city like cool sheets pulled up over a soft bed. Two days, then a third, went quietly by, until it had been more than three weeks since some vessel, but not the *Flower of Kashmir,* had carried his parents down the river, six days since a postcard, mailed who knew when and they couldn't tell where, had arrived to tell him nothing, and Mister Max, Solutioneer, had not been offered any work.

Max read away at *The Iliad* and studied maps of modern African countries for Grammie, who also expected him to keep himself informed about events current to the city and the world and to be learning about the simplest multicelled life-forms. Ari had dinner with the Baroness and raked first through her memories (which were not many, the subject being a servant) and then through Zenobia's (which were numerous and unreliable) for clues to the identity of his Martha. He kept up Max's tutoring work with Euclidean geometry as well as his own university studies. "I'm used to being busy by now. I've actually gotten to like it. A lazy life isn't interesting enough for me, not anymore. Great-Aunt keeps complaining that she doesn't understand how someone as round and soft and unnoticeable as *that little detective* can be so good at what he does. So you must have been in costume?"

Max tried not to worry about his dwindling supply of coins or become impatient with the way Pia would come so chirpily into his kitchen, bringing one of Gabrielle's scarlet-ribboned boxes. Pia looked at him with such obvious hope of an assignment that he felt more worried.

"How is your father's restaurant coming along?"

"He can't find the right location. He wants it to be in the old city, because all the other fancy restaurants are in the New Town, so his will be different. He thinks it would be a real draw," she went on, obviously quoting her father word for word, "if it were on the water. Maybe on the river? So guests could watch the boats or eat outside in summer."

"Why not on the lake?" Max asked, happy to have something to think about even if it had nothing to do with him and was in itself not particularly interesting.

"Only *The Water Rat* and fishing dories go out on the lake. They aren't very exciting to watch, or romantic, not like ocean liners. He wants his restaurant to be something special."

"Like the pet owners at Hilliard," Max observed.

Pia didn't allow any criticism of her father. "You've never even met him. So you don't know anything," she snapped. "When do you think you'll get another job?"

Max shook his head. He had no idea. He was losing hope.

Grammie seemed to understand how he felt, but Ari had his mind so full of his own search and his own studies that he didn't notice Max's low spirits. He made nightly reports over Grammie's suppers of his unsuccessful efforts to locate his Martha.

"I've asked Zenobia all the questions I can think of, in all the different ways I can think of, and she isn't any help at all," Ari said. "So I decided to look at the servants' rooms. Just in case. Just on the off chance. Just because . . . because I can't think of anything else to do."

"Keep thinking," Grammie advised. "You have to keep thinking about things like this, these stubborn knots of problems. Maybe Alexander the Great could cut the Gordian knot, but the rest of us have to unravel them, patiently, following the string around and around."

Max pointed out, "The Gordian knot doesn't have anything to do with Ari finding his Martha."

"You *are* disagreeable today," Grammie answered. "More moussaka?"

Ari ignored them both. His voice was thoughtful, his eyes worried. "I had to go up about fifty stairs, and there wasn't much light because it's the back staircase, to get to the attics where the rooms are. There were four bedrooms off in one direction and four off in the other. Each room had only one bed in it, one window, one little table by the bed with a lamp on it, one small dresser, and two hooks on the back of the door . . ." His voice trailed off. He took a couple of bites, remembering. "I wouldn't want to live in a room like that," he said. "Nobody would."

Grammie didn't agree. "There are worse places to live, much worse. The Baroness's servants have bathrooms, don't they? Aren't the rooms warm in winter? Are there windows in the bedrooms?"

"It looks like I'm not the only quarrelsome one," said Max, disagreeably.

They both ignored him.

"Yes, there's one bathroom for each wing, and electricity, and each room has a small coal fireplace. It's just Zenobia and the two Marthas who live there now, but Zenobia is old, and the stairs are steep. You'd think the Baroness . . ." He fell silent. "There wasn't even a bookshelf, Mrs. Nives."

"I'm not saying I want to move there," Grammie told him. "I'm just saying that there are worse."

"What difference does that make?" Ari demanded. "If I were the Baron Barthold, and had servants, I'd give them decent rooms, not way up in the attic, and with wardrobes, with bookshelves and bureaus and a table to write on. I had no idea my Martha was being treated like that."

"You *will* be the Baron Barthold," Grammie pointed out.

This dismayed Ari. "But I don't want to be. I don't want anyone thinking I'm like the rest of them, and I don't want to live in that castle, with all those things in it. I don't want to be rich or important. I don't want any of it. You didn't think I did, did you?"

"No, of course not," Max and Grammie assured him. "No, we never, we know you better than that."

Ari went on with his list of horrors. "It's not just the castle. There are farms and herds of dairy cows and herds of sheep in the hills. There's the ironworks and the Barthold Bank and the shipping line. The Baroness has to keep track of all the records of expenses and profits, taxes and wages, contracts, production figures, yields . . . You don't know how much work it is."

Max was having an idea. He couldn't speak it out loud, but he very badly wanted to. If he'd had some job of his own to be working on, he wouldn't have had any trouble holding his tongue, but the desire to give Ari advice was clawing its way up into his throat, like a mountain climber approaching the summit, stubborn and determined. Max had to chew fast and swallow hard to block its progress.

"It's a lot of work being done by a lot of people, a lot of jobs and not just for the workers, for lawyers and accountants, too," Ari told them. "And all for one old baroness." Then his fork stopped halfway between his plate and his mouth, and his eyes lit up again with what Max recognized as hope. "All those records?" His words came faster. "The Baroness must keep account books for the castle, too. So maybe my Martha's real name is in one of those books!" he cried.

The mountain climber in Max's throat loosened his grip and slid back down, out of danger. Oddly, even though it was what he wanted to happen, Max felt a little disappointed, too, as if, like that adventurer, he had lost a chance to stand at the top. He couldn't even tell Ari that he'd had the same idea.

That evening, instead of joining in for a game of hearts or a lazy conversation, Ari left as soon as the dishes were washed and put away. "If I do an extra hour of study tonight," he explained, "then I can get to the castle tomorrow afternoon and start looking through the account books. What if I knew her real name?" he asked, to apologize for rushing off. "I never even knew her name, I never even asked. Can you imagine that? I knew it wasn't Martha, but I didn't even bother to ask what it was." He shook his head slowly, and his cheeks grew red with embarrassment at remembering the kind of young man he had been. He looked at Grammie, at Max. "She deserved better than me."

Neither of them knew how to answer that, so they said nothing. They just wished him a good night's study, a good night's sleep, good luck with his researches.

After Ari had left them, Grammie refilled their mugs and said to Max as she sat down again at the table, "I almost never see you alone these days."

Something about the way she said that alerted Max.

"And I don't want to make you talk about your personal business in front of Ari if you don't bring it up yourself," she went on. "But if your supply of coins is running low . . . ?"

"I'm fine," Max mumbled. This wasn't exactly true, but if he ate only bread and jam at home, what with his good dinners here, he could last through another week using Ari's rent to buy food and leave him ten in his pocket for next week's painting lesson. Grammie didn't need to be worrying about him.

"I don't think you've had any new jobs come in," Grammie went on.

Max couldn't deny that.

"I have a job for you," Grammie said then.

"You do? *You* do?" This was not at all what Max had expected to hear.

"It's not a big job, or an important one, or . . . Well, it is what it is," she said. "Now that I see I have your full attention," she teased.

A job was not a teasing matter. Max nodded, businesslike.

"We have a little problem at the library, worth maybe seven—"

"Fifteen?" Max suggested. Then, at the expression on her face, "Ten?"

She nodded. "Agreed."

Max got right to work. "What's the problem?"

"Do you remember that children's weekly magazine, *The Toy Chest*? When you were little, you'd make your mother bring you to the library early on Fridays and you'd spend hours poring over it. Even before you could read."

"It was all the pictures," Max explained. "I still remember some of them. There was a hut in—"

Grammie interrupted. "Our copies of *The Toy Chest* sometimes disappear. Not all of them, maybe only one every month, but . . . Magazines are periodicals. Periodicals have to stay in the library. I've never seen anyone trying to check one out, and neither has my assistant. So I thought of you. You're the Solutioneer," she reminded him. "The library can hire you to solve its problem."

Max had thought of a difficulty. "It won't look bad that I'm your grandson and you're hiring me?"

"If my position doesn't enable me to help out my grandson, what's the point of having it?" Grammie asked right back. She must have already had the same doubts.

"All right, but you know, if your grandson can't charge you the going rate . . ."

Grammie laughed, but she didn't raise her offer. Max

decided that if he had to choose between not working at all and earning less, he'd choose the latter. After all, less was more than nothing. "I'll begin observation tomorrow."

Grammie had a request. "Can you be unrecognizable?"

Early the next morning, a businessman hurried up the steps and through the wide doorway into the library. He wore a dark pin-striped suit and a tall hat. His shirt had a stiff white collar, and a gold watch chain crossed over a black brocade vest. His shoes shone with polishing and he strode across the foyer, crossing in front of the circulation desk before he took off his hat, so occupied with his own affairs that he had to be someone important, perhaps a banker, perhaps a company manager, in need of information. As he strode past, he didn't even glance at the gray-haired librarian seated at the desk. She looked briefly up at him, then back down at the papers she was studying, then sharply up again, this time with a small smile.

Max, in the suit his father had worn to play Banker Hermann in *The Worldly Way* and with a smaller pillow than the one he wore for Inspector Doddle, took a chair by one of the long windows of the reading room, where magazines were spread out on long tables and newspapers hung from racks. He chose the day's copy of the London *Times,* which, it being a Friday, had a particularly thick financial section. He opened to news of recent patent applications, and waited.

The reading room offered newspapers and magazines from all around the English-speaking world, with back issues neatly arranged on clearly labeled shelves. Grammie took pride in her reading room with its comfortable chairs and broad tables, its bright light, and the alcove where children could sit in smaller chairs at smaller tables to read the publications ordered especially for them, *Saint Nicholas, The Toy Chest, The Youth's Companion.* Set out on a central table, where it could not be missed, was the framed announcement: PERIODICALS MAY NOT BE REMOVED FROM THE READING ROOM.

All morning long, Max read articles about money and markets, about home decoration and social events, about conflicts—over territory, over beliefs, over new or old laws, even over education and medicine. It was surprising how much people found to fight about. There were even arguments about books and paintings. He read recipes for roasts and gardening recommendations. He read crime reports and the reports of government committees. It was sometimes discouraging to learn what was going on all around the world, and it was often dull. Only the sports news and the comic pages could be called amusing.

While Max was reading, he also studied the people who came and went in the room. They tended to be men and to be looking for something specific, a particular newspaper, a particular magazine article. The few women who sat in the chairs, reading a fashion magazine or a society paper, were clearly filling in an empty hour before it was time for something else, an appointment, a coffee, a lunch, a store to open. Most women wore day dresses and small summer hats; they carried wide straw shopping baskets. One younger woman, who arrived just before lunchtime, wore a dull gray blouse and skirt, which hung around her thin body as if they had been intended for someone plumper, although her pale brown hair was neatly arranged and she seemed perfectly clean. She was carrying three magazines when Max noticed her take a chair at the big table. She sat studying them, one after the other, until the clock tower bell rang twelve, at which sound she rose and darted out of the room. She carried no shopping purse, wore a kerchief around her neck but no hat, and her shoes were clumsy, thick-soled laced boots. After she left, the library closed for lunch, which Max did not eat with Grammie.

During the afternoon it was city clerks who came in, on business, and then boys and girls, with and without mothers, to find books to read, for school and for pleasure. Not until Max at last got out of his chair to leave the room for the day did he notice the odd assortment of magazines the gray girl had left on the table: *The Well-Dressed Woman,* a ladies' fashion magazine filled with picture after picture of the newest styles of skirt and gown and hat, *The Toy Chest,* and a popular monthly that told the news in photographs, *The Rotogravure.*

Max arrived home to an empty house and a note from Ari saying that he had looked at the castle account books and found some of the same names he had seen in the record books of the farming properties up in the hill villages. He was off to investigate and would return when he had found out all he could. Maybe, the note concluded hopefully, he would return with his Martha. Max changed out of Banker Hermann's suit and back into his ordinary shirt and trousers. He was about to leave the house when Pia arrived, bringing strawberry tarts, and Max was actually glad to have someone to talk to, although he told her she couldn't stay long.

She stayed long enough to tell him news from Hilliard ("They notified all the parents that they've hired a guard for the gate, after a *recent distressing event*. That was you!"), to register her usual complaint ("boring boring boring") about the schoolmates she didn't want to rejoin when vacation ended, and to react to Ari's plan ("He's always so hopeful. Do you think he'll ever find her?"). Then she suggested to Max that if he needed work he should talk to her father and offer to solve the problem Mr. Bendiff was having finding a location for his restaurant ("I don't know if he'd be willing to pay you. Should I ask?"). When they had finished the pastries, he saw her off on her bicycle, then mounted his own. He rode by the Starling Theater to see that all was well there and then crossed the river to The Lakeview. He needed to take a long, fast ride. He had not enjoyed sitting still all day, even if it was a job. He wasn't looking forward to sitting still all the next day, too.

23

The Library Job

• ACT II •

It was the only job the Solutioneer had, so Saturday morning found Banker Hermann once again seated in his chair by the window, once again opening the financial section, which, he was relieved to see, was much thinner than it had been the day before. Time passed slowly. Max had difficulty staying awake.

However, when the same pale young woman, dressed in the same shabby clothes, entered the room late in the morning, he woke up enough to watch her over the top of his newspaper. At noon, she closed the same three magazines she had looked at the day before and left them out on the table, not slipping any of them under her blouse or into the shopping basket she carried. He followed her anyway, out onto the street. She might have nothing to do with the missing periodicals, but she might; she was the only unusual thing he had seen in the reading room. Besides, how long could he ask himself to sit quietly, waiting to catch a periodical thief in the act?

One and a half days, he answered. This young woman was a guess, but maybe she would prove a good guess. Certainly he was ready for a walk through the warm mid-May noon. He hurried along the sidewalk, twenty feet behind her.

She was a small person, narrow-shouldered and narrow-hipped. She walked fast, but without energy or eagerness, and looked neither to her right nor to her left. He followed her along the boulevards and across the avenues of the New Town, where she drew curious glances in her shabby clothing and heavy boots, and then into the crowded, winding streets of the old city, where a banker was the one who looked out of place.

The young woman was unaware of Max. She was unaware of everyone and everything. She walked in a cloud of fear, her head down and her narrow shoulders gathered in, her arms folded across her chest. There wasn't anything very unusual about her, and Max wondered why she was so afraid, or was it embarrassment? She puzzled him. Her straw-colored hair was in neat braids, she had a sharp little nose and chin, and she seemed ordinary, so why did she walk along the street in that cringing way? What bad thing was it that she expected to happen if someone noticed her?

She hurried down River Way until the buildings of the old city gave way to the district where boatyards and warehouses sat beside workshops in which carpenters and blacksmiths, stonecutters and brickmakers labored. Max followed, now a good distance behind. Just after the buildings gave way to riverside meadows, she stopped at a wooden gate, wide enough for a mail coach with its six horses to enter. Max hurried to catch up with her, but she slipped through a small door cut into the gate and disappeared from sight. He caught only a glimpse of a dirt courtyard within, enclosed by low buildings, before the door shut behind her and he heard a key turn in the lock.

Max stood in front of the gate wondering what to do next. On his right there was a brick wall, two stories high with three windows on each story, to all appearances a house. On his left another two-story wall had only one blank window, at ground-floor level, beside which he saw a metal tablet tarnished with neglect. He crossed over to it. CHARITABLE WORKHOUSE FOR THE ELDERLY AND THE INFIRM, it said. ENTRY FROM DAWN TO DUSK DAILY.

Max turned his back to the building and looked across the road to the broad river, where painted fishing dinghies floated among tall masts of yawls and sloops, and a small tugboat on its way to the Queensbridge docks struggled against the current. In the far distance, apple orchards were in bloom. Except for the grim building behind him, this was an entirely pleasant spot, and he lingered unnoticed, enjoying the view, before he returned home.

On Sunday Max was free to paint, and that is what he did. The May sky lay closer overhead, its blue deeper and warmer, its clouds whiter and fluffier. It is what seems to happen in May, as if the sky itself bends down to inhale the scents of damp soil and new grass, of jasmine and hyacinth and primroses. It was the kind of perfect day that should bring only good news—that a war has ended or that lost parents are found. The news that day, however, was of a storm at sea and a great ship going down.

Max might not have heard about this until the next day if Grammie had not gone to hear the band that played in the park on spring and summer Sundays, and rushed home with the Extra edition of the *Queensbridge Gazette* so they could "Read all about it! The sinking of the *Miss Koala,* as told to our special correspondent by Captain Eustace Trevelyn!" Only the captain, the ship's head cook, and one officer survived, rescued from their lifeboat after days on the open sea, eventually brought safely to land in Portugal, where they delivered their tragic news.

Before she gave him the paper, Grammie reminded Max, "We got a postcard, remember?"

Max read the article and reminded her, "There was nobody on the *Miss Koala*'s manifest that sounded like them."

Aloud, they agreed, "I'm sure they weren't on board the *Miss Koala*."

But each of them had doubts. Max's parents had been well enough to send a postcard weeks ago, but Grammie and Max had no idea where they were when they sent it. They had no idea where they were now.

As the afternoon and evening went on, each tried to convince the other not to worry. The *Miss Koala* hadn't come to port in any place where the last letter of a postmark would be *A*. Still, the fact of any ship's sinking was a shock. Max had imagined many unhappy ends for his parents, and that one of the worst had actually come to pass—even if not for his parents—was terrifying. Max couldn't help thinking of those passengers, imagining their terror and confusion, all that death. Grammie mused on the precariousness of life, how you never knew in the morning what might happen before dark. Neither one of them slept well that night.

Lucky for Max, the Solutioneer had a job and a plan of action for Monday. As soon as the shabby young woman came into the reading room on Monday morning, Max picked up his banker's tall hat and left. She did not notice him go, because she was immediately engrossed in the new issue of *The Toy Chest,* which by Monday had already been read aloud to many small children and looked through by a few of the older ones. He bicycled home at top speed, changed into his dog-catcher's costume—minus the net—and bicycled back. As he was walking up the wide steps to the library entrance, the young woman was hurrying out through the doors.

He was just another city official, and she didn't lift her gaze from where her heavy boots were being set down, first on the steps and then on the pavement, so that when Max tapped her gently on the shoulder she froze, taken by alarmed surprise. He stepped around in front of her and her eyes grew wide.

"I wonder if I might have a word with you, Miss," he said, taking his cap by its long, stiff brim to doff it and speaking quietly so she could know he meant no harm.

She said nothing. She stared at him for a long minute. Then she burst into tears, covering her face with her hands, hunched over in misery.

"Now then, now then," Max said, trying to soothe her. "Now then, Miss."

"I didn't do nothing," she blubbered. "I didn't mean to. I won't never again. What did I do?"

"Come along," Max said in the same soothing tone. A little crowd was gathering around them, which did not suit Max at all. "Make way, please, let us pass. The young woman is upset, please let us pass by." He held her gently by the arm and moved her down the sidewalk and across into the park. She didn't resist. She didn't protest. He sat her on a bench and waited for her tears to cease, then handed her his large red bandanna to wipe her eyes.

"Better now?" he asked. Head bowed, she nodded, and Max nodded, too. "May I have your name, Miss?" he asked, as if he had every right to be asking her questions.

"Nance," she answered, without taking her eyes off her hands where they twisted the bandanna in her lap.

"How old are you, Nance?" he asked.

"They tell me I'm sixteen but I've been there more than

two years but maybe it's written down somewheres?" She did look at him then. "Would they write me down?" she asked.

"It's very likely," Max said, in the language of government officials. "You are presently domiciled—" Her confused, lost expression caused him to rephrase the question. "You live in the workhouse?"

This reminded her. "I got to get back, Sir. They'll be angry."

He shook his head and laid a hand on her arm to keep her from bolting up off the bench. "You must answer my questions first. However, I'll walk home with you to explain your delay. May I continue?"

"I got to get back," she repeated urgently.

"We have reason to think you have taken some magazines from the library," Max said quickly.

Relief washed over her face and she explained, "That's what a library is for. Anybody knows, they told me, you take things home from the library."

"Not magazines. Not newspapers. Not reference books. Didn't you see the sign?"

She shook her head, looking down again to her hands on her lap.

"It's right there," Max pointed out. "It says, 'Periodicals may not be removed from the reading room.'"

"I *thought* it said something," she announced, pleased at her own cleverness.

"You can't read," Max realized.

"How could I?"

"You learn at school."

"People like me don't go to school."

"Like you?"

She nodded, on this subject confident. She tapped her finger against her temple and told him, "Without the usual. Short a room upstairs. Simple Simon. Blockhead. Noodle?" she asked helpfully, thinking he didn't understand. "Thickwit?"

"Ah," he said, speaking officially. "I see."

"I know numbers. I can do adding and take away. Not times," she concluded sadly.

"I see," Max said again. "I see." His stomach growled and he had an idea. "Will you come with me for some ice cream? While I think about those magazines."

"I won't never, not no more, not now I know I oughtn't," she said. "Can't I go home now?"

"The store is on your way home," he told her. "Come along," he said, as if he had every right to tell her what to do. She obeyed.

Nance refused to enter the ice cream shop with him, but she did keep her promise to wait outside, and she ate the chocolate ice cream cone with apparent pleasure, although it didn't slow down her anxious pace along the street beside him.

24

The Library Job

• ACT III •

Ari was still off on his search, so Max and Grammie ate alone again that evening. She wanted to talk about Ari's chances of success, but Max wanted to avoid that topic. He was afraid he would give in to the temptation to tell Grammie his guess about Gabrielle so that when—as he confidently expected—he was proved right, someone would know how clever he'd been. He diverted her attention by telling her how easy it had been to solve the library's problem and return the missing copies of *The Toy Chest* that afternoon once he had talked with Nance. Grammie reached immediately for her purse and paid him. Then she went back to her dinner and said, "I wondered about her. She was always slipping in and out. Like a ghost."

"It's how she lives." Max didn't know how to tell his grandmother what he had seen at the workhouse. There were no words dull and flat and gray enough to do the job, no combination of letters to spell out the hopeless and lifeless atmosphere of the place. "It's so *sad*" was all he could think of, and he had to immediately correct that. "Not that Nance is sad, she seems—she's not happy either, just—"

"Resigned?" Grammie suggested. When he shook his head, she tried, "Defeated?"

He shook his head again. They were eating a minestrone, thick with vegetables, and there was dark bread to dip into the broth. Both of them ate slowly, and Max's words came out slowly, too, without organization, the ideas chopped up and mixed together like the potatoes and zucchini and carrots in the soup. "Nance grew up in the orphanage, from— Somebody left her there, wrapped in a blanket, a baby. They told her at the workhouse that she's sixteen."

"That means she left the orphanage two years ago. What did they train her to do there?"

"I suspect they sent her away younger, because she says it's been five winters she's worked for Master and Matron. I don't know *how* old she is, but it's not more than eighteen, it could be— And she's the only servant, Grammie, she does . . . There are three old men and two old women. And the Master and Matron, they're middle-aged and in good health, but Nance still does everything. Cooks and cleans, does all the shopping, all the workhouse laundry. There's no running water in the workhouse. They use zinc tubs, an outhouse. Except for the Master's apartments. Do you know why she took the magazines?"

"To look at the pictures, I assume. I assume she can't read?"

"In their rooms? They just have candles and oil lamps. Not even gas lamps. The Master's apartments have electricity, of course, and he has a bathroom, too. The workhouse bedrooms have brick floors; the building must have been a stable, or a factory. It was never meant to be a place for people to live. Nance didn't understand about borrowing library books. She can't write her name, either."

"Is she perhaps simple-minded?" Grammie guessed. "I wondered that. Her timid expression, her . . . She seemed to always be at the edge of the room, scuttling."

Max nodded. Nance had waited for him, as obedient as a dog, and had never thought to ask why he'd give her ice cream. "She never even had ice cream before," Max told Grammie. "It's not right, not a bit right. She has to go across the road and wash the laundry in the river, even in winter, I think. She wasn't complaining when she told me all this. Except Master and Matron's laundry; she carries that to a laundress. Grammie? She thinks if she leaves, the police will put her in prison. It can't be legal, what she's . . . What's being done. Can it?"

Grammie asked, "Did you talk to this Master person?"

"What do you think?"

"I think you should have, so I think you must have. What did you find out?"

"He says she signed a contract, she's an apprentice. But if she can't read—"

"Exactly," Grammie said.

"I don't know what to do," Max said.

"You'll think of something," Grammie told him. She tried to console him. "You did find the missing magazines. You earned your fee."

Max didn't feel consoled. He couldn't feel consoled when Nance had—and had always had—such bad luck in life, and where was there a place in the world for someone like Nance?

Tuesday brought another perfect May morning. Max rose early, troubled by memories of the day before and grateful for his luck, his own house, with electricity and hot and cold running water, clothes washed in the machine he shared with Grammie, grateful for having gone to school, for enough to eat, and good food, too, and for time to paint if he wanted to. Even if he had lost his parents, or they had been taken away from him, or they had abandoned him, he still had a lot to be grateful for. He sat down to finish the geometry problems Ari had set him, in case his tutor returned in time for their lesson. He had no idea when to expect Ari back, and he wondered what his tutor might have discovered, up in the high valleys. He wondered also if Ari's feelings about the quiet up in the hills, the simplicity of life in that clearer air, would have changed over the years. In which case, he wondered if Ari might just stay there, disappearing from Max's life into an entirely new life of his own, the life he had been dreaming of since he was a boy.

Max doubted that, but he wouldn't know if he was correct until Ari had returned. Or failed to return.

Homework done, Max went out to the front yard with his easel, but instead of painting a new skyscape he studied the two best April pictures, a cloudy sky that promised a spring thunderstorm and an early-morning sky that promised a windless day. He thought about which looked more like April. After not very long he threw back his head and laughed, as victorious and booming a laugh as his father might have let loose in the final scene of *The Worldly Way,* when, as the humble manager, he foiled Banker Hermann's scheme to take over the lumber mill and force the impoverished mill owner's pretty daughter, as played most pitiably by Mary Starling, to marry him. Max laughed out loud, clapped his hands together twice, and went to the kitchen to write a brief letter. As he sat down, pen in hand, he thought that he needed not only business cards but also stationery, all declaring his profession, MISTER MAX, SOLUTIONEER.

The butler at 111 The Lakeview had just opened his mouth to say something unwelcoming to the plump, seedy man in his pork-pie hat and not overly clean bright blue waistcoat when the fellow thrust an envelope into his hand and turned on his heels to walk away. The butler had no time to refuse to accept the envelope or to demand that the fellow identify himself. He didn't even have time to pin down a vague sense that he might recognize the man, although he certainly didn't *know* him. It was the odd eyes—the color of brandy spilled on the stone cellar floor?—that struck him as somehow familiar, but it was only the man's back that he could study, searching for a memory, watching the questionable character go down the drive with the side-to-side rolling gait of an overweight man or an old sailor. Then the butler looked down to see that the envelope was addressed to Mr. Bendiff, and he shrugged. His employer was a curious character, not at all what the butler had been used to but generous in his dealings with servants. Mr. Bendiff entertained some odd people at the house, and while he was himself—as the butler knew; he would never agree to work for someone of questionable morals—an upright and honest man, some of his business brought him into contact with the kind of people who seldom set foot on The Lakeview.

Max went from Pia's home to the castle, where the Baroness wanted someone to complain to. Max had his own business to conduct, so their conversation did not run smoothly. The Baroness greeted him crossly from her throne-like chair, "I've lost my heir."

"I've found you a scullery maid," Max responded, standing in front of her with his round hat in his hands. He did not twist or rotate the hat; he did not fiddle with it. He might be dressed as the Unsuccessful Suitor, but he was playing Inspector Doddle, who always got his man.

"The boy won't live here, he doesn't want the money, he doesn't even want the title," the Baroness complained.

"This girl is simple," said Max, as dry and undramatic as Inspector Doddle reading facts from a file. "But young and strong and of a good disposition. You aren't young, and neither is Zenobia. A pair of strong shoulders will come in handy."

"On the other hand," the Baroness admitted, her voice growing less sharp and unhappy, "he does come to see me. He keeps me company sometimes. He is willing to overlook"— she chose that word because she could not think of herself as someone who might need to be forgiven—"my error."

"This girl will have to keep her own name," Max warned the Baroness. "She can't be asked to make that change, any more than Zenobia could."

"He can't escape the title," the Baroness concluded with satisfaction. She regarded Max. "I have two Marthas working here already. What do I need with another?"

"This girl will never marry. She has no family. She comes from the orphanage and is now much misused in the workhouse."

"I am not a soft-hearted do-gooder, Mister Max. I thought you understood that."

"You don't need to be. You might, however, want to show your great-nephew that it's possible for wealth to improve the lives of others," said crafty Inspector Doddle.

"Humph," said the Baroness. "As if he weren't smart enough to already know that. I hope you don't expect any further fee for finding this new Martha."

"Her name is Nance," Max said.

Thursday afternoon, Max, wearing the town official's uniform, walked through the old city and out along River Way to claim Nance away from the workhouse, where, as he arrived, the Master, his dark suit brushed clean, his white shirt collar starched stiff, was just entering an automobile with an ornate *B* painted in gold on its shiny black door. The Matron was in too much of a state of alarmed excitement to question the official's demand to see the contract Nance had signed. He read it over slowly. Then he lay a finger on the wavery *X* with which one of the parties had signed and looked into the woman's face. He was William Starling as the Queen's Man, fighting to save Her Majesty's reputation and the life of her infant son from the plots of the King's evil brother. He kept his eyes on the Matron's face as, without a word, he tore the paper along its length, once, twice, a third time. With a stern look, he handed the pieces back to her. "You wouldn't want that to come to anyone's notice," he advised.

"Especially not now," she agreed unapologetically. "Not when the Master is about to move up in the world and take me out of this place."

She cared entirely too little for the way they had treated Nance. He warned her, speaking with all the power of displeased royalty behind him, "This malfeasance will not be forgotten."

That *did* distract her, but only briefly. "It was the Master's doing. I'll tell him when he returns, but now—take the girl, go about on whatever your business is with her. It's better that she be gone. And I've plans to make."

Nance was not surprised to see him and did as he told her without question, packed all her possessions into a shawl, gathered its corners together into a knot, and clutched the bundle to her chest as she followed him into the open brick courtyard. "I like your eyes," she told him. "Friendly, like the fireplace before I scrub it clean. Do you want to see my fireplace?"

Max did not.

"Did you come to give me more ice cream?"

He had to stop off at his house to change into the Unsuccessful Suitor's suit that Inspector Doddle wore and was relieved that Nance was undisturbed by this. "Now you're fat," she told him, seating herself behind him on the bicycle. "Pretty vest," she added, perfectly happy. She asked no questions when he took her to the castle, and curtseyed clumsily to Zenobia when he introduced the two. Then Max led her up the narrow back staircase to her new bedroom.

For a long minute, Nance stood silent in the center of the small room. Then she set her bundle on the bed and went to look out the window. She returned to sit on the bed. She turned on the little lamp, then turned it off. She covered her mouth with her hands. "For me?" she said from behind her fingers. "Just for me?" She lowered her hands to tell him, "There's a light." She switched it on and off again and twisted around on the bed. "I can see the sky out there," she said. "May I stay here? Please, Mister?"

Back on The Lakeview, heading home, Max rode slowly. He was proud of his solution to the problem that Nance hadn't even understood she had. He felt entirely satisfied with himself, as his feet pushed the pedals around and the lake shone silver off to his right. He was good at his work, resourceful and imaginative. He'd never been so good at anything before in his life, he thought, going through the Royal Gate and back into the old city, taking the shortcut through Misery Lane. But his happiness lasted only until he walked into his own kitchen.

Because the house was empty. He had known it was empty, but standing in an empty house, solitude spreading out around him, he had to remember: When he paid Joachim for his next lesson, he would have only fifteen in his pockets, and no other job awaited him. All the activity of the last few days had distracted him from that reality. He could no more think of having business cards and stationery printed than fly to the moon. Worse, he had to recognize that without earnings his independence was at risk.

But independence was all he had left. Max had a sudden bleak black intuition that he would never hear from his parents again.

He fled from that thought. It was better to worry about work, and less frightening, too. How could he drum up business? He wasn't thinking well about this problem, he knew. His only idea had to do with whether he could take that phrase literally and wander around the New Town with a drum—wasn't there a drum in the prop room, for *A Soldier's Sweetheart?*—proclaiming his own name to anyone passing by, in case anyone knew anyone with a problem needing solving.

It was a relief to hear a ringing at the bell and to know by almost immediate opening and closing of his front door that Pia had decided to come pester him again. At least she would divert him, and maybe at best she would ask him some nosy question that would give him an idea. He needed an idea. He needed five ideas. He admitted that to himself as he went to welcome her.

As usual Pia was dressed in her school uniform and carried a white box wrapped around with a scarlet ribbon, and as usual she had an irritating mysterious smile on her face as she charged into the kitchen. What was not usual was the long envelope she put down on the table beside the box. *Mister Max* was typed on the front of it. Also not usual was her failure to start talking, although he could almost *see* all the words she wanted to speak crowding up in her eyes and pushing up the ends of her mouth. Silently, she opened the box. Silently, she watched Max open the envelope.

Inside were two tens and a five, folded inside a typed note, *For services rendered,* signed only *Bendiff.* Then, before Max had time to work it out for himself, Pia's words burst out of her. "He thinks it's the perfect location, and he's already talked to the Mayor about buying it from the city. His architect will look at it Monday, and he's putting those two in charge of a pub in the New Town. If they succeed at the job, that's fine by him. If they fail, it's too bad for them. He thinks," Pia announced, taking a large bite of apple turnover, "they'll fail."

"But what about the—?"

"The old people are being moved into private homes. The city will pay for their care. It will cost the city less *and* they'll be much more comfortable. Poppy will make sure of that. So, what do you think? Wasn't that a good idea of mine?"

Max thought: He could make it through another week and maybe two, and that was a relief but no solution. He thought: Pia could teach Nance to read, at least enough to keep her from ever getting into that kind of trouble again. He thought: These turnovers look delicious, and he reached for one.

The box held four turnovers, as well as two thick slices of a lemon sponge cake with lemon curd between each of the three tall layers and a light lemony buttercream frosting, and also, piled one on top of the other, four square pieces of linzer torte. "Everything looked good," Pia explained. "Besides, what if she *does* go to work for my father and stops selling them?"

Max hadn't eaten any lunch and was hungry. He'd finished one turnover, was halfway through his piece of cake, and had begun the argument with Pia about teaching Nance—"Why should I? It's not as if I have time on my hands," she was arguing—when Ari entered the room from the back garden.

He looked tired, his clothes were rumpled, and the light of hope in his eyes had gone out. Pia asked if he'd found his Martha, and he shook his head. Max asked if he still wanted to live up in the hills. At that question Ari did smile, his old sad smile, and say Yes; but he added right away, "It's not possible, of course. Other things are more important."

"Didn't you find out anything?" Pia demanded. "You were gone for days. I'm sorry," she added.

"Oh, I found my Martha's family. Named Glompf," Ari told them, "and I found out that the Bartholds aren't the only ones good at staying angry, or judging harshly and holding grudges. When I told them their daughter had been absolutely and definitely proved innocent, all they said was that so much damage had been done to their reputation, they didn't think it would ever be repaired. They didn't even spare one thought for her. They have no idea where she disappeared to seven years ago, and they don't care. Except that she used to send them most of what she was paid, and they are still cross at losing that. I tell you, both of you," Ari announced, "I hope I never bear grudges like that. Great-Aunt at least acknowledges that she was wrong. But those people . . ." He fell silent, took a breath. "I'm going to unpack and have a quick bath, then we'll have a lesson, Max." At the dining room doorway he turned to say, "I did find out her name anyway. It's Gabrielle," and he turned away, valise in hand.

Max clamped a hand down hard around Pia's wrist to keep her from saying one word. When Ari's footsteps could be heard going heavily up the stairs, he released her.

"Our Gabrielle?" Pia asked, whispering.

He nodded.

"Why didn't you tell him? Why didn't you let me? Did you already know?"

"I know what I'm doing," he said as firmly as Lorenzo Apiedi talking to the lawyer who was advising him to do whatever it took to save his own life. Like the young patriot, Max repeated it slowly. "I know what I'm doing."

Pia wanted to disagree but decided not to. "Hunh," she grumped, then shrugged and picked up a linzer torte, took a bite, and took up their quarrel where it had been left off. "What if I just don't *want* to teach someone to read? Someone too stupid to have learned how before?"

They both had red angry cheeks when Ari came back into the room. He still carried a battered briefcase, but that was all that was left of the penniless student. Now he wore brown gabardine trousers, a soft golden sweater, and soft leather shoes. Now he looked wealthy and possibly important, like one of the redheaded Barons Barthold, although he lacked their imperious eyes. He interrupted the quarrel. "What's wrong? What *is* this? I thought— What's going on?"

Pia started telling Ari about Max's impossible request, which had grown to seem ever more impossible to her as the quarrel went on, and more difficult, and even less to her liking. Ari nodded and said only, "I see, I see." He looked at Max with a calm expression. "I see," he said, and nodded. He opened his briefcase and set his volume of Euclid out on the table as Pia went on about the pointlessness, anyway, of trying to teach someone who couldn't read at this person's age.

Ari nodded. "I see, yes, I can't argue." He reached out to take a turnover, asking politely, "May I?" and pointed out to Max, "Pia is much too young. *And* immature. Well, that's only to be expected at her age, but she's right. She can't teach someone simple-minded. The way she lives? How can you expect her to understand someone so very different? Even if she could do that, if she were that kind of a girl, do you think you could ask her to work that hard? I know just how you feel, Pia," Ari concluded, and he bit into the golden-brown tip of the pastry.

"I am not too young," Pia answered, and turned her impatience on Ari. "You can't say I'm spoiled, because I'm not. Not one bit. I'll show you," she told him, eyebrows drawn together over stormy eyes. "I'll do it, and I'll do it so well—"

But Ari had stopped listening. He had swallowed his bite of turnover and, still holding the pastry in one hand, reached out with the other to take Max's fork—this time without a polite apology—to take a bite of the lemon cake. He ate that bite and then another. Then he looked from one of them to the other, too stunned to speak.

Pia looked at Max. Max looked at Pia. Then they both looked back at Ari, who was now sinking his teeth into a linzer torte square. After savoring and swallowing, "Where did these come from?" he asked, almost whispering, as if he didn't dare to speak something out loud.

"Pia brought them," Max said. He had decided, since he had just won the argument, to let Pia have the pleasure of telling Ari where, as always on a Tuesday afternoon, Gabrielle Glompf was to be found.

Ari forgot that he was supposed to be giving Max a lesson. "It has to be her," he told them. "Nobody else can bake like that. Do you think it's her? I have to go—I'm going to—I have to—" and he was out of the room, out of the house, on his way, his eyes bright with hope.

25

In which what was lost
is—in a way—found

Max had made up his mind not to waste a day
worrying. In the morning, he ate a quick breakfast
and took his easel out to the back garden to see if he could
paint the overcast morning sky's shades of orangey-pink-
streaked gray. It was a pearly light he was trying to capture
on paper with color and water and his hand, too. In painting, he thought as he painted, it was literally your hand that
made things happen, whereas in other things—in the theater, in business, at Grammie's library—it was a metaphorical hand at work. Gabrielle's literal hands mixed and shaped
her pastries, and Captain Francis's hands steered *The Water
Rat,* but it was metaphorical hands—whose? the Master's

or Matron's? the city's?—that had created the unhappy and cruel situation at the workhouse, where Nance had lived like a slave, or some misused pet. His Solutioneer hands, Max decided, could work either literally or metaphorically, and he rather liked that.

By the time Ari brought his cup of morning tea outside to sit on the back steps and take a look at this first new morning of his renewed life, there were two finished watercolors, neither of them entirely satisfactory, although Max was pleased with the pink underbelly of one of the clouds. Max was ready to be disturbed. He took off his red beret and turned to his tutor-tenant-friend. "Well?"

Ari knew what he was asking. He held the mug of tea in cupped hands and smiled, flushing with pleasure, then he shook his head gently, in puzzlement or sorrow or perhaps just the confusion of so much happening in so short a time. "She was glad to see me alive and well. She forgives me. She let me wait in the shop until it closed, and walk her home." Then he remembered. "You already knew her, Max."

Max swallowed. "Yes."

"Did you always know who she was?"

"No," Max said, then admitted, "I wondered, when I first talked with the Baroness. I started to wonder then, because of something Gabrielle had said, but I only figured it out . . . just a few days ago."

Ari studied him. "Seven years ago, I'd have horsewhipped you for keeping quiet," he said thoughtfully. "But now I know better. If I hadn't gone looking for her myself, hadn't tried to find her myself, if I hadn't—I think she'd have sent me away again. You did me a favor by not telling me, Max."

Relief washed over Max. He hadn't been sure how Ari would react. Ari was, after all, a Barthold.

"Because of course Gabrielle knew." Ari spoke the name joyously, and he repeated it. "Gabrielle knew all along she hadn't taken the spoon, so that it could be found didn't surprise her. But she didn't know about me. I was—I still am—a question mark." Ari turned to Max, smiling, to say, "She didn't know it was you who'd found the spoon, so I could at least surprise her about that. And now"—Ari stood up, stretched—"now I'm going to tell Great-Aunt that if she can't welcome both of us, Gabrielle and me, I mean, into her life, then she won't see either one of us. Any idea what she'll say?"

Max laughed. "Not a clue."

Ari ran his fingers through his red hair. "Neither do I. She isn't exactly predictable, the Baroness Barthold." That, however, didn't worry him, not one bit.

With Ari gone and the urge to paint temporarily satisfied, the whole day stretched out empty in front of Max. He decided to do schoolwork. He mastered Euclid's fifth proposition, using a ruler and compass to construct isosceles triangles, and then made—as he said to himself, standing up to admire it—an elegant drawing of a plant cell. After that, it was time to eat. He'd had enough of sitting in the kitchen and carried his lunch of soup, bread, and cheese into the dining room, where he sat in his father's chair. Sitting, slowly eating—because what would he do with the afternoon?—Max was almost sorry that the Long-ears were no longer around. They had made things lively and given him something interesting to do.

Then he realized that the Long-ears *had* left him a possible mystery. He could wonder if his father was speaking some form of the truth, if not the literal truth, about dining in the company of a fortune. Certainly those three accomplished crooks had believed it. Between one spoonful of soup and the next, Max looked up at the many posters on the dining room walls and all the books lined up on their shelves. He didn't want to think about how few coins he had in his pocket and how few days of independence they represented, and he didn't want to remember who should be sitting in the chair he occupied and who in the chair opposite, so he sent his mind wandering over to the unlikely possibility of a fortune. It wouldn't be vast. How could the manager and lead actor of a small theater in a small city in a small country earn a fortune? But it might be something—if his father was the saving sort. He hadn't ever heard that about his father, and William Starling was an announcing sort of person, so Max would have heard that, wouldn't he? But it wasn't impossible.

The Starling Theatrical Company usually played to full houses, and it did make a profit, Max knew. Perhaps there was a precious edition of one of the plays standing on the shelf like any ordinary book, hidden in full view, Shakespeare or Molière. Grammie could teach him how to research rare editions and maybe he would ask her to do that. Or could it be the posters? It was his mother who had designed them, and a lithographer friend of Joachim's had produced three dozen copies of each, advertisements to put up around the old city and the New Town as well as to display beside the entrance to the theater. There was no chance that the posters would turn out to be the work of some famous artist, Rembrandt, for example, or Goya, or even one of the modern painters, maybe Cézanne. But could their frames be valuable antiques?

Max chewed his bread and cheese and doubted that. Even the intricately carved vines and flowers that wound around the poster of *A Soldier's Sweetheart* couldn't be valuable enough to count as a fortune, Max was sure. And the wide, gilded frame around *Adorable Arabella*—which was his mother's best role, the one she was most famous for and enjoyed the most—with its checkerboard of squares and thick knobs that looked like pawns in a chess game, even *that* frame was no more than a curiosity, or at best a unique piece of craftsmanship.

Max finished his lunch and leaned back in his father's chair, thinking idly and inattentively . . . and the idea came to him. The idea floated to the surface of his mind like a photograph appearing in developing liquid, a clear image where just seconds ago there had been blankness. He surged up from the table. He could kick himself for not noticing at the time what Pia had asked about. Granted, it was one of her many and many inquiries, but hadn't he already realized by then that among all of her chatterbox questions there was often one that he would be smart to answer? He could kick himself harder for being so slow to understand what the marriage of Arabella to Banker Hermann might mean—because hadn't his father talked about that impossible event in both messages?

Mostly, however, he would have liked to kick his father. There was no need, no need at all, for William Starling to have been so . . . so flamboyantly secretive. As if it was all a game, he thought angrily.

Then Max remembered the Long-ears and thought maybe his father's games were necessary after all.

Carefully, he took the image of the pretty young woman in her striped purple gown down from the wall and laid it on the table. The frame *was* heavy, even heavier than he'd guessed. It was also thick, much thicker than any of the others. The only reason for its weight, Max guessed, taking a gentle, experimental tug at one of the knobs, was if the frame was made of something very heavy.

Was the frame solid gold? Could his father's fortune ever mount up to the extent of that much gold? That seemed unlikely.

And in fact it *was* unlikely. Because when the little door pulled free of its fitting, like a knobbed piece pulled out of a toddler's puzzle, Max saw a little leather bag hidden in the space behind it. The leather bag held gold coins, five gold coins, and it fitted exactly into its little box of a hiding place. Max replaced the bag of coins and the door, then tried another knob, which pulled its square of wood free from the frame to reveal another little leather bag.

Max felt as if he had been tossed up into the air by some

energetic explosion beneath him, some volcano or waterspout erupting, tossing him up into sunshine. He closed his eyes and heard his father's voice telling strangers in a restaurant, "My fortune? I break my fast every morning in its company!"—a brilliant actor playing a merely vain and bombastic one. Smiling, Max returned to the frame.

Not all of the knobbed squares hid coins. Some hid only bags of gravel. Max thought that his father had planned to gradually exchange the gravel for gold coins when he had them. Only a dozen of the little knobbed boxes held gold, but that was wealth enough. On that amount, Max could live comfortably while he completed his schooling, and his university studies, too. There was more than enough to last several years, until Max was old enough to earn a living in some chosen profession. Max was dumbfounded. How could it be that his father had accumulated so many gold coins? And what was Max supposed to do with them?

Because his father *did* want him to find them. That was the secret of the two messages he'd been sent. And Max had solved the puzzle! Also clear was his father's opinion that Max might *need* them, and that was worrisome.

Max hung the heavy poster back in its place on the wall. He returned to his father's seat at the table. From there, he stared across at Adorable Arabella, just as his father had so often done, but without his father's exuberantly smug expression. *This* was a real problem.

He knew perfectly well it shouldn't be a problem. It should be a solution. It should be *the* solution to all of his problems and troubles, having enough to live on. But it wasn't, not really. Because if he had enough to live on, then he didn't *have* to work as the Solutioneer.

If Max wasn't the Solutioneer, how could he be independent?

Moreover, if he didn't have other people's problems to solve, Max would be left with just his own.

He had no interest in the coins, Max decided, and he wasn't going to tell anyone about them, not even Grammie. He wasn't about to let a fortune ruin his life. He would, however, sleep more soundly, knowing the coins were there if he needed them.

But in the darkness of deep night, the sound of the fire wagon, bells clanging and hooves thundering, woke him. The Theater? was Max's first thought. Until he heard the direction they were going in. But awake now in the darkness, he found his heart still pounding: His parents must have known as soon as they got on the boat that there was something wrong, wrong and dangerous, going on. They must have wanted to reassure him, without putting him in danger, and also to make sure he had enough to live on. They must have been trying to take care of him, in case they wouldn't be there to do that themselves. What had they gotten themselves into?

The afternoon mail the next day brought him two unexpected letters, almost as if, now that he could wait, the world decided it needed him, and right away. The first letter asked Mister Max to call at the office of a lawyer in the

New Town, on a private matter, at his earliest convenience. The second letter was from a boy at the Hilliard School who wanted Mister Max to prove to everyone that Madame Celestine always gave girls better marks than boys, which wasn't fair, was it?

Max was trying to decide how to answer this second letter and what to wear in response to the first—the disreputable detective's suit? the town official's uniform?—when Grammie burst into the kitchen. He rose, both letters in his hand, to tell her this good news. Then he saw the disarray of her hair and the frightened—or was it excited?—expression in her eyes. "What's wrong?" he asked. "Grammie? Are you all right?"

She put a newspaper down in front of him, right on top of his letters.

"What are you doing?" he cried. "What's wrong?"

"Look. Just . . . Look!"

He looked.

It was a newspaper published in Rio de Janeiro. Grammie held it folded open to one of the back pages. Her finger pointed to a photograph.

The black-and-white picture was blurry, but he would have known those smiles anywhere. He had seen them hundreds of times on stage, accepting applause. No matter how his parents might be feeling, no matter how well or badly either one of them might have performed that evening, they always smiled just this way, smiled out over the audience with just these same proud and joyous expressions, as if never before had applause been so welcome. There could be no doubt: It was his parents.

His father wore a close-fitting military-style jacket with gold braid on the shoulders and cuffs and a broad sash, hung with many medals, diagonally across his chest. His mother wore a tiara that gleamed white in the photograph and a pale low-cut gown with long pale gloves that went up to her elbows and jewels around her neck and wrists. They stood, smiling, each with one arm stretched out wide and welcoming, the other hands clasped between them.

"What *is* this?" Max whispered, without taking his eyes from the picture. "Who is that?" He pointed to the only other person in the photo, a shadowy figure in what looked like a military uniform standing off to stage right, behind his father.

"Read it," his grandmother advised, and moved her hand so that he could see the caption under the picture.

"It's in Spanish!" Max protested.

"Oh. That's right," said his grandmother, the librarian and former teacher, so disturbed and distracted that she had forgotten that important fact. "I had to go to the University to find a translator."

Max kept his eye on the photograph while Grammie recited, "The newly crowned King and Queen of Andesia."

Max looked up at his grandmother. "That's all?"

Grammie nodded, not happily.

Max thought. "Well . . . at least? We can be sure now they weren't on that boat," he said.

Grammie nodded and after a long minute reminded him, "The *Miss Koala*."

"That one," Max agreed, without taking his eyes off the photograph. Then he looked up. "Andesia?" he asked. "Where's that?"

"South America. It's a tiny country, mountainous, situated at the point where Ecuador and Colombia meet, not far from Peru. The soil is thin and rocky, so for a long time nobody cared about it or wanted it, just the people who lived there in their villages, with their animals. But silver and copper were discovered, and with the mines everything changed. These days, the common people barely scrape a living, while the people who own the mines are extraordinarily wealthy."

Max raised his eyebrows.

"I looked up anything I could find about Andesia," Grammie explained. "I've gone back over old newspaper reports. It seems that the Andesian royal house was the worst kind of monarchy, greedy and cruel; it treated the people—except for the mine owners, who only had to pay heavy taxes—like animals. Last summer, the people got up in arms—well, spades and pitchforks, mostly; they couldn't afford weapons, knives, too, probably, scythes, hoes—and revolted, and no wonder, but . . . The ruling powers in the neighboring countries got together to offer political asylum and a safe home to the royal family, and then they sent in their own joint army to reestablish peace. They put a man whose mother was Andesian and father Peruvian in control, as military governor. Temporarily,

they said. Ha!" Grammie had lived too long to believe everything she was told.

Max was not to be distracted by what nations said, or newspapers, or politicians. He touched the photograph with the tip of a finger. "It's them, isn't it."

"Max?" At this point Grammie sat down beside him, as if her legs could no longer hold her up. "I read the articles carefully. More than once. This man they put in power? His name is Balcor. It's probably him in the picture." She set her finger on the shadowy figure.

Grammie spoke slowly now, as if she didn't want to be telling this part of the story. "First, this General Balcor announced that the royal family had been betrayed, tracked to their mountain fortress and murdered in their beds, all of them. It was a gang of gypsy robbers, he reported. All the jewels and treasures the royal family had taken with them into exile were stolen by those same gypsies. It was a national tragedy, a tragedy for all of South America, and the General promised that he would find the culprits and hang them. He swore to return the jewels and treasure to the people of Andesia. He said the people of Andesia needed a king to lead them, and when the Andesians said they'd take *him* for their king, he declined. But I don't trust him, not for a heartbeat.

"Then he announced, this was last March, it was in the newspapers, he announced to the country that there was a distant cousin of the late king, now living in a foreign land, and with the death of the entire royal family, this cousin was the heir to the throne. Do you see where this is heading?" Grammie asked.

Max did.

"What have your parents gotten themselves into?" Grammie wondered, and Max thought he had never heard her sound so upset, so anxious, so helpless, and he had only the vaguest idea of what kind of trouble his parents might be in. All he knew was that it was trouble not of their own choosing.

"They were tricked," he said. He couldn't take his eyes off the two smiling people in the newspaper photograph. "Do you think they're prisoners?"

"Whatever his plan is, this General Balcor needs them alive and well," Grammie said, sounding a little calmer, now that she had shared her fear.

Max agreed. "So they're probably safe enough for now." He hoped that was true, because he had noticed—and decided not to tell his grandmother—the way his father held one of his mother's hands clasped tightly in one of his own as they opened their free arms to accept the praise of their people. This was the bow that meant trouble. Whatever performance they were in, it wasn't going well.

Grammie said, "So our problem is, What do we do? Or is that your problem? You're the Solutioneer after all. I'm just your librarian, just an information source."

"I don't know what we *can* do," Max answered, "not right away, not until we know more. I only know we can't say anything to anyone. Absolutely no one. Not even Ari, not even Pia. Not even Joachim."

"Yes. Because this General Balcor needs to think he's getting away with whatever he's up to. As long as he thinks that, he needs your parents. I wonder what his plans are," Grammie said, studying the photograph.

Max looked at the situation from a different angle. He wondered if he could get a message through to his parents and, if he could, how he could, and what it would be.

He reminded himself that not only were his parents alive but also they had been located. That had to be good news. It was good news, mostly. Because if you know where someone is, you know where you have to go to get them out of whatever trouble they're in. You might not know just what, precisely, the trouble is, but how to discover *that* was Max's next job.

He'd done all right with problems so far, he told himself reassuringly. If this one was more distant, and difficult, that didn't make it insoluble. He looked up at his grandmother, and smiled doubtfully.

She looked back at him, and smiled doubtfully.

We're in this together, Max thought.

"At least we're in this together," Grammie said.

"We know where they are," Max reminded her.

"Yes," Grammie agreed. "And we also have the Solutioneer on our team," and now her smile had no doubt in it at all. "This isn't getting dinner on the table," she said, and turned to leave.

"I think I'll go outside," Max said, and he was already thinking hard. "And paint."

Join Mister Max on his next
adventure in solutioneering!

THE BOOK *of* SECRETS

Turn the page for a sneak peek.

Dear Mister Max,

Your name was given to me by one of our prominent law-yers, Fredric Henderson, who offered as reference also the Baroness Barthold. Both parties spoke of your per-spicacity and your discretion. Those are qualities I am in need of. I will be aboard The Water Rat *Sunday morning when it leaves the city docks for its nine o'clock circuit of the lake. I will be standing at the bow, regardless of wind and weather. I ask you to meet me there, where we can talk privately on a matter of importance to the city, and to the welfare of the country, too, quite possibly. Thanking you in advance I remain yours sincerely,*

Richard P. Valoury

Richard P. Valoury, Mayor, was typed underneath a sig-nature so scribbled that among all the letters, only the *V* was recognizable.

Grammie was reading over his shoulder and "Why do people have such terrible handwriting?" she demanded. "Maybe I should go back into the classroom, and improve things."

Max was surprised. "Do you want to teach school again? I thought you really liked the Library, with all the books and magazines and newspapers, with all the different tasks the job needs you to be able to do."

"Things don't always go the way we want them to,"

Grammie told him gloomily. "You should know that by now, Max."

What the Mayor of Queensbridge saw that windy Sunday morning was not what he expected. He had been told by Fredric Henderson—but, he reminded himself, Fredric Henderson had only been repeating what his wife said and the Mayor had met Henderson's wife, a birdbrain if ever there was one. So she was likely to have gotten it all wrong when she told her husband that this Mister Max was a poor student, a brilliant poor student perhaps but nonetheless threadbare and a little underfed. He'd probably be glad of any kind of work, Fredric Henderson had advised the Mayor. Since this, at least, was just what the Mayor hoped, he was happy to believe it.

He also discounted the Baroness Barthold's report that Mister Max was a round little fellow, comical really, dressed in a nasty bright blue waistcoat that might be his Sunday best, but did nothing for his pumpkin-shaped figure. Was he clever? Or merely lucky? The Baroness couldn't swear to one or the other, but the detective seemed to care about the downtrodden, if the young woman he had brought into her employ was any example, and he *had* persuaded the Bendiff girl to do some tutoring in her kitchens, and in the Baroness's opinion that looked like a difficult child to persuade to do anything. So perhaps he was clever. Yes, he *had* done the Baroness good service but, really, she couldn't swear that that hadn't just been luck. Also, he wore this ridiculous pork-pie hat . . . Noting the Baroness's advanced age, the Mayor had decided that her eyes must be bad and that her memory, also, could not be relied on.

So, on balance, he was expecting an impoverished student, although perhaps not quite so thin as Mrs. Fredric Henderson had reported.

What he saw, however, was a dark-coated figure striding toward him, as slender as a rapier. The man had draped a long white aviator's scarf around his neck. The wide-brimmed black fedora gave him the look of some kind of artist, some poet probably, some bohemian free spirit. His back turned to the bow of *The Water Rat,* the Mayor faced the approaching figure. If he hadn't known that Captain Francis was watching, he might have feared for his own safety, although he couldn't have said why. There was something dangerous about this man, this Mister Max, this Solutioneer. When the figure came nearer, the Mayor was made even more anxious by the man's eyes. They were a strange, indefinable color, like the charred timbers of one of the wooden buildings, burned in the recent fires of the old city.

That thought, however, reminded him of his urgent need for Mister Max, and his hope that the man—of whom he'd never heard until just recently—might be able to do what neither the police nor the various powerful citizens he had consulted had been able to. Even Hamish Bendiff couldn't help, and something that Hamish Bendiff couldn't do anything about was a serious problem indeed.

The Mayor stood up straighter and held his hand out

importantly. He might be in need of help, but he was still the elected mayor of Queensbridge, the man chosen by a large majority of the people. He cast a quick look up at Captain Francis, standing at the bridge, took a deep breath to steady his voice against the wind, and said, "Thank you for agreeing to meet with me."

What Max saw was an ordinary gray-haired man, dressed in an ordinary gray pin-striped suit, stiff white collar and cuffs showing, a homburg on his head, a narrow briefcase at his feet. He saw the Mayor of Queensbridge, an important man who did not look like such an important person.

Max had chosen the hat and coat worn by the spy in *The Queen's Man,* in part because it seemed to him that was the best role for this morning's private meeting, and in part because the only other time the Solutioneer had boarded *The Water Rat,* this was what he'd worn. It would not do to underestimate Captain Francis's curiosity about his passengers, especially those who were not familiar to him. He strode boldly up to take the offered hand and shake it firmly, asking, "What is it I can do for you, Mayor Valoury?"

He might be dressed as a subtle and slippery spy, but he was Mister Max, the Solutioneer, on a job.

"You don't waste time," the Mayor said with an approving nod. "I like that, and this trouble is certainly serious enough. Let's sit," and he led Max over to a set of benches built up against the curving prow of the boat, freshly painted a bright white. The wind that morning was brisk, so the other passengers kept to the cabin, but even if it had been a calm, hot day, the two would have been able to speak privately. These benches, in fact the entire bow, were reserved during the summer months for the exclusive use of any royal party that boarded the little ferry to go from one lakeside village to another, and sometimes even on an outing into Queensbridge. If no royal party was on board, the benches remained empty unless—as happened that morning—Captain Francis awarded their use to someone. "Sit here," the Mayor said, indicating the space beside him.

They sat so close together that, were the wind to carry sound back to the main deck, or the passenger cabin, or even the bridge, their words would be confusingly mixed together and thus indecipherable. Max grew even more curious. Whatever could the Mayor want of the Solutioneer? That required such secrecy.

The Mayor took an envelope from his briefcase. It was a plain envelope, addressed in square capital letters to THE MAYOR. He put the letter on his knees and set the briefcase on the deck, between his feet. Max studied his potential employer.

The Mayor had a thick, graying brown mustache and lively brown eyes, with bags beneath them. Deep lines ran along his forehead and down from his nose to the sides of his mouth. He was a heavyset, well-fed man, and everything about him was self-assured as he turned to face Max, one hand holding the envelope firmly down, so it wouldn't blow away. He was a serious man on serious business, and a worried man, too. He asked, "You've heard about the recent vandalism?"

Max nodded. "There have been fires as well."

The Mayor nodded. "I suspect—I strongly suspect—that something is going on. For one thing, it's always some small shop that gets broken into, or where a fire breaks out. Greengrocer, cobbler, newsagent . . ." He looked out over the lake water, recalling. "A bakery, a milliner, a fishmonger. Is that eight?"

"Six," said Max, who had been counting.

"There are two more." The Mayor thought. "A butcher and—there was one that surprised me, you'd think that would be the easiest to remember . . . Yes, it was a florist." .

"What was surprising about the florist?"

"The shop was outside the gates, not in the old city. Granted, it's only four steps beyond the West Gate, but still . . . All the other victims are in the old city."

Max understood the significance of this, the difference between the rabbit warren of streets and lanes and alleys that was the old city and the wider avenues and boulevards of the New Town. "What do the police say?" he asked.

"That's the problem. The police don't have anything to say." The Mayor sighed and told Max, "They're suspicious, of course, but nobody will talk to them. Nobody has filed a complaint. Not one. The shopkeepers shrug, *bad luck,* they say, *faulty gas line, some dray horse must have thrown up stones.* This would be cobblestones from the streets. What hoof is ever going to throw cobblestones? Up from under flats filled with lettuces and peas and radishes—so they're all so tossed around and trampled that everything has to be thrown away? That's a whole day's earning lost. Lost by a man with five children to feed."

The Mayor waited, for Max to take in this information, to think about it.

After a minute, Max asked, "Where have the attacks—if they are attacks—taken place?"

"As I said, mostly in the old city, but they aren't limited to one street, or even to one district, any more than to one type of business. I have a list, names and addresses." He reached down for his briefcase but Max had a question.

"Are the shopkeepers all in one family, or joined in any way?"

"Not a one of them has anything in common with any other, except that each is in business alone and most of them have families."

Max considered all of this. The ferry's motor rumbled steadily as he thought, and the boat made its way through little waves up to the town dock at Summer. The Mayor waited patiently, as if he understood the value of thinking. Both of them ignored the business of landing—Carlo, the Captain's son, leaping onto a dock and making the vessel fast before unlatching the low gate to let passengers debark, off-loading whatever boxes or crates or animals the ferry was delivering, and then welcoming new passengers on board before untying the boat and leaping back onto the deck, to fasten the gate behind him and call up to his father, "She's set to go, Captain."

When on board, at work, Captain Francis and his son kept things official. They might go home to the same little house in the evening, and eat supper together, and call one another Dad and My Boy, but once on board, they were Captain and crew and nothing more.

As *The Water Rat* chugged back out into deeper water, now moving around the base of the Promontory from the top of which the summer palace overlooked the peaceful scene, Max broke his silence to ask the Mayor, "What about places that haven't been vandalized? Where there haven't been fires? Is there any pattern to those?"

His question apparently came as a surprise, but it didn't take long for the Mayor to realize, "None of the warehouses, no larger stores, not the theater—Do you know the Starling Theater? It's empty, will be for weeks I gather, maybe months, everybody knows. But nothing's happened there. You'd think, thieves? You'd think they'd at least take building supplies from that restaurant of Bendiff's. All the renovation he's doing. Although I think he has dogs there, now, but they never went near it, even before the dogs, even with all that lumber and piping in piles, just asking to be stolen. You're right, Mister Max. It's curious. Why only small shops? What do you think?"

"Why are you so sure there's something going on?" Max asked now. He himself agreed. There had been too much vandalism and too many fires for it to be a coincidence. But he wondered why the Mayor seemed so certain.

The Mayor nodded his head, as if he had hoped for and expected this question. "When there had been—I can't remember, maybe four? or five? and not one complaint? I got curious. Worried, really. I called in one of our best young policemen and asked him to look into things, ask around, keep his ear to the ground. He knows the old city. He grew up in it, went to school there, lives there." The Mayor sat up a little straighter, to tell Max, "Just because his own home and his offices are in the New Town, that doesn't mean a mayor doesn't care about *all* of his citizens. And maybe, the less important citizens—not that any one of us is more or less important than the other, you understand. I never think that."

Max smiled. The Mayor obviously thought of him as a voter.

"These are my people, these shopkeepers. Everyone is my people and it's my job to take care of my city. Also . . ." He hesitated, as if he didn't want to have to say it, but he made himself go on. "Not three days after I asked Officer Torson to look into things, I received this."

He held the envelope out to Max. Max took it, and removed the sheet of paper from it. The words had been cut out from the *Queensbridge Gazette* and pasted onto plain paper.

Mr. Mayor, You will do yourself and Queensbridge a favor if you forget about sending your policeman around asking questions. People don't want to hear those questions, in case you hadn't noticed. So call off your dog and you can tell him we know where he lives, we know his pretty wife and their three children. Things can get worse, Mr. Mayor.

Max looked up, across the sparkling water of the lake. They were approaching Graffon Landing, close enough now so that he could see the small waterfall that tumbled down the rocks into the center of the town, tossing tiny rainbows out into the air. The houses of Graffon Landing were painted in bright colors: whites and yellows, mossy greens and rusty reds. The houses gathered together, like friends around a campfire, between the steep cliffs and the blue lake, under a sky that shone with warm sunlight, and was home to a flock of soft little clouds.

It would have made a perfect watercolor sky for the month of June, for Max's imagined calendar of skyscapes, and for a moment Max was sorry he was on *The Water Rat* being the Solutioneer instead of being himself, a twelve-year-old boy who was learning from Joachim how to paint skies, in watercolor.

The scene was lovely but the note he held in his hand was ugly and he asked, "Has Officer Torson seen this?"

The Mayor shook his head. "How can I show it to him?"

This, Max was sure of, and he said it plain and clear, "You should." Saying it, he was Mister Max, the Solutioneer, who knew trouble's ugly face when it popped up in front of him. Even if he'd never before seen trouble like this.

The Mayor sighed again. "You're right. I'll tell him first thing tomorrow morning. Because if anything happened . . ." He couldn't finish that sentence. "*Will* you help? We'll pay anything you charge, there's no problem with paying you. *Can* you help us?"

"What do you want me to do?"

"Find out what's going on and who's behind it. Figure out a way to stop it." The Mayor had been ready for that question. He smiled a tired smile, removed another sheet of paper from his briefcase, and snapped it shut. Then he looked at Max, looked right into Max's eyes. "You're my last hope, Mister Max." He gave Max the list. "And we only have five weeks before the Royal Family arrives. I will *not* have my city in disarray, especially not while the King is here."

When he said that, he sounded quite fierce. "I don't want anybody in the entire royal party to even start to suspect. Think of the uproar." His eyes flashed as he imagined it. "Soldiers stationed all over the city. Or they'd pack up and leave and take all the coins they would have spent here away with them. We don't want that," the Mayor announced.

Max sat and thought. He didn't agree to take the job, and he didn't refuse it. He thought about it. Eventually, he asked, "Officer Torson couldn't find out anything?"

"Nothing. But he noticed that they got right to work rebuilding, repairing, mending, restocking their shops, as if—as if they knew it wouldn't happen again. He's a good policeman. Smart. Observant. I trust him."

So did Max. Grammie had taught Sven Torson in grade school and she thought well of him, but he didn't tell the Mayor that. Instead, he thought some more. "I don't know quite how I will go about finding anything out," he said.

"So you'll do it?" the Mayor asked. "You'll try? I'm a little desperate," he added unnecessarily, and held out a purse.

"Here's an advance of double what they said is your usual fee," he said.

Mister Max, the Solutioneer, costumed out as the Queen's chosen spy, a dangerous man who knew how to take care of himself in almost any situation, pocketed the purse. He smiled reassuringly. "I'll do my best."

The two shook hands, sealing the contract.

Captain Francis watched this from his position at the bridge, at the helm. He had known the Mayor was meeting with someone. Every now and then the Mayor had such private meetings on the foredeck of *The Water Rat*. Usually, Captain Francis knew the men with whom the Mayor wanted such private conversation, or who didn't want to be known to have an appointment with the Mayor. But this man he didn't know. Although, he remembered seeing him once before, earlier in the spring, accompanying a lady up to Graffon Landing and then later in the day and still in the same lady's company, making the return trip to Queensbridge. Captain Francis had already been curious about the man—artist? foreigner? confidence man? dancing master? He couldn't tell. Now he was even more curious. He looked down on the dark hat and dark-coated shoulders, and wondered. He couldn't remember the face. Possibly, he'd never really seen it.

When they docked at Queensbridge, Captain Francis called down to Carlo to make the boat fast and then make it ready for the afternoon passage around the lake. "I won't be long," he called, but said no more. "Put in a few extra stores, it's Sunday, there'll be the afternoon trippers. Can you manage?"

"Sure thing, Captain," Carlo called back. "I know what to do." Carlo didn't ask where his father might be going or what he might be doing. That wasn't their way. When parent and child lived so close together, and worked together as well, it was important that each should have his privacy. Carlo himself had slipped off alone, several times recently, and Captain Francis had not questioned him about that. His son was a grown man, after all. Probably it had to do with a woman. Captain Francis hoped so. They had been living alone, just the two of them, since the death of his wife, when Carlo was just a boy, just twelve years old. A woman would be a welcome addition to the family and Carlo would confide in his father when he was ready, when there was something to confide. Captain Francis just wished he could be sure exactly what was going on, because Carlo had seemed low-spirited in the last two or three weeks, slow to laugh and quick to fall silent, maybe even anxious, which wasn't like him. Young men, Captain Francis knew, could get themselves into trouble, and they were often too proud, or kind, to ask their fathers for help.

For now, however, Captain Francis's attention was on the Mayor's mysterious companion, who had melted into the group of passengers crossing the ramp from the ferry down to the dock, well behind the Mayor, who had been the first off, in deference to his position in the city. The stranger crossed behind the large berthed vessels like someone who knew where he was going, but Captain Francis crossed behind him like someone just out to enjoy the warm midday sun.

In this way they wound their way through the streets of the old city, until the stranger turned into Thieves Alley and went through a gate and up the pathway to a small stone house. Captain Francis strolled on to the end of the street, just a passerby, a wandering Sunday passerby. But he had read the sign that hung on the gate through which the man went: MISTER MAX, SOLUTIONEER.

Captain Francis returned to his boat, none the wiser, really, but knowing something he hadn't previously been aware of.

For his part, Max had no idea that he had been followed home. He was busy thinking about the problem the Mayor had asked him to work on, determining how to find out what he needed to know in order to solve it.

CYNTHIA VOIGT is the author of many books for young readers. Accolades for her work include a Newbery Medal for *Dicey's Song* (Book 2 in the Tillerman cycle), a Newbery Honor for *A Solitary Blue* (Book 3 in the Tillerman cycle), and the Margaret A. Edwards Award for Outstanding Literature for Young Adults. She is also the author of *Homecoming* (Book 1 in the Tillerman cycle), the Kingdom series, the Bad Girls series, and *Young Fredle,* among others.

You can visit her at cynthiavoigt.com.